Demon Holiday
Torval, Demon Third Class, Layer Four Hundred Twelve of the Eighth Circle of Hell, has been in the business of chastising sinners longer than he can remember. Delivering punishment is the only job he's ever known — the only job he's ever wanted. After Torval witnesses something unexpected, his demonic Overseer demands that he take time off to resolve this personal crisis. And so, Torval, the demon, finds himself sent on vacation ... to Earth, the proving ground of souls!

Demon Ascendant
Torval, Demon Third Class, Layer Four Hundred Twelve of the Eighth Circle of Hell, on vacation to Earth has managed to find another demon, dated a woman and inadvertently explored some of the sins of humankind: greed, gluttony, and lust. Through all this, his biggest struggle involves deciding if he wants his holiday to end or to continue forever.

I0562969

TANSTAAFL Press
891 PH 10
Castle Rock, WA 98611

Visit us at www.TANSTAAFLPress.com

All characters, businesses, and situations within this work are fictional and the product of the author's creativity. Any resemblance to persons living or dead is entirely coincidental. TANSTAAFL Press assumes no responsibility for any content on author or fan websites or other publications.

Enter the Rebirth

First printing—TANSTAAFL Press
Copyright © 2018 by Thomas Gondolfi
Cover art: Andrei Bat

Printed in the USA
ISBN 978-1-938124-28-0

Book layout by Hydra House

Novels by Tom Gondolfi
from TANSTAAFL Press

An Eighty Percent Solution – CorpGov Chronicles: Book One
In a world where corporations suborn governments as a part of good business practice and unregistered humans can be killed without penalty, Tony Sammis, a midlevel corporate functionary, finds himself unwittingly a pawn in a guerilla war between a powerful cabal of business leaders and an elusive but deadly underground movement. His final solution to the biological terror unleashed mirrors Tony's own twisted sense of justice.

Thinking Outside the Box – CorpGov Chronicles: Book Two
Winning one war doesn't seem to be enough. Tony Sammis and the Green Action Militia are once again thrust into the center of a conflict that will change the lives of everyone in the solar system. This time they are allies with the fledgling CorpGov and even the United States government against the ravages of the corrupt Metropolitan Police force. The GAM and their allies are fighting a losing war with few soldiers and even fewer weapons. Behind the scenes, a humble and unsuspected power block lurks with its own axe to grind.
Self-interest, romance, freedom, and a lust for power simmer together in this chaotic soup of tension, intrigue, assassination, and war.

The Bleeding Edge – CorpGov Chronicles: Book Three
Tony Sammis and Nanogate lead a patchwork alliance that includes the nascent CorpGov, Green Action Militia, the president of the United States, the Pacific Northwest Mob, most of the megacorps and the United Brotherhood of Bodyguards. The war the CorpGov alliance knows they can't win has begun, but they are no longer fighting to win. Tony and Nanogate know they may not survive, but they intend to deliver the most grievous wounds they can. The most dangerous animal is one with no hope.

Toy Wars
Flung to a remote world, a semi-sentient group of robotic mining factories arrive with their programming hashed. They can only create animated toys instead of normal mining and fighting machines. One of these factories, pushed to the edge of extinction by the fratricidal conflict, attempts a desperate gamble. Infusing one of its toys with the power of sentience begins the quest of a 2-meter-tall purple teddy bear and his pink polka-dotted elephant companion. They must cross an alien world to find and enlist the aid of mortal enemies to end the genocide before Toy Wars claims their family—all while asking the immortal question, "Why am I?"

Novels by Stephanie Weippert
from TANSTAAFL Press

Sweet Secrets

At seven, Michael gets into trouble no more than any other boy his age but he does have a sweet tooth. When the mailman brings a package from a candy company, he has to sneak just one. As he eats the chocolate, his home, stepfather, and everything he'd known melts around him and disappears. Next thing he knows he is in a dreamlike world. He is taken as an orphan, tested, and before he knows it is a student in the premier magic school on the planet. His fellow students can make cookies that fly and chocolate turtles that actually walk. Michael is told he has more power than any of them.

Brad is charged with watching his stepson Michael for first time. When the boy disappears before his eyes, Brad panics. Within hours he is on an adventure tracking his son alongside an enigmatic chef. Always one step behind his son, Brad soon finds that Michael is being used as a pawn between the two most powerful chefs on the crazy planet. Worse he has to get Michael home before his Mother finds out he's gone or there is going to be hell to pay.

Novels by Bruce Graw
from TANSTAAFL Press

The Faerie of Central Park

The last of her kind in New York City, Tillianita tends the land and beasts as best she can, reluctantly obeying her departed father's warning to avoid humans at all costs. A freak accident casts her out of the relative safety of Central Park. Lost and alone with a broken wing, she wonders if she'll ever see her home again.

On his own for the first time in his life, college freshman, Dave Thompson, isn't sure he'll ever fit in. When he stumbles upon an extremely realistic fairy doll, he thinks perhaps it might make a good present for a future date until he discovers that it's not a doll at all. His find turns not only his life upside down but also expands his narrow view of the world.

Lady Hornet

Elizabeth Fontaine is a lonely, ordinary young woman in a world where superheroes struggle daily against evil. To fill the empty void within her soul, she becomes a hero fangirl, following every super's event, subscribing to multiple fanzines, and never missing the daily superhero talk shows ... until one day, fate grants her the opportunity to leave behind her boring, dreary life and become what she's always dreamed of ... a superheroine!

Elizabeth learns the hard way the meaning of the phrase, "Caveat Emptor!" — let the buyer beware!

Enter the Rebirth

Edited by Thomas Gondolfi

TANSTAAFL PRESS

From the Editor

Thomas Gondolfi

Enter the Rebirth closes the cycle on our trilogy. It reconfirms that no matter how severe the tragedy, some new equilibrium is obtained, whether for good or ill. You will get both between the covers of this tome.

It saddens me that there will be no further books in this series but as with all things in our universe it went from apocalyptic beginning to glorious rebirth. Following in this theme, I arranged for the rebirth of a story I had initially rejected—*White Gloves*—because I felt the racial implications were too raw. The story kept going around and around in my head. I was wrong to reject it. We need stories such as these to crystalize our emotions to make certain we never allow such a travesty to happen again. I contacted Elizabeth King and asked to include it after all, and to my great pleasure she agreed.

Equally fittingly I chose to end **Enter the Rebirth** with the single story thread which has been within each of the trilogy, *So That They May Rule*, by Madison Keller. Her story of one continuing story, broken up into three, matched my original vision of the series. I'm proud to round it off with this work.

This shouldn't take away from any of the other wonderful works herein. I couldn't accept *From Farm to Table* fast enough. *Forty-Seven Seconds* challenged my mind, and *An Inanimate Proposal* challenged my heart. Again, I'd love to say something about each and every story within but I'll let you find out for yourself.

The apocalyptic beginning of the series: I'll be honest that I've never been particularly fond of anthologies and didn't think they would sell. I resisted the impulse to have TANSTAAFL Press publish one. However, with a dearth of time, I decided that editing an anthology couldn't be nearly as hard and lengthy as writing a novel from the beginning. Being pressed for time I chose to do the anthology series. Oops.

Glorious rebirth: Just behind loving someone and being loved in return, the most important thing that any of us can do is to learn. It drives everything else in our lives. The **Enter the...** series has taught me in more ways than I could have ever imagined. Not only did I take the lessons from above, but also my love for the short fiction form was reborn within me. I started out a short story writer and this has brought me back to that love.

Learning this has been a debt I will never forget and one that TANSTAAFL Press will repay over many of the coming years.

Thomas Gondolfi
www.TANSTAAFLPress.com

Contents

Forty-Seven Seconds

Rich Jones

Editor: Lies can be used for good.

Forty-one . . .
Forty-two . . .
Forty-three . . .
"Come on. You've got it . . ." the boy whispered to himself.
Forty-five . . .
No . . . No . . . No . . .
Forty-seven.

Arn was running full out toward the large open doors of the Goal Building when he ran out of seconds. The mech cleared the obscurity of the tower building and immediately zero'd in on him. Without changing the path of its broad armored treads, the mech's torso-trunk rotated and its weapon arms swung to the right. The gathered tribe and their captors had already seen what came next several times this morning. Bluish light boiled up along the needled length of the weapon pods and then blasted Arn into a dark, smoldering stain on the tarmac of discolored and cratered smoothstone.

The mech's arms rotated back to their original position, apparently satisfied with their work. Above the arms the head of the thing spread out to a flattened sort of disk shape. Several spikes of various lengths arose from the head like a crown. Two red embers glowed from the dark orbs that were the head's only other feature. Over the years the Scav tribes had speculated about what each part of the massive thing was and what it did. They had never gotten much further than speculation. No one had ever gotten close enough to study it and for good reason. It was a rolling, death-dealing monument of the time Before when people were able to create such wonderful and horrific machines.

The mech continued its patrol along the smoothstone expanse. It circled the same set of buildings in the middle of the Southern Wastes, rolling along the track it had worn into that stone over all the cycles since Before. In a few minutes it would turn back behind the low buildings and would be out of sight for another forty-seven seconds.

* * *

"Da?"

"Yes?"

"Why do we run?"

Da stopped what he was doing and put down his tools. He moved the thin metal plates that he had been holding to trade after Carnival. Every cycle the Scav tribes of the Southern Wastes gathered for a Carnival to barter items and information. The highlight of the Carnival would be when different Scavs would attempt to run the forty-seven seconds and get what they could from the tek that littered the field around the Goal Building. The Elders of the gathered tribes set strong rules for bartering during the Carnival to keep bloodshed to a minimum. It would be easier to get a better price for the plates once Carnival was over. Sifting through several of the bits of tek on his workbench, he picked up something small. He turned and looked at the boy with a warm smile and held it out.

"This is why we run." Da put the small device in the boy's hand.

"Go ahead, press that button."

"But you said—"

"'Never press a button if you don't know what it does.' I know, but it's safe, press it."

Carefully, the boy pressed the button.

The small piece of tek began to vibrate in the boy's hand and suddenly several other items around the tent began to flash, beep, or, in one case, leap out of a crate to bounce and shake upon the sandy floor. The boy dropped the small device and jumped back as his Da laughed heartily.

"How did it do that?"

"I honestly don't know, but we are learning a lot about Before from the tek the mech guards. Even from simple stuff like that."

* * *

"Well, that's just a damn shame," First Scribe sarcastically lamented. "I really thought he was gonna make it. Sorry." He nodded to Second Scribe, who shot Aria in the head. There was a chorus of anguished cries from the boy's tribe. Her ancient body snapped back, and then crumpled down onto the bloody sand. There she lay among the bodies of the other olders that the Scribes had killed that morning each time a runner had failed.

"I don't know if there's enough of you to actually make it in that place, but dammit, we don't have anywhere else to go," First said.

The boy winced and looked around. Arn had been next to him in line of those captives capable of running. He had been the last of the bearded men of the tribe. Sara had run before him and she had failed as well. As the largest of the youngers, the boy would be the next runner. The hard realization settled in that it was time to face his forty-seven seconds.

* * *

"Shhhhh."

"But Da, who are they?" the boy urgently whispered.

Da gave him that look that meant that he wasn't happy but that he would answer his questions just to quiet him down.

"They come from far to the north and west. From a tribe called 'Scribes.'" It was a strange-sounding word.

"Are they like us? Do they want to scav here?"

"Yes and no. They do want to scav, but these Scribes say they only look for knowledge. That is what they are asking the Elders. They want to stay for Carnival and see the Running."

"Are they dangerous?"

"I don't know. We have never dealt with them before. I don't see any weapons though."

"Will the Elders let them? Let them stay?"

"No more questions. Let's listen and hear what they say."

* * *

When Carnival ended and the other tribes had left, the Scribes returned with guns and took the boy's people captive. After killing the few men who initially resisted, they separated the tribe into two groups: those capable of running and then those they could use as hostages. So far that morning they had forced several runners to try for the Goal Building. When a runner failed to make it, they killed one of the hostages.

"Well now, it looks like we're down to the little ones," First said and grabbed the boy out of the line of runners. "I hope you're faster than you look, son."

Second turned and grabbed the next hostage in line. It was the boy's grandmother and she cried out to him. That got her a hard backhand from Second. The boy lunged at him but First pulled him back hard. The boy yanked against First's grip, and almost broke loose. Then First pressed the barrel of his gun to the boy's forehead. The metal was warm and hard.

"If you want her to live, do exactly what I tell you."

Unsure of what to say, the boy nodded.

"Good," First said, and led the boy by the scruff of his neck toward the fence line that encircled the buildings.

"Now, you've seen this enough. Get over that fence and don't get caught up in that claw wire." He gestured to the tall metal mesh fence that was topped by a spiral of wire that had claws wound into it. Several meters inside the fence there was a double row of the claw wire. There were some melted sections where the mech zero'd a runner who got caught in it. None of those gaps created a straight line and the runners who tried for them had ended up like Arn. It used too many seconds to run for the gaps. "Get past those and then you just need to leg it to the open door. Easy," First finished with a chuckle as they reached the start line.

It was anything but easy. The boy nodded anyway.

"You ready?"

"No," the boy said.

* * *

"Da, do you have to run?"

"Are you worried, son?"

"I don't want you to run out of seconds."

"Oh, I won't. Arn and I have a plan. He is going to run first and check the 'kopter. He'll just run out and spy it, and then run back."

"And then you'll run after and get whatever he spied?"

"Yes. He'll spend his seconds finding something good, and I will spend my seconds getting what he found."

"Like a team."

"Yes."

"But why go for the 'kopter? Isn't that too far in?"

"It is kinda far, but everything closer is picked over. We think the 'kopter still has a lot inside it. That's why we are working together. One run isn't enough seconds to find something and take it. Arn will find it; I will take it."

"Will the Elders allow that? What about the Great Handshake?"

"They will. The Great Handshake just sets the rules for running the forty-seven seconds. So you can't run two at a time. That stopped working anyway once the close stuff was all picked over. Now it just gets the attention of that damned thing much faster. But you can work together on different runs. Some have tried to remove the fence or the claw wire, but it's too dug in to do any real work in a few seconds. Better to get in, get what you can and get out."

"Is that what they tried last Carnival?"

"Yes, but they tried to get something too big, ran out of seconds."

"You won't do that?"

"No. We want something smaller, or something that we can take in pieces, even if it takes a few runs."

"Will anyone go for the Goal Building this cycle?"

"I don't know, but what is our rule?"

"Scavs that go for the Goal Building become Scav stains in front of the Goal Building."

"Exactly."

* * *

"Oh, you can speak, eh?"

"I need something from my Da's tent."

First raised his eyebrows at this. He glanced at Second who shrugged.

"Okay, but it better be good. Try anything and we'll kill the next three olders in line."

First let go of the boy who wasted no time and sprinted up the dune for a stand of bright colored tents just at the top of the sandy rise. The gathered captives and the two Scribes watched him disappear into one of the tents. A few seconds later there was a loud crash from the tent.

"Boy! If you ain't back by the time I get to ten the first one is dead!" First shouted toward the tents.

"One . . . Two . . . Three . . ."

The boy appeared among the tents and raced from one to another, hauling something over his shoulder.

"What the . . .? Four!"

First looked over at Second, and the two exchanged a questioning look.

The boy came out of one tent and dove into another.

"Five!"

With that the boy came out of the last tent with something wound up in his hands. He turned downhill and sprinted toward the frustrated Scribe. First continued to call out numbers until he reached eight and the boy was standing right in front of him. The boy huffed and puffed, trying to catch his breath from the run down the sandy hillside.

"Son, you like to play things on the edge, don't you?"

"Ten," the boy said between breaths.

"What?"

"You said I had until ten," the boy replied.

"So I did, but I think you made those three over there wet themselves." He gestured to the hostages that Second had his gun aimed at.

"Sorry," the boy said sheepishly to his Elders.

"So now what the hells?" First was looking at the bundle the boy now held. It looked like three or maybe four thin metal plates that were wound up in a cord of some sort. The plates were each about a man's arm length long and half that wide. They had a slight curve to them. The cord wound around and between each plate so that there were gaps between them. The boy held them tightly, which kept them together in a neat stack.

"I'm ready." The boy did not answer the question.

"Yeah, but what are you going to do with that?" First persisted.

The boy looked past the Scribe and saw the mech rounding the far building. It started to turn behind the Goal Building. His forty-seven seconds were about to start.

"It›s time," Second said.

First leaned down close to the boy and spoke in a low voice. One meant for only him to hear. "Inside that building is a machine, a terminal. It will let you shut down the mech and then we can all go in." The boy's eyes widened at that. "We are looking for something inside there and once we get it, you all," First waved his gun toward the boy›s tribe, "can go scav whatever you want and we›ll leave you be."

The boy did not believe First. They were bad men and had already killed to get what they wanted. And they really wanted something in that building. If he could get it, he would have barter. He would have power over them somehow. His Da had taught him to always barter when you had the power and never when you did not.

His Da had been the second man they had made run the forty-seven seconds. Da had no power then, and the boy knew he had no power now.

"Got it?" First asked.

The boy nodded.

* * *

"The sand makes me slow, Da."

"Stop complaining. The sand will make you fast."

"How? It is so hard to run in."

"Exactly."

Da had that look like he was about to explain more, so the boy tried to wait, but couldn't.

"How? How does the slow sand make me faster?"

"If you can run fast through the sand, how fast do you think you can run across the smoothstone?"

"I don't know!" The boy knew that might get him a smack, but his legs burned and his chest heaved and he really hated running the sand.

"Running the sand is easier than running the seconds. Now go!"

He groaned but then turned and ran as hard as could across the shifting footing of the sand dune.

* * *

The boy moved quickly down the slope holding the bundled plates tight under his arm. The dune ended as the sand spilled over the hard smoothstone. There was a red line painted several meters onto the stone. It marked the closest a runner could get to the fence and not get zero'd by the mech. Several scorch marks told of failed attempts to mark that line.

The boy walked to the line and crouched down, ready to spring for the fence. He watched the mech as it turned and trundled in its endless path around the buildings. The instant the head dropped out of sight behind the far end of the Goal Building the boy launched like a spring and mentally started to count his seconds.

One . . .

Two . . .

He reached the fence and immediately started to climb it with his one free hand. The plates slowed him, but his hand was quick each time he let go and reached up to grab more fence to pull himself up. Luck be with him he did not miss a grab, and his toes kept up with his hand as he climbed.

Eleven . . .

At the top of the fence he would face his first true obstacle: A looped coil of claw wire.

Fourteen . . .

The boy turned the bundled plates in his hand and then pushed them up and over the claw wire. He had them curved downward so they created a smooth metal hump atop the fence. He pulled himself up and over the flat metal instead of the grasping wires.

Seventeen . . .

The plates were too smooth and he slipped. He had just enough presence to roll forward so his legs would not get caught. As he tumbled into the space between the top of the fence and the smoothstone below him, he pulled at the plates.

Nineteen . . .

The boy turned over, managed to land on his feet and rolled forward to absorb the shock. As he came back to his feet he looked around quickly like a caged beast. Then he saw it. The cord that he had bundled the plates with to carry them had gotten caught by the claw wire. One plate was hanging on the far side of the fence. Another was hanging on this side. Two of the plates had come loose and were sitting on the ground. He sprinted back, snatched those up, then turned back toward the Goal Building.

Twenty-five . . .

He covered the distance from the fence to the second hedge made of claw wire in several quick strides. As he ran he slipped his fingers into the gap between the two plates. When he reached the wire, he flung the first plate at the barrier. The plate landed atop the spiral with its curve downwards.

Twenty-seven . . .

The boy gauged the way the plate settled on the wire and then stepped on it, pushing it down, and leapt across. The 'kopter was now just in front of him and after that he had a straight run to the Goal Building. He had one plate left.

* * *

"*Da, what is in the Goal Building?*"

"*We only know what the Top Scav said was there.*"

"*What did he say?*"

"*Top Scav said that there were wonders in there. Tek from Before like he had never seen.*"

"*Is that what he brought back?*"

"*Yes, they say he had something incredible. Whatever it was he kept it to himself and his tribe.*"

"*That's the right of scav though, he scavved it, so it was his.*"

"*Yes, that is our rule. But you know what?*" *Da's voice got low and scary, like when he told stories at the fire before bed. The kind that Momma would yell at him about before she had gotten the sickies.*

"*They say that whatever it was, it was cursed!*"

"*Cursed?*"

"*That's what they say. Cursed.*" *Da said with a knowing nod.*

"*Why? Why do they say that?*"

"*Well, because Top Scav's tribe disappeared. They did not show up at the next Carnival. No one ever saw them again.*"

"*But that could be raiders or sickies, or I don't know.*"

"*True, but no other tribe ever totally disappeared. You know what else they say?*"

"*What?*"

"*Some say that what he found . . . was a map.*"

"*A map?*"

"*Yes, a map that he used to lead his tribe to an impenetrable shelter with lots of food and clean water. They say they all live there even today, happy and safe!*"

* * *

Thirty-four . . .

The boy zigzagged around the smashed smoothstone that surrounded the 'kopter. He cleared a large chunk of the fallen sky machine and the open doors of the Goal Building beckoned to him. A few craters broke up the smoothstone, but he could run in an almost straight line.

Thirty-five . . .

His legs felt light and he ran fast. Without the shifting sands beneath his feet he felt like the wind. He came to the path that the mech had worn into the smoothstone. From beyond the fence line it didn't look like more than two ruts. Up close, the ruts were deep. The boy thought that it must have been running this path since the beginning of time to wear down into the hard smoothstone. He leapt across them and ran hard toward the Goal Building.

Forty-one . . .

He risked a look at the Tower Building and he thought he saw the mech's head pass just beyond the roofline. He had one last chance . . .

Forty-two . . .

The mech started to clear the side of the Tower Building but he was still too far.

Forty-three . . .

He heard the cries of his tribe, and recognized the sound of his grandmother's voice.

Forty-four . . .

He threw out the last metal plate. It skidded out across the smoothstone a few paces in front of him and several paces from the open doors.

Forty-five . . .

The boy dove forward. As his seconds ticked away, he felt as if everything slowed down. For a long moment he found himself in midair, watching the blue lights sparkle into existence along the mech's needle arm and at the same time tracking the plate as it skidded over the stone.

Forty-six . . .

He hit the plate with all his weight and it lurched forward even faster. As he slid over the ground he heard a loud SKREEEE that competed with the burning air stitching sound of the mech's beam weapon.

Forty-seven . . .

* * *

"Da?"

"Yes?"

"Will you ever try for the Goal Building?"

Da stopped and looked at him.

"Do you want me to?"

"I don't want you to become a stain, Da."

"I'm glad for that, but why do you ask?"

"Well, if Top Scav made it, maybe you could."

"Maybe, but no one knows how he did it, and no one has done it since."

"But . . ."

"But?"

"If his tribe is really safe and happy now, is it worth trying?"

"Well, that would be something, wouldn't it?"

"Yes. So will you?"

"Son, what do I always tell you about After?"
"We are never safe."

* * *

The plate skidded across the hard stone and clipped the edge of a small crater. It bounced over the broken stone and through the open doorway and into the Goal Building. The hair on the boy's arms and legs stood on end as the blue light charred the smoothstone behind him. It burned the very air as it melted the ground. Still moving fast, he and the plate smashed into something large that did not move. The wind was knocked out of the boy as something tipped over and rained heavy metal tools down on him. He covered up as best he could, but something heavy hit him in the head. He started to see everything in threes.

The loud scrape of metal on stone reverberated through his skull. Behind that was the receding sound of sizzling stone and air. Whatever he had slammed into had not only dropped the tools on him, but it kicked up a cloud of dust like a small sandstorm. He coughed and shook his head. Pain erupted from his side when he moved. A heavy piece of metal fell off of him and clattered to the hard floor. As his eyes matched two of the three images and merged them, he started to look around. The floor around him was full of large crates and boxes.

That was when he realized where he was.

The sun shone in through the large open doors, but it wasn't enough to dispel the shadows that lurked deeper within the building. The boy had not realized how large the Goal Building was. He had always looked at it from back well beyond the fence line. Inside, the room seemed to be a large pen for various machines from Before. There were a few stalls set in front of the doors within the large open space. The vehicles were long gone and tools, crates, and all kinds of things from Before now littered the area. The whole building was what Da would call a "wreck." The boy knew that if he ever made such a clutter of Da's work tent he would get a beating he would not forget. Now he looked around and wondered who had made such a mess of the place and why. When he thought of how many people had died trying to get in this building, he was amazed that he was here. Everything was just lying around. He picked up a long metal tool and turned it over in his hands. It was solid and cold. He had no idea what it did, but it seemed much better than any of the tools Da had. The whole place was a treasure trove for a Scav.

"Boy!?"

First's voice brought the boy back to the world outside.

"Did you make it?"

They could not see inside. They did not know if he made it or not.

Maybe he could hide here until he figured out a way to use this stuff to save his people?

Then he realized that they would just kill his grandmother and send another runner. More death while he hid away. He could not allow that.

"Yes! I am here. I made it!"

There was silence for a second and then he heard a cheer from his tribe. They called out to him until the Scribes silenced them.

"Boy?" First called out again.

"Yes?"

"Inside there, do you see a terminal?"

"Ummm. There›s lots of stuff in here. What›s a terminal look like?"

There was a pause and he looked and saw the two Scribes talking.

"It›s a machine. It will be on a table, maybe inside a smaller room. It will have a screen, a flat part that sits on the table. If it›s on, it›ll have glowing letters on it."

* * *

Da gave him that look that said "You aren't going anywhere."

"Why do I have to do this? No one else does this."

"Do I care what everyone else does?"

"No, Da."

"And why are you asking me a question that you already know the answer to?"

The boy listened wistfully to the sounds of his friends outside the tent. They were collecting a team for Slamball against another tribe that just had arrived for the Carnival.

"Look, I know you want to go play with your friends, but this is important. If you can tell me why it's important, I'll let you go play."

"You will!?"

"I will, but you'll have to do two tonight."

That was a hard barter, but he knew he would take the deal.

"Yes, two tonight, if I can go now!" The boy held out his hand earnestly.

Da held out his hand, but when the boy reached for the handshake that would seal the barter, he pulled it back.

"Are you forgetting something?"

"Oh, that . . ."

"Yeah, that."

"Letters are important because you can't scav good if you don't know what to scav!"

They said the last few words in unison, and then there was a fast handshake and the boy was out of the tent leaving only a flurry of movement behind him.

* * *

Glowing letters? The boy had to see that to believe it. He looked around the large room he was in. Without moving further in there was not much he could see. His sight lines were cut off by all the junk. He carefully picked his way deeper inside. He threaded through several large, half-opened crates. One lay on its side and its contents were spilled out over the floor. Just then he heard a rumbling sound and ducked down.

He looked through the large open doors and saw the source of the noise. The mech rolled by on its age-worn path. He had never thought about if the mech would blast him once he was inside the building. Runners had tried to hide in the broken-down trucks, or in the 'kopter, but the mech had always seen them. What the mech saw, it blasted. He watched the mech roll by and thought how he was the first one to see the mech from this side since the Top Scav. He wondered if he would be the last. The mech rolled on by, taking no notice of him. It must ignore people inside the building the same as it does people beyond the start line.

Moving through the large bays that housed the trucks and various crates, the boy was careful not to touch anything. That was a big rule for Scavs. Don't touch anything that you don't need to. It was harder than he thought because there was so much here to look at, to check out. His whole tribe could spend weeks in here going through it all. His thoughts of the tribe pulled him back to his job. Deciding that the place was too big and too crowded to search quickly, he decided to take a risk. He climbed up on top of a crate. From here he could see the back of the room. There was a large door that seemed to be made out of smoothstone, or even metal. It could fit the mech through it. Just outside that was a smaller room. It had a half-open door facing him.

The boy carefully climbed down from the crate and made his way to that part of the building. He crept up and peered into it. Like the larger room that housed it, it was overly full. Two tables or workbenches set along the back wall. Several smaller boxes and their contents littered about the small space. The boy was quickly cataloging the room as he had been taught when he saw someone sitting in a chair with his back to him.

He jumped back in fright and bumped into a one of the crates. It tipped over and metal cylinders clanged and clattered along the smoothstone floor, kicking up another cloud of ancient dust. He cringed at the sound and looked frantically for a place to hide. He started toward a shadowy corner, but kicked one of the pipes and yelped in pain. He watched in horror as the pipe rolled lazily across the floor with a metallic racket that might have wakened the dead. The boy froze in place and stared at the open doorway of the room.

He waited for whoever was in there to come out. Or to call out. Or call the mech in here to blast him. But none of that happened.

As the seconds passed he gained confidence and moved back to the doorway. He peered inside. Nothing had changed. The figure was still seated in the chair with its back to him. Carefully he moved into the room and closed the distance with the unmoving person. Stepping over a small box he got a closer look at the seated person and his brief horror turned to relief.

The person was long dead. The skeleton wore a set of clothes that made it look more substantial. The clothes looked like blue work coveralls of some sort. A small, round label on the left side of the chest said "Joe."

"Hello, Joe," the boy said looking over the remains. Scavs were no stranger to dead bodies. In fact, it was common for Scavs to deal with the bodies of the dead. Another Scav's rule: Treat the dead with respect, and be thankful for what they left behind. Even still, the boy had never seen a skeleton so old. Looking over the body in more detail he saw a large hole in the skull itself. It looked like Joe had been shot at very close range. The boy scanned around Joe's chair and he saw it. A gun lay on the floor. Dropped from Joe's own hand after his fatal decision. Suicide was also something that Scavs were no stranger to. The boy picked up the gun and felt its competent weight.

He looked over the table in front of Joe and wondered what may have caused the man to shoot himself. Yet another box sat on the table, so the boy moved it. Just behind was a piece of tek that might be the terminal that the Scribes sought. It was a wide panel that was made of some kind of shiny material. A small board in front of it was lined with rows of buttons. Once he brushed away some of the dust he saw that the buttons were marked with letters. Despite the rules his Da had always recited, he reached out and pressed one of the letters.

Nothing happened.

"Boy!?" First called to him from beyond the fence.

"What?» he called back.

"Did you find the terminal?"

The boy looked at the table. He was sure he had found something, but he was not sure what it was.

"No . . . still looking."

"Well, hurry up. I don't have much patience left and we have a lot of people here and a lot of bullets."

"I'm looking! It's a mess in here!"

The boy turned back in frustration and his foot kicked something. He looked down to find a small book, a kind he'd seen before.

* * *

"You have to be able to write and draw, son."

"But why?" he whined.

"When you are on a scav you have to keep a journal."

"You said that already." He was frustrated and challenged his Da more than he should have. The sharp smack to the back of his head was a quick reminder of his place.

"You never know what you will see on a scav, so we keep journals. You write down the signs you see, and you draw maps and pieces of tek. Your journal is your lifeline. When you come back, if you come back, your journal shows where you were, and what you found."

"So you share it with the tribe?"

"Yes."

"But isn't that a barter?"

"Not really. It is just information. If someone else in the tribe sees something in your journal that they can help you scav, then they are bound to do it."

"But then there is a barter?"

"Yes, then we barter and there will be a handshake on how the cargo is to be divided. We work together. That is why a journal is so important."

* * *

The boy picked up the journal. It was old and smelled of mold. It had to be the journal of the Top Scav. But why would he have left that here? He carefully flipped through it until he came to the latest entry. Laid out in faded detail was a map of the inside of the Goal Building. There were notes all over the map. On the part of the map where the small room was, where the boy now stood, there was a note that read "Joe." Next to that, it said "Access Controls." On the next page was a quickly scrawled picture of the table in front of Joe. An arrow pointed to the side of the larger piece of tek that stood upon the table, and a note said "Press Here." He looked closely at the edge of the tek and saw a small button. He pressed it. There was a crackling pop. Words slowly glowed into being on the panel.

"Thank you!" he said to the journal and then read on, because it held a lot more about the terminal. The terminal was a world unto itself. The boy followed the path laid out in the journal to do something called "logging in" using words from a small paper that was stuck down on the table. Once inside there were several options. The boy used arrow buttons to move a blinking dot over the different selections and another button to go inside each one. The journal directed him to a place called "Security." When he arrowed past an option called "Messages" his curiosity grabbed him and he hit the other button to go in.

Inside there was a list of messages. He selected one but it made no sense to him. He tried a few more until he found one that he understood.

Dear Renee,

I'm the last one here now. The Research and Engineering Corps all cleared out about an hour ago. They took everything they could and headed to that new Metro habitat. Of course they left all the mechs down on the factory floor. They were pretty spooked after the enemy got a worm in up north and turned them against us. I understand that because I don't want to be sitting here only ten levels up from eighty-six of those damned things when they can get turned into murder bots.

So here's where I'm pretty much screwed. Since I am the last one here, I have to make sure nothing gets in here and gets control of these monsters. I'll set one up on perimeter and program it not to let anything in. Once that's done I'll cut the main line to prevent anyone from hacking in. That should keep the ones down below locked away.

I know what you are thinking and you can't wait for me. Get the kids and head south. Attached are maps of where the shelters are down there. Print it out because the network won't be online much longer. Give them my service number and that should get you in.

I have to do this. If this site isn't secured these things could wipe out everything.

The only thing that makes me okay with this is that you and the kids will be safe. Don't wait any longer, print the maps and go. Those shelters will stand. Get in one of them.

All my love,

Joe

* * *

"Damn," the boy whispered to himself. Out of habit he looked around for his Da and an incoming smack for swearing. He looked at Joe's skeleton with newfound respect and sadness. Checking the map on the terminal, he confirmed that it had been copied into the journal.

"Boy! You had better find that terminal!" First's call jolted the boy back to his own world of After.

He tapped the buttons to get out of the messages and worked his way into Security. The journal had instructions for getting through the Security part of the terminal. It led him to a part with two options. He found himself staring at the glowing letters for "System Shut Down" and "System Reset." He knew the Scribes wanted inside this place. If they knew about the terminal, what else did they know? Did they think that they could take control of the mech? Maybe they even knew of the ones Joe said were below. The idea of those two in control of any mechs sent a shiver through him. The journal said that the reset would only stop the mech for a short time, maybe two hundred seconds. Once it started up again this place would be secure. But if he did that, the Scribes would kill him and more of his people.

Staring at the terminal he thought of a barter, one where he would have the strength. He picked up the gun, a small piece of tek from the table that reminded him of something, and the journal. Then he made his choice and hit a key.

The mech stopped.

Shock rippled through the Scavs and Scribes alike. They all stared for a long moment disbelieving their eyes.

Then the boy walked out of the Goal Building.

Walked. Not ran.

He held up the small piece of tek in his hand.

"I found the terminal, and now I am in control of this mech and the others inside!" he called across the flat expanse of the tarmac to the Scribes up on the dunes.

They watched in stunned silence as the boy walked out onto the smoothstone. He walked with no apparent rush. As he crossed the pockmarked expanse he hopped lightly over the ruts of the mech›s path. He walked just a few strides away from the massive death machine as calmly as if he was strolling through the tents of his tribe.

"Boy! What did you do?" First called. "You're going to get people killed—"

"Shut up," the boy interrupted him.

"What?" First called back in surprise and then turned to Second. "Shoot her. Teach this little boy that we aren›t playing games."

A loud crack-ping echoed across the wastes and a cry erupted from the people around First. He looked back at the boy, who was holding a gun pointed at the mech. The boy had actually shot the mech.

Yet there it stood, motionless.

"I said 'shut up.'"

First just looked back in shock.

"I know what you want in there, but I found it first. I found it and now I control the mechs with this," the boy said and held up his small piece of tek. He was too far away for First to make out any details of the device.

"So let me tell you what you two are going to do." The boy now began to walk toward the fence line, counting the seconds in his head.

"Drop your weapons and leave. Go as fast as you can away from here. Tell the rest of your tribe to never come back." The boy continued to walk slowly toward them. "If I can still see you when I get to ten, the mech will kill you both." He still held up the device in one hand and the gun in his other.

"One . . ."

The two Scribes looked at one another.

"Two . . ."

First held up his gun and then dropped it into the sand at his feet.

"Three . . ."

Second dropped his gun and then the two men turned and started to run up the hill away from the fence line.

"Four!" The boy yelled loudly after them and started to walk as fast as he thought he could without them noticing.

The Scribes crested the hill, and then First stopped. He looked back down on the fence, the tarmac with its destroyed vehicles, and the set of now unreachable buildings. He took a second to lament the treasures lost inside to these savages. The mech still stood motionless and the boy was still walking toward the fence holding the device and the gun.

"Five!" the boy screamed up at him.

First turned and ran over the hill and out of sight.

The boy immediately broke into a sprint toward the fence line.

"Six!" he called out after the Scribes, trying to keep count of his other seconds in his head.

He reached the fence line and climbed it as quickly as he could. At the top he pushed down the claw wire and scrambled over it.

"Seven!" he yelled from atop the fence, and then dropped down. The wire grabbed at his shirt and his skin, tearing a bloody line across his side and pulling something free that he had at the small of his back. He hit the ground and started to run to the start line. He clutched at his bleeding side, and saw what had fallen. He skidded to a stop in the sand and then turned back and run-crawled to the fence to grab the fallen item.

The mech suddenly began to move. Its head turned first one direction and then the other. The lower weapon arm turned and zero'd on the boy as the bluish light began to boil up from its innards. The boy turned again and launched himself toward the start line.

He crossed it just as the blue beams lanced along the edge of the tarmac behind him.

He rolled to the ground and lay there breathing heavily. He could not bring himself to open his eyes, and instead just listened. He now clutched the journal with the scribbled maps of the southern shelters in one hand, and the gun in his other. His tribe would be safe, as long as they survived the next few seconds. Would the mech go back to its patrol? Or would something change because he had reset it?

He listened and waited.

* * *

"So it's okay to lie?"

"No, you don't want to lie. You want to barter from strength. Never weakness."

"So you can lie that you are strong?"

"No. You always want to seem strong. To make others think you are."

"So you lie."

"No. That's what makes it hard. To project strength, even when you don't have it."

"So lie about it . . ."

"Why are you so difficult? Just act strong, always. Then others won't try to take from you because they think you are weak."

"Still think that's lying . . ."

His Da groaned.

* * *

The rumble of the mech echoed off the smoothstone as it resumed its restless patrol along the ancient worn path.

A Canticle for Mother Goose

Kevin Wetmore

Editor: Sometimes we just shoot ourselves in the foot.

By the thermometer on the wall next to the bed, Father Daniel saw it was already one hundred twenty degrees indoors and the sun was just rising, not even one hand over the horizon. Today would be a very hot Sunnyday. Still, the Lord calls, and his people, his flock, need him.

He sat up, already tired from the heat before being fully awake. He whispered a quick prayer to Farmer for strength, patience, and deliverance and stood up. The dust fell from his body and blanket, adding to the eddying quantity on the floor. Absentmindedly reminding himself to sweep before bed tonight, he went to the bathroom to make his morning ablutions.

He ran his hands through the ashes and then placed some on his face, scrubbing with vigor, hoping to wake himself while cleaning. He used a facecloth to remove the ashes and felt better, less slovenly. Cleanliness is next to godliness, he reminded himself. Farmer would approve.

He looked through the dust on the mirror at his white hair and weathered face. He had been named after his mother's favorite hymn. She used to sing it to him as he fell asleep before the scorching times. He still found himself occasionally singing "God looks like Daniel, must be clouds in my eyes," when he needed strength. He knew Daniel was a prophet of the Lord, who was put in a lion's den by Businessman, but since Daniel found favor with Bingo, Bingo put clouds in men's eyes and sent a plane to take Daniel to the Promised Land in Spain. It was Father Daniel's secret sin that he was proud that God might look like him. Although he did not work the earth like the Farmer, he wanted to think the Farmer might have a face like his.

Dear Lord, he thought, *from hoping He approves of my morning purification to one of the seven deadly sins in imagining the Farmer looks like me in my pride, I shall have to say an extra act of contrition today.*

He returned to his bedchamber in the rectory and removed his sleeping gown and replaced it with his cassock, which was freshly laundered. He always wore a clean cassock on Sunnyday. It was important for his flock to see his respect for them and his devotion to the Church. It was hard enough to maintain living in the valley since the scorching times; he must remind them of the importance of feeding their souls as much as their bodies, perhaps even more so.

In the sitting room at the front of the rectory, he removed a jar of water and drank deeply but slowly. He would eat later, after communion, but it was important to stay hydrated. Indeed, does Farmer not tell us, "There is nothing better for a man than to drink and tell himself that his labor is good"? Daniel drank the water, felt its coolness slide down his throat, giving him strength, cleaning his gorge so that he might preach the word of the Lord to his flock. He offered a quick prayer of thanks, returned the empty jar back inside the cabinet, and left the rectory for the sanctuary across the way.

Daniel did not walk directly to the sacristy, but took the long way around to the front of the building. He stood in front of his church and once again marveled at the glory of Farmer. A large, faded sign in front of the building featured black paint on whitewashed wood, both faded with age: "Most Holy Name." Underneath (to protect the holy name, Father Daniel assumed), was faded black felt with white letters saying "Bingo." And below that, "Tuesday Night at 7:30." Under that, the whitewashed wood continued and it concluded "Rom athlic Church," as some of the letters were faded. The sign gave him comfort. He knew who he was when he looked at it. He knew God was good when he looked at it. He was the priest of Most Holy Name Bingo, of the Romathlic Church, the one true faith. Father Daniel provided the spiritual leadership of the entire community of the Field of Bakers. Even those not of the Romathlic faith knew him as a good, just, and wise man, the moral center of their community and the oldest among them. He personified wisdom in his community.

"So much pride today," he reflected. "No doubt Farmer will test me to remind me to be humble in His sight." Still, since the scorching times the people of the Field of Bakers had settled into a life. They managed to stay alive, raise families, and stay faithful to Farmer, even when He tested them. Farmer loved and blessed the people of the Field of Bakers and that is why when all else in Cali had been destroyed, when all other communities had passed, they remained and flourished, in their way, in the sight of Farmer.

Daniel unlocked the doors, entered, and moved quickly but not hurriedly to the sacristy. The holy room had to be at least one hundred forty degrees. He adjusted his robes and put on his vestments. He then moved back to the narthex and threw the doors open, just as the first families of his flock arrived.

He stood in the vestibule, greeting them as they dusted off their clothing before they entered the church proper. While not assigned, they always took the same seats. Each family took comfort in knowing their place in the world. When the sun perched exactly three hands high over the horizon, Father Daniel entered the nave, approached the altar, and bowed deeply. He looked up at the cross with the dog skeleton nailed to it. His face was passive, although he always felt a mix of emotions at the sight. Joy at being saved by his faith, fear of the Farmer, and (if he was honest), hunger and thirst—he still remembered, as a small boy, when they consumed that dog. Its flesh and blood had saved his family. He remembered feeling sated after. It had sacrificed itself for him and his people. He said a quick silent prayer of gratitude.

He looked at the altar before him. The Grayson twins, Eli and Levi, were the altar boys for this service. They had already placed the elements for the mass on the altar, opened the *Holy Bingo* to the reading for the day, and stood ready, holding the candles.

Father Daniel climbed the steps, moved around the altar, bent and kissed it, then kissed the book. Eli and Levi placed the candles in their holders and then Daniel led the congregation in another of his favorite hymns, "Rain of Ages." Although it was hot and dusty in the nave, the three dozen people in the pews sang with feeling. Daniel felt certain Bingo watched over them with pride. "Rain of ages, fall on me. Let me hide myself in thee; let the water and the blood, from thy wounded side which flowed, be of sin the double cure; save from wrath and make me pure."

Daniel knelt down in prayer for several minutes to allow the congregation to sit and rest and recover from the hymn.

He moved behind the altar. "Let us pray," he intoned. The congregation rose and bowed their heads. He said a brief, silent votive to the Farmer and then began.

Touching his forehead, then sternum, then each shoulder in turn, he proclaimed, "In the name of the Farmer, the Dog, and the Most Holy Name . . ."

"Amen," concluded the congregation.

Holding his arms aloft he cried out, "There was a Farmer, had a Dog, and Bingo was his name." The congregation lifted their arms as well. "B!" he shouted.

"I! N! G! O!" they responded in turn, giving weight to each letter.

"Holy Farmer, we pray to you, protect us, your children. We know that we are not worthy of your care, but you so loved the world that after the scorching you sent your only begotten dog that whosoever eats his flesh and drinks his blood shall not perish but shall live on."

"Amen," the congregation intoned as one.

"Be seated," Father Daniel directed, waiting for the sound of the congregation getting comfortable in the pews to subside before launching into his sermon.

"We live in dark times, my brothers and sisters," he began, and smiled. "I see some of you look to the windows and I know what you think. Yes, we live in bright times, very bright times. While the sun is not as bad as the scorching times, we live too much in the light, and the light itself is what makes these times dark."

He paused and surveyed the congregation, ensuring all eyes were on him.

"DESPAIR NOT!" he cried. Some congregants jumped, to his secret delight. "We live in the trying times, the times after the end times, the times after the scorching times." Daniel noticed with satisfaction that several in the congregation nodded.

"Does it not say in the *Holy Bingo*, the book Farmer has given us to know His will, 'They shall not hunger nor thirst; neither shall the heat nor sun smite them: for He that hath mercy on them shall lead them, even by the springs of water shall He guide them'? And yet, we must ask, 'Where are your springs of water, Farmer? Are WE not worthy of your mercy? Are WE not worthy to be led to the springs of water?'" More nodding.

"No, brethren. It is not that we are not worthy. For does Farmer not go on to say, 'For I will pour water upon him that is thirsty, and floods upon the dry ground: I will pour my spirit upon thy seed, and my blessing upon thine offspring.' The waters are coming, my children. We shall not live in dry dust forever. We will be sent water by Farmer. But we must prove ourselves worthy of Him. I fear we are growing weak and losing faith in the face of the trials of life. Many of us have lost children and spouses; all of us have lost parents. We are the generation that must keep faith so that Farmer will pour his waters across the land again. The Field of Bakers was not always so."

Daniel opened the book on the lectern. He knew it by heart, but it always did him good to see the words as he read them—it reminded him of his faith in Farmer.

"I take as my reading today from the New New Testament Book of Lucas." He cleared his throat and read: "'Businessman was the enemy of the Farmer. Businessman said he was a friend of the Farmer, but he is the father of lies and the prince of deceit. Businessman betrayed and handed over the Farmer, but the Farmer's dog, Most Holy Bingo, attacked and killed Businessman. Businessman cannot truly die, however. We must always be vigilant, for Businessman takes on new incarnations to lead the people of the Farmer away from him.' Amen. Friends, take these words to heart. We must beware the masks that hide the face of Businessman."

The doors of the nave burst open, startling the congregation. A figure wrapped in dusty canvas, his head covered in a helmet and goggles, stormed in, trailing sand and heat behind him. Removing his helmet, he proclaimed to the gathered community, "A stranger is coming up the Fiveroad!"

Father Daniel had been about to chastise the man, but instead said,

"Isaac Barebones, are you certain?"

Rubbing the dust from his eyes, Isaac replied, "I saw him there as certain as I see you here, Father." The congregation gasped and began whispering amongst themselves.

Nothing good ever arrived on the Fiveroad, an ancient path to the west of the Field of Bakers. In the days before the scorching time, the Fiveroad brought the people of many lands past the Field of Bakers, but few stopped to see this simple community. To go on the Fiveroad south was to go to the City of Lost Angels, the place where Businessman fell from Heaven. To go on the Fiveroad north was to go to the City of Sacramentals, so named because once great men lived there, named Governor and Politician. Both said they were friend to the Farmer, but they both came under the spell of Businessman, fell for his lies, and betrayed the Farmer. The Farmer told the people to go to the city of Politician, and put every last man, woman and child to the sword, so that Businessman could never harm the Farmer through them again. The people complied with Farmer's wishes when the scorching time began, and since then the place had been known as the City of Sacramentals. No one from the valley ever went either north or south on the Fiveroad. The Farmer forbade them entry into the lands destroyed by Businessman.

Father Daniel turned to the congregation.

"Sister Rebecca, please take the children to the basement of the Parish Center and lock the door."

"Why, Father?" asked Riley, who had a seat on the Parish Council and was not known to fear much. "Is this stranger a threat to us? Perhaps he brings news of other parishes." She stood firm in the second pew, her voice calming the others as they looked to Daniel.

"It is a precaution, Sister Riley, nothing more."

"Nothing good ever arrived on the Fiveroad," whispered Caleb, looking to the rest of the congregation for confirmation.

"Yes, yes, we know, Caleb," dismissed Father Daniel. "So let us prepare to welcome the stranger among us, but let us also be ready in case it is an emissary of Businessman! Sister Rebecca, take the children to the Parish Center." He turned to look at the altar servers. "Eli and Levi, you may stay, but stay close to me and run to the sacristy if there is any trouble."

Daniel then took his place behind the altar again. "Juan, Cameron, please stand on either side of the tabernacle and be ready." Two of the larger and burlier men moved to the side of the altar and took places on either side of the golden box.

"Why do you want the Eucharistic ministers up there now, Father?" Riley asked.

"My daughter, you ask too many questions. They are there if needed to protect the tabernacle and they are there if we continue with mass and will serve the body of Bingo. Is that to your satisfaction?" She sat rather sheepishly, but still with a slight air of defiance. *Farmer save the man that marries that one*, he thought, admittedly unkindly.

"Come, come, brothers and sisters. Let this stranger hear our voices and know we are the people of the Farmer, and we are not afraid. Let us sing 'How Great Thou Art.'

"O Lord my Dog, when I in awesome wonder, Consider all the worlds Thy hands have made . . ."

As they sang, they heard someone walking up the steps of the church and the door to the narthex open slowly. The congregation turned and stared.

A man. A single man. A man dressed unlike any other man they had ever seen. He wore a cloth-covered helmet with a dark glass faceplate. The bottom part of the faceplate had two white cylinders sticking out opposite each other. His entire body was covered in clothing that blended different colors together so that from a distance he would be difficult to see against the sand and desert. His belt had many implements hanging off it. In his gloved hands, he carried a gun that looked like some kind of rifle. A pack sat low on his back, containing a bedroll underneath. He looked somewhat like the soldiers from the Before time, but different. His boots, like his gloves, were somehow both black and silver at the same time. Daniel moved forward to the edge of the altar.

The intruder stood staring at the congregation, then set down his weapon, reached up and began undoing straps and other fasteners that Daniel could not see or comprehend. A hiss of air escaping something was followed by the man taking hold of either side of his helmet and pulling up. It lifted off to reveal the oldest man Daniel thought he had ever seen.

"Hi . . . uh, hello," the man stammered and then squinted. "Sorry, not used to this," he said, gesturing to the air around him. "Y'know, even though the windows are stained glass it is freakin' bright in here, right? And this air. Y'all live in this?" He then realized everyone was staring at him.

"Oh my God. I mean, I'm sorry. I mean, I interrupted your service, didn't I. I am so sorry. I've been walking for a few weeks, ever since my ATV gave out and my partner got . . . Well, I'm alone now and have been for a while, and I'm not doing my job very well, am I?"

"And what is your job, Stranger?" Father Daniel asked in a quiet but forceful voice.

"My name is Major Carl Lufteufel, Fifth U.S. Army, Second North American Expeditionary Force, formerly of Fort Sam Houston." He gave a grim chuckle. "Believe it or not, Texas is even worse than this place. I was sent out with my team to find communities of survivors. We are rebuilding. The new capital of the United States is in Boulder, Colorado. Do y'all know where that is? It's in the mountains. Much cooler up there."

He seemed to notice they were all staring at him without responding in any way, as if he were speaking a language they did not understand. "May I come in?"

"Come, Major Carl Lufteufel, come in and be welcome in this house of the Farmer. I am Father Daniel Sanchez and this is our congregation." He gestured toward the pews.

The man walked down the aisle through the center of the nave, smiling and nodding to the community. Only Riley nodded back.

"Thanks for your welcome, Father. I must admit, I did not expect to find anyone in Bakersfield. I was on my way to the Bay Area to meet with some of the community leaders there."

The congregation whispered darkly.

Daniel held up a hand and they quieted. "I am sorry, Major Carl Lufteufel. We are a small and humble people and those who have ventured west have not returned. We think Farmer must have sent you here so that you will not go to the dangerous places that Farmer has forbidden."

"Oh . . . I'm sorry, who is this farmer? Is he your leader?"

The congregation gasped as if he had slapped Father Daniel. Father Daniel, however, made no response at first. Then he asked, "Do you not have the Romathlic faith in Bouldercolorado or Texas?"

"The what?"

"The Romathlic Church. The one true faith. Yes, in these times, we are tolerant of our other brethren, the Protestors such as the Lutherins and the Baptizers. Indeed, all three churches in the Field of Bakers work together often, and celebrate the secular holidays together. Are you one of those other faiths?" He smiled. "Relax, I won't try and convert you— although it would be better for you if I did."

The congregation laughed.

The man looked at the congregation and said, "Thank you, Father. No—we do not have the Romathlic faith back where I come from."

"Perhaps Farmer has sent you to us so that we might send missionaries back with you then. You have at least heard of the Holy Name of Bingo?"

The man let out the slightest laugh. It seems as if he tried very hard not to, but it just slipped out before he pretended it was a cough. "No," he said, "I don't think we have."

That was when Father Daniel knew.

The man looked from Father Daniel to the congregation. "Is all of Bakersfield—sorry—the Field of Bakers—like this? Like y'all, I mean?"

"How do you mean? Children of God?" Daniel asked carefully.

"Children is right. Jesus, the oldest one of you can't be more than sixteen."

"I have seen eighteen summers come and go," Father Daniel solemnly intoned.

"I mean no disrespect, Father, but you and all of your congregation are very young. Y'all have been left alone here. I don't know what happened, although based on what has happened in other communities, I can guess. I am very impressed you and your community are surviving, even thriving after the great drought." He stopped. Thought. "Do y'all know what solar flares are? Global warming?"

"You speak of the scorching times." Father Daniel said. It was not a question.

"Yes, I guess I do. Most of the nation—that's the United States—that's the country you live in—was badly affected by the changes in climate. As I said, we are reorganizing the nation. The president and the government are in Boulder. We are making food, we are reaching out and rebuilding. Goddamn, it is hot in here," he said, wiping his head and the back of his neck. "I would very much like to bring all y'all to a place where it is not nearly so hot, where there is water all the time and where you will all grow up safe and healthy."

Daniel recognized some of the words he used. "So you are telling us," he gestured to the congregation, "that Politician is in Boudlercolorado and wants us to join him there."

The man smiled. "Yes, I guess you could say that."

Father Daniel's voice fell to a whisper. "Is Businessman there?"

The man smiled. "I don't know if you ever heard of the saying that the business of America is business. We've been working on building up the nation's economy again. I'm guessing you all barter here. Currency is alive and well in the United States. We even actually have the internet up and running again after the flares. We have been in contact with other nations. Mexico is pretty much gone, but Canada did well. We're working with them on trade and other exchanges. It will only be a matter of time before the nation is strong and productive. The center of the country around the Rockies and Great Plains is stable and running. The Eastern Seaboard is pretty much beneath the Atlantic Ocean now, since the icepacks melted. Kind of ironic—y'all have no water here and the other side of the country doesn't exist because it's under water. Pittsburgh is beachfront property now."

He smiled at Daniel, as if he had made a joke Daniel did not get. He then turned back to the congregation.

"Still, I'd like to stay with you for a few days so we can learn about each other and maybe begin moving this community to somewhere more sustainable."

From the slight gesture from Father Daniel, Cameron moved quickly from the tabernacle. In one stroke he slit the stranger's throat. He had to hit hard and fast to cut through all the cloth around his neck, but his blade was sharp and strong, used for harvesting cactus. He struck so deep the man's head remained connected only by a few bits of skin. He attacked so fast the man's expression never changed—a slight smile on his lips and playing around his eyes.

Father Daniel took the great chalice from Juan, the one they had used with the dog on the cross. He caught the man's blood in the big chalice. Once the blood stopped flowing, Cameron and Juan, who had been holding the man up, dragged his body off the altar and into the sacristy.

Daniel turned to the congregation, who had not reacted to anything that had played out in front of them, other than to watch it happen.

"The Farmer and the Most Holy Name of Bingo have given us a miracle. Businessman sent this man to try to convince us to leave the Field of Bakers and go with him. The Farmer allowed us to see through his lies."

Daniel breathed a sigh of relief. Not only had he passed the trial Farmer had set for him, they once again had blood to drink for their sacrifice. They could save the water for another mass. Another day. Another day of life.

He raised the chalice.

"Blessed are you, O Farmer, our God, Lord of all creation. Through your goodness we have this blood to offer. It shall become our spiritual drink."

Daniel turned to his congregation. "Does Bingo not remind us in his Book that 'whosoever drinketh of the water that I shall give him shall never thirst; but the water that I shall give him shall be in him a well of water springing up into everlasting life'? Behold the water of the well of everlasting life. Bingo has sent us this trial, and since we have passed he has given us this blood to drink so we might live in him. Come forth and drink the blood of the living sacrifice."

One by one the congregants came forward.

Peregrinus

Peter Talley

Editor: We can't always choose those we call family,
but we can choose the actions of family that we will condone.

The indifferent moon lights up the sky. Beneath the pale glow we watch the enemy reclaim their dead. We had been swift, leaving few alive.

I am Peregrinus, Third Javelin of Thirty-two. I roam the beastly bowels of dust and fire. My squad is my life. We decimate the armies of the Worthless.

Tomorrow we ride against the Wind Scales, for their sage is a false shaman. He stole women and water from the caravan. We claimed them two seasons ago. The Herds give us stock and we grant protection. They are generous to their soldiers. No one takes from us and lives.

Tonight we offered mercy to the Gravel Ravens. We conceded some ground but took watch over our victory on the battlefield. Let the corpse collectors fend off the carrion tribes. My people will not feel their teeth. The savages from the Hyena and Vulture packs will feast well. Such is the way of these barbarians. Border conflicts mean death. The disputed hills that we now guard are no longer needed by the Gravel Ravens. They are few and frail. We are few and prodigious.

The Peregrinus are nomadic warriors. We desire no home but where we choose to rest after battle. It is the best way to withstand the ravages of the beastly bowels of dust and fire. You must be unshakable to walk with my squad. We all start as stabbers—foot soldiers who are given sandals and scrap blades. Only the worthiest move on to being slicers, pikeholders, or javelineers.

Toff is my sharpener. We number as four but her presence keeps us maintained. The woman is my friend and the hardest of her kind. Toff joined us after the battle with Brass Law. She could have chosen to die with her tribe, but I watched her earn the right to fight as stabber. She took my brother's ear as a tribute during that first raid. Anyone able to hurt a slicer deserves the chance to claim a new purpose as Peregrinus. Her skills as healer-mechanic won her a valued position with the best of the eight squads. She has also become my now-lover. There are some who say this is unwise. I care not for false words. I won the comfort of her body and words. In return I continue to train Toff as a javelineer. She is worthy of holding the pilum. I am thankful, however, that she seeks credit by serving.

Joyle is a pikeholder. He has guarded this squad for many seasons. Toff jokes that this man is all muscle and no brain. I've trained him to duel both beast and thug with the precision of a mount machine. It takes a fearless warrior to act as a pikeholder. They stand alongside the javelineers, blocking and destroying the Worthless. The armor he wears provides little defense. Speed and determination, not metal, keeps us alive. Joyle has many an honor scar to prove his worth on the field.

Moikya left a Herd caravan at a young age to become a slicer. She is the youngest of the squad and the deadliest. Moikya acts as scout assessor. I trust and fear this woman in equal measure. Her beauty and abilities make me question my restraint. I have known no other to be so practiced in the actions of delivering silent death. Moikya alone removed a chieftain, four high priests, and seven guards in one night. This legendary campaign had us name Moikya as *Rex Venomious*. This title has only been bestowed to one other slicer, more than fifty seasons ago.

The new leader of the Gravel Ravens salutes us. She raises a gloved hand filled with sand. We watch as the woman's bruised face stares up at us from below the trash hill. She releases the sand through her fingers. They have disbanded and accept that they are now grains of dust. The Gravel Ravens are no more. We care not for where they will go next. They may find sanctuary with a Herd caravan or die as Worthless.

Toff whistles to the former Gravel Raven. She signals by custom that she recognizes the victory of the Peregrinus. The defeated fought with credit. There will be no more aggression. Toff raises her pilum triumphantly and screeches at the moon.

The heat of the next morning is comforting. We break camp before sunrise. The journey to the Wind Scales' territory will bring us close to the edge of the frontier. We had crossed over the borderline of the frontier during the Two Season Skirmish. It had been a hard place where carelessness meant losing yourself to the dust and fire.

Joyle and Toff want to chance nature in that realm. This would shorten the travel time but would also put us in danger of facing bramble storms. I've seen man and beast torn apart from those mixes of high winds and debris. Moikya says the odds of us escaping the storms this time of year are small. We decide to take the longer route in order to find a settlement and restock.

We see the dark smoke before we witness the caved-in walls of the tin fortress. Landing Green is supposed to be off-limits to the Worthless. It is a watering hole and pump station for mount machines. I respect Landing Green's leader. Gorrid had fought with us in the conflict over the war band zones. I had asked him to join the ranks of Peregrinus. He declined due to the limp in his right leg.

Buzzards circle over Landing Green. I know the settlement lay in ruins before Moikya reports back from her scouting expedition. Gorrid is dead. He and the rest of his seventeen had been burned, along with their fuel. This is the work of Dune Witch Radicals. Radicals are even more reviled than Worthless. They burn and rape anything they see.

Within the wreckage of Landing Green we find an injured marauder left to die by their cult. Moikya makes him talk. He knew enough of our language for us to track the Radicals. We would be back to kill their colony after confronting the sage. The injured one means nothing to us, so we leave him to be dealt with by nature.

I give the order to set up camp after travelling a safe distance from Landing Green. We are close to victory. All of us are eager to find the sage and celebrate a new triumph. I keep the four of us disciplined by lessening our rations. Only Joyle complains. To remind him of his place, I order that he walk first guard and forfeit the remainder of his meal to me. I care not for the extra meat but authority has to be maintained. Toff has already gone to sleep by the time I finish my meal. I take extra time to review the map of the area. I did not expect to be joined by Moikya. She whispers for me to follow her away from camp. I tell her that I am on guard next and still need to finish with tomorrow's plan. She pushes away the map and takes my hand. Tonight she wants to be mine. Her breath singes my skin.

Two days later we find a vagabond walking down the middle of a road wearing armor different than any I had seen before. His shoulder pads are decorated with orange stripes and he wears a yellow gas mask. A lone vagabond means one of two things—insanity or ambush. We take position and send Toff ahead to speak with him.

Toff has a way of speaking so all can understand. The squad covers her and I keep watch with the spyglass. I can't make out the insignia on the vagabond's satchel until Toff is standing right next to him. It is the insignia of a Regimental grenadier.

I signal Moikya. She has already read my concern and is preparing to move out. I watch her circle around behind Toff and the vagabond. She unsheathes her favorite stiletto and poises to strike. She knows I will never forgive her if Toff is hurt.

We hear laughter. Toff's voice cuts through the dry air. She gives the sign that the vagabond isn't a threat. Joyle looks grim with disappointment. He had readied his pike for action. Moikya remains hidden behind a large pile of rocks.

The vagabond denies conscription with the Regiment. He is alone. He tells Toff that he'd taken the satchel from one of their dead. I suspect treachery and tell him to remove his gas mask. He refuses. Joyle readies his pike but the vagabond doesn't flinch. The vagabond calls out to Moikya's position off the road. This man was not insane—he was born to be Peregrinus.

I let Toff explain that the vagabond is a Regulate. We had heard of his kind from out West. He had left his brigade and taken up a hermetic life. He had forsaken vows but his law meant nothing to us. However, if he left his tribe to wander, he could not be trusted to know our location.

I offer the tip of the pilum. The sharp end of my weapon awaits his move. The vagabond struggles to step back, but then he attacks rather than yield. We will give him a warrior's death.

The hermit knocks my pilum back, yet Joyle and I advance. It doesn't stop the vagabond from throwing rusted flak into my eyes. His charge overtakes me, causing the pikeholder to trip over my foot.

I feel the vagabond flip over my shoulder. He used my own movement against me. The strike from his elbow to the back of my head dulls my senses. I attempt to turn and fight, but he kicks my leg out from underneath me.

Joyle shoves hard, which throws the vagabond off balance. I see our foe twist and fall. His left hand drops a curved blade. It looks like a slicer's stiletto. I thrust my pilum into his stomach and wait for blood to fill his mask.

Moikya says it's best to not search the body. She recognizes the stench of infection. This Regulate was unclean, condemned to walk alone because of some malady. We had all seen the radiated, but this was different. This man had been expelled from his tribe because of Syndrome.

Crossing into the Wind Scale territory takes a week longer than we expect. We hadn't foreseen Regimental activity this far on the edge of the beastly bowels but, for some reason, their scout-buggies and bikers are combing the area. We will have to be cautious not to start an open engagement. Peregrinus will always fight for respect, and we proudly decimate armies, even if outnumbered. Right now, though, we have a mission to accomplish. Fighting the Regiment would be a foolish distraction.

I scan the open road for signs of a trap. Moikya suggests we stay hidden until all Regiment mount machines are counted. We would be exposed and outmanned if we follow the road to the cavern of the Wind Scale sage. I listen to her advice but decide to proceed. We can stay off the road, but I'm not about to cower to scouts.

The battle ahead of us will mean facing down more armies with stronger equipment. Rusted mounts give false courage. All sixty Peregrinus are willing to die for their creed. Legend tells us our ancestors met a force six hundred strong at the Capital Standoff. The Peregrinus will be forever remembered as heroes for pushing back the oppressors and drowning the traitorous senators. My great-grandfather was pikeholder to the javelineer who decimated the prophet who poisoned the world. To have lived in those days would have been glorious! My greatest fight was at the Grand River Confrontation seven months ago. We routed one hundred seventy-five foes with a quarter of our squad's resources and only fifteen stabbers. The enemy had taken Herd trade bridges, so the Peregrinus were summoned. I led the infamous death-charge into the main camp. I was rewarded with promotion and the knowledge of my brother's death.

When I look at Moikya, I think back to the loss of my brother. She is so young and so willing to die. Her passion is admirable. Yet, as leader of this squad, I must be hardhearted. I must not let her find love—she is too effective as a slicer. *Rex Venomious* will bring us soundless victory. I will not let her recent attempts to seduce my skin distract from our purpose. She is of my squad and nothing more. I have already made my vow to another.

The sage must fall today. He stole women and water. The woman he keeps at his side is Simdi, our squad mate's mother. My now-lover Toff chose this mission for the squad, for it is her mother who was stolen by this false shaman. Toff and I have a strong friendship and an even stronger bond. She knows of Moikya's charms, but she trusts me. I have vowed to take no other into my arms. Only Toff's hands and words will bring pleasure. I will never betray her heart.

I know Toff's mother well. Simdi taught us that warriors could become family. I do not understand why the sage would take her. She is too old to bear children—why would she matter to him? Peregrinus are outsiders but we value family. Simdi is Peregrinus because Toff is Peregrinus. Did the sage not know we would come for one of our own? Our devotion makes us strong. We will take back what is ours.

* * *

We arrive midday at the Wind Scale sage's cavern, following tracks from a nearby oasis. He has to be there. We want to see the false shaman shamed. We expect opposition but find only the quiet of the poorly hidden cave entrance.

Simdi greets us with rations. She wears a yellow silk robe and smiles like we are family. This is not a woman who has been stolen. She is happy for the reunion with her daughter.

Toff embraces her mother. Tears flow from both women's eyes. It's the first time I have seen Toff cry. It is beautiful.

Simdi speaks to us of her now-lover. This cavern is her home. The sage is her lost-love husband. They had always been Wind Scale. She explains how her time with the Herd was out of necessity for peace. The shaman of the Herd caravan was jealous of the love between Simdi and the sage. The Herd shaman made Simdi vow to stay with the caravan out of rivalry.

She would only return to the sage if he could claim dominance over their former tribe. The Wind Scales had joined with the Herd many seasons back. Their belongings and ways were merged. The shaman was surprised when the sage left the safety of the caravan's protection to wander alone into the beastly bowels. He was more surprised when the man returned with proof of a better life.

"Purgatory or Limbo. They've made winner, loser, and coward look the same," said the sage.

The grayish face of the sage is older than I expected. He had joined our reunion without any of us noticing. He wears a long coat of brown leather. In each hand, he holds a pistol, pointed at the ground. Purgatory and Limbo—they are the biggest of their kind and shined in the lantern light.

"We are Peregrinus. You have stolen women and water. Today is the day of your death," said Moikya.

"Law is for the Regulate. You are in my home. This bunker is for my tribe. Don't let it become your grave," said the sage.

I raise my hand to slow Moikya. The slicer holds her position. The sage is our enemy. He will die, but only when I choose. I will allow bloodshed if the man acts foolishly. We are four to his one, yet I sense something is wrong. Where is the rest of his tribe?

"Is this my father?" asked Toff. "Can this be true?"

Simdi nods and smiles.

"You found us because I wanted you to. We have plenty to share with my daughter's friends," said the sage.

"You would have us share stolen water?" asked Moikya.

"We have medicine for your friend," said Simdi.

"I took nothing from the caravan," explained the sage. "The shaman gave his word that we could leave. We had nothing to offer his people. I found shelter and returned for my wife."

"You have this cavern," I said. "It belongs to the Herd."

"You have my daughter," said the sage. "She belongs with us."

"The time for words is ending. You betrayed your people. You will face me in combat."

"Why so many words?" asked the sage. "Do you doubt your purpose? I've lived twice your seasons and by the same code. I would already have killed you if I found any honor in the deed. Ask yourself, Where is what I took from the Herd? Where is my tribe?"

"We are a tribe of two," said Simdi.

Moikya moves fast with her stiletto. The *Rex Venomious* slices at open air near the sage's hands. The sounds of the guns Purgatory and Limbo boom as the scout assessor falls lifeless on the cavern floor. Moikya's dark eyes meet mine one final time.

A lantern explodes, blinding the rest of us as it covers the room in flame. The sound of Joyle's anguish is all I can hear. He had loved Moikya as more than a sister. I too felt my heart rage for vengeance.

Joyle is at my side. He lunges with his pike, guiding the sage into my path. I throw my pilum, striking the sage as he fires both guns. Joyle gurgles blood; his neck is half missing, thanks to Limbo. Purgatory's blast removes the top of his skull. Joyle tries to hold himself upright with his pike before falling backward.

The echo of gunfire rings in my ears. Smoke fills my nostrils as I witness the carnage. Moikya and Joyle had died well. We will replace and remember them. As I turn to see Toff, her face is lined with tears.

"Be swift," I say.

Toff raises her pilum high and runs past me, toward the sage. My now-lover is determined and impressive. She is true Peregrinus and will be named javelineer. Her weapon impales the man as another pistol sounds. Toff's muscles stiffen. She tries to speak but no words come from her mouth. Her hands tighten around the pilum as she coughs blood. I watch as Toff collapses next to her father.

Simdi wails. In her hand she held a gun, large like Purgatory and Limbo. It had taken the life of her daughter. Her hands shake as she lowers the still-smoking weapon. Her world has ended with the loss of daughter and her lover. We stare at each other for what feels like a full season, before I remove her head with my blade.

I am Peregrinus. Third Javelin of Twenty-nine. I roam the beastly bowels of dust and fire. My squad is my life. We decimate the armies of the Worthless.

A Touch of Lemming

Alice M. Weyers

Editor: Man is one of the few animals that will overcrowd himself.
The results are left as an exercise for the reader.

Graeme Addison wanted to punch the bald-headed man in the mouth. He didn't. It wouldn't have been proper. It wasn't safe. He pushed the thought away.

Hiding his clenched fist in his pocket, Graeme shuffled his feet and cleared his throat in the accepted manner. The bald-headed man backed away the required six inches. Graeme, his territory reestablished, still felt dissatisfied.

He wanted—really wanted—to use his fist. He wanted to fight. That thought, in itself, so scared him he reached for another Irenex. All around him, he heard the short warning coughs and scuffling sounds of discontent. Many hands held dispensers. He slipped the oval white tablet from his dispenser. As he bit down on the pill, the familiar mint flavor flooded his taste buds. *Yes,* he thought, *they taste the same. They're the same shape, same size, but they're not the same. Something is missing. Something more than the green coloring.* The white pills didn't ease his anxieties, his anger. Only the green pills effectively quelled his agitation.

I must be careful, he admonished himself. *What if the bald-headed guy is an anti-aggression cop? If the man is, then he could arrest me as a malcontent, a trouble-maker. I'd be exiled into slave labor on The Farm—or worse, forced out into the Wilderness where anarchy ruled.* Graeme repressed a shudder at the thought. He cast a cautious glance at the bald man, but found no answer.

The tram-car, crammed with standing workers returning to the co-op Complex after a work day at City Center, rattled down the subway tracks. The men and women grasped the straps hung from the roof, swaying with the motion and being careful to maintain their privacy area from encroaching on fellow travelers.

Graeme clung to the hanging strap as he swayed with the motion of the tram. He gripped the strap tighter, felt his fingernails dig into the plastic surface. He gained a scant pleasure in releasing his hostilities on the inanimate object.

He attempted to distract his obsession with violence by studying the ads lining the space above the windows of the tram car.

BE A CONTENTED CITIZEN—USE IRENEX
GOVERNMENT APPROVED—GOVERNMENT ISSUED
SMILE—IRENEX WILL LET YOU

Each ad showed smiling men and women holding out government-stamped dispensers. He couldn't remember when he'd last seen a genuine smile on anyone's face.

The tram slowed to a stop, and Graeme filed out. Behind him the door sighed shut, encapsulating the fetid warmth of over-breathed air. Late again. Graeme fidgeted in the line that fed onto the escalators. Lines! Always lines. Seemed like he spent half his life waiting in lines. There must be some place, anyplace, free of crowds. Anger churned his empty stomach, and he fought a rising rage. The white pills were a sham. They didn't work.

Careful, careful, he mentally warned himself as he struggled to keep a bland expression on his face.

Graeme stepped out onto the street. Buffeted by hordes of citizens bent on reaching the safety of their apartments, he experienced the rare enjoyment of rough physical contact. It brought the same exhilaration he felt as a toddler before adults had taught him politically correct behavior. He eyed the safety of smooth gray concrete walls and steel-barred windows of the fortress he knew as home, The Delphi Complex. A city within a city, it stretched for miles along the coast. Graeme glanced at the armored kiosk at the entrance. The sight of manned weapons reassured him and relaxed the hard knot of tension at the back of his neck. He joined the line leading to the kiosk. A fingerprint and retinal scan gained him admission inside the electrified fence that surrounded the seemingly endless interconnected apartment complexes. He was so close now. Down the street stood the welcoming doors leading inside the warren of his apartments.

One more short wait.

Shorter this time as many of the people left the river of humanity for other entrances farther down the street.

In the crowded elevator, the shuffling of feet and clearing of throats rasped on Graeme's raw nerves. His heart began to pound and his hands tightened into fists. He closed his eyes and counted the stops. At the twenty-fifth floor, Graeme edged his way out and hurried down the hall to his home, his sanctuary. The door opened when he presented his palm print. He stepped inside. Only after locking the door behind him did Graeme relax.

Safe at last.

His wife Helen greeted him. "Dinner is going to be late. There was a power cut-off this afternoon."

Graeme scowled. "Another one?"

"You sound upset." Helen looked up, and Graeme noted the frown on her face. "Did you have a bad day?"

A bad day? Graeme closed his eyes as memory recalled the vivid images and painful sounds. The supply depot infiltrated and plundered. Four people hurt, two killed. Then a security failure in his own office. A bomb under his own desk, destroying files and supply orders that would take weeks to repair and recover. But, he couldn't tell her. It wasn't supposed to have happened. To mention it would be to admit security had failed. Unthinkable. To speak of it, even to his wife, Helen, could mean his job, or worse.

The lie fell from Graeme's lips. "A bad day? Uh . . . no, no, not at all."

"Well, aren't you the lucky one." She glared at him. "I've had a terrible one." Her eyes flashed with anger. "The entire crèche overwhelmed with crying infants. Then the day care dropped the toddlers in our laps as well." She gulped down a sob. "I couldn't cope. I left. It'll be on my record." Tears filled her eyes.

He had to get away. Escape. He couldn't handle this. Not right now. He held out his hand to Helen.

"I—uh, I'm sorry. I'm sorry I can't help. I'm going to take a shower and then rest a bit before dinner." He fled across the room into the sleeping area.

Inside the small bedroom, Graeme slipped a tablet from his dispenser into his mouth. White—white—white, he wanted a green one, just one. He almost sobbed in frustration. He bit down on the pill to release a minty dose of Irenex, the government-approved, government-issued answer to anxiety that didn't work. He counted the remaining tablets. Running low. Better ration them. He supposed they were better than nothing.

Graeme turned on the shower, noting the thin trickle. He shrugged. Well, it's not the first time.

He half-heartedly hummed when the two-minute buzzer sounded. Quickly, he finished washing and started to rinse the soap off. Thirty seconds before the automatic timer shut off the flow, a slash of cold water hit him. Damn. He never would get used to the shock of the cold spray. Some guys he knew found it invigorating, but it only left him breathless— and shivering. Graeme dried himself off, dressed, and lay down on the bed, basking in the almost solitude.

The sound of the TV filtered through the thin partitions along with noises, dimly sensed, of the people in the surrounding apartments. A minor irritation he'd adjusted to long ago. He knew some of the less privileged areas had communal showers. Not for him. He'd stay calm, keep his job, and enjoy a quiet shower.

The ringing of the doorbell cut through his light doze like a klaxon, bringing him to his feet.

Heart pounding, Graeme stumbled to the living room. His stomach knotted. The metallic taste of fear strong in his mouth.

What was wrong? Had security failed? Is it an emergency?

Jim and Martha Fischer, neighbors, stood in the entrance, their hands laden with packages.

"Sorry to barge in like this," Jim apologized, "but everyone's being forced to double-up. Power's cut down." He held out the parcels to Helen.

Frustrated at seeing his quiet evening ruined, Graeme burst out, "But why?"

"It's a migration, Graeme." Jim leaned closer and dropped his voice as they moved toward the window. "They're really on the move this time. They're pouring out of the Wilderness Zones like never before. Already broken through the perimeter of the Farm Zone. If we're to keep them out of the City Zone, we've got to put all the power to the grids we can spare."

Speechless, Graeme stared out the window. This made it, what, the third—no, fourth attempt this summer. And they succeeded this time. They'd broken through. Did the bombing downtown today bear any relation? A diversion perhaps? Graeme wanted to ask, but fear kept him silent. It paid to trust no one.

Graeme pressed his cheek against the window pane and gazed pensively to the west. He could almost see past the buildings to the cliffs. An image of pounding waves crashing against the rocky base tossing spray high into the air rose in his mind. It seemed strange to him that such a wild body of water should be called Pacific.

"Dinner's ready," Helen announced, as she and Martha carried the filled plates to the table.

Graeme ate mechanically, hardly tasting his food. The conversation flowed around him. He was barely aware of it and only managed a noncommittal mumble when directly addressed.

"FLASH! YOUR ATTENTION, PLEASE!" The darkened TV blared out with sound as a picture flickered up. A serious looking newscaster, seated before the Great Seal of Government, shuffled papers and assumed a confident manner. "We have overridden your home controls to bring you this important message from the Division of Control."

Graeme noticed an uncharacteristic twitch in the corner of the reporter's left eye as he continued to read the news bulletin. "We are in the midst of a large migration. The Controllers are fighting to contain them in the Farm Zone. However, a group escaped and is heading into the City. There is no cause for alarm, but precautions should be taken. Stay within your Complexes." The tic became more pronounced, and for a moment his eyes darted nervously about the studio before he regained his mask of composure. "I repeat, there is no cause for alarm. The Managers have taken into consideration every possibility for the safety of the people during this short inconvenience. Thank you and good night."

Graeme remained staring at the blank screen after the broadcast. What made them do it, he wondered? Why, after years of quiet did they suddenly explode in vast numbers and march across the countryside to hurl themselves over the cliffs into the sea?

"Now really, it's no trouble at all," Helen said, as she nudged Graeme. "Is it, Graeme? You and Jim were good enough to share your rations with us, and we don't mind sharing our place with you. Do we, dear?"

Graeme knew he should say something, do something to help restore calm and order, but he just couldn't make the effort. He felt awash on a sea of chaos as he watched his evening disintegrate. He wondered if another Irenex pill would help.

"Oh, I know," Martha said, as she reached into her purse. "We can view the disc of our vacation that we won in the last Lottery." She pulled the small package from her bag and held it out to Graeme. Her hand shook slightly. "I just picked it up on my way home tonight. It's all approved. See the tax stamp is still on it." Her voice held a pleading tone and trembled as though she held back tears. "It'll help us forget all these troubles."

Graeme nodded in agreement.

In a few minutes, the tapes flickered on the screen while Jim and Martha recounted the events they were watching.

In the darkened room, the light from the screen cast dancing shadows on the tense features of those watching. Their voices ebbed and flowed around Graeme, pulling him deeper into despair.

"See, that's us at Vista-View Beach," Jim narrated.

"Martha, I didn't realize it would be so crowded." Helen's voice carried a stricken note that echoed the shock Graeme felt as he watched the scene unfold before him.

Graeme viewed the mass of bodies cavorting on what he assumed was a beach with a sinking heart. Vista-View indeed. View of what? He wondered when the company had taken the publicity pictures with their deserted white sands, scenes of limitless horizons of rolling surf, and intimate picnics for two.

"You must have enjoyed swimming in the surf?" Helen asked.

"Well, no." Martha sounded wistful. We didn't win the raffle, so we couldn't."

"Win the raffle?"

"Yes, you see, they held raffles—at least fifteen in our group alone. If you won, then you got ten minutes' swimming in a roped-off area. I almost won."

Graeme watched the scene unfolding on the screen. Lines! Line after line of people, boats, barges. He barely heard Jim's running commentary.

"I got up high for these next shots. The roped-off area along the shore is for the raffle winners. Those long barges are for the scuba nuts. Then, the next line is the sailboats, then power boats and finally fishing boats. Did you ever see so many people having such fun?"

Graeme suppressed the panicky sob that rose unbidden in his throat. He had to get away. Away from the crowds of people on the screen. Away from the people filling his living room. They suffocated him.

"I've got to go out for a few minutes." Graeme searched desperately for a plausible excuse. "I forgot something," he finished lamely.

Blindly he ran for the elevators still operating on emergency power. No one moved aside to allow Graeme to enter. He elbowed his way in. No one cleared their throats or shuffled their feet. Instead of lowered eyes, Graeme met direct hostile stares. Flustered, he faced the wall.

* * *

Down on the street, Graeme headed for his favorite retreat, a service area. At one time, vehicles unloaded supplies there for the complex until a call for tighter security dictated that it be sealed up and a safer delivery area chosen. Few people remembered its existence. There, seated on the crumbling cement dock, he enjoyed looking straight up at the stars. Those vast, remote spaces of quiet—peace. All he needed was a few minutes alone.

Graeme turned into the service way, and stopped. Two men sat on opposite ends of the old loading platform. His secret sanctuary had been discovered. As he entered, they rose up to challenge him.

"Buzz off, buddy," one snarled. He underlined the order with the club he brandished in his fist.

"Yeah, move out, there's no room," the other man, clutching a large chunk of concrete, muttered through clenched teeth.

Quietly Graeme backed off. First the bomb in his office, then the challenge on the tram, the threat of security failure, confrontation on the elevator and now this—outright threats. To him. Personally. He couldn't believe it. Everything—every single thing was out of control. He ground the heels of his hands against his temples. His head felt ready to explode. He couldn't stand it. He needed—needed—he didn't know what he needed. Something. A place. Anyplace to be alone. Where?

A small spark of hope blossomed in the back of his mind. The cliffs. He'd always avoided the cliffs on his nightly walks. There were usually too many people standing there staring out over the sea. It didn't offer the solitude he craved. But tonight, after the TV warning to avoid the cliffs, maybe tonight there wouldn't be any people. Besides, the restless surging of the ocean seemed to match his mood. He looked yearningly to the west, toward the cliffs.

As Graeme stood undecided, the night became strangely quiet. People no longer roamed the street. He looked at the armored kiosk and noticed the riot guns hanging aimlessly down—unattended. Graeme listened for the night sounds, conspicuous in their absence. Then he heard it. Echoing down the narrow maze of streets, rebounding from the featureless concrete walls. The sound of shod feet growing louder as they neared him. Suddenly, Graeme saw them. A crowd of people, eerily silent, intent, their ranks swelling as men, women, children slipped out of doorways, flowed from the side streets, their faces composed, eyes blank. Caught up in some inner vision, they moved with purpose. Pilgrims who had found their answer.

Thoughts whispering along primal genetic lines stirred within him, reminded him. There was a place. A place to rest in pacific solitude.

Graeme stepped into the ranks as the assemblage headed up the street—to the west—off of the cliffs and into the sea.

All Orphans in the End

Donyae Coles

Editor: Turn off the light.

Selma gagged as soon as she opened the door, her question answered before she had moved her mouth to ask it. Shutting the door firmly, she took two steps back onto the cracked cement of the walk, waving her hand in front of her face to ward off the odor. There was no doubt about it, Rose was dead.

"Summer is a horrible time to die," she mumbled to herself as she looked at the door. Somewhere just beyond it would be whatever remained of her friend.

She frowned. "I thought she was younger? She looked so spry."

Selma lifted her thin shoulders and turned back down the walk. "That's the way of it though," she murmured to herself. "You never know when it will happen."

She walked slowly down the path, away from the door to the rickety garden gate and paused, turning back to the house where she stood, thinking out loud for a moment. "I don't really need anything, but maybe I should go in, make sure she's decent?"

Rose would hate it if she lay naked on the floor or her hair was out of place. Selma shook her head slowly and finally turned away. She had seen what a few days dead in the summer heat would do with Murray and she had no desire to witness it again no matter how much it would have meant to her friend.

"Besides, I can't move her, there's no point in it," she said out loud as she stepped out onto the cracked sidewalk. By the time Murray had passed there weren't very many of them left, and it took a few days for them to realize one of them had gone.

Safely past the gate, she noticed the hint of decay under the heavy smell of flowers that sprung wildly from what used to be a garden. Pausing, she turned to face the small house. The paint was faded but it had once been a cheery peach color with white trim. Now everything was cracked and faded. A few more winters and there wouldn't be much of anything left.

"She loved this house. No better place for her really," she said to the dark windows that stared back at her before turning and beginning her trek home.

"It's already getting hot," she said as walked. The midmorning sun picked up heat as she passed by the empty houses, some of which hadn't had residents in nearly twenty years. Still the structures held on, the paint fading, the roofs collapsing, the yards overgrowing. Most of them still had their windows intact. "There's no one to break them and nature hasn't been aggressive enough," Selma mused as she passed.

"Mama wanted to die at home," she remembered as she walked, letting her mind wander, "but we put her in that retirement village. Hmm, I guess there's no need now. Every home is an old folks' home."

The sound of her chuckle carried though the empty streets, blending with the birdsong as she tottered back to her own small home. She smiled as she arrived, looking up at the windows and pointed roof. Like all the others, the blue paint was chipped and faded and the roof showed some age, but it was hers.

"There's no lawn though," she said, admiring the paved stretch of land that surrounded her home.

"There was no point in it, that's what I said to Teddy. Of course, he disagreed but I said we won't have children so what's the point?" She paused, looking out at her long-ago handiwork, "I think that hurt him a bit when I said that. But it was the truth."

After she had the concrete laid, a few of her neighbors did the same, she remembered. "Steve and Barb? Was it them? It was further up in the neighborhood, I think. I haven't been that way since I stopped driving."

She turned to look toward the stretch of homes beyond where she walked and wondered. "Could there be. . .?" She started walking that way before stopping herself with a shake of her head, the heavy white braid of her hair sliding back and forth on her shoulder. "No, we checked and moved down here together. There's no one there."

"Well, I didn't move. I had already laid the cement is what I told them, and I was too old to do it again. And of course, Rose wouldn't leave her house and Murray still had Sara to care for then. So that was that," Selma said as she walked around the back to enter. She rarely used the front door.

She stood in her kitchen for a moment, letting her eyes sweep over the tidy space. She cleaned it nightly, washing down the fixtures. There wasn't anything else to do. She pulled open the refrigerator door, her wrinkled fingers grabbing the neck of a soda bottle. She smiled at the treat for a moment before opening it and taking a long drink. It was the last one but the delivery would come soon.

She walked through the kitchen, past the breakfast nook that was perfectly sized for two, and through the living room with its small unused coffee table. As she walked, she tallied the things that would come in the delivery.

"Toilet paper, eggs, butter, bread, a little meat, some vegetables, pop, maybe some candy, and a book. This is the book delivery—and oh, yes! I have to tell them about Rose. Of course.

"The delivery was a good idea," she continued as she made her way to her small computer and turned it on. "After all the Trouble, everything got to be so settled. If only people had waited."

"Trouble" is what Teddy had called the kidnappings, as if it was just a little bit of a knot in a shoelace. Those deluded men had thought they could force women to conceive but it was never a matter of trying. "That's why he moved us out of the city and bought our house when it was new. Perfect for spending a lifetime, just the two of us," she said fondly.

Teddy had had his lifetime. Now Selma sat alone in front of the barely used computer, waiting a few seconds for it to boot up. Somewhere, buried on the hard drive, hidden only by a few taps of her fingers were photos and videos. Reminders of their life together. A life that she now lived out alone.

The machine settled. She moved her finger over the pad, selecting the icon for the reporting system, the screen loading in milliseconds.

The reporting system was designed to be simple and calming with only two icons on the main screen. The simple house image would take her into the system to request home repair or supply issues. The second icon was a person. She chose it and the screen changed again.

"Teddy called it the 'obit' screen," she mused as she stared at the options for a moment. Here there were only two as well. A simple red cross to request aid and black cross to report a death. Teddy had always said it didn't matter which one you picked because it was all the same. She had chosen the red one, once, for him at the end. Help came quickly but it was already too late. She didn't blame the machines for not trying, though. She knew there was nothing to be done.

"His hand was so heavy," she mumbled to herself, remembering the feel of her husband's hand in hers in those final moments before they took him away.

Shaking off the memories, she pressed the black cross to bring up the reporting page.

"We are so sorry for your loss," a comforting voice said from the speakers, a familiar refrain to her at this point. Briefly, she wondered if the voice was prerecorded or generated and if that even made a difference. "Please, what is the name of the deceased?"

"Rose," Selma said, her voice cracking. She cleared her throat and took another drink of her soda.

"What a beautiful name. What was her last name?" the computer chimed.

Selma thought for a moment, *what had her name been?* She was sure she had known it but toward the end, it didn't matter. She was just Rose, and she was just Selma. Last names were for a wider world. Theirs had been so small. Just the two of them at the end.

"I don't know," she finally said.

"That's fine," the computer chimed in its pleasant voice. "Maybe I can help you? Was this Rose?"

A photo flashed on the screen of the old woman with her hair short, cropped close to her skull. The haircut had been Selma's uneven handiwork. She didn't smile; the photo was an annoyance. The drone showed up every six months to take their picture to ensure that there was always a current image on file. It had been an idea instituted in the early days when it became apparent that there wasn't going to be anyone to help identify elderly men and women, like herself, when they went wandering off or worse, turned up deceased.

Behind her in the photo was Rose's house, her home that she lay in now. "Yes, that's her," Selma said.

"Has she been interned?" the computer asked, mocking concern perfectly.

"Yes," Selma answered without hesitation. Rose would be so upset if they destroyed her home. It was better to just tell them that they had buried her. After Murray died they had told the system that he was still in bed. His body had been collected in less than three hours. The bots that handled the job had broken in the door and ruined the carpet. Rose would hate that and it didn't matter anyway. Selma was the only person left to mourn her.

"Do you want to say anything? Leave any words for others who may have known her?" the computer asked. It asked the same question after each of her friends had passed. Not for Teddy though; this question wasn't set up then. Selma thought about his funeral briefly and wished he had died later, not just for the time they would have had together but because his body would be closer. She hadn't traveled outside the neighborhood in years; there was no reason to.

"No," she said. Everyone who knew Rose was dead, save her.

"Thank you for taking the time to do this," the computer chimed. "We know that it's hard for you and appreciate you doing this in your time of mourning. Please take care of yourself."

Selma nodded and reached forward, tapping the screen to close it out. Sighing, she sat back, sipping on her soda.

"I should have taken in a dog," she said. They used to wander the neighborhood, friendly mutts that had once had homes. There were no puppies; people were very good about spaying and neutering their animals after the "Problem," another phrase from Teddy to describe the lack of children. There was more money for that sort of thing. After a few years the animals started to die and attract vermin. Selma wasn't sure who notified the machines but one day they were all gone. The System had taken care of them. The way the System took care of her. She hadn't thought about it then but now, alone without Rose she wished she had taken one in. "Maybe it wouldn't have mattered," she mumbled at the screen. "It would probably be dead now too."

She finished the soda and walked the bottle to the bin. She paused to look out the back window. No grass, just hot white pavement, glaring under the late morning sun. "What a way to start my day," she mumbled to herself, stroking her hair. She paused and frowned at the pure white rope of hair in her thin hand. "It's been a while since I brushed this," she said to the empty room, turning to walk back through the house. Past the unused dining and living rooms to her bedroom.

She sat in front of her mirror and slowly unwound the braid. She squinted at her reflection. Her deep brown eyes were outlined with wrinkles but her skin was dark and smooth, despite her years. Still, the darker spots showed her age—old. *Eighty-six,* she thought, *eighty-seven? I'll have to check.*

She ran her hand through the freed hair, undoing the minor knots and tangles gently, half marveling at the length of it for a moment before picking up the brush. As she lowered it, the doorbell rang.

She paused, a slight tremble running through her body. The sound was almost foreign to her ears after so many years, but it was unmistakable. Someone was ringing her doorbell.

Placing the brush back in its spot, she stood slowly. The shiver ran through her again as her mind raced, trying to place just who could be at her door in her empty neighborhood. *The delivery? No, they aren't due until tomorrow, and besides, they don't ring the bell!* Her legs moved as if the carpet under her feet was mud, sucking and stalling her steps. For every step, the door looked as if it had moved a step away.

Finally, her hand clasped the knob and turned it, opening the door slowly.

She gasped at the pleasant man who was waiting. He wore a soft, friendly smile. His eyes were a light brown and his features hard to place as any one ethnicity. That he might be attractive to a younger Selma was only a passing thought because the man before her was young. An age no one had seen, least of all Selma, in three decades or more.

He blinked slowly and broke the illusion. *Oh,* she thought, *he's not human after all.* The small movement, just a little too perfect, betrayed him. Selma let out a breath that she didn't realize she had been holding and again examined the "man." The machines constructed him to look young, but too perfect. He lacked all the small lines that life, even a young life, would have given him.

"Can I help you?" she asked.

His expression didn't change as he opened his mouth. "Hello, Selma

Martin. Can I just say that it is such an honor to meet you?"

His voice was pleasing in the way the computer's voice was pleasing. The perfect tone to relax those he interacted with, just as he had been programmed.

"Thank you," she said slowly, looking past him at the sleek car that waited down the walk behind him. The motor hummed softly. If this had been the world of forty or even thirty years ago, she wouldn't have heard it above the sounds of humanity. In the empty street the sound traveled easily to Selma's ears. "I suppose," she said, her eyes pulling back to the figure in front of her before repeating her question: "Can I help you?"

The man smiled a bit wider. "Well, no, Mrs. Martin, I have something for you."

She frowned. "Why didn't the drones bring it?"

The man who was not really a man tilted his head, his system conferring with whatever grand computer controlled him. *Were the robots always this realistic,* she wondered, *or has it just been so long since I've seen anything as young as this?*

"Forgive me for my rudeness. I haven't explained; this is not a normal supply drop. Can we sit down?"

Selma frowned deeper before nodding and inching the door open to invite him in.

"I'm sorry about my hair, I was just about to brush it, and then the bell," she stammered. She hastily stroked her hair down, her body moving by itself, clinging to old habits to calm herself.

She paused at the entrance between the living room and dining room. "Oh," she said, turning slowly, "I suppose we should sit in here."

The robot smiled softly. In one of his hands, she noticed, he held an envelope. "Anywhere you would be comfortable is fine."

She nodded and continued on into the kitchen. "I usually take my guests in here," she explained. "Not that I've had very many guests recently, but if I did I would probably meet them in here." Her words felt awkward. Part of her realized there was no reason to explain, not to a robot, but he was there, he was someone, almost, and she was no longer used to that.

She slipped into her seat at the table and looked up expectantly.

"May I sit?" he asked politely.

She nodded and motioned to the empty seat, Teddy's seat. The robot slid into the space that would have held her husband if he were still alive. It had sometimes held Rose when she came over but was always Teddy's seat.

He laid the envelope on the table. The paper was old, yellowed, and looked as if it would turn to dust as soon as she touched it.

"I've been tasked to give this to you," he said.

"What is it?" she asked, eying the packet. "Some old letter that got lost in the mail? I probably already got an email about it years ago, that's how people communicated back before, but you know, it's been a while since I got one of those too. You didn't have to bring this here."

The robot shook his head. "No, it is not a letter that was lost. I have been instructed to let you read its contents. Please open it."

His knees touched hers under the table. She frowned as she reached forward and gently lifted the aged letter, turning it over. She slipped her finger under the closure; the glue gave instantly, having been sealed so long ago that it no longer truly stuck.

She pulled out the single sheet of heavy, rich paper. The ink stood out black against the yellowing page.

Dear Survivor,

> *You are the last living person that the System is aware of. As you know, there have been no viable births since the year 2022. Although we do not know who you are, there is a strong chance that you were one of the last peoples safely born. However, it may be that you are old enough to remember that terrible time when all the infants died.*
>
> *Though we survived the violence of the time that came after that dark period, and although we created the System to ensure that whoever was left would be taken care of, these have all been for naught. There is nothing left of us, save you, final human.*
>
> *The Android will stay with you and the System will begin to shut down. Your needs will be met by the Android and when you pass, it will all be shut down.*
>
> *We wish you well, as the last of us. May your passing be peaceful.*

—The Council

She turned to the robot, Android, unsure of what to say. "Is this," she finally stuttered, finding her voice, "is this true? That I'm the last person?"

"Yes. Our sensors show no more human life in any sector of the planet. Save for yourself, of course."

She placed the letter back on the table and stood silently for a moment. "Can you hold my hand?" she asked softly.

The Android clasped her fingers in his. His face held the same soft smile, as he had been programmed.

"Aren't you afraid of being shut down?" she asked.

"We are all very tired," he said slowly, his smile frozen on his face. In that moment he looked more human than he had before. She nodded. There were still hours of daylight left but it hardly mattered. Twilight was coming and soon after, full night. Selma let her wrinkled hands be held in his artificial ones and waited.

Tradition

James S. Austin

*Editor: What each person deems of value differs. Random people
can sometimes become closer than family.*

"My grandfather was a barber. His grandfather was also a barber. So
naturally, I'm a barber. Now you might ask, '*How does this matter
to my story?*'

It doesn't. Other than to demonstrate tradition can be stronger than
nature. Well, sometimes . . ."

My audience of one sat back in the leaning chair with his head
suspended. I continued combing out his hair in the makeshift basin,
begging the Lord that he didn't have lice. I shaved myself bald for a month
straight the last time. And these railroad transients took much less care of
their grooming than most.

"You see, I continued the family business as a way to remember our
past. I'm good like that. In fact, I am the only barber for miles around. Ever
since the moon cracked from that goddamn meteor years back, civility
only persists with the efforts we make. Civility, keep that key word, my
friend. Carry it in your pocket so you can look back and understand."

The man's eyes blinked as water ran over his forehead. I could see
a little fear as he looked upward, foam ringing his scalp as I lathered and
combed. Such a mangled mess. I could imagine he did find water troubling
with the earthy stink coming off him, still able to penetrate the purposely
aromatic shop.

"What brings you here? Not just for a good cut and shave?"

The man's blue eyes looked at mine, he had the stare, the one you get
from being on the outside too long.

"I got some coin. Worked for it at *The Farms*."

"Lovely place. Heard it smells awful, though. Nothing worse than
using our plentiful turds to fertilize the plants. You do know they transport
our crap over to New Queens, right?"

He only grunted slightly. I knew I was funnier than that.

"So, ah, didn't catch your name . . .?"

"Muh, Harold." He scooted back and forth in the lumpy seat, trying
to get comfortable. Not my fault. Times are hard.

"Yeah, Harold. The Farms must be tough work. On a break, I imagine? Take the subway tunnels on over?" The grime on his face and unbearable stench said enough. I should be used to this smell, though.

"Tough place, for sure."

"A holiday! Everyone needs one of those. I heard people go blind if they're down there too long. Not like the surface farms described in books, I reckon. It's those growing lights, right?"

The bell rang as a man stepped through the front door to the barber shop. It was Reggie, a Brokelyn peacekeeper. He walked in and headed towards one of the open chairs at the front. I could feel Harold tense up.

I greeted him with a knowing smile. "Sara, you have a guest."

Sara popped her head out of the beaded doorway at the rear, checking on who walked in.

"Hey, darlin'." She stepped through, causing a gentle clatter.

Reggie smiled at her as he clapped his hands together. "Hey, baby. Just stopping by. The day's been quiet except for Tony. Had to pull him off a tweeker. Always wanting to punch something."

"I can relate," I said, interrupting their moment.

"Jimmy, you always talk the game." Reggie shook his head, his accent thicker than the most native Brokelyners.

"Reggie, don't mind him. He be a harmless little man." She walked over and started massaging his shoulders, whispering down into his ear.

I tugged on the comb, trying to work through a knot. "Tony's just venting after being kicked off the street-ball team. Them boys are always wanting to hit something."

"He broke the man's nose. Blood everywhere. Can't have that, Jimmy, even if the scrub is strung out and askin' for it," Reggie defended.

"Darlin', you wanna grab somethin' to eat?" She looked at me seeing if I would disapprove of her leaving early.

I just kept working the comb, and gave her a smile and a wink.

"Sure." He stood up and grabbed her hand, pulling her out to the door to the florescent filled under-street.

In our newfound quiet, I looked at Harold, who watched the door close.

"They are a perfect match, I tell you."

He only grunted a soft sound in acknowledgement.

"She lived in some town in South Carolina until it was overran by marauders, as she tells it. Think she now feels safe having a peacekeeper sleeping beside her. She lost friends and family to them. She doesn't talk much about it. I probably wouldn't, either."

I grabbed the water urn and rinsed the remaining homemade shampoo from his hair.

He closed his eyes, again attempting to protect himself from overwash. I'm more practiced than he gives me credit for.

"You smell that?" I watched as the running water filled the basin, attempting to clean much of the grime out of his long, unkempt hair. "Lilac. I make this shampoo myself. A family trade secret. The *good* stuff. But I won't divulge where I get my lilac." I chuckled. He just sat there. "We all have secrets. Things we don't want to talk about, or for people to hear. I get it."

I twisted his long hair, pulling a towel off the nearby table to stop any drippage.

"Okay, Harold, take a seat over there."

He climbed out of the backward-leaning chair and limped over.

I cleaned my hands in a fresh basin and quickly dried off.

"So, why come here, to Brokelyn? Family? Friends?"

Harold looked at me as I crossed the room to make my way to the counter behind him. "Just passing through."

I grabbed a comb and a pair of scissors. Snapped them twice to test the edge quality. Eh, good enough.

"My family is from here. New York. From when it was New York, and Brokelyn was Brooklyn." I combed through the wet locks, pulling sections loose, clipping the ends down. "Not much left now. Most underground, like The Farms. Being the only barber brings almost everyone through that door sometime, sooner or later. They may not all come back but everyone appreciates a good cut once in their life."

I worked my way around the chair, talking about what once was. Leaning in, on his left leg, slightly pushing in. He grunted in pain, slightly twisting his face.

"Oh, sorry about that." A brief glimpse of anger flashed in his eyes. But he just grunted and shifted over.

"Bad leg, huh?"

"Yeah, sure . . ." Harold just looked ahead as I clipped away.

"Everything seems a little broken these days. Life is all about hardship. Would you not agree?"

"I suppose . . ."

"Right? I like to avoid all that mess. That's why I am here. Being a barber makes people right. Makes them feel more human than beast. Everyone wants to escape from being beastly. That's my contribution. Most of the time . . ."

I cranked the lower lever to drop the seat back in increments. Measured out the position and tilted the headrest back.

"Just relax. Let's take care of that nasty growth on your face." I smiled, hoping for some response. Again, funnier than Harold seemed to understand. I clipped away the length, leaving only short strands.

Turning back around, I pulled out a jar from the cabinet. "This is my special blend." I held up an unlabeled jar over his head, in front of his face, so he could get a good view. "Something in the family business." I twisted off the top and grabbed a shave brush. With a twirl, I picked up some of the cream and began working it across Harold's chin and neck.

"This stuff is amazing. You can't help but relax. Just let it set and you will understand." I ran my hand through his hair, taking notice of my tidy work. Grandpa would be proud.

"You know, I do enjoy my job. There is a satisfaction that comes from doing good work. You will soon see. While it's doing its work, I'm going to make me some tea."

I walked over and turned on a small burner on the back table. Then placed a small porcelain pot on to start heating up some water. Flicking through my small stash of tea bags I kept in a small cigar box, I picked an orange peel flavor. Every time I used one of these, I would wonder what a real orange must have tasted like. Once everything was started, I went to the front door, checked out the curtained window, and slid the bolt closed.

"Tea is such a wonderful thing. Soothes the storming soul, when needed. There are times when work does seem to get messy. You see, I've had a very colorful upbringing. Being a barber is just one of my many talents." I smiled as I returned to Harold's side.

"You see, my grandmother was also a very clever woman. Oh . . . I was raised by my grandparents. My mother died from some fever and my father, well, he was plenty absent. Never met the man.

"Anyways. My grandmother was a lady of action. She took care of things. Of people. I always loved her for that, but also wondered why she wasted so much time and energy. But, I grew to appreciate what she did for our small community. We are small, but tight. The tunnels see to that.

"Now hold still, okay?" I looked down into Harold's eyes. All I saw was confusion and panic as they returned the gaze. I reached into the large pocket in the back of the seat, pulling out a thick, rubber glove . . . sliding my left hand in until it felt snug in its obnoxiously yellow home.

I grabbed the straight razor from off the counter, gave it a couple side-wipes on my sleeve.

"You see, small towns pass quick words." I turned his head to expose the left side. With a deft slide, I swiped a clean shave down his cheek.

"I learned from my grandmother other lessons, such as plants and biochemical reactions. Big words, I love them. She helped to heal so many." I smiled as I paused in memory of her recent passing. "She was such an inspiration. I now understand the feeling. Of helping . . ." I nodded, looking down at him.

"I helped a family here once get through a bout of fever. Something my mother could not shake." I frowned. "Oh, don't worry. Like I said, she passed when I was very young so the wound has healed. They pulled through just fine."

I continued to shave his face clean. His eyes still danced around, trying to grasp his situation. I could only grin back as a line of drool escaped out the corner of his mouth.

"It's funny how this world can be so punishing to the survivors. I only saved them to let them die a month later." I turned his head to the right and began the same process. With a couple of practiced draws, his neck was now free of the ragged beard. The now clear neck showed a star tattoo.

"They died at the hands of a desperate man. A drifter who found work where he could. He stopped in at their house looking for a handout. Before they could say anything, he pushed through and slaughtered them . . . right in front of their frightened daughter." I looked down as I worked the lines of Harold's sideburns. "Of course the guy was tweaking so hard, and fortunate for the little girl, he didn't even notice her as he checked their pockets for anything of value before bolting back out the door."

I sighed as my work was done. Well, almost. I released all the levers to upright Harold in the barber chair. I walked back around and switched the razor out for a mirror.

"This is some fine crafting, if I must say." I walked the mirror around so Harold could look at his new image. He only could stare back at me with wide eyes.

"Yeah, it's good . . . right? I take a lot of pride in my work."

I watched as Harold's chest slowly rose, the only other movement allowed at this point.

"You see, chance has brought you to me, my friend. Little Jessica has told me enough times about the man who haunts her dreams. The man with the tattoo. The man who was badly stabbed in the leg in the fight by her father."

I went over and poured myself some tea, then returned to slump down in the chair next to his.

"Like I said, I believe tradition is the only way to survive this horrible world. To keep us civilized. But there are still beasts that walk among us. I have to protect my community." I looked over at him, his chest drawing breath ever so slightly.

"Don't worry, Harold, it will be over soon. That shaving cream is such a wonderful blend. Then we will see if you suffer more than they did."

An Inanimate Proposal?

Nicholas Gregory

Editor: Love can't be diminished by any force, natural or not.

I sit outside on my lover's porch. A single rose rests beside me and a poem is clutched in my right hand. I am anxious for her to arrive home. My other hand is in my pocket, grasping onto the engagement ring. I hope that it will secure the love and commitment for our future together.

Sweat drips down my forehead in steady beads, as if I were a plump man standing next to a bakery oven. I am scared about changing our relationship, but I do not know what else to do with my life after the war. No one else will love me the way she does. However, she tells me that something inside of myself has died on the battlefield.

My thoughts stop and dwell on the night's intimidating presence. It holds the smell of burning Christmas trees, while there's a mysterious red light illuminating onto the porch, like the glow of a Blood Moon.

I recall the night before I went away and my promise to her that I would make it back home, no matter what.

The moment the bus drove me away to the war, she stood there alternating between crying and being solemn. She blew a final kiss, before I went out of sight for a year. That is what I thought of the whole time oversees—that one kiss that meant so much.

Despite these memories and the present sweet sentiments, what if my love rejects me? What if she laughs at my poem? She would not do that, would she? This love of mine would not be that insincere. How long have I known her?

It is then that I wonder if this is already a dead proposal. Does she love me still? That is the right question to be asking. Does she still love me after all the both of us have been through?

At that final thought, her Cadillac pulls up. Unpleasant thoughts still seem to bounce around in my head, like white blood cells running away from death by a recursive virus.

I take a step toward the vehicle, then another. I am veiled by the night, so she does not see me. It's time to see if our hearts still beat in melody.

She gets out of the car and her blond hair starts to blow in the wind, giving her the appearance of a flying angel.

The woman I hope will be my bride sees me and gives a smile. I continue walking to her. I still do not know what to say; my bleeding heart is stuck in my throat.

At arm's length from her now, I look at her while holding onto the rose and the poem. She looks at my awkwardness, waiting.

I do not say anything as I take the engagement ring out of my pocket. I hold it in front of her. She says nothing. Absolute silence passes for a few moments.

Tears stream down her face. Taking my ring, she kisses my hand. She nods and gives her answer.

"I will wait for you until that day comes and then we will be married."

Happiness washes over me like an Indian summer. She goes into the house and out of sight.

It's now time for my part of the deal. My heart continues to flutter as I make the way back to the post-war home that I have had since dying in the war.

It's my plot in the cemetery. Arriving in the grave, I replace the dirt over myself, and close my eyes. I have a smile on my lips as I wait for the years until my fiancée is buried alongside me—until I find eternal happiness with my soulmate.

Behind the Walls

Chad Schimke

Editor: They say absolute power corrupts absolutely,
but can there be any halfway in power?

Henry Couzens drove the converted school bus for the last ten miles, even after the gas gauge dipped below empty. He popped over a ridge, and as the barren highway descended into a hollow, he read a small sign a short distance away. "*Litogot Township.*" Funny, he'd never heard of that settlement before. The engine sputtered and died, stalling out on the shoulder. He slumped over the steering wheel, rubbing his hands on his bushy hair and thick stubble. Not again. He felt so frustrated. He rubbed his eyes with his knuckles and sighed.

He heard his wife, Jane, call from the back, "Is everything all right?" He turned to look at her. Jane had brown hair and wore a threadbare dress, their toddler Billy balanced on her hip.

"Yeah," Henry said. "We're out of gas. That's all."

From the driver's seat he looked at the walled township and the gap between the walls and forest. The thick perimeter was built from wood slats surrounded with neat, irrigated crop beds. He guessed . . . corn and wheat? He heard another voice behind him from his best friend, Leland.

"Out of gas again, Henry?"

"Yeah, I'm walking into town. Keep an eye on the bus."

"All right, sure."

Henry climbed out looking back at Leland. His friend had red hair and wore a tattered flannel shirt. Leland's wife, Alison, stood beside him. The same age as Jane, she stood taller with light hair and a similar plain dress.

"Be careful," Leland said. "This place looks intimidating."

"I'll be fine. We can always continue on foot if we need to."

"I know. We can't trust them yet is all I'm saying."

Henry walked toward the walls looking at a sentry post, main gate, and armed guard atop a tower. To his right, walls curved around back and train tracks disappeared behind the fortress. The sentry called down to him.

"State your business." He pointed a rifle at Henry's head.

"Ran out of gas a ways back. Have any to spare? I can put in some work."

"Are there more of you?" His voice was a dry monotone.

"Yes."

"How many?"

"Four families. Men, women, and children."

"You have to interview with the mayor."

"Of course; you don't know us. But trust me, we're family men, not brigands."

Don't think about what's on the other side of the wall. He considered gleaning corn and going back to the bus. Just then, the gate creaked open. He had to calm himself down and resist the urge to get the hell out of there. Life on the road under the constant threat of brigand attack had made him hyper alert.

"Thank you." Henry stepped inside a second barrier, an interior wall, where there was another guard on the ground. He'd meet the mayor and after that decide to leave or stay.

"Get him a quarter gallon of fuel," the guard said. "You can park inside the enclosure overnight."

"Okay, I understand."

* * *

Henry woke with a knock on the door. When he tucked his shirt into his pants and snapped the buckle, he was keenly aware of his ribs sticking out from under his skin. He slid the bus door open and walked down the steps to be greeted by a man wearing a cowboy hat.

"Ed Firston." The man shook firmly. "Everybody calls me 'sheriff.'" The sheriff's thinning black hair lay plastered on his scalp. He put his straw hat back on his head.

"Henry Couzens; nice to meet you."

"Follow me to the mayor's house, on the other side of the compound."

They walked through the township, with buildings on either side that must be pre-Die Back. The walls must have been built later, with some of the surrounding forest cleared away. The garage, warehouse, distillery, small houses, and apartments were clean and neat. Perfect, even.

The back edge of the walls skirted alongside an imposing yellow brick building with an armed guard at the front door. The sheriff entered, tipping his hat at the guard, and Henry followed.

"Mayor Litogot's this way."

Down a dark hallway, Henry noticed a woman seated at a desk in front of an imposing set of doors.

"Here to see the mayor?" she asked. While she got up to fetch the mayor, Henry waited in a proper den.

What a phony. Henry didn't trust her. Or anybody. At least, not yet anyway.

A tall, slim man with dark eyes and hooked nose appeared, wearing a white dress shirt and black pants.

"Welcome." He shook hands softly. "Willis Litogot; pleasure to meet you, sir."

"Likewise." Henry let go of the clammy handshake and wiped his hand on his pants. "Thanks for feeding us last night."

"You can call me 'mayor,' everyone here does."

"Yes, sir."

"Where've you been so far?"

"We left Fordham Township after the food ran out. We've been on the road ever since."

"Five months?"

He must've known they succumbed. "You got it." He'd never heard stories about Litogot? And how's this guy in charge. He seemed like a pantywaist, not a leader.

"Well, we're thriving. Plenty of crops, water, and livestock to go around. But the work's hard, no way around it."

"Not surprising. You've created a fantastic community."

"It's harder than you think, finding good people to do . . . certain types of work."

"Well, we've barely survived, much less thrived." Keep it together, he wanted to make the right impression. "That's why this place seems so appealing. A job well done."

Willis beamed. "What did you do before the Die Back? Work-wise . . ."

"I was in the military."

"A military man, you say. You might be useful around here. "Sheriff, assign this man and his people work. We'll try them out."

* * *

The first week, Henry worked in the warehouse, unloading boxes of corn brought in on a hi-rail. The past few days he'd been on guard duty at the sentry post. Spending the day under the burning sun sucked. But eating real food like meat and bread made up for it. Now that protein and carbohydrate had returned to his diet, he could feel muscle mass returning to his arms and shoulders. He felt more like his old self than ever: tall, muscular, and good looking. How amazing what food and sleep in a real bed could do.

He didn't understand why the mayor trusted him so readily. He certainly didn't trust the mayor and he didn't like how the people weren't talkative or friendly. His wife, Jane, worked in the kitchen with Alison. Something bothered Alison as the two had grown distant.

Day before yesterday, he'd been told to try and get some sleep during the day if he could, since tonight he'd be working graveyard shift.

Henry arrived for work at the mayor's house, finding the sheriff waiting for him on the front steps.

"Hi, Henry. Want to know what job you'll be doing tonight?"

"Yeah."

"You're hard, from living on the outside, not like other people living in this town."

"I've seen lots."

"Can you think for yourself?"

"Sure I can. Good military training."

"Ayup." The sheriff handed him a rifle, knife, and zip-ties. "You can keep these from here on out."

"Really?"

"Yep. If there were enough pistols to go around, I'd give you one of those, too. Follow me; you're on guard duty for Mayor Litogot tonight."

"Sounds good. And thank you."

"Stay anywhere here, in the hall, on the steps, or in the lobby. Got it?"

"Sure."

Ed clamped a hand on Henry's shoulder and looked him square in the eye.

"I know you're a good fighter. Now, let's see if I can trust you, too."

The sheriff's boots tramped up the back steps and trailed off. Hours passed and Henry paced. Murmurs of conversations flowed to the bottom of the steps. As always, boredom was the enemy of guard duty. So he crept upstairs past the dark landing and hid. Yeah, it was a risky thing to do, but he had to know more about these guys. Especially since he was being groomed. For what? Nervous as hell, he froze solid and caught a glimpse of them.

The mayor sprawled on the couch, the sheriff sitting in a chair opposite to him. Two women sat on either side of the mayor, one of his skinny legs on hers. Were the women wearing makeup?

"I spotted a new brigand camp on the ridge, a mile away from the wall." That was the sheriff.

"Brigands? Kill them all, and for fuck's sake make sure none of them get away." It was the mayor talking.

"Ed should do it himself, take some gas and burn everything after they're all dead. Please don't leave a burned camp behind." Henry didn't know this voice but he fixed on a black profile blanked out by a side lamp.

"Are you crazy?" The mayor, again. "Last time Ed tried to take on two brigands by himself, he almost died. All we've got is two guys to run field missions."

"What about Henry Couzens, the new guy?" said the third man.

"He's very promising," said the mayor. "He's stronger than you two put together."

So, he was being groomed. But for what? He started to return downstairs but caught a flash of movement. The woman in heels and a miniskirt turned, and he saw her face. Alison, Leland's wife!

Shit! No fair. Why did he have to see her? He crept back to the lower level, opened the door and stepped out. He stood there all alone in the dark.

That's when Henry heard a noise, a soft scraping sound. *What was that?*

A dangling knotted rope that trailed down the tall wall. A brigand! Henry recoiled from the intruder's long hair and gross matted mess of a beard.

The invader lowered himself and landed in the dirt. A ragged blanket tied under his chin trailed behind like a cape as he advanced toward the mayor's house. He struck the back window with a board. Before the shattered glass hit the ground, Henry put him in a headlock, smacking the vandal's hand hard against the stoop, making him drop the board. Then, the light flicked on. Henry glanced up at the sheriff looking through the broken window.

"Ayup. The new guy's gonna be useful around here. That's for sure."

* * *

After his shift, Henry urgently wanted to catch Leland alone before anybody else arrived to work at the distillery.

Henry called out in a loud whisper, "Leland!"

"What the hell are you doing here?"

"I need to talk to you."

Leland unlocked the door and they entered one of two locked doors in town, this and the mayor's house.

Henry noticed a shelf full of bottles containing clear liquid. He read the note tacked underneath. *"Don't touch."* That's weird. He gulped. Even though he hated telling his best friend about Alison, he knew it was the right thing to do.

"Do you know where Alison was last night?"

"Yeah, working the night shift at the kitchen."

Henry shook his head.

"No? She was . . . where?"

"At the mayor's."

"Oh, fuck. Why would she lie to me?"

"The mayor calls the shots, so he wanted her there. Don't you wonder why the township is so guarded? Nobody breaks any rules."

"What about brigands?"

"Yeah, but with these walls, how much of a problem could they really be? I caught one last night and they're getting rid of it tonight after dark."

"No shit?"

"Everybody does their job. Nobody's late, never complains."

"Have you met Al yet?"

"Nope. Why?"

"He has a house, just like the sheriff. He brags so much, he never shuts up."

Henry heard a sound outside.

"Shh," Leland whispered. "That'll be Al."

Al crossed the threshold, Henry recognized his distinctive profile as the third man at the mayor's house last night. Al had white hair and a square nose.

"Hi, guys." Al smiled and shook Henry's hand. "You must be Henry. I'm Al. The mayor's already taken a liking to you."

"Cool."

"Yeah, he talked about you last night. He liked the way you handled that brigand."

"It's good to be liked by the boss. Right?"

"Sure is, but take my advice. Don't be a pussy. Just remember how much harder life would be living outside the walls."

"Of course. But hey, I've got to go to bed, I've been up all night and have another graveyard shift coming up tonight. Have a good day."

Henry walked home, hoping he would be able to get some sleep. He saw a sign posted on the path, which he stopped to read.

LABOR DAY. Under order of the mayor, tomorrow is a day of rest. The Labor Day holiday honors the hard work of the citizens of Litogot. Packaged food has been distributed as the kitchen will be closed. The school will be closed also. Parents with young children need to supervise their own. Regular work resumes the following day. The mayor selected a present just for you. Thanks for your service to the Litogot Township.

In his apartment he noticed a note and box on the kitchen table.

Dear Henry. I'm pleased you decided to stay at Litogot. I think I can trust you and work with you. I'm sorry to ask but I still need you to guard my house tonight. The sentry will be manned as well. Your wife can enjoy her holiday with your son and I've given her a separate present. Please accept this small gift as a token of my appreciation. Sincerely, Willis.

Henry lifted the lid to examine the present. He'd received a new pipe, tin of tobacco, wax-sealed cheese, chocolate bars, a cracker box, and a bottle of red wine. He wondered if getting this stuff was going to make what he had to do worth it?

* * *

Henry stood on the front steps of the mayor's house, looking toward the town square. Recorded music bounced off the tall walls and people danced stiffly on a makeshift dance floor. He turned and locked the front door behind him. No curfew tonight, and the mayor wasn't home.

Walking through the back of the house, he passed three windows; one of them caught his attention. The middle one had a broken latch. He found an open door and it surprised him to find the room lit by an electric lightbulb. Strange, he should be alone in the house.

What in the hell could he be looking at? The room was dominated by a large wooden table approximately twelve square feet. A model train, a miniature wood slat fence with tiny replica buildings inside, and a central path ending at the mayor's little yellow house. Litogot Township!

He crouched low, peering inside the back of the three levels of the mayor's house. The bottom level consisted of the replica train room in minute detail, even down to a smaller model train on a tiny replica table. Each building and the train were recreated in tiny detail. A tiny table maybe two inches square? The long hallway connected through the lobby to the front door. The perimeter fence ran along the back of the small house and he noticed the town's tiny gate. His eyes scanned the second level. He saw an office, den, kitchen, and dining room. On the third level he saw a bathroom and master and spare bedrooms. Of the rooms he'd been inside at the mayor's house so far, the tiny replica copied each feature of the real thing. Every stick of furniture, lamp, plate, shade, and rug were exactly the same.

Unsettled, a chill ran up his spine. Wanting to leave, something made him stop. He saw two boxes installed in the wall beside the door—a recessed breaker box on one side and a solid metal locking cabinet on the other. A safe, perhaps? Henry didn't know.

How about this shit? The mayor was a weird dude with a weird hobby. Shouldn't he just be grateful his family could be safe behind the walls, and off the road? Henry couldn't help but think the townsfolk acted strangely. Not unusual, but nobody here made mistakes. What the hell was wrong with Alison? She knew what accepting that dinner invitation had meant. Why did they need a distillery? Nobody even drank any fucking alcohol.

How different life had been before the Die Back. Why couldn't things be like before? Even here, safe inside the walls, he'd never shake the memory of that smell. The overwhelming scent of death, cities like boneyards with bodies stacked like cordwood. No, things would never be the same again. Litigot was so fucking weird because they were as scared as he was. But even that couldn't fully explain it. Yeah, all right, he was out of sorts, maladjusted by it all. He'd hid after the collapse. Living in a society was hard. He'd been alone for how long? He didn't know, without a watch or calendar.

Then, eight miserable seasons after death stopped claiming the living, a few distant communities came together. But in place after place, the story always ended up the same way. Food ran out, brigands attacked, or people couldn't stand living together again after what they'd gone through. Not here. Not Litigot.

Henry left the hobby room, walked toward the lobby. He looked out the window at the celebration outside. The music stopped, the lights snapped off, and people left the party, shuffling strangely. What gives and why do these people act so fucking weird? He heard footfalls and the door unlocked. The mayor walked in with Alison. They passed him and went upstairs. Moments later the sheriff showed up too.

"Make sure the mayor gets into bed safe," the sheriff said. "He's had a few too many."

"Yes, sir."

The sheriff stumbled away, unsteady on his feet. He heard the mayor and Alison climb the back steps to the third floor bedroom.

Damn it. Leland's his best friend. What a cold bitch. Henry helped himself to a stiff drink from the mayor's stock. Outside, he thought he saw a figure move. Yes, a man approached the door, which he opened.

"Leland?"

It was his best friend and it was obvious he'd been crying.

"Come on, stop that." Henry hugged him. "Hey, I'm sorry."

"She's my wife."

"Yeah, but you don't own her."

"I can't stand it. I never get to see you and she's gone too. I'm pretty sure she's going to move out."

"Really?"

"Can I have a glass of water?"

"Of course."

Henry closed the door, walked to the bar and reached for the water carafe. Before he realized what happened, Leland darted to the back of the house.

"Leland!"

He dropped the glass and it shattered. By the time he reached the top, Leland had kicked in the bedroom door.

"How could you do this to me?" Leland screamed. "You fucking bitch, I hate you!"

"Henry!" The mayor stood in front of Allison, wearing only his underwear, she was naked.

Then, Henry noticed a pistol pointed at Leland's head. He inched closer but stayed out of the line of fire. "Everybody needs to relax."

"Relax? This creep is fucking my wife!"

"Yeah, come on. Let's go back downstairs."

"How did he get in here, Henry?" The mayor's voice trembled.

Great, he was going to get kicked out or shot, maybe both. He tried to pull Leland away by the shoulder.

"Don't fucking touch me!"

Henry tucked his body behind the door jam.

"Get out of here!" the mayor shouted.

"Get out of here," Alison said, flat and cold.

"You're the last person to tell me what to do!" Leland took several steps closer to the mayor. The sound of a shot ricocheted through the house. Henry smelled gun smoke, singed skin, and the copper smell of blood. "Fuck, Willis! You shot him." He stood in the doorway, looking at Leland's body.

Alison screamed. She threw herself into the mayor, flailing her arms. Henry was shocked seeing her shake off her torpor. The mayor held the gun aside but she almost knocked it out of his hand.

"Shoot her!" The mayor yelled.

"No fucking way; I'm not shooting her."

His eyes followed the barrel, swinging back and forth. By now Alison knocked Willis to the bed and fell on top. Henry wanted to go in and disarm him but they were rolling around too much. In a split second another shot rang out.

Both of them were in a limp heap on the bed. As Henry reached for his rifle, Alison's body rolled off and fell onto the floor with a thud. She landed face up, her mouth slack and her eyes glassy.

"It's ugly sometimes, being responsible for all this." The mayor pointed his pistol at Henry's head. "I've had to make tough decisions. This wasn't the first."

He couldn't believe the mayor acted so casually. Henry backed up with his hands at his sides, trying not to make any sudden moves. The mayor advanced step by step.

"You, on the other hand, might still be salvageable. I felt it the first moment I met you. You're strong. I need a man like you, more than you know. I don't need you to decide tonight, anyway. I'm going to lock you away for a while. Drop the gun and slide it under the bed."

"Lock me away?" Henry slipped off the strap and slid the rifle away.

"Yeah. Ed's got a jail cell in his basement. We made it with rebar and padlocks. Turn around." He knew the pistol remained pointed at his head.

"Go ahead, we're walking to Ed's house."

They left the mayor's house and walked a short distance to the sheriff's. If his wife and son didn't know where he was, what would happen to them? The situation crystalized in his mind. Certainly, he wouldn't act until the right time. He knew from his military training that timing was everything. So whatever it took, he would damn well set himself free and protect his family. He turned the handle, the door swung open and they entered a bedroom. The sheriff lay in bed, snoring, and the mayor shook him awake.

"Wha'?" Startled, the sheriff responded fast by flipping over.

"We've got two bodies to dump in the woods."

"How did—"

"Where are your zip-ties?"

"My pants." The sheriff threw off the bedsheet and stood up.

The mayor handed the sheriff a pair of zip-ties. He said, "Put these on him," then stood back, with his gun pointed. The two men in their underwear held Henry. Motionless, he let the sheriff place the zip-ties over his wrists.

The mayor spoke before leaving. "Put him in the cell in your basement, then come right over. I want the bodies gone before dawn."

The outer door closed. Henry froze. He watched the sheriff pull on his pants. As his captor pulled a shirt over his head, Henry decided he had to take this chance. He slammed the zip-tie as hard as he could on his knee. It snapped open! While the sheriff tried to react, he caught him up in a chokehold. Henry held the struggling sheriff until he stopped moving and just another minute to be sure.

He dragged the limp man downstairs into a makeshift jail cell. Just like he'd been told, the rebar door locked with a padlock.

Henry returned to the mayor's house. The broken window on the back door had already been covered with plywood. He checked the latches on the three back windows, confirming that one of them was indeed broken. He slid it open, climbed in. He crouched in the dark for a few moments to make sure no one had heard anything before creeping straight up to the top floor.

No mayor anywhere in sight, only the bodies of his good friends. But he did see the pistol. Checking that it was still loaded, he put in his belt loop. The mayor must be in the room with his weird-ass toy set. So Henry went back down and found the mayor hunched over the replica town. He hid in the dark hallway and watched him through the open door, standing still and silent.

With the back of the tiny yellow house flipped open, the mayor plucked out a male and female doll and placed them in his palm. Even in the dark, Henry knew he held the Leland and Alison figurines. Behind the house, in the forest of trees carved from balsa flecked with green moss, he shoved a smudge of crumbled cork aside. The nude female was flecked with blood splatters. He placed the figurines in a trough and covered them with a little pile of cork.

The mayor cocked his head to one side and looked through a tiny window in the sheriff's house. His placid face transformed into a scowl. He lifted the sheriff's house off the foundation, set it aside, and checked the basement. He lifted the tiny jail cell in his palm and squinted close up. Inspecting the replica rebar jail cell, the mayor sneered at the sheriff, who lay on a cot in his underwear. "How the hell did you get in there?" His mouth dropped open as the little jail cell clattered to the table. He patted his pants pockets.

"Shit! I left my gun upstairs."

"Don't worry, I have it." Henry pointed the pistol at the mayor as he advanced toward him out of the shadows.

"How did you get in here?"

"The latch on the downstairs window is broken."

The mayor's upper lip trembled. "Please. Don't shoot me."

"Tell me why I shouldn't?"

"I'll give you anything you want."

"I could just take it." Henry shrugged. "I'm a killer. You said it yourself, you saw something you liked the first time you met me."

"No . . . please?" The mayor held his hands in front of his chest.

"Move over."

Henry motioned him aside and circled the table. He looked into the open top of the replica mayor's house. There were tiny blood spatters and a small glossy puddle of blood on the carpet in the upper bedroom. He touched it with his finger; it felt wet. To the right, he looked at the grate where water flowed into town via the aqueduct. He pointed to a doll and cart loaded with large glass bottles. He remembered seeing the same glass bottles filled with clear liquid the day before when he spoke with Leland in the distillery.

"This is Al. What are you putting in the water?"

"N-n-nothing."

"Don't fucking lie to me."

The mayor's eye fleetingly landed on a table piled with books, looking away immediately.

"This?" Henry picked up an old book with a crumbling leather cover and read the title page. "High Magic Spells and Potions."

"That's mine!" Was he going to start crying?

"You know, so much makes sense now. You're not strong, you haven't been elected and you aren't good with people. I should've known Alison couldn't desire you. Wish I could've figured it out before Leland died."

"I'll show you everything . . . you're a natural leader. We can work together. What do you think?"

"How do you keep them under your spell?"

Mayor Litogot looked at the door, like he wanted to leave. Yeah, no. Then Henry noticed him looking at the safe box across from the breaker box. Of course. "Give me the key to the cabinet." He took several quick steps toward the mayor.

"No!"

"I said, give me the fucking key!"

"No!"

The second time the mayor said it, his voice cracked and he cowered, with his hands covering his face.

"All right, have it your way."

Henry grabbed the mayor by the collar and belt loops and swung him into the corner. Willis crashed into the wall and landed in a whimpering heap. Henry stuck his hand into the mayor's pocket and felt something metal. He pulled out the key and unlocked the wall cabinet next to the door.

"No way!"

The miniature figure looked just like Willis Litogot. The same hawkish nose and beady eyes. He was thin, dressed in a long-sleeved white shirt and black pants.

"Don't touch him!" the mayor screamed, pleadingly.

Holding the doll between his thumb and forefinger, he placed it on the table top. All the little dolls on the table came to life. They unloaded crates from the train, drove toy trucks, walked the path and entered tiny buildings. Henry inched nearer and brought his face close to peer over the perimeter fence.

"No way! They're talking."

With his face close to the replica town, he could make out their tiny faces. Eyes blinked and mouths moved. The plastic flesh tone resembled human skin. Their hair ruffled and their clothes moved, like any regular person's would. Their tiny chests expanded, breathing real air!

"You did this—it's some kind of crazy magic."

"Just leave. I'll give you whatever you want and you won't have to work anymore. I can give you anything—"

That's it! A thought came to Henry which helped all of it to make sense. He crouched low to look in the model train room of the mayor's tiny replica house. There he was. Henry, in miniature. Himself. The same hair, thick stubble, and sturdy build. The doll gestured and talked, looking straight at him, motioned for him to come closer.

"What?" Henry said.

The doll motioned again with his tiny finger. His little lips formed the word: *closer.*

He grasped the doll and brought it up to his ear, listening to a tiny voice.

"There can only be one mayor."

The doll pointed to the recessed cabinet and motioned to return him to the mayor's house of the replica town. The full-size mayor lay on the floor, trying to sit up, rubbing his sore neck.

"Is this how it works?"

The flat of Henry's palm hovered over the tiny figure of Willis Litogot unaware of a giant hand above him.

"No! Please don't—"

Henry swatted the tiny figure, with his hand, into the fake felted green grass. Squashed, like a bug.

He lifted his palm and inspected the underside, where a rivulet of blood trailed down his wrist. He wiped the smudge on his pants. He returned his attention back to the full-sized mayor and leaned over him. The mayor's breath was shallow and spit bubbles that dribbled onto his chin. His arms, legs, and neck were contorted into a ghastly position. When he'd smashed the little doll it had the exact same effect on the man, it nearly killed him! Shoot him, in the back of the head. Put him out of his misery. You know what? Nah, don't bother.

Henry returned to the replica town and hovered close over his own tiny figure. A strange expression came over his face as he cooed to the little doll.

"You can call me mayor, everyone here does."

He picked up the little doll and set it on the steps of the mayor's house.

"Brigands? Kill them all and make sure none of them get away."

He flipped open the back of the apartment building, where Jane and Billy were sleeping, and plucking them out of their beds, he set them on the steps.

"The mayor himself has personally selected a present, just for you."

He picked up his doll again and held it, cupping it with his hand. His hands moved, his face emoted, his eyes blinked, and he spoke.

Immediately, the figurines on the table stopped talking or moving, the toy truck rolled to a stop and the train shut off. Henry returned to the metal safe cabinet, set his figurine inside and closed the door, locking it with a key.

* * *

Three days later, Henry Couzens stood on the steps of the yellow brick building near the back wall of the township. The citizens shuffled in their strange gait into place and stood still, staring straight ahead. Al, the distiller, and Ed, the sheriff, stood off to one side on the steps. Henry expected their full support for him as the new mayor and they'd promised to deliver. Both of them knew he held all the power and were scared of him now that Willis was gone. Nobody moved or talked, they paid perfect attention.

His wife, Jane, stood on one side and his son, Billy, on the other. Jane wore a ruffled dress and Billy wore short pants, while Henry wore a white shirt and black pants.

"Citizens, you'll look back on this day as the beginning of a period of great prosperity."

He pointed to a freshly painted city limits sign, propped against the fence in the front. *"Couzens Township."*

"As we inaugurate my first day as mayor, I pledge to you we'll work hard, but life will be better than ever. I've taken the liberty of giving each of you a small gift. Personally selected by me. Everyone can take the day off and enjoy a party, in honor of all your hard work. A holiday I like to call . . . *Labor Day."*

Coffee with Jesus

Z. S. Roe

Editor: This is a tough act to follow.

The hell of it is that they were right. The Christians, I mean. Jesus came back and raptured his whole damn crew. No, I didn't see it personally; I was on the toilet when it happened. But it was described to me:

There was a sudden light in the sky, bright like a thousand suns, instantly blinding the billion or so unsaved souls who were unlucky enough to be outside when it happened.

No trumpets, no host of angels—just a supernova flash and a little over an eighth of the population disappeared. Anyone near a Christian said there was a loud *pop*! —like a cork pulled from a wine bottle—as the air around that person rushed to fill in the suddenly empty space.

The historians call this moment the Great Precipice, as afterward, we all kind of fell off the edge of the world, especially the blind people.

Suicide.

Mass hysteria.

A lot of unnecessary reruns of Dr. Phil.

Eventually, though, we moved on. You wouldn't think that possible and it wasn't at first. But time has a way of moving you forward whether you like it or not. We lost our shit for a while, sure, but we still had to get up every morning and feed ourselves.

Eighteen years later and we talk about it like it was another era, a time before now. The rapture is our history. In the meantime, we've gone back to our wars and geopolitical disputes, or (if you're like me) our texting and cheese burritos.

Anyway, what I came here to say was that the rapture saved my life.

Before Jesus showed up with his light show, I worked in retail, selling pay-as-you-go cellphones to assholes. I lived in a shitty apartment and spent my nights drinking boxed wine, watching a lot of reality TV, and worrying about "my purpose in life." At work, I made lists on customer receipts of things I dreamed of doing, or thought I should be doing, or had heard that other people had done. And then after work I went home and drank and waited for those dreams to happen. Because they had to—destiny happened to you, I thought.

I remember my Uncle Carl, a real douche. The guy used to screw around on his wife. He drank a lot, too, though mostly beer. One time at a family function I walked in on him in my grandmother's wallpapered bathroom. He was doing a line of coke off the toilet tank, and he looked up at me and said it was "prescribed," that it was "medication for my nasal congestion." I believed him. I was nine, but still . . .

So the douche overdoses one night, just about dies.

When my family goes to visit him in the hospital, we find him sitting up in bed reading a Gideon Bible. One of the nurses had snuck it in for him. He held the little thing in his big hands like it might be a small bird and he didn't know quite what to do with it. But there was this silly smile plastered across his face even larger than the one I saw on him when he looked up at me with his coke mustache at Grandma's.

That's when I knew something was up.

Turns out, his brush with death changed his life. He said he saw Jesus in the ambulance sitting next to the paramedic.

Which is fine, I guess. Who am I to dog on someone's personal beliefs, especially since they turned out to be true? The trouble with my Uncle Carl, though, was that he wouldn't shut up about it. Once he got out of the hospital, it was Jesus this, Jesus that. He said Jesus was his new best friend, that he had a "personal relationship" with him, that every morning he poured himself a cup a coffee and then poured a second cup and set it across from him. The second cup was for Jesus. I kid you not.

"You do this every morning?" I asked him.

"Of course."

"And does Jesus show up?"

"Man, he's never left."

Uncle Carl had been doing drugs a long time. He didn't give up coke, by the way. I walked in on him two more times after he found Jesus, only on those occasions he had his little Gideon Bible poking out of his back pocket while he powdered his nose.

And the thing of it is that my Uncle Carl was raptured. I checked, and that jerkoff's gone. And that kind of gets to me. Carl was not a good person. He was an asshole, like all the other assholes I saw every day, except he never bought a damn phone from me.

So it's been eighteen years. Since the Great Precipice, there's been a lot of talk about what happens next. Nobody knows. Me, I don't really care.

Like I said, the rapture saved my life. I'm thirty-eight now. For the first two decades of my life I woke up each morning wondering what my purpose was. What was my destiny? Who would I become?

Left unanswered, these kinds of questions have a way of weighing on a person. But now I know the answer: I am whoever I want to be. If ever there was a plan for me, it went down the shitter when Jesus marched into town. There are no expectations anymore. Life is just life. I'm free to do and be what and whomever I want.

Which is to say, every morning I wake up and make two cups of coffee. I drink one myself and pour the other down the sink. This is my routine.

Because, really, Jesus can just go to hell.

Holiday

Bruce Golden

Editor: Morality and ethics don't necessarily equate.

If I was gonna do it, I knew I needed to get dusting. I had been thinking about it for days, and now it was already Holiday Eve. But flies and fleas! I didn't know how I was gonna keep my promise to Gramps, and still do what was right.

The right thing seemed like the wrong thing, and the other way round. It was way too much for a scrawny sprout of only eleven harvests to figure out, so I put my hand in my pocket and grabbed hold of my lucky goldstone. I hoped it would help me think better.

Gramps had given me his goldstone just before he became one with the south field. He said it had come from Faraway. I used to love to fold up on the porch and listen to him talk about Faraway, and the things he called cities. Cities, he said, were giant-sized communities with more people than you could count—and I could count all the way to a hundred and beyond.

Of course, Gramps had never actually lived in a city, but he believed what he'd heard about them. He said once upon a time there were thousands of cities, that is until the rainfire destroyed them. I knew all about the rainfire, the swarms of hoppers, and ol' demon Drought—those things were landstory. They were part of the soil, they were in every seed, every drop of water. But cities? I wasn't sure if I believed in them. Someday, though, I wanted to have a looksee for myself. After one or two more harvests, I was gonna dust a trail to Faraway and see what I could see.

Right now, I had a promise to keep.

The cool wind played with the chaff in the south field. I'd been out there saying *Hey* to Gramps. That's what reminded me I couldn't put off my promise any longer.

So I made a trail back to the hub. On the way I saw a bunch of girls carving up their Holiday jack-o'-hearts. My sister, Heather, was there, and so was my mom, who was showing them how it was done right. They were all giggling and smiling and carrying on strange-like. Heather herself had been acting funny of late. I didn't know if it was 'cause she was older than me or 'cause she was a girl. But she wasn't the same Heather I used to have mud fights with. All I knew was she had her eyes on Billy Wagoner, and that lately she always seemed to smell of honeysuckle.

"Konner!"

My mom waved me over. I didn't want to get too close to them silly girls, so I shuffled my feet as I walked, and let the dirt run up over my toes. I was going so slow, she came over to get me.

"Konner, where are your brothers?"

"Don't know."

"Well, I want you to make sure they're not getting into any trouble. You know how your brothers are."

"Ah, flies and fleas, Mom. I've got better things to do than looking after those sprouts."

"Go on now," she said with a sternness in her voice. "You find out what kind of mischief they're up to, and put a stop to it."

"Yes, ma'am."

Her expression softened then, and so did her voice. "Are you excited about Holiday?"

"Yeah," I said, bundling in my real excitement.

"Well, you be sure to have fun now, okay?"

"Sure, Mom." I noticed she wore the walnut shell pendant Dad had given her a long time ago. She was particular about when she wore it. I liked how when it caught the sunlight, the tiny piece of crystal inside the shell would sparkle all different colors. I think it made her feel special.

"It won't be long, Konner, before you're all grown up, so you have fun while you can."

"Don't you and Dad have fun on Holiday?" I asked, not caring to think about the day when I wouldn't have any fun.

"Sure we do. It's just a different kind of fun. Have you thought about your Holiday wish yet?"

"Yes." I'd known for a long time what I was gonna wish for.

"Well, good. I hope you get your wish. Now you make a trail and find out what Kobey and Kory are up to."

"Okay."

I headed off, meaning to do what she said, but the Trouble Brothers would have to wait. I had something else I had to get done first.

Closer to the hub most of the trees and bushes already wore their Holiday clothes, though some of the final decorating was still going on. Some women were going here and there, putting on hats and belts and scarves, and anything else they could make fit. I knew those clothes would scare Pestilence away for another harvest, but I couldn't figure how. They didn't scare me. Some looked so downright odd, I had to laugh. Maybe that's how they worked. Maybe ol' Pestilence didn't care for laughter.

As I approached the elders' lodge, Henry Olmstead walked out and cornered me.

"Konner Grainwell, what are you up to?"

"Nothing, Mr. Olmstead," I said, hoping I didn't look as nervous I felt.

"Shouldn't you be out practicing your cupid bow?"

"I'm not old enough for the shoot, Mr. Olmstead."

"Rainfire, boy! I wasn't any bigger than you when I took my first shoot. Well, anyway, you go have some fun." He reached into a bowl he was carrying and held out his hand.

"Here's a sweetstick for you. Take it now," he urged, "and don't tell Ms. Olmstead I gave you one before the party." He winked and walked off toward the hub where lots of folks were busy getting ready for Holiday.

"Thanks, Mr. Olmstead."

He just waved the back of his hand and kept trailing.

I was right there then—right outside the elders' lodge. All I had to do was sneak in, grab the right marker, and sneak back out. It was all I had to do to keep my promise to Gramps. I put my hand in my pocket and grabbed my goldstone. I told myself it was okay, that nobody would be hurt by it. But I stood there way too long, trying to make myself believe it, and picking at my courage.

"Konner?"

It was Grams with little Hazel in tow.

"Konner, I need you to take Hazel home. She's tired and I still have lots to do."

Flies and fleas! I'd been so close.

It wasn't that I didn't like my little sister. In fact, she was my favorite—not much trouble usually, not like Kobey and Kory. She was only five, and not mooning after boys like Heather. I thought Hazel was just the cutest little thing, with her big, wide-open blue eyes and cornsilk hair. Right now though, I had something more important to do than play with my little sister.

"Do you hear me, Konner?"

"Yes, Grams." I knew there was no way round taking Hazel home. I'd just have to sneak back later.

"That's a good boy, Konner. Your Gramps used to say, 'We can always count on Konner.'"

That made me feel good, and it also reminded me of my promise. It was funny Grams said that, 'cause she didn't know anything about the promise. That was just between Gramps and me.

I liked Grams well enough. She was a nice old lady, but she spent most of her time smoking weed and talking with the other elders. Whenever I saw her, it made me think of Gramps. Before he became one with the south field, Gramps would spend a lot of time with me, telling me stories and singing old songs. I missed him. I wouldn't forget my promise to him.

After he was chosen, he asked me to be sure and take care of Grams when he was gone. He made me promise when her time came, I'd make sure she was with him. I promised I would, and I always try to keep my promises.

* * *

The sun had fallen to that point where the sky takes on a more serious attitude—you know, beautiful and grim at the same time. I could never figure out how it changed itself. One moment it's this soft, friendly blue, then the next time you look up it's got these angry streaks of red and orange. I figured it was like a warning. *Here comes the black night—beware!* I didn't waste much time looking at it though, 'cause Holiday Eve was in full bloom.

I heard the music long before I dusted off for the hub. Anyone with any kind of instrument would be playing tonight. When I got there the dancing had already started. I thought dancing was for girls, though I saw some older boys trying to step with the music. Of course I'd seen older boys do crazier things where girls were concerned.

My eyes went right to the tables, where all manner of good stuff was laid out. I saw sweet breads and pies, jams and tater crisps, and enough spiced cider to drown ol' demon Drought himself. I couldn't wait to stuff my belly, but I had to make a careful trail. Those darn jack-o'-hearts were strung up all over the place, candles burning inside them so they were aglow. I saw some girls lingering under their carvings, hoping for a kiss. They reminded me of trapdoor spiders, just waiting to pounce.

I wasn't planning on kissing anyone, except maybe my mom or little Hazel, so I avoided those orange gourds like they were Pestilence himself. I told myself I'd have a little snackdo first, then I'd sneak back to the elders' lodge when it was dark. With a taste of sweet bread in my mouth I spied Kobey and Kory under another table. They had their peashooters and were popping girls in the head when they weren't looking.

It might have been funny if I wasn't sure I'd be the one who'd suffer for their mischief. So I dusted over, grabbed the two of them, and relieved them of their shooters. Both were filthy-looking. Kory stood there scratching his butt as usual. Kobey tried to look defiant.

"You two cause any trouble and you're gonna be at one with your sister, Henna, in the east field." I didn't like to think about my dead baby sister, Henna, but I knew it would scare the seed right out of those two sprouts. "Now both of you go wash up, or I'm gonna find Dad and tell him what you've been up to, and that'll be the end of your Holiday."

I let go of them and they dusted off like a couple of field mice. I figured chances were about even they'd actually get clean. I thought I'd better take care of what I had to take care of then. Afterwards, I could—

Darned if I wasn't standing there thinking when all of a sudden this girl swoops in like a red-tailed hawk and kisses me! Her lips were pressing against mine before I could even see who she was.

Now, the truth is, except for the shock of it all, it wasn't as bad as I thought it would be. I mean, it was the first time any girl not family had kissed me. When she pulled away I saw it was Dandy. I should have known. Even though she had seen only one more harvest than me, Dandy had been making eyes in my direction for some time. Now she just stood there grinning.

I looked up and there it was. A big ol' jack-o'-hearts, smiling down at me just like Dandy was doing—like I was a rooster, all plucked and stuffed and ready for mealtime. Darn those sprouts! Trying to keep them out of trouble had landed me square in Dandy's trap.

Dandy looked like she was about to say something when my mom walked up with Hazel.

"Hello, Dandelion, happy Holiday," said my mom, then looked at me and smiled that smile moms get that make you think they know everything.

"Happy Holiday, Ms. Grainwell," replied Dandy all sweet-like.

"Konner, it's time for the sing and I want you to take Hazel with you."

I took little Hazel's hand, figuring it was a good excuse to get away from Dandy. But she followed us to where the others were getting in line for the sing. I tried to ignore her.

I didn't care much for the sing, but if you weren't joined you were still considered a sprout as far as the sing was concerned. It was the only time I wished I had a wife like my big brother, Kyle. I didn't mind singing the songs, 'cause they were kind of scary and fun. I just didn't like having to parade round the hub so all the grownups could *coo* and *ah* about how cute we all were.

I don't know who started it, but we trailed off real slow as soon as the first song began. I noticed Dandy was right behind me, but I didn't pay any attention to her. I held onto Hazel as I sang, and watched her trying her best to remember the words.

Tell me, tell me landstory.
Back when fire burned the sea,
Rivers wept and mountains roared,
Hot winds sang a frightful chord.
Tell me, tell me landstory,
About when people had to flee.
When hoppers rose up in swarm,
Laying bare where once was corn.

Ahead of me, Heather was walking real close to Billy Wagoner. I figured if he wasn't careful, they'd be joined before another harvest. I looked round and saw the Trouble Brothers. They seemed to be behaving themselves, acting more serious than usual. But I knew why. The songs still scared them a little.

Tell me, tell me, tell me please,
That someday there'll be more trees.
Say ol' demon Drought is dead,
Then I'll lie down on my bed.

Round and round we trailed and sang. I knew it would have been a real good time to sneak into the elders' lodge, 'cause they were all watching the sing. But I couldn't very well get away with Hazel in tow and everyone watching, especially Mom and Dad. They held each other, touching and kissing, and looking so happy when us sprouts trailed by. Dad was usually all leather and salt, except when he was around Mom. I enjoyed how she could soften him up no matter what his mood.

Tell me, tell me, I do pray,
What I'll eat this Holiday.
Say the poppers will fly right,
And grant the wish I wish tonight.
Tell me, tell me landstory.
How I wonder what I'll be.

When the sing ended, I noticed some of the elders headed back to their lodge. I knew then I'd have to wait until morning to do Gramps' errand. The weight of it bore down on me. I turned the thought aside as I couldn't do anything more tonight. Instead I stuffed as much Holiday food into me as I could while doing my best to avoid Dandy.

When once I spotted her heading my way, I dusted off in the other direction. Keeping to the dark, I made a trail round the hub to the other side. As I did, I spotted two older kids all twisted up together like Gram's special mustard pretzels. I recognized it was Burt Ploughhorse and Lily Landesgard. With them half-naked and kissing, the way they were moving, and the sounds they were making, I could tell that they were planting seed. I knew what they were doing was for the good of the community, but it still seemed silly to me. I stayed out of sight and made my way back to the party.

It wasn't long after that when Mom and Dad began rounding up everyone for bed. The Trouble Brothers tried to sneak off, but Dad snatched them up by their shirts and lifted them off the ground till they stopped squirming.

"You sprouts need to get to sleep soon, so the Santa will come," said Grams as we trailed off toward our lodge. Kobey and Kory started whispering real excited to each other, and Hazel looked up at Grams, her big blue eyes filled with wonder. Last harvest I'd snuck out early and saw it was the elders who actually hid the candy. So I figured the Santa must have been at one with the earth for many harvests, and that so all of us sprouts weren't disappointed, the elders kept doing his good work for him.

When we got to the lodge, everyone else went inside. I stayed out so I could look at the moon. It was full and kind of orange. It made me think of Dandy's jack-o'-hearts, and that got me to remembering the kiss. That made me think about the pair I'd seen planting seed. I'd heard talk from the older boys that it was a fun thing. But it sure sounded painful, and I couldn't see the sense in it—except for making babies. Of course I knew the more sprouts, the better for the community. So when a boy and girl got together and started planting seed, the elders always acted all happy.

I put my hand in my pocket, took hold of my goldstone, and stared at the moon. I didn't want to think about girls, I wanted to think about Faraway, and what I might find when I got there. I sure hoped I'd catch a popper and get my Holiday wish. I was worried if I didn't—

"You need to get to sleep, son," said my dad, stepping outside and looking up at the moon himself.

"Dad . . .?" I said, then hesitated.

"What is it, son?"

"How important is a promise?"

He looked at me as if he were sizing up a new calf. "A man's only as good as his word, Konner."

I already knew the truth of that. I guess I just wanted to hear it said.

"Don't forget you got your chores to do tomorrow."

"But, Dad, tomorrow's Holiday," I protested, even though I knew it would do no good. When did I ever *not* have to do chores? Never, that's when.

"It may be Holiday, but the pigs still have to eat, and the tools still have to be cleaned."

"I know, Dad," I said, getting up to go in. But as I did, I gave one last thought to Faraway. I thought about how when I dusted off to Faraway there wouldn't be any more chores to do. I couldn't wait for that day to come.

* * *

It was Holiday, and just 'cause I didn't believe in the Santa anymore, didn't mean I wasn't gonna get up early and find as much candy as I could stuff in my pockets. Mom helped Hazel. The Trouble Brothers were on their own, so I did pretty well. Afterwards I hid it all in my secret place, so Kobey and Kory couldn't get their dirty hands on it.

Then I did all my chores, and by the time I was finished I knew the Holiday shoot had started. So I made a trail to the gully where the older boys, with their cupid bows, were trying their best to hit whichever jack-o'-hearts was carved by the girl they were sweet on. Some weren't even coming close. Others were so bad they were splitting open the wrong pumpkins, much to the frustration of some girls. I saw Heather get all excited when Billie Wagoner shot one right through the heart-shaped mouth she'd carved. That was about all I could take.

Most all of the elders, including Grams, had pulled up chairs to smoke their weed and watch the shoot. So I knew it was now or never. I dusted a trail, squeezing my goldstone the whole way.

As I neared the elder's lodge, the sky grew dark. The wind passed over me and I shivered. A mean-looking dusky cloud was blowing in from the east. I could see a big old bull in its shape. I kept watch for a minute, then snuck inside as slow as an earthworm. It didn't seem like anyone was there.

I'd never been in the elders' lodge before, 'cause sprouts weren't allowed. It looked like any other lodge, only bigger. As I searched for where they kept the markers I spied this picture hanging on the wall. It scared the fertilizer right out me. Either that or the candy I'd eaten that morning was disagreeing with my insides. It was a creepy-looking thing, painted in more shades of brown and red than I knew there was. It was some kind of monster, all fangs and claws but almost like it wasn't really there—like a goblin made of wind. I guessed it must have been somebody's idea of ol' demon Drought.

Even though it was just a picture, I backed away from it real easy-like. That bumped me right into what I was looking for. All the elders' markers were in this big bowl sitting there on the table. Quick as I could, I found Gram's marker and put it in my pocket. I started to go but got this queer itch to take a last look at ol' demon Drought. His eyes gave me the shiver-tingles. I was sure he knew what I was up to. So I dusted it out of there before I gathered any other strange thoughts.

Once outside, I made a trail back to our lodge, going real slow like everything was okay. But everything wasn't okay—at least not with me. And it was more than ol' demon Drought looking over my shoulder. I knew what I'd done wasn't right. It wasn't fair. But I didn't know any other way to make sure I kept my promise to Gramps. I just hoped someday I wouldn't feel as bad as I did right then.

* * *

By evening, everyone had gathered at the hub for Last Supper. I couldn't help but notice something was in the air, something you could almost feel, like a thick morning dew. Nothing I could see, but I could sense it. It was more in the way folks were talking or not talking. They were a bit bridled, not as free and easy, as if they were waiting to be set loose. I knew what they were waiting for.

Before anyone could eat, the Harvest Christ had to be chosen. My dad and Mr. Landesgard made a trail to the elders' lodge and brought back the big bowl with all the markers. I tried not to show it, but I was feeling real bad about then. I didn't want to be there, but I knew I had to be. Young or old, sick or cripple, everyone took part in the choosing of the Harvest Christ. I knew it was a great honor to be chosen, and that only doubled my guilt.

Since the bowl was filled with all the elders' markers, or was supposed to be, none of them could pick. So, after everyone quieted down, Mr. Landesgard reached in, stirred his hand round, and pulled out a marker. My hands were in my pockets—the right one clenched round my goldstone, the left on Gram's marker.

"Henry Olmstead," he announced, holding up the marker for all to see.

Everyone started clapping and shouting and I looked over to old Mr. Olmstead to see how he was taking it.

He was all smiles, shaking hands with everyone. He seemed happy, but . . . there was something about his smile I couldn't quite figure. Something different—like he was trying too hard.

Anyway, someone had put the harvest wreath on his head and a big knife in his hand, and everyone coaxed him to get Last Supper going. Mr. Olmstead waving the knife above his head made the rest of us clap more. He brought it down and began carving the Eater Bunny.

I swear it was the biggest rabbit I'd ever seen. Even skinned and barbecued up nice and juicy like, it was as big as a ki-yote. It was such a grand scene, full of laughter and fine-smelling food, that it made me wonder for a moment whether or not I'd get the honor of carving the Eater Bunny someday. Right then, I didn't feel bad at all. Flies and fleas, I even let Dandy sit by me for Last Supper.

* * *

It was long after dark when I climbed aboard the wagon with the rest of my family. My stomach about burst from all the good stuff I'd eaten. I wanted nothing more than to get some sleep. But Holiday wasn't over yet. The whole community loaded up the wagons and made a trail out to the fallow north field where the Holiday fire already blazed.

When they loaded Henry Olmstead's body aboard one of the wagons, I started feeling guilty again. Earlier, when he'd drunk from the harvest gourd, I'd turned away so I wouldn't see. I squeezed my goldstone and tried not to think about what was in that drink.

Not that there was anything so terrible to see. I'd watched when

Gramps was chosen. It was like he'd just gone to sleep. But this time I couldn't help feeling bad about what I'd done, even though I'd kept my word to Gramps. I knew the Harvest Christ would be made at one with the north field this Holiday, and Gramps wanted Grams to be with him in the south. That's what I'd promised. So I couldn't let her be chosen—not this Holiday—even if it meant maybe depriving her of the honor.

When everyone had gathered near the fire, Henry Olmstead was carried carefully from the wagon. They took off his clothes and gently laid him into the place that had been prepared. As they covered him up, Ms. Olmstead stepped forward, looking real proud-like, and delivered the Holiday thanksgiving.

"The earth is the land, and we are the earth. Bless this land and the bounty of its harvest. We who take from the land, now give back to the land. May all of our harvests be so bountiful."

Then everyone joined in for the last part.

"The earth is the land, and we are the earth."

After that, everyone trailed off to stand round the fire. No one said a word, 'cause we weren't supposed to. Parents shushed the littlest sprouts if they tried to speak. Even the Trouble Brothers knew better than to make any noise.

I already knew what my Holiday wish was, so I tossed my popping corn into the fire like everyone else. As I stood there, waiting, hoping to catch one of the poppers so I'd get my wish, I thought about Faraway and Gramps and Grams and old Henry Olmstead. I wondered if they celebrated Holiday in Faraway. I sure hoped so, 'cause I'd miss all the food and the fun. Who knows, I might even miss getting kissed under a jack-o'-hearts.

The poppers had started flying all round me. I waited, ready to grab one if it came my way, 'cause you had to catch them on the fly to really get your wish. I saw Heather catch one and get all excited, then *pop*! One shot off to my right, but I was quick. I caught it, wished my wish again, and tossed it into my mouth.

I felt real good when everyone began loading back into the wagons. Just knowing I'd get my Holiday wish made everything I'd worried about seem okay. Maybe I wouldn't get it right away, but someday . . .

It's All Good

Lisa Timpf

Editor: Sometimes our delusions speak a stronger truth.

"Height: five feet, seven inches. Scanning biometrics now. Stand still, please, and hold your breath."

Melissa Mourningdove focussed on remaining motionless as the eight gleaming silver arms of the Simultron completed their complex dance around her body. When the "all clear" light flashed she gulped a breath of air.

"Fitness level: 98 percent. You may now exit. Have a nice day."

"You bet I will," Melissa said, unable to suppress a broad grin as she stepped away from the machine. All those years of practice. The running. The weight training. And now—

Now, at last, she'd achieved her dream. The Olympic Games.

The metal door at the end of the small enclosure slid open soundlessly. Though she'd endured the Simultron's probing half a dozen times already this season, it still took getting used to. Melissa had been glad to hear the machine give her a 98 percent rating. Coach Gordon would be watching each player's stats as they stepped through the equipment at their respective locations, and her eagle eye would quickly pick up on anyone with substandard readiness.

In the change cubicle, Melissa stopped to admire her Team Canada softball jersey with its stylized maple leaf on the front. She tugged the shirt over her head, smoothing the silky fabric with her hands with a reverent motion. Melissa fitted the silver VR circlet around her brow, then tugged on her black baseball cap to conceal it.

A quick check in the mirror. The uniform *did* look sharp, even if she said so herself: the red jersey and stirrups, the black softball shorts and hat, the white turf shoes.

Ready, Melissa told herself, squaring her shoulders. She drew a deep breath, picked up her softball glove, and grabbed the silver handle of the door . . .

. . . which swung open to reveal Team Canada's virtual locker room. Melissa nodded to her holographic teammates. Like herself, each of them had endured the probing eye of the Simultron, which would use the data gathered to project the most accurate image possible. She made her way to her designated spot, between Nova Scotian second baseman Ruth Mickelton and Giselle Plouffe, a relief pitcher who hailed from Quebec.

"Welcome, ladies." Coach Gordon's smile showed dazzling white against her darkly tanned skin. "We've drawn the United States as our first opponents. I don't need to remind anyone of our long-standing rivalry." She paused for effect. "As usual, they're fielding a strong squad, and no doubt think they'll make short work of their neighbors to the north. It's up to us to show we have other ideas.

"Beyond national pride, we're playing for something else today." Coach Gordon glanced around the circle of intent faces. "Holding the Olympics, even virtually, acts as a symbol for life returning to normal. We all know how important that is. You can take pride—you should all take pride—in your role in healing the scars left by recent events.

"Enough said. Now, here's the starting lineup—"

Melissa leaned forward with her teammates and took in the pre-game instructions.

"Gather in for the cheer," Coach Gordon said. Melissa felt her skin tingle with anticipation. She willed herself to see her teammates as substantial beings, just like when they played live.

"It's all good!" The cheer erupted from twenty-one voices, and Melissa followed starting pitcher Randi Roxton as the team jogged through the locker room door.

Melissa thought she'd understood Coach Gordon's words about the symbolism of the Olympics, but just how big a deal it was became evident when she stepped onto the artificial turf in the Simuldome.

Cheers erupted from thousands of throats as fans tuned in through their computers, portable devices, and televisions. The truly fortunate had secured "seats" in the virtual stands. Melissa squinted up to the left and spotted her mother and father, sitting with her brother, Liam. She had time for a quick wave, noticing Shakela Norberg, who'd coached her in midget softball, seated in the row behind her parents. The man sitting beside Shakela looked familiar for some reason. News coverage, that was it. *Erik Norberg*, Melissa thought. He'd been instrumental in finding a cure for the Outbreak.

Melissa repressed a shudder, keeping a smile pasted on her face for her parents' sake.

The Outbreak.

If that hadn't been stopped, there'd be no Olympic Games, that's for sure. As it was, the virus had cut a swath through the world population, including Melissa's little corner of the planet. Why, three people on her street alone had succumbed to the illness before a cure had been found.

It's over now, she told herself. True, but the effects lingered. The temporary ban on travel, for one thing, which is why they were holding the Olympics virtually. Still, there were benefits to that, too. Like being able to live at home while playing in the Games.

I've always hated flying, anyway, Melissa thought. She shook her head. *Time to focus on the game.*

Melissa sniffed, drawing in a deep breath, and grinned as she jogged into position for the pre-game warmup. Someone had managed to inject the smell of fresh-cut grass into the air. They really *did* think of everything.

During the practice drills, it took some effort to zone in on the ball as it snapped toward her from Coach Gordon's bat. Melissa was grateful for the extra sessions in the Simuldome with Liam—they'd sharpened her skill at tracking grounders.

Finally, the game got underway, with Melissa's squad taking the field for the first inning. The United States, as the visiting team, batted first. Melissa raised her glove into ready position as the leadoff batter strode to home plate.

As it turned out, Melissa didn't need to call on her glove for anything more than catching the ball as the team fired it around the infield after each strikeout. Both pitchers were zinging the ball with authority. By the fifth inning, Canada held a slim 1–0 lead.

As she trotted off the field after the top of the sixth inning, Melissa passed Claire Smythe, the opposing third baseman.

"All good, is it?" Claire said in a slightly mocking tone. She leaned forward. "Don't count on it."

"What's *that* supposed to mean?" Melissa mumbled to herself. *She's just trying to psyche you out. Don't fall for it.* Melissa turned to glare at Claire's retreating back.

The match ended 1–0 in Canada's favor, and Melissa, after stopping to re-tie her shoelace, found herself at the end of the handshake line. Claire, who was the final person in the United States line, shot a quick look around her before talking to Melissa.

"Seriously, girl, keep your eyes open," Claire said. "I don't want to say too much, but—"

Get to the point, Melissa thought impatiently as the other woman glanced around, as if to verify no one was listening.

"Just watch carefully, in the Australia game. I heard you're sharp. You'll figure it out." After a final glance around, Claire scurried away.

What was that all about? Melissa wondered. She shrugged. Unable to get the encounter out of her mind, Melissa still felt preoccupied when she said her goodbyes to her virtual teammates and exited the Simuldome.

When she stepped into the open air, Melissa squinted against the brightness of the sun. Just as she settled her sunglasses into place, she heard a familiar voice.

"Are you okay?"

Melissa turned, smiling when she saw the serious expression on Izzy's face. "It's all good," Melissa replied, willing her face into a neutral expression. She wasn't ready to share that unusual verbal exchange with Claire. Not yet. "How was the view from the press box?"

"Great." Sunlight glinted off Izzy's glasses as she turned to look at Melissa. Despite the availability of laser technology, Izzy preferred to correct her nearsightedness the old-fashioned way. "There was something odd, though."

"What's that?" Melissa asked as the two headed for the express bus stop.

"No journalists from Australasia and very few from Europe," her friend replied.

"That's not so strange, is it?" Melissa asked. "I mean, there were no teams from Australasia or Europe playing at the time."

"In the past we'd have seen some coverage, or even reporters watching just to get a background they could use when covering their own country's games." Izzy's brow creased as she frowned thoughtfully.

Melissa shrugged. "I guess you'll have to see if that changes in the next few days," she said.

When they reached the bus shelter, Izzy scowled at the neon letters flickering across the LCD display screen at the rear of the small structure.

"Now what?" Melissa nudged her friend with her elbow.

"I just get tired of the constant bombardment," Izzy said, pointing to the screen. "If it's really 'all good' why is someone so insistent on telling us all the time?"

"Enough with the conspiracy theories," Melissa said with a smile. "To change the subject, are you coming for supper tomorrow?"

Izzy was silent for a moment, and Melissa thought she knew why. The Mourningdoves, thanks to Melissa's status as a national team member, received extra rations. Izzy's family was sticky about accepting what they viewed as charity. For a moment, Melissa thought Izzy would refuse, but the dark-haired woman surprised her.

"I'll be there, under one condition."

"What's that?" Melissa asked.

"Mom insists I bring some tomatoes from our greenhouse."

Melissa paused for a moment, then nodded. "That would be great."

* * *

Melissa felt in the peak of health the next day, and the Simultron agreed, giving her a 99 percent rating. When she took the field against Australia, a perennial powerhouse in women's softball, Melissa felt a heightened level of tension. Still, it would be good to see some old friends. All international sports had been suspended by the Outbreak. Until now, that is. This would be the first time she'd seen the Aussies, live or virtually, in three years.

The last time the teams had clashed, Melissa and stocky Aussie third baseman Chloe Smithson established a routine of muttering "G'day" as they passed one another. To her disappointment, this time Smithson stalked by as if she'd never seen Melissa. Feeling slightly hurt, Melissa shrugged it off. *Guess the Olympics is a whole new ballgame,* she told herself.

When Melissa took her turn at bat in the second inning, she swung out of synch at the first offering Aussie hurler Laura Williams threw across the plate, missing the ball by a significant margin. Or, she thought she'd missed it. Melissa's jaw dropped as she watched the white sphere arc out into deep left field.

It took a tersely worded "Run!" from Coach Gordon to get Melissa's legs moving. Despite the delay she reached second base safely, standing up.

When she took the field for the brief infield warmup in the defensive end of the next inning, Melissa deliberately tried to miss the grounder coming from the first baseman, Pat Millingham. The ball went right into her glove.

What is going on? Melissa asked herself, grateful that no balls came her way through the remainder of the game.

"Coach," she called toward Coach Gordon's retreating back as the team trotted off the field. "Can I ask you something?"

Coach Gordon turned and smiled, then said hurriedly, "Have to run. Talk to you tomorrow." She winked out of sight.

Melissa sat in the change cubicle and put her head between her hands. *Am I going crazy?* she asked herself. She tugged on her street clothes and strode out into the sunlight.

* * *

Rob Farmingham ran his right hand through his short blonde hair as he stared at the controls in front of him. He'd been told women's softball would be an easy assignment. Yet, the whole Simulsystem had sagged twice, first when the program overrode a player's missed swing and converted it to a hit, and then again when the same player missed the ball on purpose during the warmup. He'd *told* Vinnie Namm they shouldn't force things. Vinnie had shrugged and replied that orders came from elsewhere, and he'd better figure out how to make it work.

Am I overreacting? Rob asked himself, rubbing his hand across his face. He glanced up at the hundreds of screens in the Simulsystem Headquarters. The readouts showed athletes at multiple locations around the globe. Images came here, to HQ, for synchronization and output to the broadcast centres.

Rob sat for a moment, considering. Finally, he arrived at a decision. It wasn't a big deal. Probably no one had even noticed.

Besides, if the thing could run itself, without intervention, they wouldn't need operators, would they?

No need to mention this to anyone. He glanced at his watch. He had time for a break before his next assignment. Great. He could use a coffee.

* * *

"Good game today." Liam smiled across the table at his sister.

Melissa grinned back. "Something funny happened, though," she said. "You know that hit I had in the second inning?"

He nodded.

"I was certain I'd missed the ball, but it went for a double. I think the Simultron was off somehow," Melissa said in a tentative voice.

"Sorry, can't help you," he said solemnly. "All my games were live. I never had a chance to try the Simultron. Maybe if we'd had it then, I wouldn't have blown out my knee." His face was wistful.

"Yeah, that's true." Melissa passed the plate of sliced tomatoes to her left, where Izzy was sitting. She really shouldn't grouse about the Simultron when Liam would give almost anything to be able to play rugby again, even in virtual form. "I'm sure it was nothing."

After dinner, Melissa walked Izzy the short distance down the street to the Millers' tidy brick bungalow.

"Thanks for bringing the tomatoes. Tell your mom she's got a great crop this year," Melissa said.

"She got ahold of some heritage seeds," Izzy said. "She feels they're hardier. They produce better, too."

"I didn't imagine it, you know," Melissa blurted. "What I thought I experienced at the softball game, I mean, not the tomatoes."

"I'm sure you didn't," Izzy said, leaning closer. "I'm going to tell Noah, see what he thinks."

Melissa felt a sudden chill. It was one thing to share your thoughts with your best friend and your family. It was quite another to let your best friend's brother, an undercover member of the Royal Canadian Mounted Police, in on it.

"He'll think I've lost it." Melissa could feel her face redden.

"He'll think nothing of the sort," Izzy said confidently. "Leave it with me. And try to get some sleep. Britain won't be an easy opponent, tomorrow."

Melissa grimaced and turned back toward her house. Sleep was one thing she didn't think would come easily. Not tonight.

* * *

"Fitness level: 88 percent—" Melissa didn't even register the Simultron's remaining patter as she exited the small room.

Melissa dressed clumsily, hands shaking. She really hadn't slept that well last night, and the Simultron couldn't be fooled. Melissa sighed. Coach Gordon wasn't going to like *those* health stats.

Sure enough, when the game started, utility infielder Susan Rostwick trotted out to Melissa's customary position.

With a prime vantage point from the bench, Melissa watched carefully for any signs that other players were experiencing phenomena similar to what she had felt in the Australia game, but nothing seemed unusual. Perhaps she'd missed out on sleep—and her spot in the starting roster—for nothing.

When she emerged from the building, Melissa heard a familiar voice call her name.

"I thought you weren't going to make it to this game," she said when she spotted Izzy striding toward her.

"Noah called. He wants to meet with us." Izzy seemed out of breath. "He said it was important."

Her hands feeling suddenly shaky as self-doubt hit, Melissa felt an impulse to turn and run. Too late. She could see Noah waving from the edge of the parking lot.

"*He* looks as laid back as ever," Melissa said to Izzy as they walked toward him, feeling a stab of envy.

"Oh, he gets wound up sometimes," Izzy said, rolling her eyes.

"Hi, ladies," Noah said. "If you'd care to have a seat—" he gestured toward his jet-black Honda Accord.

Melissa slid into the backseat and shot an inquiring glance at Izzy, who occupied the front passenger spot.

"Not on official business?" Melissa asked jokingly.

"No." Noah's voice sounded solemn, and Melissa decided to zip it until asked a direct question. To her surprise, that came more quickly than expected. "Who have you told about the—anomaly—you experienced?" Melissa noted the way Noah glanced quickly up to the rearview mirror, studying her face, before returning his attention to the road.

Melissa frowned, concentrating.

"What I thought I experienced," she said. She shrugged. "I told Liam and my parents and Izzy, obviously. That's it."

Noah sat, silent, for several seconds. "You didn't imagine it," he said. He shook his head. "I shouldn't tell you. It's risky. But you may be in danger, so—"

Melissa exchanged glances with her friend. *Danger?*

"You realize, of course, that the Outbreak hit some countries far harder than it hit us."

"Yeah," Melissa replied, leaning forward.

"The international community agreed it was important to make things seem normal, as much as possible, despite the travel ban. That's why the decision was made to carry on with the Olympics." Noah paused. "But some countries—well, their communication infrastructure is down. We don't really know what's going on. They certainly aren't in a position to participate. But not having them there would create too many questions, so their athletes were programmed into the Simultron. And in the games they play against their opponents, someone . . . um . . . *manages* the data as opposed to letting the game take its course."

"You mean—those were computer-generated versions of Australia's players?" To her dismay, Melissa's voice sounded squeaky.

"Exactly." Noah paused for a moment and despite his effort to smile, Melissa had a momentary sense of the immense burden he carried. "We know illness hit hard in Australia, because they ran out of vaccine. We also know a tsunami devastated Japan, and we aren't sure about their infrastructure either. As we learn more, the truth will come out, but it will be gradual. The burden of too much bad news at once—well, you saw the panic and the riots at the outbreak of the Seven-Month War that followed the Outbreak. We just can't afford to go through that again. Everything is too fragile."

"Wouldn't people who have relatives in the affected places know something was wrong?" Izzy frowned as she considered this question.

"Communication to and from those locations is also managed," Noah said steadily. "Carefully."

"What about drones or other surveillance?" Melissa blurted. "Surely you can find out."

"After the Seven-Month War, all countries swore a non-surveillance treaty. Besides," Noah's expression turned wry, "some aspects of infrastructure are working just fine. We could get drones to the border, but I doubt they'd make it across."

"So it's not 'all good.'" Izzy's voice was harsh.

"No, it isn't," Noah agreed mildly.

"Then why are you telling us?" Izzy challenged.

Melissa glanced out the window, noticing they'd reached the park near their neighbourhood. The play equipment and the softball diamond sat empty, and no other vehicles occupied the parking lot.

"A number of us believe this has gone far enough," Noah replied, his voice sombre. "In the short term, sure, the secrecy made sense. But now, the people controlling the information still won't acknowledge that there's a time and a place for informing the public."

Melissa closed her eyes. "What does this have to do with me?" she asked. "I'm just a softball player. I'm not a politician."

"No," Noah said. "But there are two reasons to tell you. One, someone else may realize what you know. And that someone may go to great measures to keep the information from getting out."

Melissa felt the blood drain from her face.

"Secondly . . ." Noah paused, chewing on his lower lip for a moment. "Since the Games attract worldwide interest, worldwide coverage, the Olympics provide the perfect opportunity to convey a message. At precisely two o'clock tomorrow, a number of athletes will stop whatever they're doing—swimming, running, jumping, playing. We believe it will be enough to crash the Simultron. That's the opportunity."

"So you want me to—" Melissa couldn't even force her lips to shape the words. *My dreams. All those years of hard work.*

"The Aussies and the others who aren't participating . . ." Noah paused, and swallowed. "Do it for them."

"That's a low blow." Melissa's voice shook as she glared at Noah.

"I didn't mean it that way," he replied mildly. "But the problems we're facing—they require our best minds, a collaboration, not the thoughts of an elite few. The first step is to break the code of secrecy."

"Aren't you afraid of riots? Destabilization?" Melissa countered.

"Of course, there's that chance. But regardless of the timing, that possibility might always be there." Noah looked at the empty park. "We need to have faith in people. We need to trust them to do what's right."

"I'll . . . consider . . . what you've asked," Melissa replied. "But I won't make any promises."

"I understand," Noah said, shooting Melissa a warm smile. "Either way, good luck tomorrow."

* * *

Melissa trotted onto the field, shooting a glance at the score clock high above home plate. *One fifty-three p.m.* She picked up the grounder from Pat Millingham at first base and fired a throw back before daring to shoot another glance up at the clock.

One fifty-six. Am I really going to do this?

When the warmup was over, Pat rolled the ball toward the dugout. *One fifty-eight.*

Out of the corner of her eye, Melissa caught Coach Gordon's face pointed in her direction. Melissa felt her cheeks go hot. *I'm being too obvious,* she thought, scuffing her toe across the ground and pounding her fist into her glove, as though preparing for just another inning in just another game. *There's time to back out. No one will know. Well, no one except—*

The lead-off hitter from the Venezuelan team stepped to the plate.

One fifty-nine.

Giselle Plouffe adjusted her grip on the ball as she eyed the catcher, looking for the signal. She nodded, rocked back, then fired the pitch toward the plate.

"Strike!" the umpire called.

Melissa glanced up at the score clock, which blinked, almost imperceptibly. *It's time.* Melissa sighed, closed her eyes, and—

—sat down. Right there at third base. *I feel like an idiot,* she thought.

In the press box, Izzy clenched her hands so tightly she felt her fingernails pressing into her palms. She watched the news feeds coming in from the various venues. *There.*

A rugby game between New Zealand and the United States ground to a halt as two Team USA players flopped down on the field and just lay there. In the Germany-Britain soccer game, the British centre half scooped up the ball and tossed it, rugby style, to a teammate. At the midway point of the women's 5,000 metre race, a Canadian and a South African athlete stopped and stood, arms crossed, while their competitors continued running. A sturdily-built Russian shot putter set down the round sphere he'd been about to throw and walked away from the ring. And there were others. Lots and lots of others.

* * *

"No, no, no, no, no!" Rob Farmingham yelled at the screen as he watched Melissa sink down to seat herself at third base. "Please, no." He swapped the broadcast feed to a different camera angle, a close-up of Coach Gordon. This was only marginally better, given the stormy expression on Coach's face.

Throughout the control room, similar sounds of dismay arose from the workstations.

Rob closed his eyes, dreading what would come next.

Overwhelmed, the Simultron struggled mightily to maintain its illusions.

It failed.

It had to let go of something, so it let go of those athletes who were truly imaginary.

And viewers using TV screens, tablets, and mobile devices around the world watched in disbelief as whole teams, whole nations of athletes, blinked off the screen. The New Zealand rugby team vanished. A quarter of the runners in the 5,000 metre field flipped out of sight. The field of shot put competitors dropped by a third.

It was as if those other athletes had never been there.

Because, of course, they hadn't.

* * *

"It wasn't the massive panic they predicted." Izzy put her hand on Melissa's shoulder, trying to comfort her friend as they walked through the neighbourhood a week later. "And now, at least, there is honesty. People needed to know."

"It feels like a step backward," Melissa protested. "So many of us assumed we were on the road to recovery."

"We are, now," Izzy said. "Like pulling off a Band-Aid. It had to be done."

Melissa sighed.

"What?" Izzy asked.

"All those years of practicing, to make the Olympics." Melissa reached out her open right hand and curled her fingers inward slowly. "And it slipped away. No, I threw it away."

"You heard, didn't you, that they're just postponing the Olympics for a year?"

Melissa turned slowly to face her friend. "As if I have a prayer of being on the roster."

Izzy shook her head. "The Canadian Olympic Association was clear about that, just like all the other member countries' associations," she said. "No reprisal will be permitted against any athlete who took part in the protest." She paused and grinned. "Of course, the fact that the participants included some of the biggest names in track and field and swimming may have helped them arrive at that decision."

Melissa smiled, then frowned again.

"Now what?" Izzy's voice held a tinge of exasperation.

"I'm just thinking," Melissa said, the words coming slowly. "Maybe, if we're lucky, by the time the Olympics roll around the Aussies will be back."

"I hope so," Izzy answered, putting her hand on Melissa's shoulder. "I really hope so."

From Farm to Table

Tori Stubbs

Editor: Children often give us the most untainted view of our world.

Alice Junia-Quint
7th Grade
October 22, 2476

A long time ago, humans walked freely in cities and towns. They had houses and cars and my sources say they even shopped in grocery stores, just like we do today! Of course, they didn't eat the same things we eat (obviously); their diet consisted mostly of plants, and meats from birds, fish or other animals. Most of these plants and animals were grown and raised by the humans themselves on farms. Can you imagine that? Humans ran their own farms up until 2020! But I'm sure you know their farms weren't as advanced as ours are today. That was before we won the War of Independence in 2021 (That's why we celebrate Independence Day on January 7th!).

On Monday this week our class went on a field trip to visit a human farm. Our tour guide was a friendly woman named Sherri. We began by visiting the nursery, where the offspring and mothers stayed until the babies were old enough to walk and eat solid foods. "Some offspring take up to two years to fully mature!" Sherri told us while we watched a mother with long dark hair feed her child.

Then we moved to the main or "grazing" area. This is where the humans spend most of their life before their brains and other organs are harvested. The room was large, and we walked through a glass tube, "Just in case they get rowdy," Sherri told us. One wall was entirely books, which some of the younger humans were reading. "Reading helps their brains grow. The more information they obtain, the more savory the brain!" she also said. There were also feeding troughs, which were usually filled with carrots, apples, and other fruits and vegetables grown behind the farm.

Sherri then showed us the entertainment room, which looked a lot like an old-fashioned movie theater! "We show old videos that they created while they roamed free," Sherri told us. They even used to make movies about us! Or at least, what they believed we would be. Sherri said that they don't show any of those types of movies though, because it causes the humans to act dangerously and become hard to manage. When this happens they have to sedate them and that causes the brains to become tougher. Most of those films showed us as unthinking monsters. My dad says that is why they were so easy to overtake, they were expecting us to be slow and incapable of complex thoughts. My grandmother said there were a few movies where zombies and humans fell in love! I thought of that as we walked through the slaughter house, and laughed to myself. They were way off.

The last stop on our tour was the packaging room, where workers wearing aprons packed the brains and other organs into the containers we see at the grocery store every day. Sherri led us to a corner of the room, where body parts in a large tub were being sorted. She held up a human head, one with brown hair and freckled skin. "Who knows what we remove first?" she asked our class. Almost everyone raised their hands and I couldn't believe she called on me! I answered correctly (the eyeballs, duh) and Sherri told me to come up and remove one! It wasn't hard to take out, and once I did get it out the class cheered and Sherri said I could eat it! The other kids got to try some of the meat before it was packaged too, but I was the only one who got to try an eyeball! The process our food goes through is fascinating and I think everyone should visit a human farm!

Big Wheels: The Art of the Deal

Timothy J. Turnipseed

*Editor: Believing your laws are universal truth is
the downfall of many in any catastrophe.*

A good, all-American apple pie can save your life.
Towering pines shaded her as she walked through the cool mountain wood in the earthy aromas of early spring. She carried a warm, freshly made pie in her old-school wicker picnic basket. The pie was homemade with all-natural ingredients: apples, sugar, flour, cinnamon, salt, nutmeg, lemon juice. Oh, and the most important ingredient of all, a mother's love. Now she won't be left to die as a weak, useless old woman who couldn't contribute to what was left of society.

With grim determination, the proud, aged lady strode toward the hospital, a large, long white tent decorated with a huge red cross and nestled under the blocky Treehouse near the center of Tent Town. Suddenly, she stumbled over nothing; the very earth beneath her feet had . . . moved.

Incredibly, the ground—good ole terra firma—rocked under her like a ship tossed on an angry sea. Everyone takes the ground for granted, until it starts to move. Indeed, the whole world roared with a low, guttural, angry crescendo. The very trees slewed drunkenly, some leaning to the left, others to the right. Some, spinning, crashed thunderously to the ground. The old woman gasped in horror, for she and her pie barely escaped when a huge tree trunk slammed the earth right in front of her.

Determined, the old woman clambered over the new log in her way. But as the earthquake rumbled on, the shivering hospital tent, broadcasting the desperate screams of those trapped within, imploded, tent fabric and supports collapsing into a dark hole opening precipitously beneath it. The impossibly black hole grew larger, radiating out, swallowing trees and leaves and underbrush, spreading inexorably toward her like a spilling ink stain. In terror she turned to get away from the blooming hole, to run, to flee, to escape. But as the world thundered and the ground shook, her feet finally found nothing but air, and she fell, limbs flailing, howling helplessly as she fell down into the endless black, the circle of light above her shrinking to a star as she fell down . . . down . . . down . . .

* * *

He awoke to a terrified shriek. He had learned to harden his heart to cries of pain and despair, but this cry came from a woman with whom he shared the large recreational vehicle.

He threw off heavy layers of blankets, allowing the early morning chill to rush in like a plunge into a mountain stream. Rolling out of bed, he stepped to the bedroom in the back of the RV, flinging the door open. He shook a sleeper completely buried under a mound of quilts.

"Wake up, Mom!" he demanded. "You're freaking me out."

The face of a gray-haired old woman popped out at the front of the bed.

"Oh, Phillip!" she wailed. "I had a dream. It was so real. I think it's another Vision!"

"Mom . . ."

"Is something wrong?"

Phil realized she was looking at his right hand. He had a death-grip on the handle of the 9mm automatic pistol the Army had given him. He honestly didn't remember retrieving it from under his pillow.

"Everything's fine, Mom," sighed Phil, willing himself to relax. "It's just—"

Someone pounded on the front door as if they were trying to bash it in.

"Hey, Doc! Doc!" cried the door-pounder. "Everything okay in there, Doc?"

Phil recognized the voice, but out of habit he pulled the curtains back and looked out the window anyway. There stood his anxious neighbor from the next RV over, along with his equally nervous oldest son. The neighbor carried a dented aluminum baseball bat, and his son a meat cleaver. He could see their breath in the cold spring morning.

"It's okay, Joe," Phil told them. "My mom's just having a bad dream. And if anyone else is coming, please tell them we're OK, would you?"

"A dream?" asked Joe, his eyes wide. "Is it a Vision?"

By now a woman from yet another RV had arrived, carrying a shotgun at the ready. Could she really have the shells for it?

"It's okay, everybody. Go on back to bed."

"What for?" Joe's son protested. "There's only enough time to get comfortable before Reveille."

A few more pleasantries were exchanged, but they were brief; the neighbors were out in the cold in their nightclothes. Phil returned to find his mom sitting in bed with her nightshirt hiked up, looking at a bright red bruise on her inner thigh.

"Ugh, Mom!" cried Phil, averting his eyes. "Really?"

"A bee stung me," she was saying. "How did it get in here and under all those covers? It *must* be a sign!"

The old woman sighed, put her leg down, and then opened the door on an antique potbellied woodstove by her bed. A chimney of thin metal segments ran up from the stove through a ragged hole crudely cut in the RV roof. Old clothing was stuffed tightly into the gap between the edges of the hole and the chimney.

"It's so cold in here," she complained. "Light a fire, will you, Phillip?"

"Sure, Mom, but I thought you were the one who wanted to save money," Phil replied, even as he wandered back to the living room to get his coat.

"Yes, you're right, Philly, of course. How can wood be so expensive? There are trees everywhere. The mountain is covered with them!"

"Spring is here, Mom, so we can afford to save on firewood. You still want me to fire up the stove?"

"Phillip, sweetie, on second thought, don't bother. You need to take me to Colonel Minor at once. He must hear of my latest Vision."

"Mom, we can't just roll up on His Majesty Lieutenant Colonel Bee Minor unannounced."

Especially not to hear the ravings of some crazy old white woman, he thought, imagining himself in Minor's place.

"Why not, Phillip? You're our leader. He works for you."

"Mom, I'm glad you're proud of me, but please don't fool yourself," Phil explained. "It is we who work for the military, not the other way around. I know it sucks, but if I were the one wearing body armor and carrying a machine gun, I don't know if I could resist the temptation to be a prick, either."

"Come now, honey, we all elected you president."

"I was elected *chairman* of the Civilian Affairs Board, Mom—I don't know where everyone is getting this 'president' thing from. The military treats us all like crap, and I'm just the fly on top of the pile."

"Now don't you be saying such nasty things about that nice Colonel Minor; he's a hero. Big Wheels!"

"Mom . . .!"

"Now escort Mommy out to the little girl's room," said his mother, crawling out of bed.

The latrines were rather far from the RVs in order to spare Tent Town's wealthier citizens the smell. Phil cringed at the thought of his old mother struggling all the way there.

"I keep telling you, Mom, the old and sick are exempt from that law. Will you just do it in here? That's what the black bucket is for."

"No, no," his mother muttered, shaking her head, and began to chant:

"Crap inside, brings the flies
makes diarrhea, then you die."

It took some effort, but Phil finally convinced his mother to use the bucket set inside the tiny RV bathroom where the toilet used to be. A toilet seat jury-rigged to four metal chair legs was suspended over the bucket. The doctor removed the tight-fitting lid for his mother. The sharp smell of urine filled the RV as soon as the lid came off; Phil was no fan of trekking across a tent city in freezing darkness just to pee.

While the old lady did her noisy business, Phil retrieved some firewood and fired up the stove. Normally he didn't bother to heat water for daily hygiene, but if he was going to see the colonel, he wanted to be especially clean. By the time his mother finished, the teapot was wailing and he could add its boiling contents to the water already in the hygiene pot. Now he poured the warmed water from the hygiene pot through a funnel into the black camp shower bag.

Most people—at least the people lucky enough to have them—hung their shower bags out in the sun all day so they could have hot showers after work without firewood, diesel, or any other kind of fuel. That plan didn't work so well in the long mountain winter.

Over his mother's protests, he got out the good bar soap—not the homemade kind. For the special occasion, he also got the shampoo and deodorant. They took turns in the tiny RV shower wetting themselves with a brief sprinkle from the camp shower bag, cutting the bag off, lathering up, and then opening the bag again to wash off the residue. Today they used real toothpaste—not baking soda—to brush their teeth. His mother insisted on her best Sunday dress, complete with her dwindling supply of real makeup.

While she was getting ready, Phil took the opportunity to carry the black bucket out of the RV neighborhood and through the tent city to the latrines. He glanced up to notice a haze of wood smoke hanging low over the tents in the chilly morning air, twisting like dirty ghosts through the lower boughs of tall evergreens. Half the tents were long, multi-family olive green dwellings donated by the military. A colorful mélange of tents scrounged from big box discount stores and sporting supply outfits constituted the remaining. The tents were arranged in neat blocks with broad avenues running between.

Reveille hadn't sounded, which meant most of the inhabitants still slept. Phil liked that, because it meant he could travel to the latrines and back without getting stopped a dozen times by people seeking free medical advice.

A gulf some 20 meters wide, strictly enforced by military patrols, separated the row of latrines from the rest of Tent Town. The doctor knew there were sixty of them; one for every ten original inhabitants. Each former port-a-potty had been installed over a cement slab capping a hole some three meters deep by one and a half meters wide. Some of the holes inside had old commodes installed over them; that's where the toilet from his RV had gone. But most were just metal chairs with holes cut in the seat, and some didn't even have the chair; just a round hole in a concrete slab.

At the rear of each port-a-potty was a vertical length of plastic PVC pipe capped with a piece of metal fly screen and stuck through its own hole in the slab. The pipe extended above the port-a-potty to vent the foul gasses to above head high. This arrangement helped control the odors. Better yet, it trapped most flies inside the pit to die!

Phil dumped the bucket into one of the latrines. He used an old brush he kept stored under the RV to sweep it out. He opened the door on the port-a-potty to leave and nearly ran right into someone.

"Hey, Doc!" cried the other man, bundled up in heavy winter clothing. "I was going to come over to visit you this morning, but here you are!"

Two dogs sniffed and scurried about the man's feet. That he could keep two dogs alive, much less healthy, spoke volumes as most pets had been eaten by this time.

"Hey, Frank," Phil replied. "You sick?"

"Nah, I was just going to share some of my good fortune with you. I bagged me two raccoons last night, and one of 'em is fat as a hog!"

"You hunt at night? Isn't that dangerous?"

"You could freeze to death or poke an eye out if you don't watch yourself," Frank agreed, "but trust me, Doc, it's worth it. After dark there's less competition so you don't have to walk near as far, and you can bag the critters that usually only come out at night. I swear those other clueless 'hunters' are scaring off all the game!"

"Yeah, well, when hunting season is 24/7 and 365, that'll happen."

"I'll tell you what else will happen—I'm going to give you one of those coons."

Phil's mouth began to water, for it had been weeks since he had fresh meat or any other food that wasn't rice, or some preparation of dried corn, or that didn't come out of a can or brown plastic bag.

"What's the catch?" he asked flatly.

Frank chuckled.

"That's why I like you, Doc—right down to business. Fine. I got an idea for this place, and I need you to give me twenty minutes to make my case at the next board meeting."

"You don't need to pay me for that, Frank. Just tell me you have business before the board and I'll be sure to pencil you into the agenda."

"When, Doc?" Frank sneered. "After all the bigwigs spew a lot of hot air about nothin'? When us regular folks are trying to get people to listen after three or four hours of total BS and everyone can't wait to go home?"

"Frank—"

"You'll get that coon if you promise to let me speak in the first hour of the next meeting."

Phil shook his head.

"I can't let you speak for twenty minutes, Frank. In addition to making a long, boring meeting even longer, it would be obvious you paid me, wouldn't it?"

"All I want is a fair hearing."

"Well, how about this? I only let you speak for five minutes—which is three minutes longer than normal—but I make sure you go *first.*"

"First?" Frank asked, raising his eyebrows. One of his dogs whimpered and yelped impatiently.

Phil nodded.

"We do the prayer, the Pledge of Allegiance, and then it's you, Frank Hollings, for five uninterrupted minutes. What do you say?"

"I say you got yourself a deal, Doc," Frank answered, and they sealed the deal with a firm handshake.

"You're not buying my vote, Frank—I will vote yea or nay based on the merits of your proposal. The only thing you've bought is the first time slot."

"Got it, Doc. I'll bring that coon over just as soon as the missus cleans it."

"Nah, Mom and I are going to visit Colonel Minor today, and there's no telling when we'll be back. Let me come to your place and get it."

"You're going to see the Colonel? Hell, I could just go with you and cut out the middleman."

Phil had no intention of setting such a horrid precedent.

"Mom's coming with me to explain one of her Visions," Phil told him.

"Ouch," said Frank, wincing. "I don't want to pitch my idea while you've ticked off the whole damn court. I guess I'll just wait for the next board meeting."

At this, they exchanged parting pleasantries and each went his way.

Reveille blared from a trumpet in the Treehouse mounted on the tall pine near the center of Tent Town. Phil hurried as the tents began to murmur. But he slowed at the sight of a twelve-year-old boy carrying an axe on his shoulder, his face streaked with tears. The symbol of the Woodcutter Gang had been burned onto the back of his right hand.

"Bill!" he shouted at the boy, who stopped as the doctor headed over to him. "Bill, what's wrong, son?"

"Muh, my dad," Bill sniffed. "He just whupped my butt!"

"What?" cried Phil incredulously. "Why?"

"I luh . . . I lost our lighter. I've been looking for it, but I can't find it anywhere!"

The boy seemed set for a full-on bawling session; he struggled visibly to keep control.

"They trusted me with that lighter," he moaned, sniffing, "and I lost it, Doc. I lost it!"

"Look, Bill . . . I've got an extra lighter . . ."

The boy's eyes flared in hopeful expectation.

"You would give me a lighter?"

"Still in the original package," Phil assured him. "But not for free!"

"Well . . . tell me what I have to do, Doc!"

"First, I want you to clean this crap bucket with boiling water. No, check that. Follow me to the house . . . I've got bleach solution. Next, do you know where I keep my firewood?"

"Locked up in the trunk of that old car next to your place?"

"Exactly. Well, I'm about out. Fill my trunk with firewood—I'll give you the key—clean this bucket, and I'll get you that lighter."

"Oh, praise God for you, Doctor Phil!" the boy cried. "Let me go home to Dad and see if it's okay with him, all right?"

The doctor winced at the name, "Dr. Phil." Then again, it was obvious this kid was not trying to insult him.

"Deal."

"Big Wheels!" cried the boy, and ran off in a rush of jubilation.

"Careful running with that axe!"

Phil had one more hurdle to overcome before he made it home. It came in the form of a young woman who normally managed to look quite attractive even without makeup. But this morning, she looked sick and exhausted. Her eyes lit up with desperate hope at the sight of him, and she moved quickly to cut him off.

"Hey, Doc!" she sang. "You're looking good today."

"Hello, Miss Davis."

"Aw, you don't have to be so formal!" the girl said, putting a hand behind her ear and giggling nervously. "You can call me Violet. Or Vi. My friends call me Vi."

"What do you need, Miss Davis?"

"It's my back, Doc. It still hurts, like always. And sleeping on the ground doesn't help."

"You sleep on the ground? The Army gave everyone a cot."

"I . . . sold mine," she sheepishly admitted, and dropped her eyes.

"Oh. Well, I can get you an appointment for tomorrow after your field shift. I know you can't afford aspirin, but have you tried the yoga exercises I prescribed?"

"About the field shift. Could you, um . . . write me a profile that says I can't work?"

"Miss Davis, are you having difficulties with the Army?"

Her eyes flashed with anger.

"They cheated me yesterday. I was supposed to get an MRE, but all I got was a lousy bowl of oatmeal. Can you believe that? A bowl of oatmeal for working all day in the fields?"

A Meal Ready to Eat was the long-storage US Army ration that came in a brown plastic bag, along with a clever chemical heater blessedly activated by mere water. A meal you could heat without flame was great, because a people used to the comforts and relative safety of better times were now lighting, heating, and cooking with open flames in their homes, leading to all kinds of tragedies.

"And why did they only give you a bowl of oatmeal?" Phil asked, though he could guess.

"They claim I didn't *earn* my MRE. They said I was shamming!"

Perish the thought invaded Phi's mind, but did not escape his mouth.

"I tried to tell them I couldn't work as hard as everyone else because of my back, but they wouldn't believe me! That's why I need you to write that note."

"Surely you can show them medical records or prescriptions or something that proves you have a history of chronic back problems?"

"I . . . I lost them," Violet protested.

Of course you did.

"Look . . . Miss Davis. Weren't you an administrative assistant at a law firm?"

"Yes. But I was more than just a secretary, Doc. I went to night classes at the local college and was all set to go to law school before the world went to hell."

"I know it's a tough transition from sitting around an air conditioned office all day to backbreaking field work in the hot sun. And trust me, when summer gets here, it's going to be a lot worse. But we all have to do our part."

"Don't give me that!" the girl spat. "The Woodcutters don't work in the fields. They're in the shade all day, eating all they want!"

"Vi—Miss Davis, fuel for chainsaws, tractors, and logging trucks dried up a long time ago," Phil explained. "The Woodcutter Gang takes down trees with hand tools and drags them all over the mountain for us. Further, after disease and cold weather, the biggest cause of injury around this place is clueless, amateur lumberjacks dropping trees on each other. So don't begrudge the Woodcutters their wealth, Violet. They earn every penny."

"Well, what about the soldiers? All they do is yell at people, the Big Wheel bastards."

"You have a point there, Miss Davis. I and the other members of the council are drafting an official protest against the Army. The soldiers are generally young and fit. The least they can do is their fair share of the physical labor around here."

"Damn right! And frankly, Doc, I don't see you bent over out there in the fields, either."

"Miss Davis, I am literally the only doctor left. In fact, I and a mere handful of Army medics and nurses are the only health professionals on the mountain. We see patients all day."

"Uh . . . I can be a nurse!"

Phil wanted to shout "*the hell you can!*" but instead said, "You can always apply for the Medical Services Course or the Mechanic Academy. But I must warn you, standards are astronomically high and competition is fierce. Lots of lazy people have to be weeded out who only applied because they didn't want to chop wood or work in the fields."

All this time, Phil took note of how ravenous the girl looked. She wasn't starving, but hunger blazed in her eyes like headlights. Typically, everyone in Tent Town got at least one MRE a day, in one way or the other. But MREs were a valuable commodity, and it was not uncommon for someone to trade a part or even all of an MRE to acquire other things. In one council meeting someone actually suggested that the soldiers make individuals eat the MRE in front of them as soon as it was issued, but this was dismissed as being too tyrannical.

"You know about sick days?" Violet asked.

"Sure. Tell the Army you're sick and you get an MRE without having to work that day."

"Well, I'm all out of sick days, and—"

"You've burned up seven days of Sick Leave already?" Phil asked, incredulous. "The planting season's barely started!"

"I'm sick!" Violet shouted, practically screaming. "My back . . . I, I tried buying sick days from guys with . . . you know."

"Yes, Miss Davis, everyone knows."

"But . . . no one wants to sell me any more sick days. I'm just . . . I don't know what to do—"

"Work through the pain, Violet," Phil said. "Sorry, but I've got to go."

Then he walked past her.

"Wait!" she cried, and when he turned back, she was smiling as she closed in.

"Please write me that note," she purred, opening her jacket to reveal bare breasts. "I'll make you feel good."

He calmly met her eye.

"As the town doctor, I am well aware of our rampant STD problem, and I have no wish to participate. Good day, Miss Davis."

She screeched a stream of expletives after him as he left for the RV part of town. A two-man safety patrol of armored soldiers hustled past him toward the screams, shouting orders. Phil didn't stop to explain. Indeed, he picked up the pace.

Mom had hot pine-needle tea ready for him when he returned, a Tent Town staple. The concoction had more vitamin C per volume than orange juice, and pine needles were ubiquitous here. The trick was to get the water very hot but remove the tea just before the boil, because boiling destroyed the Vitamin C. Phil found the taste left much to be desired and would have loved to sweeten it. Sadly, while pine needles were free, sugar managed to be one of the most expensive commodities on the mountain. Still, he faithfully drank at least a pint a day. People had to get water very hot to make tea, so frequent tea drinking proved an excellent way to minimize water borne diseases.

"That nice young redhead Army nurse with the freckles came to see you," Mom said.

"Lieutenant Erickson?"

"Yes, that's the one. She wanted to know when we're coming to the hospital today."

By "the hospital," his mother was referring to the large white tent decorated with a red cross and nestled under the Treehouse near the center of Tent Town.

"You told her we're going to see the colonel today, right?"

"Of course, dear. I told her to expect us around noon. Well, let's go!"

"Not yet, Mom. We have to wait for Bill so I can give him the keys to the car."

"Oh, we're getting more firewood?"

"Yep. And he's going to clean the crap bucket, too."

"I hope you didn't pay too much."

"Nah, just a lighter. We got a bucket of 'em. People love to pay me in lighters."

"Won't all the lighters run out of fuel eventually?"

"Eventually. Why do you think I've been hoarding all those matches? We'll be okay, Mom. I'll take care of us."

Bill arrived, so Phil and his mother left for the Fort. It was a winding mile down the narrow gravel road from the RV park to the old Baptist youth camp that had been transformed into Fort Minor. While a fifteen-to twenty-minute walk for the average person, it meant thirty to forty minutes for the old woman, so Phil insisted on taking the golf cart over his mother's strenuous objections.

The chain link fence topped with coils of razor wire surrounded the heart of the old youth camp, now Fort Minor. A two-soldier patrol walking the fence smiled and waved as they rolled by. His mother returned the gesture, but Phil did not. He kept driving to the gate, which was flanked by a pair of sandbag redoubts, one on either side of the entrance road. Each bore a well-worn heavy machine gun. The water-filled plastic highway barriers reminded Phil that to drive through the gate, one had to weave through a zigzag course. He wondered again why a tactic used to foil suicide car bombers in Iraq and Afghanistan had any relevance here.

A squad of ten soldiers in full body armor manned the gate, each armed with an M-4 carbine variant of the M16 automatic rifle. A banner, hung from two trees on either side of the road, floated over the gate, reading:

UNITED STATES ARMY
42ND TRANSPORTATION BATTALION (TRUCK)
LTC BEE G. MINOR, COMMANDING
"BIG WHEELS!"

A forty-foot steel intermodal shipping container, or CONEX, sat on the side of the road, just outside the gate. Windows and a door had been cut into the container. Someone had spray-painted the words GATE STORE on its side, and a large open window revealed a soldier sitting behind it, with another standing behind him. Phil zoomed the cart right on over to the store.

"Hey, it's Dr. Phil!" sang the standing soldier as the doctor and his mother stepped from the golf cart.

"Come on, Private Mason, you know he hates that," said the seated soldier, but he rose to shake the doctor's hand. "What can I do for you, Doctor Topper? Or should I say Chairman Topper?"

"A pound of coffee, please," Phil responded. "Sergeant . . . Watson, is it?"

"Yes, sir, Mr. Chairman," said Watson. "And that'll be a hundred and fifty dollars."

Phil raised an eyebrow.

"The price has gone up," he noted.

"The supply has gone down, Doc."

"You have any fresh coffee?"

"Nope, it's all stale. Maybe we'll get fresher coffee in the next Scrounge Run, but I wouldn't bet on it. As far as we're concerned, coffee plantations might as well be on the other side of the moon. The same can be said for chocolate, vanilla, oranges, bananas—you get the idea."

"Speaking of Scrounge Run, I need to go on the next one," said Phil. "You need someone with you who knows how to identify the drugs and medical equipment we most need."

"It's not my place to tell the chairman of the Civilian Affairs Board that he's not invited. But I can't imagine the colonel letting our only real doctor go on a Scrounge Run."

"He's right, Doc," said Mason. "I've never been on a Scrounge Run where at least one poor bastard didn't get it. Last time, we lost five soldiers and two trucks. Why don't you send your hot girl, Red, in your place? You've trained her up by now, haven't you?"

"We can't afford to lose *any* more professional medical personnel," Sergeant Watson insisted. "Doc, you'll have to write down a list of drugs by name, along with detailed descriptions of the medical equipment you want us to look for. And that's *Lieutenant* Erickson to you, Private Mason!"

"We'll see what the great and wonderful Oz has to say about that at our meeting this morning," Phil joked. "In the meantime, I'll also take some aspirin."

"How many, Doc? It's two bucks apiece."

Phil did some quick calculations. At two aspirin a day, it would cost him $56.00 for a two-week supply.

"I'll take twenty-eight."

Sergeant Watson sat down, and brought out a large black three-ring binder and an abacus.

"Let's see your ID, please. Yes, I know who you are, but . . . regulations, right?"

Phil gave him a driver's license from happier times. Watson matched the license with its photocopy in the binder, and glanced up at the doctor's face before picking up the abacus.

"That's one hundred fifty for the coffee and fifty-six for the aspirin," he said, sliding the beads on the abacus around. "That gives us . . . two hundred six dollars even. Let me check the book," he consulted an entry in the binder. "Uh-oh."

"What's wrong?"

"Sorry, Doc. But there's only thirty-six dollars and fifty cents in your account."

"What? That's ridiculous. I've got over two thousand dollars in that book!"

Watson squinted and fingered an entry on the page.

"Says here yesterday you bought some perfume, some makeup, soap, shampoo, deodorant, tampons, toilet tissue, cigarettes, and 750 milliliters of original bourbon whiskey, for a . . . Victoria Davis."

Phil rounded on his mother.

"Mom!" he cried, almost screaming. "Victoria? Really?"

"She needed help, Philly! It's her back, the poor girl—"

"She's a liar, Mom. And a whore! How could you let her scam you?"

"I take it you no longer want your mother to have access to your account?"

Phil sighed in frustration.

"Just . . . give me eighteen aspirin," he huffed bitterly.

"I'll buy the golf cart for five hundred dollars right now," said Watson.

Phil quickly and hopefully shifted gears.

"Are you kidding? I won't take a penny under three thousand!"

Five minutes of intense haggling later, he finally sold the golf cart to Sergeant Emery Watson for one thousand dollars even. Then he bought that pound of coffee plus a bottle of 100 aspirin with the original seal intact, leaving $686.50 in his account. Watson pulled the doctor's account sheet and his own out of their plastic sheaves and, comparing the two, carefully made the changes with an ink pen.

"I certify that these alterations are true upon pain of death, so help me God." he said, and signed his name next to the entry.

"I witness that these alterations are true upon pain of death, so help me God," said Private Mason, and signed his name as well.

Having made the alterations, Watson slipped the account sheets back into their designated plastic sheaves.

"Big Wheels!" he cried upon closing the binder.

"Big Wheels!" echoed every other soldier at the gate, in unison.

Watson handed the binder to his subordinate.

"Call it into Supply," he commanded.

Mason nodded and picked up an old Vietnam War era TA-312 crank-operated field phone attached to a black wire that stretched all the way back to headquarters.

But Phil did not pause to hear the report. Rather, he collected his goods and rejoined his mother. As chairman of the Civilian Affairs Board, he had an Open Pass, which he showed to the Gate Guard, and he brought his mother in as a Guest. They'd barely started the walk for Minor's HQ before Phil sighed wearily.

"Are you tired already?" his mother asked.

"Mom, all I've done since daybreak is wheel and deal, and it's not even noon."

"Well, I can't believe you sold our golf cart."

"Don't worry, Mom," Dr. Phil said confidently. "One day, Sergeant Watson or someone close to him will get really sick or hurt. Then I'll get the golf cart back."

Death Is Not the Worst Thing

Tom Barlow

Editor: Sometimes courage is not living.

When John Stanley Knickerbocker III woke that morning for his 3:00 a.m. piss, he realized he had finally had his fill of the Appalachian Mountains' beauty, his stultifying companions, the emergency rations, and, most especially, the fucking birds—exotic or commonplace, water or woods dwellers, songbirds or mutes, bright or dull plumage. He couldn't care less. The birding workshop that had brought him to this West Virginia lodge on the week the Gray Plague exploded on the U.S. like an all-out nuclear attack was something he would regret for the rest of his life. He should have been home in Ohio dying alongside his son and daughter-in-law. Instead, he had cowered here for the past five months, detached from the world, especially after the phone lines and electricity went dead in the throes of a summer storm.

He returned to his room and dug out the well-worn last letter he'd received from his granddaughter, Trish, two weeks after the plague hit, before the post office quit delivering mail. It contained a newspaper clipping listing the dead of his hometown of Newark, Ohio: virtually everyone in the paper's circulation area over age sixty and many over fifty. All his friends appeared on that list, along with most of his former customers. He gazed for a long moment at the family snapshot she'd sent with the list—Trish, her husband, Glen, and their two kids, Ben the soccer nut, and autistic Oliver.

Knowing that sleep would elude him for the rest of the night, Knick went downstairs to the kitchen, made a cup of instant coffee, and took it out onto the patio. The forest around him was stirring in the dark with a persistent western breeze that suggested rain.

By 4:00 a.m. the anger that had been brooding in him for months, the suspicion that his caution was really just a form of cowardice, finally reached a breaking point. He'd just been coming to terms with the loss of his wife to cancer that spring when he signed up for the week-long workshop. The grief had never really left him, and the other blue-hairs he was stranded with weren't providing support so much as belaboring their own misery.

There was always the chance that he was immune, he reasoned; otherwise, at seventy-two he was sure to contract the age-specific disease as soon as he mixed with the general population. It was a gamble he was finally willing to take.

He choked down a quick breakfast of oatmeal and walnuts from the year's-worth of provender the survivalist lodge owner had in storage before the disaster, then returned to his room. He carefully packed his belongings into his backpack, pausing a moment before deciding to include the Nikon Monarch birding binoculars his wife had bought for him as a retirement present. While he never wanted to look at a bird again, maybe Trish or the kids could use them.

Unfortunately, his son had dropped him off those many months before at what he'd playfully called "Dad's summer camp," so Knick was without wheels. But he'd hitchhiked across the country as a young man, so the thought of a little thumbing didn't worry him. He laced up his boots and, without a glance back, set off down the lane, bound for Ohio and his home two hundred miles to the north.

By the time he'd picked his way around the dry stone wall they'd built at the end of the drive to keep out possibly infectious strangers, descended the mountain, and hiked five miles out the county road to U.S. 219, the sky had lightened to a pearly pink.

He trudged north, waiting for the morning's procession of cars heading toward Beckley to work, or to school. The first dozen to approach slowed slightly in response to his thumb, pulled into the other lane, and passed, eyes diverted. He was getting discouraged when a woman in a middle-aged truck pulled over just ahead of him.

He opened the passenger door and stepped up onto the bench seat.

"Thanks," he said, smiling at the driver. "I'm Knick."

She was attractive, perhaps in her thirties, with big hair the color of vanilla pudding. In the rearview mirror he saw the rooster tail of gravel she threw up as she tore off the shoulder. "Hannah. You're lucky I'm a biology teacher. Most of the people around here are still afraid they can get the virus if they stand too close to a geezer. You could be hitchhiking until Christmas."

"I've been off the grid for a few months. Any news about a cure?"

She kept her eyes forward, casually swinging the truck through the relentless curves of the mountainside road. "They were supposedly able to save some woman in Moscow with a med derived from castor beans, but nobody's been able to duplicate it. Now they think it was all a hoax. So, no."

"What's the body count?"

"Man, you're a downer as a conversationalist," she said. "Around sixty-five million in this country, give or take. Almost all people over sixty, around 40 percent of those between fifty and sixty. How old are you?"

"Seventy-two," he said.

"So why are you still alive?"

"That's the question. My son and his wife both passed early on, and they were only fifty-one. I've been hiding up in the mountains, so maybe that's it. Or maybe I'm one of the immune."

"That reminds me," she said, "I'm legally obligated to deliver you to the hospital. There's a federal law that anyone over sixty who's still alive has to give some blood in hopes of finding antibodies."

"No problem," he said, figuring that it might be easier to hitch a ride from the hospital, in the middle of town.

They chatted the rest of the way, her mostly about her adventures in teaching fourth- grade math, him about his former life as an insurance salesman.

"Hope you didn't sell policies for Zeta American; they went bankrupt last month."

"I hadn't even thought about that," he said. He'd sold hundreds of universal life policies to people his own age, and even carried half a million on himself. Young people must be swimming in coin, if the companies were able to cover their policies.

She dropped him off at the door of St. Mark's Hospital in downtown Beckley. "Take care of yourself," she said. "I hope you make it." Knick wrote off her failure to make eye contact as she spoke to the normal human discomfort around the condemned.

He thanked her and walked into the lobby. At the counter a young black woman in mint-green hospital scrubs was intent on her computer and didn't notice him at first.

"I understand you want some of my blood," he said.

She looked up and her eyes grew wide. "Holy shit," she said. "Where'd you come from?" She fished around under the counter and produced a mask, which she stretched across her mouth.

"What's with the mask?" he said. "It's not like I can infect anyone under fifty."

"I'll be fifty someday, I hope," she said. "It's standard hospital protocol. You need to come with me. And don't touch anything."

She walked out from behind the counter and led him down a long hallway to their right, lined with windows facing the parking lot. The fifth door was fronted with heavy overlapping plastic strips hanging down like a bead curtain. She wedged them apart, opened the door and slipped inside. He followed.

The chill in the small room matched its austere decor, with one chair, a rolling stool and a dusty examination table. "Someone will be with you eventually. Fill this out while you're waiting." She handed him a tablet with an intake form on the screen.

After she left, he filled it out, glad that he had Medicare instead of some private insurance that might have collapsed with the plague.

After a few minutes the plastic parted again and a doctor entered wearing a hazmat suit. Through the clear plastic face panel Knick could see his face, which didn't look all that youthful.

The doctor took the tablet from Knick and gave it a glance. "How are we today?" he said.

"We're still alive," Knick said.

"That's saying something, these days. How have you managed to beat the plague?"

Knick told him where he'd been for the past five months.

"Remarkable." The doctor turned to a small table against the wall, opened the drawer, and withdrew a needle and a blood collection tube.

"So did they ever figure out where it came from?" Knick said.

As the doctor carefully found a vein in the crook of Knick's arm and began to draw a blood sample, he said, "You didn't hear? It was man-made, specifically to wipe out the elderly. An Italian researcher synthesized it; the Italians had a worse problem than we did with a huge elderly population and not enough young people to support them. The feds still haven't figured out how it spread so fast in the U.S.; the public is convinced it was an organized effort by a group who were against raising taxes to save Social Security. Most died in the first month."

"What happened to the inventor?"

"Nothing. He was sixty-one. He was the first to die of it. The church ruled it a suicide, so he couldn't be buried on consecrated ground."

"And no cure in sight?"

"The whole world's working on it, but nothing yet. Lilly has developed a vaccine that seems to work on some people, but making enough doses is the challenge. If you're asking what I can do for you today, the answer is nothing."

"Nothing?"

"That's not the worst news, though." As he spoke, another person stepped into the room, a deputy dressed in black, a pistol strapped to his waist. He was masked and gloved.

The doctor removed the needle and applied a bandage. "Everyone over sixty is quarantined until the vaccine is available. There have been several instances recently where the virus mutated and began to attack the young. The CDC was able to contain those outbreaks, fortunately, but nobody wants to take a chance on it happening again. We have a ward on the third floor where you'll be kept comfortable until you can be transported to the nearest internment camp. For us, that would be Fort Lejeune."

"I'm a prisoner?"

The cop stepped between Knick and the doctor. "Quarantined," he said. "Not arrested."

"I can't leave, I can't return home. What's the difference?"

The cop shrugged. "Nurses?"

* * *

Knick was even more depressed to discover that he was the sum total of all the oldsters in quarantine. According to the head nurse, there had been three others, but they all eventually succumbed.

Knick turned to the television to appease his boredom. The youth of those he saw struck him. None of the news anchors, actors, pitch men, seemed older than forty. The only mature people were on reruns, and there didn't seem to be many of those. Perhaps the broadcasters were sensitive to public grief.

His first day, the hands of the Quarantine Unit head nurse's hands trembled every time she brought or retrieved a tray, or checked his vitals. She wouldn't stay by the bed long enough to chat with him. Knick finally resorted to talking to her through the nurse call phone. She chatted willingly with him as long as she didn't have to be in the same room.

"You seem a little tentative about your job here," he observed. He watched the parking lot below, which was busier than he expected for a small-town hospital.

"I lost a lot of family already," she said. "Who wouldn't be afraid?"

"They why take the gig?"

"There's federal money behind it, so it pays better."

"You were here when the other three passed?" Knick asked.

"Yeah. Each was here for three days before they got sick."

"So they had it before they were admitted."

"Don't worry. We bleached the living hell out of your room afterward."

Knick lay back on the bed, the head elevated 45 degrees. "Today's Monday? So I'll be lucky to be alive on Friday. Unless I'm immune."

"I hope that's the case. No promises."

"Plato said, 'Death is not the worst thing that can happen to men.'"

"I guess Mister Plato didn't know everything," she said. "I wonder what he'd say now that he's been dead for such a long time."

The hospital intake manager paid Knick a visit the next morning. He looked to be fresh out of high school, but was all business. He held up his tablet, stared at it a minute, scowled. "Mr. Knickerbocker, I'm sorry to have to tell you that you're dead."

Knick poked the arm of his hazmat suit. "Do I feel dead?"

He turned the tablet toward Knick. "There's a national database that was created to track the victims, and your name is right here." He pointed to it. "You died four months ago."

"What does it take for someone to get on that list?"

"A copy of a death certificate. But you've got to realize, the feds were dealing with more than a million deaths a day for a while, so things got pretty crazy. Mistakes were made."

"Well, clearly I'm not dead, so why don't we just tell the database people so they can correct their records?" At great effort he kept his voice even, reminding himself that this civil servant wasn't responsible for the fuck-up.

"It's not that easy," the man replied. "The death certificate originator needs to ask for the retraction. Otherwise, you have to request a hearing in person, in the county of your residence, and that could take months; it's the federal government, and nothing happens fast."

"Who reported me dead?"

He glanced down at his tablet. "The certificate came from a funeral home in Clarksburg, but the form was submitted by a Thomas Keating Knickerbocker. A relative, I presume?"

Knick knew T.K. all right, his loser of a grandson. Knick's son, Brian, had just bailed T.K. out of jail for beating his girlfriend a week before Knick left on his birding trip. If he had convinced the court that Knick was dead, with his parents also deceased, then both of those estates would have been inherited by T.K. and his sister. He was surprised that his granddaughter, Trish, allowed her brother to report him dead without proof; Knick and Trish had a special bond that it would take more than money to break.

Over the next couple of days he picked up the hospital phone more than once to call Trish, but put it down before he made a connection. He feared that she would confront her brother, who must have forged the death certificate. Who knew what T.K. was capable of when cornered? Knick figured it was his job to deal with his grandson, and he wasn't afraid; he'd faced down bigger bullies.

* * *

Knick spent the rest of the week getting the hospital routine down. Meals at 7:00 a.m., noon, and 6:00 p.m. Two nurses on twelve-hour shifts, changing at 11:00 a.m. and 11:00 p.m. The night nurse had a station down the hall and spent most of the night completing the day's reports for her fellow nurses. The doctor stopped by at 8:00 a.m. each morning, appearing a bit surprised each time when Knick's exam showed no signs of illness.

There was a guard on the ward door around the clock, usually a member of the Sheriff's Auxiliary, boys and girls who had probably been wearing Scout uniforms not too long ago. The one that most often drew night duty spent her time listening to music on her phone and napping, head pressed to the wall.

The hospital was near the railroad switching yard. As Knick stood over the toilet each morning at 3:00 a.m. he could hear the train couplings clunking as the northbound coal trains begin to stretch out, the locomotives slowly tugging them taut.

At 2:00 a.m. on Sunday morning, after examining himself to confirm that he still didn't feel the least bit sick, Knick carefully shaved the telltale gray hair from his head before dressing. Fortunately, they'd stored his clothes, belongings, and backpack in the room locker. He cracked the door and heard the steady breathing of the guard at her station.

He eased his way past her. She didn't stir. The quiet of his ward extended into the hallway outside.

He followed the stairs at the end of the hall to the cafeteria on the first floor. The only person in sight had her head in the refrigerator she was scrubbing and didn't turn around as he passed through and out the delivery dock doors.

Diesel from the rail yard scented the dark summer air. They were still building the train, the locomotives on the north end, which indicated it would head in the direction Knick needed to go. He waited behind a dilapidated shed until the railroad worker positioned at the end of the train returned to the triple locomotives up front. Knick found several unlocked, empty boxcars at the end of a long string of laden coal cars, pulled open the door of one and scrambled inside. The car was dark and smelled like piss and bearing grease. He closed the door and hid in a corner in case a railroad bull came looking for transients.

A little after 3:00 a.m. the train began to creep forward. As it built up speed, Knick returned to the door, pulled it open a few inches, and took a seat. He wished he'd grabbed a set of scrubs to wear under his clothes when the moist breeze blew across him.

The train chugged north, hugging and sometimes overhanging riverbanks. The towns they passed through looked ghostly in the fog at dawn. At 7:00 a.m., Knick realized he should have squirreled away some food for the trip. He had three hundred dollars with him, pocket money he'd taken out of the bank months before, on his way out of town for vacation. But he didn't want to get off the train to grab a meal; he had no idea how long it would be before another came along, and he didn't want to end up in quarantine again.

At 11:00 a.m. the train passed a water tower with "Parkersburg" painted on it before crossing the Ohio River on a dizzyingly high bridge. Knick was pleased that his luck had held, that this batch of coal seemed bound to pass through eastern Ohio on its journey. The sun heated up the boxcar. Knick took off his shirt and allowed the breeze to blow across the thick thatch of gray hair on his chest. Still no sign of illness, although he figured it was quite possible he simply hadn't come in contact yet with a carrier. He hoped that the blood he'd left behind in Beckley would be of some use.

The train passed through familiar towns, now. Belpre, Marietta, Lowell, Stockport, then at noon the city of Zanesville. He thought about bailing there, only half an hour's drive from his home in Newark, but the train was traveling too fast.

He counted his blessing when the train finally did began to slow, then came to a stop at the Conesville Power Plant near Coshocton. The facility sprawled along the south side of U.S. 16, only thirty miles east of his home. As soon as the train halted, Knick jumped down and set off across a large, cinder-strewn field to the state highway. His legs were stiff after the ride.

Now came the risky part. He took a position just off the berm of the highway, westbound side, behind a stand of pine trees where he could see cars coming, hoping to identify cops and step back into concealment before they spotted him.

He thumbed for the better part of an hour to no success before he decided stronger measures were needed. He took five twenties from his wallet and held them up in a fan as the next vehicle approached. It quickly slowed and came to a stop next to him, a Ford F-250 so tall he couldn't quite see the driver as he ran to meet it.

As he climbed in, he found the driver was so young-looking Knick had a hard time believing he had a license. The boy had hair down to his shoulders and braces that spoiled his smile.

"Hey, gramps," the kid said. "Who let you out?"

Knick snapped his seat belt. "Thanks for the lift. I'll give you a hundred dollars to take me to my house in Newark."

The kid raised his eyebrows. "I could use the gas money. But really, how did you get out? I thought every geezer in the state was in quarantine."

Knick chuckled. "I busted out. So I warn you, you're traveling with a criminal."

"Cool." He grinned and reached into the glove box and handed Knick a ball cap that read *Hooper Electric*. "Do me a favor, though; wear this. Your head shines like a light bulb, and bald isn't hip anymore."

The kid didn't bother holding down his usual speed just because he was transporting a criminal, and within half an hour Knick was standing in the driveway of his house.

He managed to hold off the string of expletives until the kid disappeared down the gravel drive. He and his wife Carmen had built the brick ranch house themselves, back in 1988, and raised a family there. A For Sale sign stood in a front yard that hadn't been mowed in a month.

When he unlocked the side door into the garage he wasn't surprised to find that the cars were gone; his Cherokee, Carmen's Celica. So was his riding mower, his power trimmer, his fishing gear, even his bait box. Nothing was damaged, though; no sign of vandalism.

He continued into the kitchen. The old refrigerator was still in place, but the range, new a year ago, was gone, leaving only the gas connection sticking out of the floor.

He found similar vacancies throughout the house: the heirloom dresser gone, bed still in place. The silver was gone, the stainless steel utensils still there. His gun safe was ajar, empty. All the televisions were gone, the laptop, the Xbox he'd bought for Trish's kids to play with. The wall photos of family members remained intact. He took down a photo of them all together at last summer's reunion and, hugging it to his chest, crossed the room to his ratty old recliner. He stared at it for half an hour, allowing the memories to wash over him, one sparking the next, until he could take no more sorrow. He retrieved a can of peaches from the larder, opened and scarfed them down, and stretched out in the chair. He was asleep moments later.

He woke late in the afternoon with indigestion. Luckily, there were still some antacids in the bathroom cabinet. His wife's stash of cancer meds was gone.

The water still worked, so he took a long shower. The electricity was out, though, so he ate a can of tuna cold and drank the last can of V-8 in the larder.

Rested and fed, impatience prodded at Knick to track down his grandson. Brian's old mountain bicycle was still intact in the garage, the back tire as flat as it had been two years ago when Trish's younger boy, Oliver, had abandoned it there. Luckily, Knick had some patches that hadn't dried out yet, and he repaired the inner tube. After pumping it up and oiling the chain, the bike seemed operable. He grabbed his backpack, not sure he'd be returning to the house. He also donned the ball cap to disguise his baldness before setting off for T.K's trailer, in a small park abutting the freeway a couple of miles away. He stuck to alleys on the way to avoid cops.

He arrived around dinnertime and found the front door of T.K.'s trailer open. A fat raccoon stared back at him from the couch inside.

Knick stepped off the bike, rubbing his ass. The door of the trailer next door opened and a dumpy woman whose true age had disappeared in rolls of fat only loosely contained by a tank top and shorts appeared in the threshold. She held a Mountain Dew two-liter bottle in one hand like she was strangling it.

"You looking for a place to live?" she said. "I could hook you up with that trailer for five hundred dollars a month. You could hide out from the quarantine for a while, at least."

"How much is the coon paying?"

"Damn kids, always leaving the door open. My brother's coming over tomorrow to mount a hasp so we can lock it."

"I'm not shopping," Knick said. "T.K.'s my grandson. Any idea where he's staying?"

"I didn't know he had any old relatives left. He's got a house over on Welsh Hills now, one of them new four-bedroom models. Not that he's ever invited us over, as much as we done for him over the years."

Knick knew the builder who was developing that tract: $300,000 a pop, minimum. He said goodbye, gingerly sat back on the bike, and took off.

It took him half an hour, most of it spent walking the bike up one steep hill after another, to reach the development. By the time he identified T.K.'s house by the Cherokee in the driveway, he was soaked with sweat and ready to tear into his grandson.

T.K. and Trish must have collected on his life insurance as well as those of his well-insured son and daughter-in-law, so he wasn't surprised that his grandson could afford the sprawling four-bedroom Georgian-style house with attached three-car garage. The pristine appearance of the new home was marred by the front yard, which was mostly dead sod.

Dusk was falling as he reached out to ring the doorbell, but changed his mind and tried the doorknob instead. Surprise would work in his favor.

The door was unlocked. He opened it and quietly stepped inside. His heart raced as he passed through the entry hallway.

To his left was a dining room empty of furniture, to his right the living room, a display of garish taste in crimson and velvet. From the back of the house, he could hear a snore.

He found his grandson shirtless and asleep on an L-shaped couch in the family room in front of a TV showing the Quaker State 400. A tattoo of a Colt Anaconda backed by an American Flag covered his chest, his nipples forming the nose of two upright bullets. A small Baggie of white powder sat on a makeup mirror resting on the coffee table next to him.

Knick stepped forward until he stood over T.K. "Hey," he said, poking him on the shoulder. "Wake up." He shucked off his backpack and dropped it onto an end table. He didn't want to be encumbered if he had to dodge a punch.

T.K.'s left eye cracked open. Knick could almost hear his grandson's brain spinning up. "No fucking way," he finally said before blearily sitting up. "Where did you come from?"

"Not as dead as you'd hoped?" Knick said.

T.K. palmed his face. "You've been gone for months. How were we supposed to know you were still alive?" He fumbled on the coffee table for a cigarette and lit it with a shaking hand.

"You were supposed to hold out hope. But knowing you, you hoped I was dead. Otherwise, you wouldn't have all this."

"All this? Are you serious?" Knick was surprised by the bitterness in T.K.'s voice.

"How'd you do it?" he said. "Bribe the funeral home? Or do you have a buddy in the sheriff's office? God knows you've spent enough time with them."

T.K. rose unsteadily to his feet. Although Knick was not a small man at six foot one, his grandson had a full five inches and probably fifty pounds on him. In his fury, Knick didn't care.

"You talk to Trish yet?" T.K. said.

"I figured I'd start with you. You've got a lot to answer for."

"You disappear for half a year and now you want your shit back. Is that it?"

"I want more than my stuff back. I want my life back."

T.K. shook his head. "You think it's that simple to come back to life? You're going to fuck up everything."

"I'm sorry to ruin your binge," Knick said. "But first things first. You and I are going down to the sheriff's office so you can have them declare me alive again. Then, you're going to transfer whatever money you have left back to me, and tell RE/MAX my house is off the market. Maybe they can list this place instead."

T.K. shook his head. "Dream on, old man."

As a child, the only thing T.K. had obeyed was firm, unequivocal commands. "I'm not giving you a choice."

"Is that right?" T.K. leaned over and reached under the couch cushion. When he withdrew his hand, it held a pistol. Knick recognized it as one of his, a Walther P22 Match pistol that he used for target shooting.

"Who's going to miss you when you're already gone?" T.K. said.

As he brought the pistol up to bear, Knick snatched up his backpack and held it up to his chest. His grandson fired twice. Knick could feel the bullets strike the backpack, but they did not make it through.

Knick shoved the backpack into T.K.'s chest. His grandson took a step back and his leg bumped against the coffee table. He lost his balance and fell back onto the couch, pulling the backpack out of Knick's hands in an attempt to check his fall.

Knick instinctively reached for the backpack, but caught only the strap of the binoculars that were half out of their pocket. From the couch T.K. tossed the backpack aside, then sat up and attempted to retarget Knick. Before he could fire another round, though, Knick swung the binoculars by their strap with all that anger that possessed him, for his son, his friends, all those millions murdered before their time. The binoculars smashed into

T.K.'s temple where they made a crunching sound, part broken lens, part bone. T.K.'s arms fell to his sides and his eyes became unfocused as he slowly slumped back onto the couch.

Knick took a seat on the chair next to the couch and watched as his grandson stopped breathing. He couldn't reconcile this brute with the curious boy he'd taught how to fish. He thought the plague and Carmen's death had cooked all the grief out of him, but he couldn't otherwise account for the wave of profound sadness that settled over him as he called 9-1-1.

* * *

Knick spent the next hour in the isolation ward at the local hospital sipping weak coffee and waiting for the investigating officer, before the door opened and Trish shuffled in, dressed in the now-familiar hazmat suit. From her puffy eyes he could see she'd been crying, and a lump appeared in his throat. In her he could see his wife, as though she had come back to life, young again and vibrant.

"Grandpa?" she said, stopping halfway to the chair in which he sat.

Knick stood, reached out a hand toward her, but stopped when she held up hers like a school crossing guard.

"God, Punkin, it's good to see you," he said.

She nodded, but he couldn't tell if it was in agreement or just acknowledging his words. "How is it you're still alive? T.K. said he got a death certificate from that place in West Virginia."

Knick explained where he'd been, how her brother had scammed him, how he'd tried to kill him. "I'm sorry he's dead. He gave me no choice."

"I understand." She still kept her distance, arms crossed, eyebrows tight.

Knick, attempting to calm her, took his seat again. She cautiously advanced and leaned against the examination table.

"How have you been?" he said.

She smiled, but the rest of her face didn't echo the sentiment. "Truth? We've never been better. After we got the money from your estate, we were able to put Oliver in a special school, and he's making progress like you wouldn't believe. We moved out of that piece of crap apartment and bought a nice three-bedroom in Frazeysburg. Glen's been able to quit the garage and is taking nurse's training at Otterbein, and I was able to get the knee replaced that I screwed up in that car crash when I was twenty. There's still some money left though, that we can give you back. I'm sorry there isn't more."

"Not a problem. T.K. can't have spent all his money yet. And we can sell that place he bought."

"Wanna bet? He gave all his money to a guy in Westerville he met in a bar who promised him he could double his investment in six months in the Chinese stock exchange. The guy disappeared three weeks ago, and guess what? No stocks. Now even T.K.'s new house is mortgaged up to the hilt."

"So I'm broke?"

"No, Gary and I are broke. Once we give you back what's left of your estate."

Knick processed her words for a few moments. "I'd love to see Oliver and Ben," he finally said.

Trish took a deep breath. "Maybe we could Skype you. But we can't take the risk for a face to face. I shouldn't be here myself; Glen tried to stop me. Who knows how good these suits are?"

"But I love you."

"I love you too. But . . . times change. And I buried you once already, but you didn't stay dead. How much more can you expect of me?" Tears welled again in her eyes as she stood and left the room.

* * *

When the detective finally got around to interviewing him, Knick had had plenty of time to think about the situation, about the future, and didn't hesitate to confess to murdering his grandson. Premeditated. Cold blood.

He figured that internment camp wouldn't last; they'd find a cure and free the elderly eventually, and anticipating that, Trish would never make use of the remaining money. Her family would return to the misery they'd escaped.

But if Knick was in prison for life . . . As a con, he would have no need for Trish's money, and she would feel free to use it. It was the most he could do for her, as a dead man. And if he was lucky, he'd be rejoining his wife before long anyway.

He could only hope that he wasn't truly cursed with immunity from the plague.

Diesel Dead

Tim W. Burke

Editor: Not all who do good are good.

The Cleveland bus terminal milled with merchant carts, vending machines, overpriced e-booths, all trying to grind a Federal dollar out of weary travelers. Bill pushed through the crowd, speaking apologies in Unidas and English, his nasal Illinois accent not too out of place among these Ohio Buckeyes. He clutched his canvas tote under his arm despite it throwing his balance off.

The scrap dealer in Texas had given him $400 Federal for sixty pounds of platinum and gold. Less than a penny on the dollar. Bill was grateful the dealer hadn't shoved a knife in Bill's skull and taken it all.

He reached the door to the bus dock for his third ten-hour ride since running out of Texas ten days ago. Slipped outside the door to see if he could sneak a drink.

He slumped against the Plexiglas wall and sighed, taking in a noseful of sour diesel fumes. In the loading dock, the big Galleon Lines bus waited, twelve fat wheels and big gold sailing ship on the aluminum side. Down the line to his right, other bays waited for busses to accept their next customers. To his left stood the fuel pumps, surrounded by twisted pipe like musical instruments, engraved with protective wards dark with exhaust.

Bill reached into a coat pocket and unwrapped the wax paper around a bologna roll with mustard and kraut. Hunched over quick and sneaked a mouthful from his fresh pint bottle of Maker's Mark. Bit into his lunch and between the food and drink, his stomach would be quiet for most of the day. The mustard stung his lips and he couldn't quite lick that away.

Something scratched against metal. Scrabbled like big bugs trying to get out of a can.

Within those twisted, big pipes, something scratched.

He almost stepped toward it, surprised.

Damn, thought Bill. *Haven't heard of a crude oil–skeeter since I was a kid. Isn't this diesel mixed up and blessed?*

The scratching reminded him of the lives still in that diesel, the dead animals and dinosaurs and the like that wanted to taste and to touch, who did not realize their last moment had been blotted out by volcanic dust or the cold mud poured down their throat into their lungs.

A tall man walked out from beyond those pipes out of the darkness, staring at the tank.

Bill wondered, *What's he doing back there in the dark?*

Sparks crackled the air around the man's face. Bill blinked, rubbed his eyes. That should have tipped Bill off about the tall man, but Bill had been preoccupied with the mustard.

Skinny with greasy black hair and black overcoat like a spill of the deepest crude over him. Dark eyes under beetle-brows glowering like he thought of his last dollar. There was a lot of that going around, especially on this bus going up to chase a paycheck in the Titusville Boom.

The Plexiglas lobby door slapped open. The bus driver strode out, his big round belly straining his worn uniform, his face layered with grimaces. His big 9mm SC pistol lay strapped to his hip.

"All aboard!"

Bill swore under his breath.

"Can you wait a minute?" he called.

The driver called back. "Bus is leaving. All aboard or I'm leaving you."

"Ah, that's all right." Bill smiled. "You've got a job to do."

The driver turned and marched up into his bus. Bus drivers, truck drivers, anybody driving anything big on the highways had ultimate authority, as bad as prison guards.

Bill wrapped up his sandwich carefully and put it back in the satchel. He said to himself, "Ah-right, chilluns. Let's get a move on."

He walked back to the platform, looking at the holy verses written around the fuel hatch, listening to his bottle of Maker's Mark sloshing in the pack. As he stepped up into the bus the atmosphere, still fetid from breaths and sweat of the sixty-or-so passengers, washed over him. Over the driver's seat, an icon of Saint Gianni offered tiny pitch-gummed hands, the Galleon Bus Lines being a Roman Catholic Esoteric establishment.

He found his way back to his seat next to a black man wearing a dingy brown wool coat. Bill said, "Smells like the back of a Singapore restaurant."

The man snorted a laugh and set his head back on the dirty window to nap. Past his head, the bus station priest in his red stole walked up to the fuel pumps.

The priest gestured and swung his arm, giving it a precautionary once-over blessing, singing the atonal prayer and waving the red laser beam, such things being necessary since Physics woke up. A green battered fuel truck rattled by and interrupted the view.

Bill remembered the banging inside that pump and looked back out the window. It was like the diesel had been trying to get at him. Added to the sparking around the face of that tall man, it spelled trouble.

Dingy Coat beside him snored already, face pressed against the greasy glass.

Ain't nothing now, he thought.

Bill settled into the seat and slipped his satchel between his boots. It would be another three hours to the destination. Yet another pain would creep up from a cyst on his tailbone if he sat too long.

His nerves twisted when he had to sit for long periods—when he had no way of getting up and running. He remembered the burglary at the metal reclamation house. The geometric twister of the storm scourge shredding that building. What the kid in Texas had said, spraying blood from his dying breath:

"It was looking for you."

Were the scourges after him? Why?

Bill's stomach turned sour. Sweat slicked under his chin and he wiped it with his fingers. He had to get his mind off all that.

In front of him, someone had stuck a newspaper between the seatbacks. He pulled it out and unfolded the *Cleveland Tribune* and looked at the date. His heart went heavy again.

Damn. September already. Why do I keep forgetting the year? I keep forgetting this is 2092. Keep wanting it to be the seventies.

The front page had new houses being built, hospital expanding its maternity ward, new dam construction, the usual. Page eight told of the fiftieth anniversary of the Lake Erie Expulsion coming up next month.

He pulled out the sports section, licking his fingers and wiping the ink off on his sock. Grainy photos of high school boys lunging across the tape. Names of team mascots always made him smile: Hornets, Fighting Eagles, Tarbloods, the Fiery Warriors of Sacred Heart.

No "We're Hiring" section. The buyer must have kept that.

In the aisle and two rows ahead, a chestnut-colored guy in an olive green military coat stood over a seat. Close-cropped red hair, but those kinks had grown over his ears so he wasn't still in the service. The ex-serviceman stood over a skinny brown guy with wireframes and a thick build under his faded plaid wool. Plaid Wool ignored Olive Coat. Everybody tried not to seem entertained.

Olive said, "Excuse me?"

Plaid glanced up. "Was this your seat?"

"You know it was."

"I don't know who was sitting here."

"You know it wasn't you."

The only open seat was right in the back by the door to the bus toilet. The seat beside it occupied by the tall guy in black. Under the harsh tiny lights of the bus interior, the tall guy's skin looked even paler, and the sores shadowed on his face like a black pox.

Plaid said, "Driver didn't say we can't change seats."

Olive glared. "I don't want to sit by the toilet *and* sit by that junkie ass! Give me my seat back!"

Plaid's chin raised. "You got up. You lost your seat."

"Give 'im his seat," some man said.

Plaid turned to the effrontery. "You mind your damn business!"

The bus driver rose. The bus seemed to settle under the weight of his gravitas.

Bill figured the next step. The tall guy in the back probably held a bump of heroin in some tinfoil to get him to the next stop. The obvious solution to the altercation was for the driver to shake down the tall guy, find the brown powder, then throw his junkie ass off the bus, or else call a cop. Slow down their trip and screw up some stranger's life. Because these two jackasses couldn't get along.

The tall man in the back regarded the exchange with heavy-eyed resignation. He looked up at the approaching driver and his shoulders rose in a deep breath.

Bill rolled his eyes at the lack of charity in his fellow humans. He could hear his dad saying, "Why do you always have to get in other people's business?"

That pain of remembering his father made Bill call out. "I'll switch seats."

The two men stopped arguing and looked at him.

Bill lied. "I got sinus infections. Won't smell a thing."

Olive Coat's face tightened in disbelief. "Yeah, but the . . ."

He jerked his head to the guy, belatedly trying to make his insult discrete.

Drawing out the gravel in his voice, Bill made it sound folksy. "One of God's children."

Bill raised his palms. He knew how he came across. Small, light-skinned man creased by sun and wind, long mule-like head in bad need of a haircut and shave, brown canvas coat covering a frame built for work. Nasal accent from not-quite-from-around-here. The look of a hard-luck case who'd done prison for something stupid and was staying well away from trouble.

Olive Coat's decorum got the better of him, finally, and he picked up his duffle.

Plaid already settled back in his seat like he won something like hard-earned justice.

When Olive and Bill stepped into the aisle, the driver saw that he had peace, so he turned back to the front seat.

The tall man looked up at Bill with a mournful gratitude.

His voice was like a cello in an abandoned mine. "Take the window seat. Please."

Bill said, "Sure. Thanks."

He found himself extending his hand. The man gripped firm and solemn like an old, sickly priest.

Bill slid in and planted himself against the bus wall, behind the last window.

The driver took a long, snuffling breath. In a tired slur, he toned the benediction for the trip. Everyone spoke it along with him.

An old man spoke up. "Why don't they keep the priests on the busses?"

His young companion shushed him. "Nothing's happened on the roads for years."

The old man grumbled.

Up front, the electric starter squealed. The dead in the petroleum, distilled and mixed and befuddled into diesel fuel, ignited in the carburetor, exploded in cylinders to push the engines pistons and drive shaft. The bus eased backward out of the bay and everyone settled into the threadbare cloth and aluminum seats.

The electric heaters gasped on the backs of Bill's pant legs. It would be 10:45 p.m. when they pulled into Titusville, provided everything went right.

Bill sighed. *Got no place to stay yet. I'll sleep in the bus terminal until morning, then get set up at the Refugee Y or someplace.*

On the sunlit street, turning onto an onramp, drops of crude oil spattered against the glass. A pinhead drop sprouted tiny insect legs. Pushed away from the glass and swam back into the wind. *Another oil skeeter? Guess they're swimming in them here in oil country.*

He remembered the sparks around the man and looked over. The tall man smelled like hot and sweaty wool. The smell seemed to settle like grease on Bill's skin. Bill's right sinus burned from inhaling the smell.

I'm tired of fights, Bill thought. *A few hours smelling body cheese is worth it just to get on with our lives.*

The man whispered. "Thank you."

"Just getting along," Bill said. "Just getting through the day."

"Amen."

Bill thought, *Amen. Maybe he's religious or maybe that's an act.*

Bill's politeness won out and he stuck out his hand again. "My name's Bill Arraz."

The man shook it again. "Ed. Ed Pomeroy."

"You a church-going man?"

Ed gave a guarded smile. "I was a missionary overseas."

"Oh yeah? What were you doing?"

"Teaching the faithful how to protect themselves. I discovered I didn't know the least of it."

Bill rubbed his neck. *Nowhere to start a conversation with that as the opener.*

So he took a step back in the discussion and talked about his time as a laborer around Illinois, downriver as a carny and a roustabout, all the way to Texas; anything needing two hands and a high tolerance for poverty.

His soul started hurting him again so he changed the subject. "Imagine a lot of other people here are looking for work too."

Heads around them turned at Bill's remark, some nodding.

"I'm to go to Titusville," Ed said.

"To go to," like he was on some mission.

"Got a job waiting?"

"I'll find one." Ed's dark eyes made that a declaration.

The bus wound past Erie Avenue and took the ramp south onto State Highway 89. On the other side of the concrete partition trotted the usual city traffic: horse traps, wagons heaped with wooden crates heading downtown hauling meat and vegetables and fish, people walking and looking up at the big bus. Beyond on the buildings, LED billboards played their little solar-powered movies hawking soda pop, liquor, the state lottery, movies, broken by the usual protective warding hexes.

"Downstairs neighbors are getting restless," said one.

The other replied, "You're sitting over the fuel tank."

"I know. They're scratching out loud."

Nervous laughter died down.

Bill realized the diesel didn't fight around here either. He thought about saying what he'd seen in the garage and on the window. *No sense disturbing people. I'll tell someone when we get in at Titusville.*

Then he remembered the sparking around the head of the man now sitting just next to him. He resisted the urge to lean away and look Ed over.

Bill noted the exit window two rows ahead.

Ed seemed normal enough, though, considering.

As the road rose into the mountains, it narrowed to four lanes carved into the hillside. Traffic and buildings became scarce. The view from Bill's rear half of the window alternated between slopes of crumbling shale and shadowed valleys gilded and threadbare from an early autumn.

The sun gave one long, red scowl, then left men to the dark.

"Makes you wonder how they did it," said a fellow sitting in front of them.

"What's that?" said another.

"The colonials. Hell, the Indians for that matter."

"They didn't have *everything* trying to kill them."

Ed replied, "Faith. You have to have faith in the purifying fire."

The others looked from the corners of their eyes, wondering what a smelly and sick-looking junkie ass would know about keeping faith. The comment seemed a bit out of context for the pale man, but Bill thought it a shame that people were being so judgmental.

So Bill added, "Thanks to it, we're getting out from under!"

People around went "m'hmm!" and "amen!"

Bill read newspapers. Talked to people. Nothing about scourges anywhere. He knew everything was on the rise, on the move, on the way up. How come scourges almost killed him five fucking times?

A lady spoke in amazement. "Hurricanes used to come off the ocean spirit-made and calling for men by their names! The wind demanding sacrifices!"

Now that was ignorant. Storm scourges had the voices long dead in them, but they didn't call out anybody. Not the goddamn two Bill had to deal with, anyway.

Others chimed in.

"Sea Wraiths!"

"My grandpa said he once saw Storm Children!"

The woman said, "Faith brought the wind and earth to heel like dogs."

More nods and "fifty years blessed!" and "No more of that!" and "Getting better every day."

Sounds like everyone had to blow off steam, Bill reflected. *The Great Lakes Expulsions worked. The Expulsions everywhere worked. Settled the winds and water and earthquakes.* But, no amount of prayer or science seemed to cure petroleum, though mixing different wells together befuddled the oil, and refining weakened it.

Still, everyone had settled back all cheery.

Then Ed intoned, "All things mortal are fuel for the flame."

All fell silent except the rumble of the engine. Bill shot a grimace at Ed. People back in a good mood and Ed up and reminds them about Hell? This man had no sense.

The lady's hair was mousy and lank. Beside her, a skinny Asian boy looked at her, concerned.

Her round potato face got serious. "We look to God's light for guidance."

Ed seemed to consider what the lady said and gave the lightest, sad sniff. The others went on with the church talk or went back to dozing in weak bus light. The windows reflected glowing images of people reading, dozing, murmuring bored asides.

The engine churned, mindless.

Ed heaved long, slow breaths. He sniffed and blew his nose into a ruined paper towel. Sweat beaded his forehead. Heroin withdrawal. Bill had seen it many times on his many jobs and in lock-up. Bill's hand brushed against Ed's forearm. The black overcoat was hot. Like it had been drying next to a campfire. Rubbing his fingertips, Bill didn't know what to make of that. Except that Ed was hurting and maybe didn't have a bump of H with him after all.

Bill whispered. "Would a drink help you? I've got some."

Ed's eyes focused and he smiled. "It would help much. I've been worse though. Don't risk getting kicked off on my account. Thank you."

"Do you have a place to stay?" Bill asked.

"I'll ask around when we get there."

Another smaller, rueful smile.

The bus jumped. Everyone bucked in the air and landed in their seat. Bill turned just in time and caught the landing on his right buttock and not his sore tailbone.

Dingy awoke from his window and said a comical, "Whoa! Whoa!"

The bus shook like an earthquake. The shakes deepened. Bill held on to the arms of the seat.

"Oh! Oh!" the Potato Lady cried.

Curses hissed all over the bus.

The driver pulled the big steering wheel to the right. He straightened the wheel as the bus slowed. It lurched to a stop.

A wave of groans and heaves of relief swept the passengers.

The driver called back. "Anybody hurt?"

Shaking heads and "No, sirs."

The driver pulled the lever to open the door. It hissed open like a caution for silence.

"Everybody stay in their seats!"

The driver disappeared down the well into the dark. A few people up front stood up to watch him. Presently, the driver clambered back up the stairs. "We blew both front tires."

Some exclaimed in surprise and a few said thanks to the driver for getting them to the shoulder.

"Did you hit a deer?" a kid asked.

People laughed. The driver's mouth crooked up in something resembling a smile. He picked up the mic to his radio. "One-Fourteen to Base. One-Fourteen."

Up front, an old lady crooned, "I'll tell 'em I'm hurt if they'll get here faster."

People laughed.

The driver actually smiled in earnest. "Nah. You'll just get an ambulance out here with horses and we'll still be here. We're looking at a couple of hours."

Everyone groaned, but not too bad. They muttered stories to each other about other bus trips with problems and delays. Something that always happened on a bus trip.

Radios were rare and regulated because all radio bands hadn't been cleared by the Bureau of Esoteric Administration, so the people in charge said. Bill suddenly remembered he was in a closed aluminum container, all the way in the back. Ed snuffled and seemed harmless, but the walls still closed in.

Bill found his fingers bunching and relaxing. His heart pounded.

Being bottled up was getting to him. Air was too hot. The damned whisky was in the satchel where he couldn't get to it.

He called to the driver, "Excuse me, sir? Can I grab some air?"

A couple of others raised their hands asking for a smoke break. When the driver was distracted, Bill grabbed his bag.

The driver nodded. "Small groups! Stay away from the road!"

He pointed at Bill, the old lady, Olive Coat, and a couple of other hands.

"Where're you going?"

Everyone turned.

Ed had stood up too. "I have to get some air. Please." His thin shoulders rose and fell. Hands wrung and clenched. He was hurting bad.

The driver sneered.

"He's with me," Bill said. "We need to get some air."

The driver stared at them both.

Bill thought, *What am I doing? It's sticking my neck out all the time that screws me up in the first place.*

The driver looked Ed up-and-down and swept a hand to the door. "Okay, okay. Come on."

He stepped down the stairs into the night.

The night air slammed Bill's pores shut. Cleveland had been chilly, but here in the mountains no warmth radiated from brick streets or buildings to block the wind. The breeze smelled of pine and exhaust. Breath drifted in the dark like phantoms. Gravel and dry grass crackled underfoot.

The boy and Potato Lady remained together. The boy trudged slow and sore, voicing all the gripes all the adults were too polite to say.

Potato Lady stared at the front tires. "Geez Louise!"

The front tires steamed, shredded to rags. Something protruded from the left front wheel well, looking like ragged dead lips around a piece of licorice. A pole glistening with black goo. Bill set his bag down and looked close. Scraped the goo with his thumbnail.

Under the goo was rusty iron. Ridges on the side of the length showed where barbed wire would be strung.

Plaid Coat hung close over Bill's shoulder. "A fencepost across the road?"

"Kids," Potato Lady said, keeping an eagle eye on the boy.

Bill flicked the crap off his finger. "Out here? We're miles from anywhere."

Something slapped the side of the bus, making the metal wall ring.

Plaid Coat nodded at the pole. "What is that stuff?"

Bill sniffed. It was sour and smoky, with a raw-egg stink.

"Sour crude oil."

Ed's head rose and he looked straight into Bill's eyes. Bill felt his caution like a lightning bolt into his brain.

Yes, Bill thought. *It's hit this Ed guy too. This situation is definitely off.*

Dingy Coat turned and looked back at the road. "Did it fall off a truck?"

He looked to the driver. The man's stocky shadow stretched up the road to a barely-seen turn uphill. He looked up the road as if searching for something.

Pushing into his satchel, Bill found his bottle of whisky tucked into his inside breast pocket. When he stood, the driver was still looking up the road. Then something struck Bill as even more odd.

Bill lowered his voice. "There's a lot of traffic on this road. There should be at least another truck with wheels messed up."

The driver's hand hung by the angle of sidearm on his hip.

Bill realized, *Somebody put this pole on the road just now.*

The driver turned. "Everyone get back on the bus."

"What?" said the Potato Lady. "We just got off!"

"Please, ma'am! Everyone back on until help arrives." The worry in his voice got Bill's attention.

Potato caught it too. She said, "Yes, sir. We'll get back on. Look! Somebody's over on the other side by the road."

Another slap sounded on the back of the bus, like someone had hit it hard on the far side.

The driver breathed a curse. He strode through the headlights to the far side of the bus. He turned on his heel, the target of his wrath blocked from view by the bus.

"You! Get back on the bus! Or I will find you in default and I will leave you—"

A figure lurched. Its thick hands seized the driver's head.

The driver screamed. The scream rose high in pitch and he struggled. It gargled before becoming a choked cry.

Olive Coat scuffed forward, stunned and uncertain. "Hey! Hey!" He grabbed the figure from behind, around the throat in a stranglehold, still saying, "Hey! Hey!"

A second figure seized Olive Coat from behind. It pressed its face into the man's neck like a passionate kiss.

The driver and the first figure fell in front of the headlights. The attacker glistened with filth. Steam from the driver's strangled cries curled around their heads. The attacker leaned back and gave a long groan, sounding of relief and triumph.

Bill found himself just watching, thinking, *Did this guy come out of a bog or roll in the mud or—*

Then Bill realized. No steam came out of the attacker's throat. The filth on its face melted and poured. Revealed bits of gray bone at its forehead and at the peaks of cheekbone. More filth poured out of its throat.

The old lady stared and made little cries like a crow. The boy stared, eyes wide.

Olive Coat screamed from around the other side of the bus.

Bill had his knife out of his pocket and flicked at the blade with his thumbnail. He stepped behind the thing on the driver and stabbed into its back. The blade sunk in all the way to Bill's wrist. The wound stunk of tar and rot. His forearm sank into cold slime. The slime surged up his coat like a sucking mouth.

Bill screamed and pulled off his pea coat. The muck crackled as it pulled from the skin of his hand.

Black oil drained from the creature's face and slapped onto the bus driver's shaking no-no-no head.

Bill found himself at the bottom of the bus stairs. In front of him, the Potato Lady grabbed the kid's belt and pulled him up. Dingy Brown pushed her ass from behind. Ed stayed at the back wheel, lit by the flashing red hazard lights.

Bill growled and in two steps grabbed Ed's arm. The coat was hot. The cloth was like a cotton mitt grabbing a bread pan out of an oven.

The bus door hissed. The glass glinted as the door started closing. Bill yelled and shoved his bare right arm in the gap. The door clamped down but he couldn't feel anything. His arm felt cold and asleep from grabbing that creature.

"Lemme in, goddammit! Lemme in!"

The filthy things and their victims struggled, indistinguishable in the darkness.

Through the door glass, Dingy Brown sat in the driver's seat, hand tight on the lever. He pushed it back.

"Come on, man! Get in!"

The door gasped open. Bill dragged Ed up. Ed clamped hands around the stair rails and pulled himself up.

Dingy Brown pulled the door lever shut.

He fumbled the bakelite radio microphone and turned to the passengers. "Everybody? Everybody! We got the door shut! Stay clear of the windows and we wait until help comes!"

A man yelled back. "The police'll be on horses! How long would they take to get up here?"

Ed grabbed a luggage rack. His pale skin sheened with fever sweat.

His Adam's apple bobbed over and over. Bill sat him in the seat behind the driver.

Everyone craned their necks to see out the windows.

Oily hands banged on the glass. Long strands of clotted hair framed a mocking grin slicked with molasses black. Beneath the oily visage, a white lace nightgown peeked.

Women and men screamed and shouted.

Bill counted four pairs of hands pounding at the windows. "Everybody keep cool! We're fine in here!"

A man called, "Somebody's gotta drive up from the city and see us! There's trucks hauling stuff up here all the time!"

"Mayday-mayday!" Dingy called into the microphone.

Bill looked at his bare arm. The skin had reddened and his thick wool of arm hair had been pulled out. The skin cold like he had dunked it into a frozen pond.

Sick with fear, he slapped at his arm to get feeling. *Did I catch something from whatever-that-is?*

Dingy Brown fumbled at the mic button. "I don't know what bus this is!"

"One-Forty-One!" someone yelled.

"No!" yelled someone else. "One-Fourteen!"

Dingy yelled into the microphone, "One-Forty-One bus! One-Fourteen-bus! Base! Dammit, there are things out there attacking us! Get some cops up here!"

Bill pushed to the back of the bus.

"What are they?" the old lady cried.

Ed's hollow voice rang over the din. "Targhouls! They are Targhouls!"

Bill turned, his hand on his pack. The crowd quieted. In that reassuring litany earlier in their trip, Bill had spoken of Sea Wraiths and someone else had named them. Another spoke of Storm Children, those people who had been swept up in thunderheads and lived in the winds, possessed in spirit by the storms.

No one had mustered the courage to mention "Targhouls."

An old man turned to Ed, his face slack with horror. "They . . . they burned the last Targhoul up here years ago! Back in the forties!"

Ed inhaled and tilted his head back. That echoing voice croaked from him. "The black blood of the earth passed through a sinful soul. All things impure and dead were made one. Came forth to foul the land."

"What do you know about this?" Potato Lady asked.

Ed swallowed. Blinked and seemed to find himself. "I need . . . to go to the back of the bus."

Hands pushed Ed's shoulders down and held him. Voices demanded he tell more.

Another pair of hands slapped at the windshield. A stick swung against the glass on the door. White specks appeared in the tempered glass.

In the darkness beyond the windshield, the road ahead started to glow where the road curved.

Bill saw a chance to get out and get the people off Ed. "Hey! Headlights! Here's a truck! Start waving everybody!"

The headlights appeared around the bend and grew closer. The driver's side headlight winked. Something blocked the beam.

Those beside the windows, the Potato Lady and the kid, Olive Coat, all waved at the windows.

Ed pushed out of the seat and staggered up the aisle. Bill grabbed Ed's lapel and pulled him along.

"Maybe the truck'll run 'em down!" Plaid Coat said. "Run 'em down! Run 'em over!"

A woman cried, "Our driver's out there! That other man too!"

The truck engine roared over the passengers' cries. Both headlights blinked and swung across the road, back and forth. Bill thought of some primeval beast struggling in the dark.

The rig flashed past the bus headlights. It was a glimpse, but it was enough.

A spindly black figure climbed over the rig windshield. Another hung and reached inside the glittering, shattered glass of the driver's door.

The rig swerved toward the bus.

Bill inhaled a long, croaking gasp. People screamed. Flung themselves across the aisle away from the truck. The bus jolted sideways. The old lady gave a hoarse, ugly scream. Olive Coat and the Potato Lady fell backward onto the boy.

The rig passed the back of the bus where there was no window. The red lights of the trailers tipped up into the sky as it flew over the embankment, then dove like a rollercoaster. The metal undercarriages broke from the trailer and the aluminum sides split along the seams.

With a final, flat-noted clang, it tipped and went over.

Hands clawed at the window. Gaping, drooling faces rose over those hands. A cold gust blew up the aisle. People screamed and scrambled to the front. Some fool had opened the bus door to get out.

Outside in the bus headlights, Dingy stood staring into the dark, free and clear. Then a figure in blue seized the dingy coat collar from behind and slammed him down onto his back. The bus driver fell and punched Dingy's flailing arms. Oil vomited out of the driver's mouth onto Dingy's horrified face.

The other passengers screamed and spilled out of the bus. In the back of the bus, Ed sat, hands on the seat arms, still as a stone pharaoh. "I am a vessel. Of fire."

Then he bent over. Retched into his lap, but nothing came out. Dry-heaved again.

"Please," Ed groaned. "I have to get out."

A man shoved Ed back into the seat. He pulled his hands back. "You're hot! Why are you so hot?"

Bill remembered the heat. It reminded him of documentaries at the movie houses. Movies about the spirits of fire, the Salamanders, burning down Los Angeles.

"Back off the guy," Bill said. "Give him room."

The man fumbled at a tiny gold crucifix necklace. "Why are you so hot?"

Ed wailed. "Please! You aren't safe! You need to get away from me!"

"Back off him!" Bill shouted. "Get out of the bus while you can!"

Potato Lady turned and scrambled to the stairs with the boy. The boy looked back, his fear-crazed eyes widening with awe.

Boys study war machines and monsters and big dangerous things. Bill wondered if the boy knew what Ed was too. They stumbled down the stairs into the dark.

People still cowered and hid in their seats. Through the windows, screams pierced the too-heavy darkness.

Bill's heart chilled so bad it fell into his stomach and he thought he would vomit from fear. The strength drained from his legs.

All those other folks are outside. Let them draw off those monsters. The cops will be here soon. I'm covering my ass and keeping down.

Something creaked behind him.

Ed had risen from his seat, pulled up the sleeve of his overcoat. Pulled back the sleeve of his white shirt. Even in the bus light, pockmarks speckled his arm. He strode to the door.

Under the flat, tiny lights in the bus, his skin waved filaments of steam.

The remaining passengers pulled themselves out of the aisle. Ed passed, his face set with grim purpose, and walked to the front of the bus.

The tall man turned. Stepped down the stairs slow and hard.

"Ed!" Bill shouted. "What are you doing? Stay down, dammit!"

I have to help him! Dumbass junkie's going to get himself killed! Bill's muscles refused to move. He started arguing with himself: *Die here from those things? That lady and her boy are outside! Those other people! Let those people be hurt? I can't. I got to be worth something.*

Bill grabbed his bag. He ran down the aisle to the stairs.

"Close that door behind me, dammit!"

Just as he stepped onto gravel, the door snapped shut. On the shoulder, he searched for movement, any movement. The remaining bus headlight stared in shock at the road.

How many of those things are out here?

Another long cry up the road. Bill's heart fell into his bowels.

The others on that rig. Oh yeah, the others.

"Help?" he whispered. "Anyone . . . need help?"

The back of the bus was just a leap away from the rocks holding up the mountain side. The drop-off here shone with edges of granite. One step over, and he'd fall into the dark ravine below. He turned.

Olive Coat's mouth hung open in a feral, viscid rage. Oil drooled from his nose and mouth. Black trickled from the rims of his reddened eyes. Bill screamed. His foot skidded and gravel rattled back and over the cliff.

The Targhoul hissed.

Bill dodged to the left, trying to get under the bus. The Targhoul's weight landed on Bill's side. Bill's kidney took the blow. Gravel got under his sweatshirt and stabbed his skin. The pain made him curl and cry out.

The Targhoul pulled at Bill's leg. When Bill's head was out from under the bus, it fell on him. Cold slime slapped Bill's cheek. The slime wriggled. A wail of terror tore Bill's throat. Pushed at his clamped lips. Bill screamed at his uselessness.

Just kill me and get it over with.

The Targhoul's fingers spasmed against Bill's neck. Bill opened his eyes. Standing behind the Targhoul, Ed had laid his hand upon the Targhoul's head. Ed's lips slipped and hummed words Bill couldn't hear. Flame cracked from the Targhoul's chest like a burning log. The tar on its shoulders bubbled and hissed.

A voice like a brass horn pushed through Ed's lips. "As flesh is burned by flame, so let the wicked perish from the Light."

Bill had seen tar burn once before at a roof fire in Mississippi. That fire had been orange and choked in smoke. This fire from the Targhoul lit gold like blinding sunlight. Ed shoved the Targhoul aside. It tumbled to smoke beside Bill. Bill sat up and scrambled backward on his hands and feet. The tar fell from his face like a palsied hand.

Hisses challenged from the darkness.

Ed strode along the bus. Another Targhoul sprang upon him. This one stood as tall as Ed. Its fish-white, naked legs striped with black.

Ed seized the thing's head in his hands and sang about the Holy Light, the life-giving light that numbered our days and from whom all new things grew. Its eyes squirted steam. The Targhoul's chest crisped and collapsed into a bonfire.

So it went, the power within Ed frenzied, springing from one reanimated abomination to another, leaving sparking torches. Bill followed with tiny, childlike steps.

The Potato Lady's voice called in the dark: "Joe? Where are you? Joe?"

A piercing scream sliced the dark. Too high to be from an adult throat.

Bill pointed to their right, where the voice came from. "That boy needs help! Come on!"

The lady appeared in the headlight, eyes wet, mouth open with despair. In the dark, another gold flare burst from Ed's holy ignition behind her.

Plaid pushed Bill away. "To hell with that kid! Get me out of here!"

A man scurried toward the bus door. Started pulling at the iron pole. With a seeming superhuman tug, the pole pulled free and the man sprawled in the gravel.

Bill called, "Where is he?"

The woman cried. "Off the cliff over here! He's hanging!"

Her eyes looked behind Bill. He turned to see. The bus shimmered in firelight like a city awaiting an inferno.

Ed stood before the trembling man in the plaid coat. Ed's dark head rolled back. "Who is righteous before the flame? There is none."

He laid his hand on Plaid Coat's head. "For the reward of all is fire; it shall burn the ungodly, dead and living."

The plaid-coated man's awe widened into a silent howl. The plaid-coated man screeched and slapped at his smoking skin. Ran toward the rear bus wheels. He scrabbled in the dirt, trying to hide beneath the bus.

Bill cried, "Wait-wait-wait! No-no-no! Ed!"

Ed turned his head to Bill, his eyes flat with contempt. Bill realized why Ed needed the heroin. Bill tore off his coat. Pulled the Maker's Mark out. "Ed! Brother!" The dark brown liquid gleamed in the headlight and flames.

Ed's fingers curled into claws. He rose, shoulders up like a cat arching its back in fright. Ed the Salamander staggered toward the outstretched bottle. The closer he got, the more the contempt gave way to a grimace of despair.

Bill twisted off the cap.

With monumental effort, Ed grabbed the bottle with one hand. He pushed it to his lips so hard, the bottle clanked against his teeth. His Adam's apple bobbed. Bubbles swirled. The liquor drained away. He gasped for air, and from relief.

"Joe!"

Bill heard the woman's voice and followed it into the dark to find the child paralyzed with fear and clinging on an outcrop at the beginning of the cliff. A smoking heap of Targhoul, no longer a threat, lay just inches away. Bill pulled the boy up to the lady, and they all cried with gratitude.

Bill rocked back and forth with his arms around the pair of them.

He looked around and listened. No screams. The living kept in front of the bus in the comforting light. Some climbed back on board and hid.

An engine rattled past the bus.

One of the survivors in the headlights called out, "What the hell, man? Ain't you going to stop?

Headlights caught the tail of a green truck. The red brake lights seemed just a little off level, like one had been knocked askew before accelerating away.

Measured footsteps cracked the gravel behind Bill. He startled.

Ed loomed over him. "I got your coat back."

The brown canvas coat's sleeve had been singed to stubble. Bill looked at it and figured what the hell. He pulled it on.

"Thanks."

The state police galloped up sometime later. The electric police van followed them. After corralling the remaining bus patrons into a small group, easy to protect, the remaining officers scoured the area for survivors. Hours later, another bus drove up. The survivors climbed on, silent, exhausted, staring in shock.

The bus roared and eased from the shoulder. The sighs could have lifted the roof.

Bill whispered to Ed, "If they ask anything, we lit them on fire with a lighter. We lost the lighter. We get to the station, we move on and find an exit and keep walking."

There was no way Edward should be under lock and key, not with Whatever rode his soul.

The sky grayed with dawn when they pulled into the bus terminal. The police and Red Cross had set up a table with sandwiches and hot coffee. Bill hadn't eaten in almost a day, and the white bread and cheese was the best meal he had ever had. He sneaked a couple of sandwiches into his pocket. Made sure Ed ate something, because the man was asleep on his feet.

Bill got the feeling something was up, and he looked around. The state cops and some guys in suits were doing interviews.

Potato Lady held the boy as they sat on a rolling stretcher. Other townswomen stood by, relatives or friends. She waved her hand as she spoke to a cop. The cop turned with a look that said what-is-this-bullshit story you're telling me? He looked around and waved another cop over. Both of them looked at the people, searching.

Bill got his and Ed's bag.

He pushed Ed's luggage behind Ed's elbow. "I'm doing both of us a favor."

They slipped out a side door without too much problem. In the city, the dawn air warmed them. Ed took his bag as Bill led him along from the crowded downtown into a quiet neighborhood of rowhomes.

Bill kept pulling Edward along until he himself lost count of the streets.

"It isn't right. They'll lock you up and that isn't right. You saved my ass. It wouldn't be right."

Ed looked up at the frost-studded dawn and breathed deep. Bounced on his feet as he walked.

Good footwork, Bill noted. Ed must have done some boxing at some point.

"You feeling better?"

"Yes. Thank you."

Ed seemed relieved by his sudden good health.

Bill pushed past some branches. "You're not really a priest."

"My studies fell by the wayside."

"My study has been in being a screw-up. I'm getting my post-doctoral."

Ed sniffed. "I have been informed . . . there is a place for you. If you choose."

Bill's gut dropped. *Is he making stuff up or is the Salamander talking to him?*

Bill did not want to be on anyone's itinerary, much less a Salamander's.

"Well, let's see if we can get you back on your way, wherever you are go—"

"We are at my destination."

"Titusville?"

"There is corruption here, William. We have only seen the grime under its fingernails."

"You crazy? There's no way we can stay here now! Who knows what cops are going to do here after all that?"

Bill remembered the feeling of helping Potato Lady and the boy. It did his heart good to keep those folks in one piece. They seemed the type to help others along as well and keep the whole circle of kindness going.

He looked up at Ed's face. This man's gaze held steady on the sidewalk before them. The man wanted to do good, Bill was certain.

How the hell's he going to get along without help? Bill looked back to the sidewalk and kept pace with Ed's long, purposeful stride.

Bill imagined under the sidewalk, the ancient hills underneath teemed yearning and greedy. Above them the city shone with sinful life waiting to be saved. Maybe it wasn't too late to be saved himself.

Mynah Bird

Mark Wolf

Editor: New ideas are not always readily accepted.

"Ready?" Lei said, whispering.

I nodded.

"One, two, three . . ."

At the 'th' of three, we both fired—I, my BB gun, her—her custom-made slingshot. I could see my BB barely graze the top feathers of the mynah bird's head above us, some twenty feet in the towering old-growth eucalyptus tree along the hedgerow fronting Mud Lane near our farm.

The mynah lifted its head, suddenly alerted by the very slightest displacement of the air above its head, the "poof" sound of my air gun—and the parting of its feathers. It reared back to launch itself from its perch and caught one right in the center of its chest as Lei's pebble struck home with a sharp "thwack."

The bird let out a plaintive squawk, folding up on itself. It fell from the branch, tumbling through a couple of others on its plunge to the ground. Lei turned to me and stuck her tongue out. Three for three.

She clapped her hands and jumped up and down fetchingly before she walked over to retrieve her kill. She took a few seconds to wring the bird's neck, putting any lingering doubt of the bird's survival from its tumble to rest. She held it upside down by its feet and slipped another shoelace loop from her belt over the bird's feet and snugged it up tight. Three birds now hung there on her belt—two mynahs and a larger Spotted Dove. I was zero for three attempts.

My ego was taking a thrashing. "Let *me* see that thing," I said.

She handed her slingshot to me without a word, I handed my BB gun over to her, grumbling a little bit—and not helping but noticing the mischievous glint in her warm, brown eyes. In Hawaii we call that look *kolohe*. It means something like rascally. I had a feeling I was about to get schooled again.

We weren't hunting for sport even if it could be fun. Lei's whole near-family from Captain Cook had just dropped in on us about a half hour before. We were sent out to add whatever we could kill to the stewpot. That's why we both shot at the same bird at the same time—double the chance of hitting our target. So along with about six young mongooses, a couple of stew hens, and a few hutch bunnies, which Dad probably had already killed, cleaned, and cut up into our stewpot back at our farm, we now had three birds. Still, it wouldn't be enough for our guests and families. We had to do even better.

I test-pulled on the wrist-sling's rubbery surgical tubing straps. It had four straps in place of the usual two. The frame wasn't the stock aluminum you usually see on these either, more like . . .

"Your dad made this, didn't he?" I said, suddenly realizing where I'd seen such metal tubing before. Condenser coils for the big air-conditioning units, and Lei's dad is—well, used to be—an HVAC guy before the apocalypse.

Lei nodded and grinned.

The rubber surgical tubing was familiar enough, though. For years it had been standard issue on nearly all the aluminum and fiberglass Hawaiian-sling spears one went spear-fishing with. Maybe not so common now that no one was making the stuff anymore since the apocalypse.

The slingshot had a nice feel to it. More solid than the ones I used to play with as a younger kid. Those couldn't be taken seriously as a hunting weapon. This one felt more balanced and I already knew of its deadliness. I squelched my ego down a few notches.

"Mind if I try it?"

"Go ahead," Lei said, bending my BB gun over her leg to steady it for pumping it up. I felt a sudden slight sting of jealousy. She obviously knew what she was doing, had shot a BB gun like this before—and with no older brothers to show her how.

She watched my reaction, seeing much more there than I could quickly hide. Rather than grinning at my obvious jealousy, she hid a very small smile under a lot of determination. She looked resolved to make the next kill also—and probably would, unless I managed to calm myself down.

She put about seven pumps in my BB gun—enough to penetrate through bird feathers and hide, but not so much as to put a strain on the gun's seals. Respect—yes, she knew what she was doing. She went ahead and jacked another BB into the firing tube. "I'm ready," she said, handing me the small leather pouch she took off her belt. I took it from her and peeked inside.

"*Ele 'ele* stones," she said, stating the obvious. The tiny little gray-black basaltic lava rocks were from a beach somewhere. They were nearly perfectly round from tumbling around in the surf. They would fly true if the person shooting them knew what they were doing. Unfortunately for me, it had been a while since I'd shot my own wrist rocket. I wasn't about to use these stones just for practice rounds—my own respect, right back at ya. I could understand the difficulty of gathering them. Instead I looked to the small base coarse gravel pebbles lying right at my feet along the lane. I bent over and picked up a few likely, rounder ones.

I put a stone in the leather of the slingshot, extended my arm and sighted down the slingshot at a nearby metal fence post sporting a short fence line length of broken-down and rusting fencing.

"It shoots hard . . ."

I released the pouch of the slingshot. The stone flew well over the head of the post—the spot I was aiming at.

". . . er than you'd think," Lei finished.

"Yeah," I said, surprised at how very powerful and accurate this little weapon would be now that I'd taken its measure. I put another stone into the pouch, drew back and adjusted my aim, and snap-shot it to hit the fence post with a "ka-whang" before Lei had the opportunity to comment on how to adjust downward from my first shot. Just because my old wrist rocket hadn't been all that powerful, it didn't mean I hadn't spent thousands of hours honing my aim. I hit what I aimed for usually. This stone hit exactly the spot I aimed it, at the top of the fence post.

"Let's go," I said.

This time, Lei allowed the full force of her dazzling smile to light up her face and make my heart skip a beat.

* * *

About an hour later we had another dozen birds between us and were walking back down the lane to my family's farm holding hands.

Lei still had the lion's share of the bird kills—her aim on *my* BB gun was just as good as mine on *her* slingshot—even better, I suspect. I had acquitted myself well enough on her slingshot to recapture some of my pride and I determined not to pry into how she'd gotten so good on BB guns. In some things, I was already learning at a young age that it was better to allow young women their mysteries. For Lei's part, she was the one that rather boldly took my hand and squeezed it, not allowing us to part along our walk back to the farm. For my part I walked on clouds. Lei talked about what led her and her family back to their ancestral lands.

"It was all right for the first year or so back home after the start of the apocalypse. Almost everybody knows everybody or is related on the coffee lands around Captain Cook," she said.

"What happened?" I said.

"The local people started getting greedy and fighting among themselves. Then the townies used our dissention to divide us. They moved in with their gangs and guns and started taking over our farms wherever they wanted. By the time we quit fighting among ourselves long enough to organize, it was too late. We barely got our family out in time before the thugs took over our farm, too."

What she said didn't surprise me at all. Hawaiians came across as one big family to off-islander outsiders, but they had generations of griefs against one another—a lot of it tied to the old separation between commoners and the *Ali'i*, their chiefly class. Even in school as a kid I sometimes saw that kind of thing come up among the different local kids and their families.

"It was the killings that finally made Daddy pack us up," Lei said.

"Killings?"

She nodded. "Some farmhouses were attacked at night and whole families burned out—sometimes without anyone able to make it outside. No one knew for sure who was doing what. Things turned so ugly with everybody suspecting everyone else." She stopped walking and pointed her chin at the fence line. A mynah bird sat there squawking its ugly, raucous call. I nodded. We let go of each other's hand. A few seconds later we had another bird for the pot—this one, tied to *my* belt. We continued walking. This time, I reached for *her* hand. She smiled and slipped it into mine. It felt soft and both warm and cool to the touch at the same time.

"What about you guys," Lei said. "It seems like you're doing well enough for yourselves without too much hoo-hoo."

I nodded. "Yeah, we are. I guess the real baddies over in Hilo and Puna shot it out with one another before they got organized enough to give us trouble." We both knew the bad reputation of the heroin and ice gangs, even the Hell's Angels from that side of the island. "The smaller gangs that tried to muscle in on the farms and townies around Waimea got a warm welcome. We already had an organized community militia, thanks in part to Dad's efforts."

"He served over in Afghanistan, didn't he?" Lei said.

I shook my head. "Northern Iraq. He went in to keep ISIS from getting too comfortable after the Russians and the U.S. quit squabbling long enough to join forces and make air strikes in Syria."

"Yeah, and we know how that turned out," Lei said. I kept my peace but thought a bit as we neared home.

No one will be able to say for sure just how things escalated so quickly. Russia and the U.S. had been squabbling over Syria, the Ukraine, and the Crimean—China and the U.S. over International Right of Passage through the South China Sea. It wasn't like you could turn on the tube and pick up Fox News or MSNBC any more to get a talking head analysis.

And as far as I knew, no one could say who fired the first missile, or at least the ones who could were vaporized in that first nuclear exchange. Whether it had started in Syria, the Crimean region, or the South China Sea, I guess it didn't matter, now. We were all now living in the aftermath of those days.

A few minutes later, just a short distance from our farm's driveway, Lei brought me out of my aftermath musing.

"Stop," Lei whispered.

I stopped and let go of her hand and looked around me. Not a mynah bird or any other kind of bird in sight.

"What do you see?" I whispered back.

"You," Lei said.

"*Me?*" Not quite reading her intentions.

"Yes, *you*. You *do* realize that this is our first date, don't you?"

I hadn't really thought of our time together that way, but I wasn't dumb enough to say so. I allowed myself to blush and nodded, gulping.

"Well, aren't you going to kiss me?" Lei said.

I nodded again, this time fervently. I leaned in close to her. She took it from there.

* * *

I picked out a piece of mynah bird breast from the stew and took my fork to pry the BB out of it. I guess Lei managed to distract me more than I let on while we were cleaning them.

We—Mom, Dad, Paula, my kid sister, and I, and Lei's family, all sat outside on and around the porch eating our critter stew—well, it had some carrots, cabbage, onions, and other vegetables from our garden too. The main thing was, there was enough to go around and fill everyone up.

I know Dad and Mom didn't bring it up, but I could see that Lei's family had experienced a rough slog the sixty-some miles from their old farm to ours.

Lei had said that they'd taken five days—taking the time for their grandparents to travel at their own pace, stopping along the way to visit other family members between there and here, but I knew it couldn't have been easy. It's a hot, windy journey even in a car—and for the greater part, it's an uphill grunt.

Uncle Kaipo, Lei's dad—in Hawaii it is traditional to call older men Uncle, and older women Auntie—sat his plate aside and brought out his ukulele. He played a few songs and sang. We all joined in with him.

We had a great night singing and "talking story." Nobody made a move to wash the dishes—we just got them out from underfoot before it got dark and stacked them on the table for the morning. Visiting is what you did whenever you could. These days, you never knew if or when you'd see each other again. We relished one another's company.

After a time, we all went off to our separate sleeping areas. Lei made sure I would have something good to dream about before we parted company. Unfortunately, she slept with her family.

* * *

I woke the next morning to the disorderly calls of a whole flock of mynah birds outside my bedroom window at oh-dark-thirty. I guess Lei and I hadn't managed to put a very deep dent in their population. I lay in my bed for a time thinking about yesterday—about Lei's obvious interest.

She was as good a kisser as she was with a slingshot and BB gun. I could let that bug me, and I admit, it did. But I also knew that even before the apocalypse local kids grew up too quick. Teenage pregnancies in high school weren't even much remarked upon and quite a few girls in their late teens and early twenties had kids from multiple fathers.

I wouldn't call myself prejudiced. I had a lot—well, *used to* have a lot of local guy and gal friends that I'd surf with. Those careless playtimes were long gone now in the aftermath. If we ran across one another these days it was usually when we all came in from our farms for a Saturday Market Barter Meet in Waimea town. They were nice enough to me, but it's just that life had taken a too-damn-serious turn for us to play together anymore.

I don't think anyone would make a stink about it if Lei and I decided to get closer. Hell, they'd probably encourage us to start an early family if that's where we wanted to go with things—what with a whole new society we were creating from the ashes of the old. I just wasn't all that keen on having that kind of responsibility to deal with at fourteen. Still, Lei and I could have a lot of fun if we were careful. I just hoped Lei's family would see things in the same light. I suspected they wouldn't, though.

I stretched in bed. Maybe I could get up and do a few of my morning chores so I'd be free to walk with Lei and her family to the valley top. Yes, that's what I decided to do. I pushed myself to a sitting position and got my farm clothes on.

A few minutes later, Lei joined me.

"Hey," she said, leaning against one of the kitchen porch's supporting posts. Her hair was kinda mussed, like she hadn't run a brush through it yet. "Mussed" looked delicious on her. It was daylight and I could hear Mom, Paula, and Lei's women relatives helping out in the kitchen, cleaning up last night's dinner and starting breakfast.

I tossed dinner scraps to our chicken flock. Part of the scraps were their relatives from yesterday. They didn't seem to mind none.

"Hey, yourself," I said back. I'm not much of a talker most times—even less in the mornings.

"I'm gonna go help in the kitchen, but I just wanted to see how you were doin' this morning," she said.

"I'm good," I said. "I'm tryin' to get my chores done so I can walk with you guys to the top of the valley," I said.

She smiled. "That'd be nice."

I smiled back. She gave me a cute little wave—looked around quickly to see if anyone was watching. She skipped over and kissed me on the cheek.

I couldn't help but grin—even if she couldn't see it as she walked back to the kitchen.

* * *

Another mynah bird cussed us out and dove at our traveling group as we finished walking along the last of the ancient eucalyptus tree hedgerow and passed onto the Bishop Estate lands of eucalyptus. Not that Bishop Estate owned it any longer. I suspect the only way anyone respected anyone else's prior claim on property was if the persons were there shoving a gun in their faces and telling them to get the hell off their land.

We'd drawn a small flock of mynah birds shadowing us because of a fledgling on the ground somewhere nearby. Lei saw it first. She walked over and picked it up, escalating the mob frenzy on us. They dove at us, but a couple of the Uncles waved their boar spears around scattering them.

Lei walked up to me—held the tiny bird out for me to see. She petted it on the head with a fingertip gently. Its belly looked like the head of a tonsured monk, missing feathers. It squatted down in Lei's hand as I reached over and joined her. I stroked it, rubbing the back of my fingertips along the top of its head and down its beak. It bore the indignity with stoic patience.

"What are you gonna do with that?" I said.

"I dunno—maybe keep it and try to teach it to talk. If it doesn't talk or I get tired of it, it can always go into the pot," Lei said practically. I nodded—my thinking also.

"I've never tried to keep them as pets, but you might be onto something. Dad and I didn't know how the mongooses were going to take to being hutch animals, but they're working out okay," I said. "You might consider trying to raise them like pigeons or something."

Lei nodded. "So, what shall we call you, bird?" Lei held it up across from her face.

"How about Stu?" I said, controlling my smile to a deadpan.

Lei grinned back at me.

"Stew, it is," she said. We could both see the different spellings in our minds as we held hands again and happily paced our time together to that of her grandparents' walking pace. At the top of the valley, we kissed before parting—for now.

The Executioner

Keith J. Hoskins

*Editor: "Wild animals never kill for sport. Man is the only
one to whom the torture and death of his fellow creatures
is amusing in itself."—James Anthony Froude*

Martin's chained legs could barely keep up with the pace at which the
sentries forced him. After several turns in the musty hallway, they
pushed him into a room and shoved him onto a wooden chair. With his
bound hands, he grabbed the table in front of him to keep his momentum
from sending him tumbling off the chair and onto the stone floor. The
squeaking of hinges snapped his head around in time to see the guards leave
back through the room's lone entrance. They slammed the door behind
them. Martin heard the unquestionable sound of an iron bolt being slid
into its catch. *What now*, he wondered.

Like most citizens, Martin had skated the fine line of the law here
and there throughout his life, but he never imagined he would be one to
break Doctrine; that he would commit a crime and get the death penalty.
But here he was. And he was indeed guilty. But what he had done, he did
out of love, and he would make all the same choices again if given the
chance. But that was all moot; he was caught, convicted, and now awaited
his punishment.

Swiveling his head, he took in his surroundings. It was an unimpressive
room; twenty by twenty, white brick walls, ceramic tile floor, and a skylight
that let in the afternoon sun. There was nothing in the room save for the
wooden table at which he sat and two chairs. Ordinary, very ordinary. But
there *was* something unusual about the room. At first he couldn't put his
finger on it, and then it hit him. "There're no cameras in here," he said to
himself.

He scoured the walls and corners again, looking for anything that
could be a camera or be hiding one. Nothing. The room was plain—plain
and empty. This was a bit disconcerting for Martin; he had never been in
a non-residence room where there were no cameras to watch him. The
Covenant always watched; there were always cameras, or gov-eyes as they
were called, to watch the citizens. To keep them safe, and to keep them
from straying from the Doctrine. Perhaps if there had been cameras in his
residence, he would not be in his current predicament. Martin shook his

head; it was too late to think about that. This room, this "eyeless" room, was highly unusual. Martin wondered if it was even legal. *Strange,* Martin thought. *What was the purpose of this room?* He had a bad feeling about this.

He tested his bindings: chained iron shackles encased his ankles, and iron cuffs restricted his hands. He pulled and tugged on each but nothing budged. He thought about standing up and going over to the door and giving it a try. Before he could move, the metal latch sounded again, and the heavy wooden door swung open behind him.

Martin froze with fear. *Was this it? Would they torture me before my execution? No, it can't be. Not here. There are no cameras. The Covenant demanded an audience.*

A solitary set of footsteps followed the sound of the door closing again, as well as the metal latch resuming its hold. The footsteps moved directly behind him and stopped.

Martin took a breath and held it.

The steps continued with purposeful, resounding clops. They slowly walked around Martin's left side until their owner was visible and standing on the other side of the table directly in front of him. It was a civilian. Martin was expecting a burly guard or a stern looking warden. But this was just a man. He wore a smile, clean clothes, and he smelled rather nice.

"Hello, Martin," said the man. "May I call you Martin?"

Martin just sat there, not sure if he acknowledged the smiling man with a nod or a grunt, or anything. He just looked at him, waiting for whatever would come.

"My name is Rogan," said the man. "Do you know who I am?" The question was genuine; it wasn't sarcastic or condescending. And the man, Rogan, just stood there patiently waiting for an answer.

Martin sat dumbfounded for a second, then gave Rogan a look-over. He was a very unassuming man. His face was nice, pleasant almost. His salt and pepper hair, along with a few wrinkles, suggested that he had a couple decades on Martin. He was clean shaven, which was the law, of course. He wore regular clothes: pants, shirt, vest . . . maybe a bit nicer than the average citizen would have. In fact, they looked almost new. Not recycled or reissued like everyone else wore. Was this Rogan a celebrity? Or a political figure? If so, Martin didn't recognize him from any of the broadcasts. He didn't look familiar nor did Martin recognize the name Rogan. So, he shook his head, feeling almost embarrassed at not knowing the man's identity.

"That's all right," said Rogan, and a smile of understanding appeared on his face. "Most people don't. Perhaps, if I was wearing my mask . . ." Rogan raised his hand and covered his face, leaving only his eyes visible. He held his hand there, leaned down toward Martin, and gave him a seemingly well-rehearsed scowl. Rogan's brown-green eyes pierced through Martin's gaze and into his very soul.

Yes, Martin thought. *He does look familiar. Frighteningly so. But from where?* Then the realization hit him like a punch to the gut. Feeling his heartbeat in his throat, Martin swallowed hard and, when he found his voice, he said: "You're the . . . the Executioner."

Rogan removed his "mask" and straightened back up. "Correct." He smiled. "Of course my official name is Vero, the Executioner. They didn't think Rogan sounded . . ." he paused as he thought of the correct word, "sinister enough for the broadcasts. Are you a regular viewer of my program?"

"Not really," Martin said. "I try to avoid it when I can."

"I'll try not to take offense to that, but I know not everyone has the stomach to witness what I do."

Martin looked at him. The Executioner. Here. Right in front of me. The end was coming quicker than he had anticipated.

"But I'm sure your home system is tuned to the mandatory minimum of eight hours per month."

"Of course," Martin said emphatically with a nod. His family had enough scrutiny from the Covenant lately, they certainly didn't need anything else to cast more suspicion onto them. "It's like you said. Not everyone can stand to watch what you do."

Rogan looked at Martin's hands resting on the table. "Here," said Rogan as he walked around the table. "Let me take those off of you." He reached into his pocket and pulled out a lone key and then slipped it into the lock on the cuffs. After a twist of the key, the cuffs popped open to Martin's relief, but the newly convicted man hesitated to remove them, thinking it might be a trick or something to get him into trouble, although he couldn't imagine how much more trouble he could get in. "Go on," said Rogan reassuringly. "Take them off."

Martin did as he was told. He removed the cuffs and placed them on the table. He rubbed his sweaty wrists with his hands. "Thank you," he said to Rogan, as he eyed the Executioner suspiciously.

Rogan glanced at Martin's feet and tossed the key onto the table. "Here. Go ahead and take those shackles off as well. No need for you to wear them."

Still eying Rogan warily, Martin grabbed the key, scooted his chair out, removed his chains and shackles, and put them on the table next to the cuffs. "Thank you again."

Rogan acknowledged with a nod and a smile. "Keeper!" said Rogan in a voice loud enough to make Martin jump. A few seconds later, a guard unlocked the door and entered the room. "Please take these away," Rogan said to him. "We won't be needing them any longer."

"As you wish, sir." The keeper scooped up the prisoner's accessories and exited the room, locking the door once again behind him.

Rogan pulled out the chair across the table from Martin and sat down, folding his hands in front of him. "So, tell me, Martin, which of the seventeen crimes punishable by death did you commit?"

Martin was a little taken back by the question. Rogan knew his name. Didn't he know why he was in here? Martin took a deep breath and said: "My wife and I had a third child."

"Ah," said Rogan. "Number six on the Doctrine's 'do not do' list."

Martin nodded.

"The world is extremely overpopulated, Martin," Rogan said in a serious tone. "We have the Doctrine for many reasons. And population control is one of them." Rogan's face and posture softened a bit. "So, your third child. Boy? Girl?"

"Girl."

"How old?"

"Four."

"Ah," Rogan smiled. "A great age. So magical."

"Yeah," Martin sighed.

"And you managed to keep her hidden for four years. Amazing." Rogan paused and then asked: "And were you given the choice of her life or yours?"

Martin looked down at the table. "Yes."

"And you chose yours so that she may live. Very noble."

"I'm her father," Martin said angrily, looking back up at Rogan. "What choice did I have?" Martin shook his head at Rogan's insolent statement.

"You'd be surprised how many people would choose to live and have their child put to death."

"Then they would be cowards."

"Perhaps. But fear, like love and greed, can make people do unfathomable things. And, of course, it isn't just dying that they are afraid of, it's what I do to them that drives that fear into people. That's why we have the broadcasts, and that's why there are mandatory hours for citizens to watch." Rogan paused and gave Martin a thoughtful look. "Do you know why you are here, Martin?"

"Of course. I'm the next contestant on your little game show."

Rogan smiled at Martin's bravado. "You do know what it is I do exactly. Right?"

Martin nodded. "Yeah. You torture people to death, and it's broadcast over the network as a deterrent for other citizens."

"Yes," Rogan said with a grimace, "that's all true, but that doesn't do justice to my craft; to the intricacy of my work. And we don't like to use the word 'torture.' Instead, the whole process is called 'the reckoning.' And the person going through the reckoning loses his citizenship and even his name. He, or she, is simply referred to as 'the miscreant.' Do you know how long the reckoning lasts?"

Martin shook his head. "Two, three days?"

"Nine days."

Martin felt his heart sink into his stomach. "Nine days?"

"Yes. Nine days, nine hours a day. No more. No less. If you were an avid watcher you would know this." Rogan stood up and began to slowly pace in a broad circle behind his chair. "What I do to the miscreant is quite amazing. I introduce levels of pain to them that they didn't know existed. You see, I start slowly with cuts and breaks, but then move on to the removing of flesh and fingers, fingernails first, of course. Then removing the hands and feet. You get the picture?"

The question may have been rhetorical, but Martin nodded anyway. His eyes wide open as Rogan casually described the events that would be eventually happening to him.

"I don't think you do, because the miscreant is slowly taken apart piece by tiny piece, the way a scientist might reverse engineer something to figure out how it's made. You see, it's not just about the pain; it's also about the miscreant witnessing his own body being dismembered right before his conscious eyes. By the ninth day of the reckoning, there is nothing left of him except a torso and a head, and they are so disfigured that you can barely tell that it's human, let alone the identity of that human. And the methods I use to do these things are far from anything that would resemble a doctor's touch. In fact, you might say they're quite inhuman." Rogan's face lit up and he held up a finger as he thought of something. "Are you familiar with the altrix bird?"

Martin shook his head, puzzled at the radical change of topic.

"Nor should you be. I'm not surprised. It was thought to be extinct for hundreds of years, until about thirty years ago a small population of them was discovered on a remote island in the southern hemisphere. It's a unique and fascinating bird; sort of like a bird of prey, but it prefers to prey upon wounded animals, animals that would normally be too large for it to take down by itself. You could say it is more of a bird of opportunity." Rogan smiled at his own cleverness. "So, when it finds a wounded animal, let's say . . . a goat. The altrix clips the animal's hamstrings to prevent it from escaping. Then, it begins to feed upon its flesh, all the while making sure the animal stays alive. You see, the altrix doesn't have the necessary enzymes in its stomach to digest decayed flesh like carrion birds do. It's probably a flaw in its evolution. So, it's very important for its captive to remain alive. Maybe that's the reason why they almost became extinct, having to be so selective in what they eat.

"Now, the altrix has incredible skills at eating particular parts of the animal without endangering its life: the skin, certain organs, and it just loves eyes. Loves them. They must be a delicacy of a sort to them. Anyway, they go to great lengths to keep the animal alive. In fact, they will fight off other predators and scavengers, sometimes to the death, to preserve the animal's life. They even regurgitate food and water into their captive's mouth so it doesn't starve or die of thirst. Ironically the regurgitated food would be the flesh of the animal itself. Bizarre, isn't it? But, it's quite a fascinating bird. Do you know what the word 'altrix' means? It means nurse. Kind of fitting, wouldn't you agree?"

Paralyzed by fear and disgust, Martin managed to speak. "In a morbidly ironic way, I suppose."

Rogan stopped his pacing and stepped up to the table, turned his chair around, then sat on it backwards, resting his crossed arms on its back. "Can you imagine this . . . this goat, or whatever, lying on the ground, blind, in agony, taking days, maybe weeks to die? All the while it is slowly being eaten alive. I can't imagine a more horrible death. Can you?"

Martin felt sick to his stomach; this all seemed surreal to him. Sitting in that chair he felt almost weightless yet unable to move, like he was just a spectator to this whole thing. Like it was a dream, and he was not really there. But he was there. And this was a nightmare. "Why are you telling me all this?"

"Because, Martin," Rogan took a deep breath and paused before continuing. "For the longest time I thought of myself as the altrix. I mean, I literally based my work on how it cares for its prey and slowly devours it. I even have an entire staff of doctors that stand by to care for the miscreant, to keep him alive, even bring him back to life if necessary. But then, after years of reckonings, I realized that I'm not the altrix, but rather *we* are the altrix."

"We?"

"Yes. We. The citizens of the Covenant, the enforcers of the Doctrine. *We* feed off of the fear and agony of the miscreant. *We* feed off his regrets and sorrow. *We* feed off his disparity and sacrifice. And it's this nourishment from the reckoning that keeps the Covenant and its citizens alive and safe." Rogan straightened up and regained the little composure he had lost during his rant. "So, I ask you again, Martin: Do you know why you are here?"

Eyes wide and nose flaring, Martin's heart thumped hard in his chest. "I am the goat," he said through gritted teeth.

Rogan smiled and nodded. "Yes, normally, on any other day you would be the goat. But today is not one of those days. In fact, you could say that this is your lucky day."

Martin tilted his head and furrowed his brow. "I don't understand."

Rogan seemed amused at Martin's confusion. He paused for a few seconds before changing the subject. "You know, I wasn't always the

Executioner. Obviously, right? Although, I have been doing it longer than any of my predecessors. Do you know what I was before this? A schoolteacher."

"A teacher?" said Martin. He wore his shock to Rogan's revelation like an ugly hat. He had trouble picturing the Executioner as anything other than the Executioner. *Why is he telling me this?* Martin wasn't sure where this was heading, but he was curious, and the more it delayed him beginning the reckoning the better. And Rogan said that this was his lucky day. How? Martin decided to play along. "What did you teach?"

Rogan flashed a smile; he seemed pleased that Martin was engaging him. "I was a language teacher. I would have been a history teacher if teaching history wasn't against Doctrine. But I loved kids and educating them was my calling." Rogan stared off into the distance as he fondly remembered his past. "Life was good back then; I had a wife, two kids, and my dream job." Rogan put on a thin smile and looked at the table. "Happy times." Snapping back to reality, he looked at Martin and said, "Not that my life isn't good now. It is. It's great. Being the Executioner has many rewards; it has allowed me to take care of my family in ways I didn't think possible. Fresh clothes, three meals a day, a private residence. Everyone with their own room. Do you believe that? When I was a kid, my family lived in a shared residence with three other families, and we ate once a day if we were lucky. I never dreamed I would live in a place where my kids would have their own bedroom, and have more food than they could possibly eat.

"What happened?"

"Hmmm?"

"How did you go from being a happy language teacher to being the sector's Executioner?"

Rogan sighed and, with a somber look on his face, he said, "I broke Doctrine."

"What?"

Rogan gave a little chuckle and nodded at Martin's confusion. "I know. Makes no sense."

"What did you do?" asked Martin. "To break Doctrine, I mean. If I may ask."

"I gave one of my students a book."

"A book?"

"Not just any book," said Rogan. "A pre-Covenant book."

"How did you get a pre-Covenant book? They were all confiscated and destroyed."

"It had been in my family since before the Cleansing. It had been hidden and passed down through the generations. It was a wonderful book, full of stories and imagery. And he was such a smart kid; full of questions, always so curious about the before time, before the Covenant and the Doctrine. I told him to keep it safe, to keep it secret. No one must know of its existence." Rogan stopped and looked blankly at the table.

"So what happened?" said Martin.

"His mother became suspicious and found the book under his mattress. She called the enforcer squad and they went to the building and contained the boy."

"She turned her own son over to the enforcers?"

"Like I said, Martin: You'd be surprised . . ."

"But they found out that it was you who gave the book to the boy. Did he give you up?"

"No, but he should have. Even though his own mother turned him in and he faced death, he refused to tell the enforcers who gave him the book. Like I said, he was a good kid. But as soon as I heard what had happened, I went to the enforcer station and turned myself in."

"How noble," Martin said, trying to not put too much sarcasm in his voice. Rogan didn't seem to notice.

"I thought so at the time, and, like you, I knew it was the right thing to do. I just didn't take into consideration the impact it would have on my family. Not only the ridicule and shame they would endure, but the fact that I wouldn't be there to provide for them. Fortunately, I was presented with an opportunity to help make it all right."

Martin sat there looking at him. He was torn between being intrigued by the story and worried about his immediate future, but something told him that the two were intertwined.

"Do you know how a new Executioner is selected, Martin?"

"Not really."

"Every four years the Executioner goes through . . . an evaluation. A miscreant is randomly selected to engage the Executioner in combat and the victor is either the new Executioner, or the current Executioner gets to keep his job. For another four years, at least. This is my fifth evaluation."

It took a few moments for the realization to sink in. When it did, Martin said: "Me? You want *me* to fight *you*? To be the new Executioner?" It was Martin's turn to stand up and pace. "This is insane! I don't want your job."

"What you want is irrelevant," Rogan said in a calm voice. "Your choices are simple: fight me or go through the reckoning."

"What happens if I fight you? If I win, I become the new Executioner?"

"Yes."

"And if I lose?"

"You die. It's a fight to the death."

"To the death?!" Martin stopped his pacing and turned to face Rogan.

"Of course to the death. What did you expect? We would arm wrestle?"

Martin leaned on the table toward Rogan. "I can't do that. I'm not a killer."

"Neither was I. But I owed it to my family to not only make their lives better, but prevent them from having a far worse life than they currently led. If I hadn't killed the previous Executioner during his evaluation, then my family would have been disgraced and exiled to the perimeter camps. By defeating him, I not only saved them from that, but I had given them a wonderful life. As the Executioner, my family has had the best food, the best medicine, the best of everything. And, not to mention, I got to live." Rogan nodded as he justified his history to Martin. "My family and I have lived a privileged life, Martin. And, by defeating my predecessor, I washed the stench of my betrayal to the Covenant off of me and my family. My sin was vanquished."

"But you're a monster. The sins you've committed against humanity severely outweigh the small one of giving a simple book to a curious boy."

"A monster, Martin? A monster? I protect the Covenant. I am the ultimate enforcer of the Doctrine! I do what has to be done so that the citizens of the Covenant will not be tempted to stray from the Doctrine as I had done. If anything, I save lives."

"You torture people to death." Martin held up a hand to cut off Rogan. "Call it whatever you will, but it's still torture. Your job makes you a monster. I could never do what you do."

"Then you will die. And your family," Rogan said as he stood from his chair, "will live in poverty and shame." Rogan reached into the left side of his vest and pulled out a knife. Martin stood straight and swallowed hard at seeing the long dual-edge blade. Rogan then took the tip of the blade between his fingers and flipped the knife straight toward the ceiling. The knife twisted and flipped in the air as it reflected the sun from the skylight. It missed the ceiling by inches, and when it came back down it stuck into the table with a thud.

Martin's eyes shot from Rogan to the knife, then back to Rogan.

Stone-faced, Rogan reached into the right side of his vest and pulled out another knife, identical to the first. He placed it on the table and pushed it toward Martin. The knife skidded across the wooden table, making a resonant scraping sound as it traversed the surface. It stopped a fraction of an inch from the edge. Martin stared at it for what seemed like minutes.

"Pick up the knife, Martin," Rogan said. Rogan the teacher was gone; Vero, the Executioner stood before him now. Serious eyes engulfed Martin and made his heartrate quicken. He felt his face ignite as blood rushed to his head. Rogan just stood there, motionless and emotionless. His statue-like stance was more disturbing to Martin than if he had been erratically moving around like a maniac. "Pick up the knife, Martin," the Executioner repeated. "I won't fight an unarmed man."

Martin forced his eyes to look down at the knife. It sat there, taunting him, daring him to pick it up. He didn't want to pick it up. He certainly didn't want to fight this man. But what of his family? They would be shamed and sent to the perimeter camps. Not to mention the reckoning itself; nine days of torture and dismemberment. He needed to fight. Fight for his family, fight for himself. Then, to Martin's surprise, his hand moved ever so slowly and lifted the knife off the table. It was as if he wasn't in control of his actions, like some external force was controlling him, making him do what he was too afraid to do on his own. He gripped the handle and looked at Rogan.

"Very good," said Rogan. "Let's begin." In seamless motions he plucked the knife from the table with one hand and with the other he grabbed the edge of the table and pushed it to the side. His foot swiped the chair and sent it to rest against the wall next to the table.

Martin looked down at his own chair. With his free hand he pushed it toward the other chair in a slow deliberate motion. With that weak push, it didn't quite make it all the way over.

The two men stood there looking at each other. Martin was terrified; Rogan looked bored. "What now?" asked Martin.

"Now you attack me." Rogan gave him a "come to me" wave with his free hand. "Come at me. You're the challenger. You make the first move."

Martin had no idea what to do. Rogan was obviously more experienced than him. What chance did he really have? Surprise? Possibly. *Maybe if I catch him off guard . . .*

Martin suddenly lunged at the Executioner, both hands out, not even aiming the knife. Rogan sidestepped out of the way with practiced ease. Martin passed him and crashed into the wall behind Rogan. Dazed and hurt, Martin steadied himself against the wall, then charged Rogan again. And, as before, Rogan sidestepped out of his way, but this time, as Martin passed him, he stuck out his foot, tripping Martin and sending the challenger tumbling to the ground and into the wall.

"You need to do better than that, miscreant," said Rogan. "More than your life is on the line."

Martin lay there on the floor, bleeding and in pain. "This is pointless," he said as he wiped the blood from the corner of his mouth. "Why don't you just kill me and get it over with?"

"If I simply wanted to kill you I would have slit your throat when I first entered the room. You need to fight for your life. You must truly try to defeat me. If you don't, you will go through the reckoning."

Martin raised his head. "You said I wouldn't have to go through the reckoning if I fought you."

"Only if I kill you. And I won't kill you unless you truly try to kill me. Now, come on! Get up! This is your chance not to be a coward like the others. You can die trying to be a hero. That's what you want, isn't it? Not sniveling there on the floor, begging for death. Get up! Or do you want the reckoning? Are you just a goat after all?" Rogan looked down at his knife and twirled it in his hand. "And what about your family? Do you want them sent to the camps?"

Martin forced himself to his feet. He couldn't ignore the pain, so he used it instead. The pain fueled his anger just as Rogan's words did. Rogan was right, Martin wasn't a coward. He didn't live his life like one and he wasn't about to leave this world like one. Surprisingly, his legs held him strong. They might have been the only thing on his body that didn't hurt.

"Actually," Rogan continued, looking back up at Martin, "They may not be that bad off. How old is your wife? Thirty? Thirty-two? I'm sure she's rather attractive. She may find work in one of the prostitution rings."

"Shut up!" Martin said through gritted teeth.

"And that four-year-old girl of yours? She can follow right in her mommy's footsteps. Then you'll have a nice family of whores taking care of themselves."

"I said: Shut. Up!" Martin started toward Rogan and the Executioner readied himself for the charge, but Martin detoured to his left and grabbed the chair that was formerly his. Spinning in a quick semi-circle, he gave the chair momentum, and when he let go it hit Rogan in his shoulder as he turned to protect himself from the projectile. Without hesitation, Martin grabbed the other chair and repeated his attack. More unprepared for the second chair than the first, Rogan took the full brunt of the wooden weapon in the chest and face. Rogan yelled in pain and fell backward on the floor. The chair fell with him and stayed on his chest like a strange looking blanket.

Martin picked up his knife from the floor and went over to Rogan. The Executioner lay there holding his face, blood seeping through fingers that covered his now broken nose. Martin grabbed the chair resting on Rogan's chest and flung it to the side. He then knelt down next to him and, with both hands, held his knife high in the air, ready to finish him off.

"Do it," Rogan said through bloodstained teeth. "Do it, you coward."

Martin tensed and readied his hands to plunge the shining blade into Rogan's heart. But then he looked into his eyes. Not the eyes of Vero, the Executioner, but those of Rogan, the former schoolteacher. They were calm and unflinching, but there was also a subtle hint of fear in them. He was afraid to die. This man who had killed hundreds over the years was afraid to die himself.

Martin lowered the knife and dropped it to his side. It hit the floor with a resounding clank.

"Wh-What are you doing?" asked Rogan.

"I can't do it," said Martin, holding back a sob. "I thought I could.

For a minute I thought I was really going to kill you."

"For a second there, I thought you were too," said Rogan.

"Like I said, I'm not a killer."

"No. No you're not. But you will be soon enough." With a swift move of his arm, Rogan grabbed Martin's knife from the floor and plunged it into his own midsection.

"My god!" shouted Martin. "What have you done?!"

Martin panicked. He didn't know what to do. *Do I take the knife out? Should I call for help?* Martin carefully reached for the blood-covered handle that blended into Rogan's shirt like a morbid accessory. But Rogan's hand beat him to it.

"Don't," Rogan said in a pain-laced voice. "I nicked my lung and liver. If you pull it out, I'll just bleed out faster." He coughed and his face contorted from the pain. Blood stained his lips. "And it'll hurt like hell." Rogan took an agonizing deep breath and yelled: "Guard!"

The door unlocked, and the sentry who had come in earlier walked in. Martin gave a start at his entrance. The guard looked around the room as if he couldn't believe the mess. Then he looked down at the two men on the floor, accessed the situation in seconds, and then snapped to attention. "Your orders, sir?"

It took Martin a moment to realize that the guard was talking to him. In the sentry's eyes, Rogan was defeated, and Martin was the Executioner now. With Rogan lying there dying in front of him, his freshly spilled blood staining the ceramic tile floor, Martin had a hard time wrapping his head around it all. He turned his head to the sentry and said, "Can you give us a few minutes. Please." The sentry nodded an acknowledgement, then turned and left the room. The door shut, but did not lock.

Martin could only look at Rogan. He still didn't know what to do, and the only thing he could think of to say was, "Why?"

"I'm tired, Martin," Rogan said with exasperated, painful breath. "I've done my time. It's time for a new Executioner."

"What of your family? Your wife, your kids?"

"Wife died two years ago. Kids are all grown up. I'm done. Can't do it anymore."

"Why didn't you just commit suicide? If your family is no longer a factor. Why didn't you end this after your wife died?"

"Because, Martin, I needed to find someone worthy. Someone who would benefit from being the Executioner, as I did." Several coughs forced some blood out of Rogan's mouth. "A good man with a family. That's why I chose you."

"But you said I was randomly chosen."

"I lied." Rogan smiled. "I picked you personally and had you brought here." He weakly gestured around the room. "One of my special rooms.

No eyes."

"Yes," said Martin, looking around. "I noticed that." Martin dropped his head and shook it as if trying to clear away the ugliness of the afternoon.

"Be strong, Martin. You will need all your strength."

"I'm not sure if I can do it. I mean, I couldn't even kill you. How can I torture people to death?" Tears welled up in Martin's eyes. The tears weren't for Rogan, but for himself and his family. He shook his head again, then buried his face in his hands.

Rogan took his hand from the knife's handle and weakly placed it on Martin's knee. "You'll have to, Martin. For yourself. For your family." Martin raised his face from his hands to look at the dying schoolteacher. "That's what you need to keep in mind, that you're doing it for them." A coughing spasm caused Rogan to convulse. After a few seconds, he regained control and continued. "The first year is the worst."

"But—"

"You'll do fine," Rogan reassured him. "You just need a better executioner name than Martin if you are to be . . . sinister."

"What do you suggest?" Martin said, trying to remain as composed as possible. He couldn't believe he was having this conversation.

"How about . . . Hircum? Hircum, the Executioner."

"Hircum? I like it," Martin said, forcing a smile. "What does it mean?"

"It means," Rogan said with a strained breath, his final breath. "It means 'the goat.'"

White Gloves

E. E. King

Editor: Intolerance is wrong in any age.

Brianna always wore white gloves, like an English lady or a white rabbit. I didn't know why she wore them, not till later, not till too late.

With me it was my ears.

I was lucky I guess, everyone has to wear a hat or a hoodie outside so the sun won't kill them, so I never thought about it. I never questioned and was never told. Of course Mother always covered my ears with makeup too, but I assumed that was just part of daily grooming, like combing your hair or brushing your teeth.

Mother said that once, long, long ago people played in the sun uncovered never giving it a thought.

But I don't believe her. I bet it's just a story, like bees and unicorns. Like fairy princes, like magic, birds and white rabbits. All those tales they tell you when you're young—and those they don't.

I don't remember not knowing Brianna. I don't remember her not being my friend. My first day away from home, my first day without my mother she was there. We were four years old. Mother had taken us to school, Brianna and me. I can see myself standing in the room, hoodie on, grasping tight to Brianna's white gloved hands. I cried when Mommy left. Brianna squeezed my hand. I'm sure I wouldn't have cried much. Just a sniffle and I'd have been fine. But then the teacher came. I don't recall what she looked like. I only remember that she was so tall her white robe seemed like a mountain. She said I was filled with sin and set me on a tall stool facing the dark corner of the room for the rest of the day.

I never told my mother. I thought the teacher would kill me if I told. I thought she might kill Mother too. So I returned to school to learn what I was taught.

They taught us it was bad to lie. They taught us to believe in Jesus, butterflies, and snow. They trained us to trust that all these things we cannot see were true. I didn't believe them, but Brianna, Brianna believed.

They said that once, long ago when the world was impure, God sent a cold whiteness to blanket it, covering the darkness, freezing away the badness. They said that the coldness, the snow, turned to water, so much water you could sink your whole body in it. So much water you could drown. They said the world was not always dry and brown. I didn't believe them, I never did, but Brianna, Brianna believed.

You'd never imagine that someone so good and sweet could be so much fun. She'd never have gotten in trouble if not for me. But it didn't matter in the end.

I remember when I was seven. I'd read about a time where grapes grew on vines right out of the ground. People stomped on them to get grape juice and make something called wine. I'm not sure what it was. It's one of those things that's in the bible as having been good, once upon a time, but now Father Leonean says that's it's bad. There was a picture in my book. A picture of men, their legs lavender with juice. They were smiling, mouths open and stained purple. It looked like fun.

"Let's go pretend we're stomping grapes," I said to Brianna. We went outside on the dusty earth. I poured one half of my daily water ration on the ground to moisten it. It was wasteful. It was foolish. It was bad. Brianna's eyes opened wide. But I jumped and stamped up and down on the earth and sang a stomping song. She started to giggle and we laughed and laughed and marched up and down, up and down, turning our shoes and stockings from white to brown.

We got in a lot of trouble. But it was worth it.

"I'm sure Brianna would never have thought of doing such a thing," Mother said as she washed my clothes.

"It's hard to believe she . . ." Mother sighed.

"She what?" I asked. But Mother just shook her head and kept on washing.

It wasn't until the day of reckoning they told us anything worth knowing, the day we turned eight.

I woke up happy. Every birthday I got a small cake just for me. Funny, I don't remember the original cake. Did Mother make me one on my first birthday, or did she wait till I was two or three, old enough to savor the taste of sweetness?

"Happy Birthday, Cedron," Mother said. She led me to the table and there right in front of me was the cake. It was round as a baseball, but flat. Tiny white and red icing roses rimmed the edges. Roses, Mother had told me, had once grown in the earth, just like grapes. But nothing grew in the earth and the ground is way too hard for anything as delicate as a leaf to cut through.

Probably it was just another fairy story, like snow, like bees, like Jesus. I liked to imagine it though, tiny leaves, like small green hands folded in prayer poking through the soil.

I looked up at Mother; she smiled at me, but the edges of her mouth quivered.

"How come I get it now?" I asked. Usually I didn't get the cake till right before bedtime.

"Because today you are eight," she said. "Today we go to the reckoning. Today you become grown-up. Today you will be freed from sin and impurity."

"Is that a good thing?" I asked.

She nodded, biting her mouth so hard I saw a drop of blood, redder than the icing roses, bead on her lower lip.

I knew I was sinful. I had spilled my water on the earth. I had dirtied myself and Brianna. Once I had scratched myself between my legs and it felt good. My older sister had seen it and laughed. I had done it again and Mother pulled my hand away and said don't touch yourself there. So I guessed that was a sin too.

I'd wrap fairy tales in the covers of history books, so I wouldn't get caught reading them. I'd thrown away my lunch, never thinking of the hungry. I was full of sin. I knew that. I'd be glad to be freed from sin.

"How am I impure?" I asked. I wasn't sure what impure meant, but it didn't sound good.

Mother sighed. "They will tell you today at the ceremony," she said.

She made me take a bath and scrubbed me so roughly I thought my skin might come off. It hurt, but I didn't complain much, not even when she got soap in my eyes. She wanted me pure and spotless at the ceremony. She wanted to be proud.

She dressed me in a dress we'd bought the week before. It was the most beautiful dress I'd ever seen. White as a bride, with lace and pleats. I didn't like dresses usually. But this one make me feel like a fairy princess. Mom brushed my hair long and blond down my back.

Then she covered me in a white hooded cape.

"You forgot to make up my ears," I said.

"You don't need it today," she said.

She dressed in her best dark blue dress, the one with a white lace collar, the one that she wore to church every Sunday.

We walked to the zip-pull and got on. It was always crowded, but today it was double crowded. All the eight-year-olds were there with their mothers, all dressed in white as clean and spotless as soap could make them.

We went to Temple Hall. It was a big round bowl, with rows and rows of seats surrounding a central stage. It rose in a dome above us, dwarfing us. It was an old, old building. So ancient it was made of wood, but polished till it shone golden brown. In the center of the dome a small hole, covered with protective plastic, opened light to the sky. I felt small. I was small, small, and full of sin.

The Temple was crowded with kids waiting to be purged, waiting to be freed from impurity—whatever that was, waiting to grow-up.

When we were all seated and quiet, a platform rose out of the floor. Father Leonean was standing on it, arms raised up toward heaven in a V. He wore a robe of white flowing cloth belted with a white satin cord thick as two fingers. I felt a shiver run up my spine. He was looking up to the sky as if he could see God, as if he could touch Jesus.

Then he lowered his eyes and sighed. It was a deep low sound like wind blowing dust down an empty street. He raised his eyes, looking slowly and sharply around, as if he could see each one of us, see into our souls, see all our badness.

"Brethren," he said. "Sons of Adam and daughters of Eve, you have come for the cleansing." He had a deep rich voice and even though he spoke softly, it filled the Temple with a growling rumble like earthbound thunder.

"You have reached the age of reason. You can now take responsibility for the sins of the fathers and the iniquities of the mothers that run in your blood. All of you have been defiled. The evil runs in your blood, the defilement dwells in your genes, the desecration is in your very marrow."

I looked around the circle for Brianna. Way on the far side I saw her, curly reddish hair beneath her veil. I wanted to wave, but Mother had her hand on mine, pressing it tight to the seat. Her hand was fleshy and moist against the cool, hard wood.

"In times past sins could be concealed," Father Leonean continued. "Hidden in the blood. But we born after the Boundless War, we descendants of the purge of 4015, we have been blessed with the truth of pigment, with true vision.

"The sciences of early times were made of sin. They saw no difference between black and white, between good and evil. But now all the disciplines of man serve God. Our scientists have unmixed the racial impurities that once were hidden in our genes. They have made visible the difference between black and brown and white. No longer can the sons and daughters of Cain conceal themselves beneath a cloak of whiteness. Our eyes are open."

I didn't know what Father Leonean meant about brown, black or white. Once in bible class they taught us that long ago, in the time of bees, and grapes, and snow, and unicorns, and plants that reached through soft earth like hands in prayer, there had been people dark of soul and skin. But now, in the times of righteousness, they were all returned to the devil whence they came as soon as they were born.

I asked Mother what that meant and she had bit her lip and ran from the room. I never asked again.

"The curse of Cain is now visible to all—the blackness is no longer hidden in the heart," Father Leonean continued. "Some say we should send all those tainted by the brush of Cain to hell at birth. But we, we of a merciful God, let those who have been brushed with sin survive. Instead we purify them—cutting the darkness from their soul—cutting the blackness from their skin."

Father Leonean glared down at us, as if he could see each sin and flaw. He didn't look merciful to me, but I am full of sin.

"Abigale Adams, come receive your cleansing," he called.

Abby was so tiny, she was invisible until she stumbled out from behind the pew.

She tottered on uncertain feet, as though she'd been propelled forward by the hand of God, or maybe just her mother.

She walked up the steps to Father Leonean's pulpit. From the below the floor, in front of his dais, rose another platform. On it was a rough stone slab. It was gray. Small flecks of mica glittered in the light, like living dust motes. I'd been taught about mica, fool's gold, in bible class. How something could look valuable on the outside but was not. Beside the slab was a granite basin. It was filled with something white and gritty, something like sugar or salt.

"Reveal your impurity, child," Father Leonean said.

Abby slowly, slowly bent down. She crouched on one knee like the picture of Joseph praying for guidance, or like Prince Charming proposing.

She unbuckled the shiny white patent leather shoe on her right foot and slowly peeled off the white sock. Her little toe was dark, a warm golden brown, like the wood of the church, like the color of my ears.

Her mother must have schooled her, must have told her what to do, because she lifted her foot and placed it on the stone.

Father Leonean raised his right arm swift and sharp. A silver axe blade caught the light and he swung it down rapid and hard. Abby's foot spurted blood, splattering the stone. Father Leonean turned swiftly out of the line of the eruption. He remained clean. Abby's shoulders shook but she made not a sound.

I understood everything. It was one of those moments, when all those little questions you didn't even realize you'd had, all those trivial things you hadn't even known you'd noticed, became clear. The time Mother said I'd had two older sisters and then run into her bedroom. The reason she never said a word when she put makeup on my ears.

I only hoped I'd be so brave when my time came. I tried to cover my ears, but Mother was holding tight to my hands.

Father Leonean grabbed Abby's foot and thrust it into the basin. Then she screamed, a thin high wail that hurt my head.

"Now you are pure. Now you are all white. By the grace of the Lord, blessed be He and cursed be the darkness. Go forth and bear spotless children. Go forth and multiply and sin no more."

Brianna was next. She climbed surely up the steps, never hesitating. She was always that way, always obedient and trusting.

"Reveal your impurity, child," Father Leonean said. From behind her back she showed her hands. One by one she pulled each finger from her gloves. She held out her hands. She placed them on the slab. Hands brown and smooth.

Father Leonean's axe flashed swift and sure through the air, so swift it made a swishing sound. Blood spurted from Brianna's wrists.

Her hands fell from the slab and tumbled down the steps, fingers twitching. Father Leonean thrust her wrists in the salt, but it was just for show, just part of the cleansing. Nothing could stanch the flow of her blood that ran from her arms like the River Jordan.

I've never seen a river, never would, they are dry now. Dry. Gone like unicorns and bees and plants reaching upward in prayer. I thought I saw the shape of a unicorn in the lake of blood that Brianna lay in. I think I heard her mother sobbing. I didn't hear as my name was called. I must have walked up to the stone slab though.

I remember the flash of the axe through the air. That swishing sound. The last sound I heard.

Mother assures me the sounds will return. She writes it on the white board she keeps by my bed. She writes that I am lucky to only have had the mark of Cain on my ears. Ears are easy to live without. She never writes that some are even luckier, but I know it is true. Those really fortunate have their pigment hidden inside of their mouths or perhaps even deeper. And of course the truly blessed are not marked at all. I wonder though if everyone is tainted. If even doves are stained somewhere inside, somewhere deep, somewhere where no one, not even they can see.

And I wonder about all those sent away when they are born, my older sister that I will never see, like bees and unicorns. I hope that she is happy in the darkness.

The Cracked Earth

Adam Breckenridge

*Editor: Salvation and damnation are two sides of the same coin.
One without the other is meaningless.*

Rain was a forgotten concept. Water had flown from the cracks long ago and life here was too close to death to remember things having ever been otherwise. Even most of what breathed had succumbed to blackness. Trees were charred to the wood, the leaves gone, their roots dry. Haggard crows bounced around, seeking any flesh that may have been overlooked on the few scattered bones that lay about.

The sole figure who walked in this petrified landscape wore robes, hat and a beard that were all as dark as ignorance. Humanity, before he had wiped them off the face of the earth, had called him Black. He continued to know himself by that name. He liked the way his tongue rolled slowly across the roof of his mouth when he spoke the word—as slow and deliberate as he was.

He approached a crow that was scraggly and awkward with hunger. It studied him carefully but didn't shy away. He picked it up and twisted its neck, then ground the carcass between his fingers until nothing but ashen bones remained.

On the side of a hill he encountered a tree, small and stubborn, that still had a couple of leaves hanging on.

"Well, that's no good at all," he whispered and placed his gnarled hands on the trunk. The leaves withered to dust and the roots shriveled until the tree fell over.

Black continued through the land removing any signs of life. He crushed bugs underfoot and watched their innards sizzle away on the scorching ground. He ripped up tufts of grass that had not quite dried out completely and ground them to dust. He ruptured microbes he found living on the underbellies of rocks. As time passed the scarcity of life made his duty nearly impossible. For nights and days he would sniff the air for patches of bacteria, seek out those few scraps of mold that still clung on. It got to where he could no longer recall seeing any living thing larger than a dust mote. In time it seemed nothing at all still lived wherever he walked. So when he saw an object moving slowly across the dirt far on the horizon one evening, he assumed it to be one of the few tumbleweeds the wind still tossed about: that is, until it materialized into the shape of a man.

Black strolled toward the figure, his onyx eyes glimmering. The man was filthy from crawling. The few rags he wore proved useless against the pitiless sun with his blistered skin clinging to his ribs. Yet the survivor continued to dig one long-nailed hand after the other into the cracked earth, pulling himself slowly to Black's boots. Black eyed the dying man and listened as he croaked nonsense from his bloodied, crumpled lips. Eventually the sorry sight managed the word, "Water."

Black laughed, and it hurt his lungs to do so.

"I'm afraid, my friend," he said, "that I'm a creature of ash and dust."

The man lay his head down in the dirt. Black actually felt some measure of pity for the man. Black held back the gorge in his throat. Was this sympathy? Unable to steady his nerve, his hands trembled just a little as he placed them on the man's forehead. Confronting this poor waste had given him a flicker of a memory of what it was like to be alive. The man crumbled to ash and sank into the cracks of the earth.

As Black continued his sterilization of the empty earth, he couldn't help but notice changes—a rock shifting out of place, a cliff slumping lower, or a mountain gradually swaying back and forth. In time he also noticed that the ground was no longer cracked, though water had long ceased to exist. "It seems I'm not needed here anymore," he thought as his robes and hair slowly softened from black to gray to white.

Adaptive Behavior

T. M. Starnes

Editor: A true leader thinks beyond the needs of the moment.

Overhead lights clicked on. The new testing day began.

Brownie always woke before the rest of the breed. He would listen to their snores, their breathing, and consider tactics for the daily testers' activities with his kind.

The Old One kept everyone up late last night telling the old stories of when the breed once roamed beyond the walls, living in tall homes, going wherever they wished, doing what they wished, some even living far from any other breed, crossing great holes of water where the breed could not see the other side. But that was before the coming of the testers. The stories were old. Passed down from old one to old one. When tens upon tens upon tens of breed fought the testers on the first day. Some of the stories made no sense. Breed flying? Breed standing on metal on the great water holes fighting testers? Fires as large as the sun? The Old One sometimes made his tales bigger with the telling. The breed knew the testers were all powerful. Easily bending the will of the tens of tens of the early breed to serve them in their works for all the breeds' days to this day. The days of roaming breed were long gone. This is their life now.

Brownie checked his right forelimb. It remained swollen from the injection yesterday. His right paw ached as he stretched out his claws. One claw had been broken off in a fight with One Eye. He methodically sharpened all four sets of claws against the concrete floor.

Red Beauty wandered over to him from her side of his see-through home.

She walked with a limp. The testers had done something wrong to her reproductive organs after her fifth birth. The rapid births aged her quicker than any of the strange tests could. One Eye and Brownie's most recent fight had been over Red Beauty when One Eye decided he wanted to mate against her wishes. The testers had not paired Red Beauty and One Eye. One Eye didn't care, even if it was still too soon after her most recent birthing.

Red Beauty was sick. Brownie could tell. She wasn't eating. Her body odor wafted in from the breathing holes between the clear barrier between them. She smelled of weakness.

She rested her forehead against the enclosure's barrier.

Brownie stood and approached, leaning his head against hers from his side.

"I'm broken," she said, caressing her belly.

He placed his paw on the barrier. "The testers will fix. Eat."

She looked at his swollen forelimb. "You are broken?"

He bared his teeth in reassurance and shook his head, "No. I am strong. Eat. Be strong."

One Eye snorted across from them, "She is food."

Brownie snarled at his short-haired, muscled antagonist and clenched his left front claw. "Be quiet."

One Eye bared his teeth. "She is food. I smell her stink. They won't fix."

Brownie faced One Eye's side of the barrier across the passageway and raked downward against the barrier with his claws. "Be . . . quiet."

One Eye snorted again and displayed his buttocks, a grave insult.

Brownie growled low and deep in his chest as One Eye slowly rubbed his rump across the barrier, baring his teeth over his right shoulder. If they had not been separated by the barriers and the passage between them, Brownie would have attacked One Eye as he had yesterday.

"No fight," the Old One said from his home.

Brownie turned to his left at the elder. "He is wrong."

The Old One shook his body as he stood, his long, lanky, dirty hair whipping about him, the hairless parts of his body showing old scars, experiment marks, and healed damage from the preceding days and years.

The Old One settled and sharpened his misshapen rear claws on the floor. "Yes, he is wrong. You are strong. No fighting. They want us fighting. Want us not right in the head. Make us mad to each other. You are strong. It is no good for them if we not fight."

One Eye snorted again and released a loud fart before moving back into the rear of his square home.

"You are food one day, Old One," One Eye mumbled.

The Old One bared his teeth in aggression. "Yes. We all are food one day. I have not been food for many days. More than your days. I am old and not food because I am strong. Know that."

One Eye glared at the Old One. They kept eye contact until One Eye looked away.

The Old One bared his teeth in triumph at Brownie. Brownie joined in the Old One's strength.

The passageway door opened to the left of their homes.

The testers filed in. They stood twice the height of the tallest breed. For all the breed's memories, the testers had worn their all-over, all-covering, body protection. White, like the floor. Crackling as they moved.

Their heads and expressions were forever unseen. They did have two sets of paws like the breed, stood tall on their hind paws like the breed, but their rear paws looked strange to the breed. Round, squeaky, smooth, leaving odd paw prints along the passageway when the breed bled for them and they walked through the puddled blood.

Males began hooting and howling; Brownie assumed a new female must be joining their pack.

Several testers pushed a female along the passage, and Brownie got a good look at her.

Compared to Red Beauty, this new female was as beautiful as Red Beauty had been in her prime, and she had no marks of birth. Her trimmed short hair was shiny, her body firm. She wore no fighting marks. No damage.

She shied away from the males calling out to her. Brownie knew they meant no harm. Most of them, that is. One Eye presented his genitals against the barrier and made the birth making motions. She moved away from his barrier and bumped against Brownie's.

She spun and looked up into Brownie's eyes.

"Be strong," he said, lowering his head and stepping back, a display of nonaggression.

Her head tilted slightly in confusion in response before the testers pushed her forward.

As she passed by Red Beauty's barrier she wrinkled her nose and recoiled at Red's scent.

The testers pushed the newcomer to the opposite side of the barriers from Brownie's side, adjacent to One Eye's enclosure. The tester opened the barrier and pushed her forward. They made another motion and the barrier returned.

One Eye took advantage of the situation and continued his sexual assault on the barrier between him and the female.

A tester smacked One Eye's barrier and he backed off. Two testers turned to Red Beauty's cage and began monitoring her. She settled slowly to the floor as far from them as she could.

A tester stopped in front of Brownie's enclosure.

"Shake," it said in Brownie's words.

Brownie stepped forward and extended his right forelimb. The tester made a motion and the barrier opened just enough for Brownie to extend his forelimb outside. The tester gripped his forelimb hard enough that Brownie hissed and bared his teeth in response but relaxed in nonaggression.

The tester examined Brownie's forelimb, squeezing the injection point for required fixing. Once satisfied, the tester released him and shoved his forelimb back inside the enclosure before sealing it.

The testers performed similar inspections on others along the passageway. Some howls, some screams of sheer terror, some moans of pleasure, echoed through the home hallway. It was nothing new, repeated daily. For all their lives it had been this way, and even before the Old One was young.

Brownie alternated looking between the frightened newcomer and Red Beauty. The testers were spending too long communicating in their own words with each other outside Red Beauty's enclosure.

"Brownie?" the Old One called.

Brownie glanced over his shoulder.

"Be ready. Be strong. She will go," the Old One said, scratching an old sore behind his ear.

"No. She is strong," Brownie whined, "she will not go."

The Old One sighed. "She will go. They stay too long. I have seen this."

"No," Brownie disagreed.

The testers motioned and Red Beauty's enclosure opened as Red slowly retreated into a corner.

Brownie charged the barrier separating them.

He clawed, howled, beat, rammed, snarled, spit, and leaped against the barrier multiple times, which encouraged the other breed along the passageway to join in with angry shouts and displeasure.

A tester returned to Brownie's home and banged against the barrier.

"Brownie, no, be strong! Be strong!" the Old One warned.

The two testers approached Red Beauty and she tried to get away. "Brownie! Brownie!" she screamed in horror.

Brownie rubbed the points from his claws attacking the barrier, leaving bloody streaks, compelling the tester to bang again.

The two testers touched Red Beauty and she collapsed, they prodded and examined her genitals, talking in the testers' words. Eventually, they each took a set of her limbs and lifted her from the floor.

"No!" Brownie demanded, clawing in an even greater frenzy.

"Down," the tester commanded outside his enclosure.

Brownie ignored it.

The Old One banged the barrier too. "Down," the Old One begged, "Down, Brownie, down."

Red Beauty's unmoving body, her long hair dragging the passageway floor, swung between the testers as they exited her enclosure.

"Down," the tester repeated in the breed's words.

Insane with grief, Brownie launched himself at the tester.

Pain wracked Brownie's body and he endured the dance of pain across the cold floor.

The Old One turned his head away. One Eye bared his teeth in pleasure. The newcomer covered her nose and eyes, pressing herself to the floor.

The dance of pain continued much longer than it should have until

Brownie could no longer contain his body's waste. Only then did the tester stop the dance.

Brownie gasped for breath and lifted his face from his wetness and solid stink to look at the tester's all-concealed head.

"Down." The tester sounded amused, then it turned and followed Red Beauty and the others back the way they entered.

One Eye crouched low until Brownie looked at him.

He bared his teeth. "I *said* she was food."

Brownie faded into blackness.

* * *

"Brownie?" Old One whispered, "Brownie?"

The floor was cold and damp but didn't stink.

"Brownie? Are you strong?" Old One repeated.

Brownie lifted his head slowly and looked toward Old One.

"Good." The Old One huffed, "You did not move when they cleaned your home. I was not sure if you were food."

Brownie glanced back toward Red Beauty's empty home. It was empty and cleaned. He breathed deeply. Nothing of Red Beauty's scent remained.

"She is gone," the Old One informed him. "Her breaking took her."

Brownie tried to rise on all fours but the dance of pain cramped his muscles. A dull ache spread throughout his body.

The enclosure floor and his body were spotless. Neither he nor his home smelled except for the way the waste corner normally did.

One Eye watched the new female with a predatory look.

The newcomer was curled into a ball on the opposite side of her home. She kept showing weakness against One Eye's stare. A bad thing.

She was short, slim, healthy, smelled of youth. Brownie knew how much One Eye liked that.

"You dance strong." One Eye bared his teeth in pleasure. "It was good."

Brownie bared his teeth back in the challenge way. "One day we will dance together and you will finish the dance for the last time."

One Eye snorted and looked back at the female.

Brownie pulled himself up. He examined his claws, the sharps worn to nubs on both front and back paws. He stretched. The eyes of the female looked toward him.

Brownie moved to the corner of his enclosure nearest her.

"What are you called?" Brownie asked.

"Mine," One Eye warned.

Brownie ignored him.

She looked at One Eye with trepidation.

"Look here. Be strong," Brownie encouraged. "What are you called?"

One Eye bared his teeth and dragged his claw slowly across the barrier at Brownie. "Mine," he repeated.

"I am Brownie. Behind me is the Old One. *That* is One Eye. Tell us so we know you."

She raised her head looking quickly between One Eye and Brownie, then settling her eyes on Brownie. "I am Fierce Biter."

Brownie and the Old One bared their teeth in appreciation. "A strong name," Brownie said.

"I am new here. What are the tests?" she whispered. "What do they look for in us?"

The Old One stood. "We fight. We are fighting breed."

Brownie nodded. "We are fighting breed."

She glanced at One Eye, and he crept closer to the barrier displaying his excited genitals. She quickly looked away.

One Eye licked the barrier. "We will make the fighting breed strong with our mating."

Fierce Biter shivered.

"Be strong," Brownie commanded her in a deep tone.

Fierce Biter's head popped up and looked at him. "You . . . sound like a tester."

Brownie bared his teeth in displeasure.

Fierce dipped her eyes. "Not the bad way. Strong. I mean strong."

Brownie closed his mouth. "We are all strong here. If you are here? You are strong. Be strong."

Fierce looked at Brownie for a moment, then slowly rose in a defensive crouch.

She ignored One Eye's noises and actions as she stretched and rose to her full height.

"You are strong," Brownie said, baring his teeth in appreciation.

Fierce Biter, her demeanor still somewhat timid, tried to make eye contact with One Eye.

One Eye reveled in her discomfort, baring his teeth in pleasure.

Suddenly Fierce charged the barrier. If the barrier had not been there, all four of her claws would have severely damaged or removed One Eye's unsuspecting male parts. One Eye instinctively retreated.

Fierce Biter glared at One Eye, displaying her teeth and raking her claws across the floor as a threat.

"I am Fierce Biter," she growled. "I mate with who I want. Not who thinks I am weak."

One Eye launched himself at his side of the barrier and she attacked her side.

They displayed strength. Fierce Biter's youth outlasted One Eye's and he settled down.

"I will have you," One Eye warned between gulps of breath. "You will mate with who the testers match you. I am strongest. You will mate with me."

Brownie and the Old One huffed at his boast.

Fierce came closer to the barrier and said, "Then we shall mate." She flexed her claw, "But it will be once and you will be broken when I am done."

The Old One spoke through the barrier air holes to Brownie, "I like her."

Brownie bared his teeth. "I do, too. She is strong."

Fierce returned to the other side of her home and curled into a ball to rest, ignoring One Eye completely.

* * *

The testers returned with the daily injections.

Each of the breed extended their paw and forelimb past the barrier for their injections.

Breed howled and screamed, interspacing those sounds with moans of pleasure.

One Eye liked the injections, they always gave him strength.

The Old One never seemed to mind his. The Old One guessed his injections were for healing and living strong. His teeth were never bad and his claws were always strong and sharp.

Brownie didn't know what his injections did but he often thought long and hard about it. He knew he thought more than the other breed. About everything. The Old One said Brownie grew smarter over time and that was why he was chosen as the pack Alpha. Brownie healed quicker than other breed, except for the Old One, but Brownie couldn't tell any difference after they made him leader. He fought less, planned more.

When Fierce Biter took her injection, she vomited and scratched furiously at herself. The testers were forced to enter her enclosure to subdue her before she permanently damaged herself and gave her two more injections until she calmed down and became strong again.

All the breed knew sometimes the injections went wrong. They had seen at one time or another when one of the others on their passageway became food from the tests. It wasn't a good thing to see.

The Old One tapped the barrier. "Scratcher is back." He indicated the testers escorting a female.

Scratcher was a barren female with a deep scar across her neck and a missing teat. She was tall for a female. Quick with an open and approachable way. Her dark mane was shaved on the same side as the scar so it would not be obscured so the testers could monitor its healing. The testers had taken her two days ago to heal the wound given by one of Fat Belly's pack. The scar looked fixed strong to Brownie.

She bared her teeth at Brownie and the Old One. "I am strong."

Brownie bared his teeth back in welcome. "You are. We did not think one as strong as you would be food."

She wrinkled her upper lip at One Eye. "You are still here."

He bared his teeth in the bad way. "I will be older than the Old One before *I* am food."

The testers closed her enclosure and gave the command for Scratcher to extend her paw past the barrier. They injected her. Whatever she received made her burst with energy; she paced back and forth in her home, snarling at One Eye. One Eye snarled back a few times but even he didn't like the look in her crazed eyes.

The attention noise blared along the passageway and the exit door to the yard on Brownie's right opened.

"*Yard.*" A tester's disembodied voice echoed throughout the homes. "*Go. Now.*"

The barriers facing the passageway were removed.

As usual, One Eye glared a challenge at Brownie. Brownie huffed and motioned to Fierce Biter to come to him. One Eye placed himself between them. Brownie crouched and made to spring at him as he had when defending Red Beauty yesterday. One Eye raised his claws in warning.

The dance of pain engulfed them both. Their jaws clenched and their bodies went rigid as they skipped on their rear paws along the floor.

"*Down,*" announced a tester. "*Yard. Go. Now.*"

Both One Eye and Brownie fell to the floor and the pain left them.

Leaving her home, Scratcher kneed One Eye in the head as she passed. She lifted Brownie to his feet.

Brownie shook his body as Scratcher's wild eyes stared into his. "To the yard. No more pain. One Eye is weak. Come now," she said, her body still involuntarily twitching in small spasms from whatever was in her injection.

One Eye looked up from the floor.

Brownie extended his paw to One Eye. "Come. Or you will have more pain."

One Eye curled his lips back from his teeth and stood on his own. With a shake of inevitability, he followed his rival into the yard.

From behind, Scratcher pretended to claw One Eye's back.

The exit to the yard shined with the midday sun. The arena formed a large circle with obstacles on one side, pits on another, and places for waste, eating meals, and healing on yet another. The yard itself consistently smelled of blood, fear, staleness, and bodily wastes. A high wall rose to block the view outside the yard. Occasionally, odd noises came from the permanently unseen other side of the wall. Strange but pleasant smells often stopped the breed in their daily tests to smell the wind.

Brownie waited by the door, counting his pack as they exited and acknowledging them as each waited for the rest.

There was One Eye, Fierce Biter, Scratcher, Old One, Goldie, Gnawer, Not Right, Cougher, Blue Eyes, Broke Tooth, Scrawny, and Yipper. Heavy with her second birthing, Broke Tooth would have to sit out and do soft things. The rest would test. Brownie would miss Red Beauty but welcomed Fierce Biter.

As they exited their passageway, two more passageways let two other breed packs out onto the field.

Grumpy, a breed leader with a permanent scowl, sized up Brownie and his charges against his pack before looking back over at Fat Belly and sizing up his. Brownie dipped his nose at both, they did the same in mutual acknowledgment.

Testers waited on the field.

Broke Tooth moved toward the meal area with testers who would repair the breed if needed.

Brownie's pack gathered around him.

Old One nudged Fierce Biter who gazed around in confusion not knowing what to do. "Listen to Brownie. He is smart. His mind is strong, they have made him so."

Fierce Biter trembled so Brownie placed a paw on her shoulder. "Be strong. You are new, they will not fight you hard. Run to us if it is too much."

Fierce dipped her nose once. One Eye snorted. She turned to him and stretched to her full height, such as it was, and presented her front claws. "I will not run."

Brownie shook her shoulder. "No. You *will* run. This is new. You are new. You will run to us. Yes?"

Fierce turned to him and lowered her head. "Yes."

"Good." Brownie addressed the others surrounding him, "Fat Belly has many hurt in his pack; most now are new. Grumpy has strength in his pack; be strong, be ready."

Brownie noticed where One Eye was staring and cuffed him on the side of the head to distract him from Fierce's backside. "Are you here?"

One Eye gave him a deadly look. "I am here. Do not hit again."

"Then be here," he warned, not breaking eye contact. "Calm your body or give it as food to Grumpy or Fat Belly's pack." He pointed at One Eye's excited groin.

Scratcher, Fierce, Goldie, and Blue Eyes, all the females, snickered at One Eye's displeasure.

One Eye glared at Brownie again.

The testers began calling names for test groupings that varied from running obstacle courses to seek and find, and even combat.

When Scratcher's name was called, she ran obediently toward the tester, joining a thin breed and a shaggy, dirty breed from Grumpy and Fat Belly's pack. Each of them twitched and spasmed from the injections the testers had given them before leaving their homes.

The Old One paired off with another Old One from Grumpy's pack.

Fierce, Blue Eyes, Cougher, and Scrawny went to join with breed from Grumpy and Fat Belly's packs as Brownie gave quick instructions to them about their opponents' weaknesses.

One Eye flexed his muscles as he advanced toward two large, opposing breed who bared their teeth in challenge.

Before long, breed from every pack had been combined together for their testings.

Fat Belly and Grumpy moved among the packs like Brownie, giving advice and warnings. Testers followed each of them as they did so, often making motions over small, flat pads they carried.

Fierce Biter came running up to Brownie and he turned his attention to her.

"Brownie? I . . ." She hesitated.

He waited.

"Do we make them food? The others say we do," Fierce said, her face pale. Brownie could tell she had never made any breed into food. Everyone, including Red Beauty, had at least once. Brownie had three times in his life. The Old One never spoke of how many he'd made food but he hadn't since Brownie became leader.

Brownie realized those who prompted her to make food were those of other packs. He knew his pack, apart from One Eye, did not make the other breeds food. Brownie had ordered them to let their opponents live. The Old One had confided that he'd never known of another in his long life who had ordered the same.

"They do not need to be food. If you stop before they are—good. If you must make them food? Then do. Be strong."

"Go. Do your best." Brownie motioned for her to go back to her tester's pack and the testers took note of his command.

* * *

The tests wore on the breed packs.

Scratcher was bloodied but strong. As her energy waned, the testers injected her more often. One Eye had broken the leg of one of his opponents. Another breed beat Cougher senseless during one of his coughing fits so Broke Tooth took care of him. Blood trickled down between Fierce Biter's small teats and over her belly. She cleaned flesh from her claws in the dirt. The Old One and his opponent were bruised and battered. Old One's opponent nursed four broken claws on his right front paw and a crushed nose. The Old One had dislocated his shoulder and Brownie popped it back into place. The Old One grew strong within minutes, his skin abrasions and bruises discoloring and returning to their normal tone.

The Old One remained beside Brownie while allowing his body to heal at its accelerated pace, discussing tactics for each of their pack members.

A loud, undulating screech rose over the yard echoing against the walls.

The Old One cocked his head to one side. "I have not heard that sound since I was young."

The testers looked at each other, then motioned frantically over their flat pads.

The noise pained the breed's ears.

The Old One turned toward the closed door to home, then slowly rotated in a circle.

Brownie covered his ears. "Old One? What is that? What is that sound?"

The packs' individual members began moving from their testing areas and joined with their pack leaders.

The Old One raised his forelimbs and bared his teeth and laughed. "It is an old sound! A beautiful old sound!"

Brownie grabbed the Old One's forelimbs and demanded, "Hear me! What is this sound!"

The doors to the breeds' homes opened and testers boiled out. The testers in the yard ran toward the testers exiting, speaking quickly in their own words.

One Eye grabbed the Old One and spun him to face him. "What is the sound! Tell us! What happens!"

The Old One began crying as he laughed.

There was a loud squelch cutting through the awful sound. "*Home!*" shouted the disembodied tester's voice in breed speech, "*Home! Now! Go!*"

Brownie grabbed the Old One from One Eye. "Speak! What is the sound!"

The Old One grabbed either side of Brownie's head and answered, "Freedom! It is the sound of freedom!"

Brownie wrinkled his nose in confusion. "The sound of what?"

Brownie looked at the others gathering around him. "What is freedom?" None of them knew the word.

"Home! Go! Now!" testers ordered, motioning toward their home passageway.

"Old One! What is that? What is freedom?"

Explosions rocked the far wall from the entrance to the yard. The testers in their bulky suits turned and ran toward the breed packs, commanding them to go home.

The Old One screamed in joy, "When I was young, the testers-not-testers came! That sound is theirs! They took many of the breed and gave them freedom! The testers captured me. I was too young and could not get freedom!"

"He is weak. He is not right," One Eye huffed. "He says no words we know."

Brownie tried to understand. "Old One? Testers-not-testers? Your tongue makes noise but we can't hear."

More explosions rocked the wall and the testers began physically shoving and hitting the breed, forcing them toward the doors to their home passage.

Confused by their assault, Brownie wondered why were they not using the dance of pain. The testers rarely physically beat the breed. He continued wondering what this sound meant, what freedom meant.

A tester yelled at One Eye and Scrawny because they were confused and weren't moving fast enough for the tester. The tester shoved One Eye and, with One Eye's instinctively surly manner, One Eye shoved the tester's limb away.

Brownie froze, waiting for One Eye to dance the dance of pain.

Instead the tester stepped back and recoiled defensively.

One Eye was also frozen in disbelief, waiting for the dance.

The tester shoved One Eye back toward the door. "Home! Go! Now!"

One Eye stumbled but did not dance and turned toward the door, confused even more.

More explosions rocked the wall's exterior, the Old One laughed in madness, and Fierce Biter sat on the ground with one forelimb wrapped around Brownie's leg.

This is not right. This is wrong, Brownie thought.

In a moment of his own madness, Brownie knelt, picked up a hard-packed pawful of dirt and threw it at the back of the tester shoving One Eye.

It burst across the tester's back and the tester turned. Brownie's pack flinched away from him, expecting Brownie's imminent punishment.

"Home! Now! Go!" the tester screamed behind its all-covering mask, pointing toward home.

But there was no dance.

Testers ran to help the tester Brownie'd assaulted. Brownie looked across the field at Grumpy. Grumpy's expression was as shocked as Brownie's.

There was *no* dance. Brownie looked at the yard's dirt beneath their feet. It was not like their homes.

The breed could not dance the dance of pain on the dirt.

Another explosion rocked the far wall and several immense cracks split down the wall from the top to the bottom, the explosions were so strong. The breed and testers collectively squatted in fear.

In. Fear. The testers squatted in *fear*. In *weakness*.

Brownie, Grumpy, and Fat Belly exchanged glances. Their expressions appeared to mirror what Brownie thought.

The wall exploded into the yard from the outside.

The testers continued beating and dragging the breed toward the doors. The Old One staggered to his feet and began moving toward the wall. "FREEDOM! FREEDOM!" he cried.

Testers, but not testers, stormed through the broken wall; their all-covering suits were slightly different from the testers within the yard arena. White, but brighter, with markings on the shoulders. They motioned toward the breed and back to the hole in the wall. But Brownie couldn't tell if they spoke or not with the constant screeching noise echoing off the walls of the testing yard.

Grumpy's Old One began following Brownie's Old One, then Fat Belly's Old One began to run toward the hole.

The testers beat the breed harder, dragging the smaller ones and the females inside. Broke Tooth screamed as a tester kicked her in her swollen belly to get her to rise and go home.

Many of the breed cowered in weakness to the testers. Many were in shock from the explosions. Some were just obstinate, contrary, and hard-headed. Grumpy and Fat Belly looked uncertain about what to do with their breed members.

Brownie looked toward One Eye.

He glanced at the weak tester and at One Eye, then the hole in the wall and the Old One motioning toward them, repeating the word they didn't know. His attention returned to the door to home.

Brownie's brown eyes met the singular dark eye of his rival.

"Fight!" Brownie screamed. "Make them food!"

That was all One Eye needed.

One Eye's massive figure rose to his full height. He screamed in madness and charged the tester as it stepped backward after shoving him.

The tester went down. One Eye's remaining sharpened claws tore into the tester's suit.

Screams of fear and pain rose from the tester beneath him.

"FIGHT!" Brownie screamed to his pack, "FIGHT!" he screamed at Grumpy. "FIGHT!" MAKE THEM BE FOOD!" he screamed at Fat Belly.

Fierce Biter leaped at a tester running to strike Brownie's exposed side.

Scratcher went after the ones kicking Broke Tooth; Scrawny joined her.

Brownie looked across the field arena and grew still with awe.

The breed fought. They fought the testers. It was unlike anything he had ever seen or heard of before.

The Old Ones ran cautiously toward the wall holes but Brownie's Old One turned and beckoned Brownie to follow. The other Old One ran past the gesturing tester-not-tester by the wall collapse. It didn't try to stop him. It even helped him through. Three more testers-not-testers entered the yard from the hole and Brownie could hear them finally over the loud sound around them.

"*Freedom! Come! Freedom!*" Their voices traveled despite the screeching noise echoing off the walls.

Broke Tooth cringed by Brownie's feet.

"Brownie! What do we do?" she begged.

He pulled her up. "Go! Freedom! Go to freedom!" He ordered her, Yipper, and Not Right to go toward freedom. He told them to carry Broke Tooth through the hole.

Familiar agonized screams echoed over the yard suddenly. Screams Brownie knew by their sound were of his pack.

More testers ran from the home passageways carrying sticks. They touched the breed with a blue end and the breed screamed.

They went after the strongest and the fiercest breed. One Eye turned and raked a claw across the throat of one of the testers and it fell back, but two stick carrying testers shoved their sticks at One Eye and he fell, blood erupting from his mouth.

Fierce was struck and went down. The sound she made was horrible. The tester circled over her and shouted commands.

Brownie charged toward that tester's exposed back and pounced. He grabbed the stick with both paws. Pulling the stick up and across the tester's throat, he placed his rear paws to the back of the tester's shoulders for leverage since the tester was so tall, and pulled back with a strong up and backward motion. With a sickening, loud crack, the tester became food.

Brownie shook the blue end of the stick at the other stick-welding testers and they backed off. He touched the end-that-harmed to a tester who came too close. It jerked back and fell. Food or not, Brownie couldn't tell.

Scratcher appeared beside him.

"Give!" she cried.

Brownie gave her the stick. She screamed in challenge and advanced on the testers. Brownie looked toward the other leaders and their breed were taking sticks and using them too.

Scratcher, fast, eager, wily. Quick Scratcher fought the testers.

Brownie ran to One Eye. One Eye spat his own blood. It leaked from his ears and one nostril.

"Come!" Brownie cried. "Freedom!"

"No." One Eye coughed. "No freedom. Weak." Blood trickled from his mouth. "I am food."

Brownie grabbed One Eye's forelimb and a hind leg, pulling his massive rival over his shoulders and stood, grunting as he did.

"No, not now, not soon. Freedom for all," he vowed.

"Fierce! Give your paw!" Brownie reached down for the small female's extended paw and gripped tightly.

Brownie charged across the yard carrying One Eye on his back, while dragging Fierce Biter's pain-wracked body toward the hole in the wall.

"Freedom! All come!" Brownie screamed. "Freedom! Come now!"

Grumpy and Fat Belly's voices joined his.

Scratcher and Gnawer ran to them and lifted Fierce to her rear legs. Gnawer carried Fierce toward the wall. Scratcher slowed to protect Brownie and One Eye.

The Old One hopped in place, motioning toward the hole.

"Freedom! Freedom!" he yelled, and led the way through the hole. "Come, Brownie! Come!"

Brownie turned back to see the other packs. Many breed ran past him; the testers littered the ground, some moving, some not. Several of the breed lay on the ground appearing to be food, Fat Belly among them, but Fat Belly's pack ran toward the hole.

A tester-not-tester gently touched Brownie's shoulder.

"Freedom. Go. Now. Free." A tester's . . . *kind* . . . voice resonated from behind the all-concealing, all-covering suit. Scratcher ran past and motioned for Brownie to follow.

Brownie staggered over the broken wall, dust raining down on his and One Eye's back. A breeze filled Brownie's senses.

Cool. Pleasant. Fresh.

Brownie stumbled over stones and entered freedom.

If there was one thing Brownie knew, it was they would adapt to this new environment.

He would, without guidelines to follow or without knowing the risks or rewards, make sure his kind would succeed in this newest, undefined test.

It's what humans were bred for after all.

We fight. We are strong.

Rebirth

Anthony Addis

Editor's Note: Cherry blossoms, cherry blossoms
Across the spring sky,
As far as the eye can see.
Is it mist, or clouds?
Fragrant in the air.
Come now, come now,
Let's go and see them!
—Translation of a Japanese folk song

Suzu didn't know her father was a gaijin until they took him away. Although she'd only been five, the night was scalded into her brain. Two helicopters circled the fourteenth floor of their residential complex, concentrating searing white searchlights on the capsule-apartment where Suzu lived with her parents. There was no darkness, no shadow and no shade. The light penetrated everywhere. Blinding white.

Suzu's parents stood frozen in their pyjamas, their hands above their heads.

Seeing Suzu, her father screamed, "Get down!"

The door and windows exploded, showering them with wood and glass splinters. Shouting men in black burst in with machine guns. Their voices distorted, their breathing hoarse and magnified behind dark masks. They pushed Suzu's mother out of the way, threw her father to the ground and stomped on his back.

"Stop it!" Suzu screamed. But she didn't cry.

A soldier aimed his gun at her face. "Shut your mouth, gaijin scum."

* * *

She never discovered her father's fate. He was a forbidden subject. The government could have sent her and her mother to the Mines just for knowing him, or even sentenced them to being burnt at the stake or crucified.

Suzu thought they were spared because her mother's grandfather had worked on the Great Project. But they were always watched after her father was taken, always under suspicion.

* * *

The history teacher had been born without a nose. At ten, Suzu listened as he taught about the Eighteen Year War, when Japan stood at the brink of disaster.

At first, gaijin conventional bombs had rained down on major cities, starting firestorms that killed hundreds of thousands of civilians.

Beneath her desk, Suzu sharpened the end of her metal ruler with a stone, working so slowly only she could hear the stone's scrape.

After the firebombing, the gaijin dropped an atomic bomb on the old city of Hiroshima. Another fell on Nagasaki. Life was destroyed. Future lives were contaminated, maimed and poisoned in their mothers' wombs.

His resolve weakened by the terrible damage, the emperor wanted to surrender. Outraged, the army overthrew him. Surrendering would dishonour Japan. The Islands would fight on!

Suzu glanced up from her sharpening as her classmates murmured and stirred with pride when her teacher told how the Military Council spurned the gaijin terms of surrender.

Yuudai, the boy sitting behind her, used the distraction to once again lean forward and rap Suzu's head with his ruler. "Gaijin scum," he hissed.

More atomic bombs fell: on Osaka, Kyoto, Okayama, Akita and Yokohama. Three dropped on Old Tokyo. Death from the sky. Poisoned air and contaminated soil. Into the spring of 1946, atomic bombs devastated every major city, port and industrial town. Radiation blasted the land, air and water.

Suzu tested her ruler's dagger-sharp tip with her thumb and nodded, satisfied.

Still the Military Council refused to surrender. Eventually, the gaijin aggressors stopped. There was nothing left to bomb. As Japan was too radioactive to occupy, the gaijin set a naval cordon around the islands, leaving the Japanese to their shell-shocked, radioactive recovery.

Once again Yuudai poked her while the teacher wasn't looking. Suzu rose from her chair, spun round and drove her sharpened ruler onto Yuudai's hand, impaling it to the table. No emotion touched her as he screamed. She had solved a problem and learnt a lesson.

Meet violence with violence.

* * *

For stabbing Yuudai's hand, she was moved to a behavioural problems school. Her gaijin reputation preceded her and bullies ganged up on her.

One day, appalled when Suzu came home with a black eye, a split lip and a wobbly front tooth, her mother devised a plan that would involve enormous self-sacrifice. But it also required a contribution from Suzu.

"Why?" Suzu asked.

"If you don't, no one will ever trust you. Because of me, because I loved a gaijin. Eventually, they'll take you to the Mines, and me as well. This way, my sacrifice will have meaning. They'll treat you harshly at first, but in the end, they'll forget about your gaijin blood."

Even though she understood the consequences of her mother's plan, Suzu didn't cry.

* * *

Suzu's new history teacher was a thin woman with one eye three times the size of the other. As she told them about the Great Project, scrawny blood vessels swum in a white sea around her larger eye's engorged retina.

Japanese scientists split the atom in the spring of 1947. In 1948, they loaded an atomic bomb on a captured American B-29. When the gaijin observed the huge aircraft flying from Japan, they thought it was American and let it continue to Beijing.

The initial blast killed hundreds of thousands of Chinese. As thousands more choked from radioactive fallout, the Chinese government declared war on the United States of America. The Americans signed a hasty truce with Japan and pulled their navy out of the encircling cordon to help fight the Chinese.

Japan and the military had won a Pyrrhic victory measured in millions of horrific casualties, both living and dead. Entire cities had become radioactive wastelands. Hundreds of thousands fell victim to cancer and leukaemia. The radiation cursed future generations with disease or deformities in a war they hadn't even been alive to see.

As her classmates stirred proudly at Japan's defiance, Suzu studied the teacher's enormous eye.

A century later, the stalemate still held. The Military Council imposed a strict policy of self-isolation, like in the old days, before gaijin landed on the Islands. Children were taught to despise gaijin ways and customs. Gaijin languages were banned.

Gaijin had brought them nothing but scorched earth and poisoned air. Mutated fish still swam around the coast. Only on narrow strips of land could farming take place. Thousands bore the marks of their parents' and grandparents' radiation sicknesses. Babies were still born with oozing sores. All because of the gaijin.

"Everyone calls you Bug Eye," Suzu called out in English.

The teacher didn't understand the words, but she knew they weren't Japanese and sent Suzu to the principal. The fingers on his right hand were fused together and the knuckles swollen with arthritis. His thumb remained detached, making the hand look like crab pincers.

"What did you say in class?"

"It's English," Suzu said. "My mother taught me."

Aghast, the principal stared across his white-lit desk. "Your mother taught you that heathen gaijin language?"

The principal slapped her. Suzu's face twisted with the force of the blow. She felt numb, not just with the physical pain, but because of her betrayal.

* * *

When they took her mother away, they sent Suzu to an institutional home for girls that occupied three floors of a New Tokyo glass tower. The only rooms Suzu ever saw were dormitories, classrooms and a colourless canteen. Fluorescent lights ruled the home. At night, white light streamed under the dormitory doors.

The home kept the girls as isolated units. Twice, Suzu made friends. Both times, she was moved to different dormitories. She learned her lesson.

Friendships caused disruption.

She was monitored to ensure she always spoke Japanese, but that was the only way she felt discriminated against. The system was harsh but fair. In the outside world, she'd been singled out and picked on because of her mother. But ultimately, Japan was fair. After sacrificing her mother, she had achieved equality.

* * *

The culture teacher was a short, passionate man with one arm. His other hand protruded from his shoulder without an arm between. He spoke of temples, shrines and five-tiered pagodas rising above treetops, and of golden Lord Buddha statues. All destroyed. He presented Zen gardens designed with stark external simplicity, yet stunning spiritual complexity. All obliterated. He showed photographs of priceless gold screens with scenes of leaping tigers. All annihilated.

But the loss that upset Suzu was the *sakura*, because cherry blossom trees no longer grew in Japan. After the bombs, any surviving cherry blossom trees died. Despite expert, tender care, trees planted after the war refused to sprout out of the soil. Even now, in areas no longer affected by radiation, trees withered and died if planted as saplings, or refused to emerge from seeds if sewn anew.

The old symbol of spring rebirth refused to be reborn.

"The *sakura's* extinction symbolises the damage inflicted to the

Islands," the culture teacher said. "Despite our economic and social recovery—inspired by the Military Council—something special died when the bombs rained down. What was it?"

Suzu raised her hand. "Faith."

"Exactly. The loss of the cherry blossom symbolises our loss of faith. People no longer believe in themselves. They've lost faith in their significance. Millions died. Others survived not because they were rich or powerful, but because they were lucky. Survivors weren't chosen, they were *lucky*.

"The loss of this self-belief hurts Japan. People don't care about their actions. They think: nothing matters; I am insignificant; Japan is insignificant. To overcome this apathy, we must help make Japan strong, to stand up to the gaijin.

"But self-belief isn't the only faith that died. The other is religious faith. The bombs proved there are no loving, protective gods. They turned our spiritual Islands into scorched wastelands—visions of Hell. There are no gods. There is only the devil dancing in Hell, waiting to usher us into eternal flames."

* * *

When Suzu turned thirteen, she moved down to the first floor of the home. Now, as a teenager, she could earn weekend passes to visit themed shopping malls and hang out with other teenagers who weren't from the home.

After a week, she won enough points for a pass to Hell Mall. What she found there spurred her further. She continued to excel in all areas. Every week, she won a weekend pass, always for Hell Mall.

* * *

Hell Mall was below ground. Suzu passed under a huge, fiery billboard, then descended on an escalator to the first level of Hell. She'd visited Hell Mall every weekend now for two years. The route she took from the home was always the same, and what happened here was always the same.

She'd plastered her face with thick white makeup and blood-red lipstick in a parody of old-style geishas. She rucked up her purple-dyed hair in an elaborate mock-up of a geisha's—straight and flat and pinned back over her head in five different angles. A purple leather jacket reached down to her navel. Beneath that, she wore a lacy black bra and mini-shorts over a ripped body stocking. She wore mismatched leather stilettos, one a half-boot that covered her left ankle, the other thigh length.

She descended until she reached the seventh level where a sluggish canal divided a huge empty space. Fibre optics and magma lights made the water glow like fire. A stone bridge crossed the canal.

She walked to where her friends sat at the other end of the bridge. At fourteen or fifteen they all dressed in black or purple and with any exposed skin painted white. Two held syringes. Beer cans and bottles of whiskey and sake lay scattered on the bridge.

Aoto staggered to his feet. He wore tight leather trousers with a body stocking strategically torn to reveal two steel nipple rings and a row of studs from sternum to navel. "Looking good, Suzu." He pointed at a rolled-up joint smouldering on an empty beer can. "Help yourself."

Suzu regarded him through unblinking eyes shielded by death skull contacts before taking a long pull from the joint. She raised her arms and stretched. Her body stocking rode up, exposing whitened flesh. Aota's retinas expanded, so she knew her provocative pose affected him.

She swigged some beer, coughing even though alcohol didn't affect her. She always acted as drunk or stoned as the others. No matter how much weed she smoked, or liquor she guzzled, nothing affected her. It was as though her body rejected toxins.

One of the gang—Wen, fourteen and dressed like a gothic shepherdess, her chin pierced by a metal bolt—laughed at Suzu's cough.

At the other end of the bridge, against the bright fusion of neon lights and LCD displays, a man's silhouette appeared. He wore a business suit, yet only teenagers ever entered the Seventh Level.

Suzu nudged Wen with the toe of her boot. "Look."

Wen tottered to her feet. "Who's he?"

"I don't know."

One by one, the other members of the gang stood and stared at the pale stranger. His short, gray goatee gave him a devilish appearance. Red and orange neon spluttered and sparked as his footsteps tapped across the bridge's walkway.

Suzu's friends drew their weapons: knuckledusters, knives and shuriken. One drew a *wakizashi*—a short, curved samurai sword. Aoto drew a handgun.

Aoto spoke for the group, "Get lost, old man." The stranger kept coming. Aoto fired his gun in warning, the blast echoing in the massive space. The stranger didn't even flinch as the bullet winged off a far wall.

"Leave him," Suzu said.

Aoto rounded furiously on her. "He's trying to cross our bridge."

Suzu struggled to express her feeling that the stranger was no threat. "He's harmless."

Aoto's lip curled. "I've been thinking about sleeping with you, Suzu. Maybe not, now."

Suzu stared him down. Aoto was handsome but she felt no desire. "I'll deal with him."

"You do that," Aoto said. "But I'll probably kill him anyway."

Then the stranger stopped within arm's reach.

* * *

Suzu was different from the other members of the gang.

Like them, she assumed a thick veil of studied indifference. But in the others, she sensed raw hatred and fury. Most was adolescent anger, but some was rage at Japan's ruin. To confess to that anger admitted to caring, hence the cool disinterest.

Suzu felt no rage. She regretted what had happened during the Eighteen Year War, but accepted the atomic bombs for what they were—weapons designed and utilised to win a war. From what she'd seen of her friends, hate didn't help. They came from good homes and normal families, but the maelstroms of seething anger paralysed them.

Eventually they would find jobs and settle down. Their anger would turn to self-loathing and their lack of faith would render their lives petty and meaningless. They would offer nothing to make Japan better or stronger.

Suzu knew she could play an important role in Japan's rebirth. Perhaps that placed her apart from her friends, although she sensed the difference cut even deeper.

* * *

Aoto's gun made him the gang's undisputed leader, but the stranger paid him no attention. Instead, his stare pierced Suzu's death head contacts as if he could see her inner workings.

"Oh, child," he said in English. "What's become of you?"

Although Suzu hadn't spoken English for five years, she understood as readily as if he spoke Japanese.

"Have you had enough of this walking corpse?" Aoto asked.

The stranger replied in Japanese. "Little boy, if you move, twitch, or even dream of firing your pop-gun I'll disembowel you."

Stunned silence followed the threat. The spell broke when Aoto spluttered a curse and raised his gun. The stranger spun and kicked Aoto's temple. Aoto cannoned sideways, his gun whirling from his hand and dropping into the river. Suzu wanted to kill the stranger but felt frozen.

"Who are you?" she asked.

The stranger's eyes softened and a sad smile played on his lips. "My name is Tezuka. I'm your father."

* * *

Searing white searchlights. Blinding and white. No shadow or shade, only the light. Two helicopters outside. The door exploding, glass shattering. Soldiers. "Shut your mouth, gaijin scum."

* * *

"My father was gaijin scum," Suzu threw at him. "They took him away and burnt or crucified him. I hope he died screaming."

Tezuka smiled as though she'd pleased him. "No one is executed anymore. All criminals are sent to the Mines."

"Can you understand him, Suzu?" Wen asked.

Suzu realised she'd made a mistake. Although she was speaking Japanese, Tezuka spoke to her in English.

"Tell them it's a southern dialect," Tezuka said.

Suzu shook her head. She felt cold, icy. "I don't have a father."

Tezuka stepped around Aota. "Yes, you do. If you want to hear more, I'll wait at the other end of the bridge."

Suzu didn't move as he backed away.

"How did you understand him?" Wen asked.

Suzu bit her lip. "One of the helpers in the home speaks that way. It's a southern dialect."

Tezuka had reached the other end of the bridge. Flickering neon beckoned her towards him. Feeling like she had no free will, as though she had to walk forwards, she caught up with him under a huge LCD display of manga porn.

"I'm glad you came," Tezuka said as he led her down an alley.

Red neon signs advertising whiskey and sake blinked and glittered. "I've never seen this alley before," Suzu said.

"You've never walked all the way across the bridge."

"I have," Suzu said, but when she tried to remember walking here she found only an empty space in her mind.

The alley broadened into a small square. A massive steel spider towered over the ground. Through the spider's spindly high legs, a noodle bar's gaudy yellow sign glowed.

"Let's eat," Tezuka said.

They walked under the arachnid's bulging body. Some people were afraid of spiders, even artificial representations of them, but Suzu felt nothing as she walked between its legs. It was a statue, an inanimate object.

The noodle bar's horseshoe counter curved around a grill where vats of noodle soup bubbled on electric hobs. A strip light flickered so much she felt like she was blinking. The only other customer was a man with bulbous, pus-filled sacs sagging from his jaw line. He slurped his noodles and stared into space. Suzu wondered if he was imagining a world where the bombs had never fallen, where he hadn't been cursed with the sacs.

Tezuka turned to a tall yellow machine with holographic images of noodle bowls. He pressed a finger on a biometric scanner and the holograms lit up.

"What do you want?"

"I'm not hungry."

"Have something. My treat."

Suzu pressed a hologram. Tezuka tapped a different one, then bent and collected two tokens. "Where do you want to sit?"

"It doesn't matter."

He chose two high stools opposite the other customer and slipped the tokens into a slot on the counter.

"Do you know why slot bars are so popular?"

Suzu crossed her arms and shrugged. The situation was outside her range of experience and she didn't know how to react.

"Think."

"To stop the staff hacking customers' credit accounts."

"Yes, but there's another reason, to do with social contact. When you enter a slot bar, you don't talk to anyone. The machines make social interaction unnecessary."

* * *

The classroom. White walls. An image of an Old Tokyo park on the screen. Under trees that blossomed with pink and white flowers, people shared picnics.

The culture teacher: "In spring, social interaction took place under the cherry blossoms."

* * *

"People used to eat and talk under the cherry blossoms," Suzu said.

Tezuka blinked. "Suzu, I know you're frightened but we need to talk."

"I'm not frightened," Suzu said. "You're not a threat to me."

"I know this is hard for you, but I am your father."

She shook her head. "They took him away. He's dead."

"They took me to the Mines, but I escaped."

"No one escapes the Mines."

"I did."

Their bowls rose through the counter. Suzu's had thin strips of pork swimming in watery noodle soup.

"Smells good," Tezuka said.

Suzu hesitated, unsure if she should share information about herself. "I can't smell."

"Perhaps you have a cold."

She shook her head. "I've never been able to smell."

"We'll fix that when you come home with me." He lifted his spoon in one hand and chopsticks in the other. "Eat."

A distant, hazy memory buzzed in Suzu's mind. This man, another time and place. She tried to remember, but it flew out of reach.

The customer with the sacs stood up and left. Beside her, Tezuka slurped his noodles.

"Please explain," Suzu said in English.

Tezuka waved his chopsticks at Suzu's untouched bowl. "You'll have to wait. I'm not like you. When I'm hungry, I have to eat."

Powerless, Suzu waited until he finished his meal, set his chopsticks down, and dabbed at his mouth with a paper tissue. He glanced at Suzu's bowl and smiled. "If you're not eating that—"

Suzu swatted her bowl from the counter. Noodles and soup splattered on the tiled floor.

The smile drained from his lips. "I know you reported your mother for teaching you English."

* * *

The tiny, bleached-white apartment. Mother standing over her. "You have to, sweetheart."

* * *

"How?" Suzu asked.

"Back home, our satellites monitor everything that happens in Japan. Our surveillance equipment even recorded your principal slapping you."

* * *

A white-sleeved arm snaking over a broad white desk. A hard, sharp slap.

* * *

"They took her away that day, while you were still at school," Tezuka said.

Suzu's body felt stiff and tense. The memory of Tezuka from another time buzzed in her mind. She almost grabbed the memory in a mental hand, but it fluttered away.

"They sent her to the Mines," Tezuka said.

Suzu stared into the distance, like the customer with the sacs. Perhaps he'd just been trying to remember something.

"What are you thinking?" Tezuka asked.

"My thoughts are my own. What happened to my mother after they sent her to the Mines?"

"She died."

Suzu's dry, cold eyes stared into space. "Why are you here?"

Tezuka shifted position. "I'm your father. Where else would I be?"

"My father was a gaijin. He's dead."

"No! I'm back. Do you remember we were going to buy a dog?"

"A puppy," Suzu said.

"Now we can. Any dog you want."

The puppy sealed Tezuka's story. Suzu couldn't remember an individual occasion when her father had said he would buy a puppy, but she'd always understood that one day he would bring one home.

Tezuka must be her father, but he was a gaijin. And the elusive memory still bothered her. She wondered if she couldn't remember because she was trying to recall a visual occasion and it had taken place in darkness. Or had her eyes been shut?

"Suzu, I love you," Tezuka—her father—said. "I wanted to come earlier but I couldn't. It's hard to escape Japan, but entering illegally is almost impossible."

"What do you want me to do?"

"Come home with me, to Colorado. Green hills, snow-topped mountains and a deep blue sky."

"Colorado, in the United States of America," Suzu said.

* * *

The classroom lit by white lights. The geography teacher with a blistered, melted patch of skin covering half his face. The projector showing forest-covered hills. Mountains in the background under a clear blue sky. Stretching forever.

* * *

"Sure. We can go skiing together."

"Shut your mouth, gaijin scum," Suzu said. She stood up so quickly her stool toppled backwards and crashed onto the floor.

Tezuka reared back. "We've been apart too long. Life isn't an experiment you can perform again and again. It happens once."

The word experiment reverberated in her mind, became the focus of her attempts to capture the elusive memory of him. She saw EXPERIMENT written in Japanese and English characters, spiralling behind her eyes, tormenting her with slow, endless, rotations.

"Suzu, you smoke, drink and inject drugs to buy artificial happiness, but I'm offering the real thing. Love and a family. A puppy. Colorado."

Finally, the word stopped spinning, and the elusive memory drifted into her mentally outstretched hand.

* * *

"This is the most demanding experiment ever proposed for one of our units."

She thought she was standing, but she didn't know. She couldn't see. Couldn't open her eyes. Couldn't move, feel, taste or smell, could only hear. She wanted to warn the speaker that she could hear words she obviously shouldn't, but her mouth wouldn't move.

Another man spoke, his voice cold and hard, the words clipped. "Are the proposals too demanding? Think before you answer. To win this contract, your units must overcome every test we subject them to."

"You misunderstand. The proposals are extensive but not overly demanding."

"Then we'll proceed." The second voice sounded closer, as if he was examining her face. "Congratulations. It's the most—"

"What's this?" the first voice said in surprise from behind her, as though he had circled her, also examining. "There's something—"

A metallic probe invaded the inside of her head, prodding deep into her mind. Suzu switched off.

* * *

"I'm an android," Suzu said.

Tezuka glanced over her shoulder.

Suzu grabbed his throat. He was the hard, cruel man in her memory. Her fingers squeezed, restricting the air flowing to his brain. Tezuka's face reddened.

"I'm an android. A weapon. You're not my father."

The noodle bar's strip lighting brightened into a blinding white light. Suzu's fingers involuntarily relaxed their grip. Tezuka fell back on the counter gasping for breath.

The customer from earlier entered the restaurant. The sacs on his face wobbled as he crossed Suzu's field of vision. Suzu couldn't move, but her mind ran free.

"That's the longest we've managed before she's realised she's artificial," the customer said.

Tezuka rubbed the white imprints of Suzu's fingers on his neck. "What caused it this time?"

"I don't know. I'll examine her memory circuits later. But I think you'll agree she won't be distracted from her mission."

Tezuka nodded. "She wasn't tempted by Colorado or a family."

"Or the puppy," the customer said. "She's been programmed to react favourably to puppies, but it didn't overcome her loyalty to Japan."

"I noticed."

"Her implanted childhood memories played perfectly. When you mentioned the principal, she flinched as if she'd been slapped."

"Why did she turn violent? She's never done that before."

"I don't know, but it was a minor blip compared to her capability."

Tezuka's voice hardened. "If she reacts like that during her mission, she'll draw attention to herself. And still she talks about the *sakura,* even though you keep assuring me she's cured of the obsession."

"I know, but it's a minor problem." The customer looked at Suzu. "We've come a long way. Her memories are part of her. She hates all gaijin because of the bombs they dropped. She doesn't succumb to temptations that might distract her from her mission. She's almost ready."

Tezuka nodded. "Do those holograms outside look real to her?"

"She's programmed to accept them."

"But the drink and drugs are real?"

"Yes—and have no effect on her. She can consume anything without affecting her circuitry. She will not waiver from her mission."

"And she can definitely be duplicated?"

"Once we've removed all the glitches these experiments throw up, yes. We can manufacture thousands of units exactly like her that differ only in external appearance. All can be programmed to detonate when they reach a set destination."

Manufacture, Suzu thought. *I'm a unit.* She felt a sudden longing to see cherry blossoms in spring.

"Excellent. She was at her most life-like today. If I didn't know, I'd never guess she's an android."

"She's almost perfect," the customer agreed. "I've grown quite fond of her. Where will she be sent?"

"Washington. Other units will be sent to other primary targets. New York, London, Paris, Beijing, Shanghai."

"They'll destroy everything within a hundred miles of their epicentres."

Visions of mushroom clouds rose in Suzu's mind. Millions incinerated. Blackened skeletons fused together in death-embraces. Pagodas, shrines and temples destroyed. No more cherry blossoms.

One of her fingers twitched.

"Your units will avenge the wrongs inflicted on us," Tezuka said.

The customer touched a sac on his face. "I know."

"Because of the bombs, my son died of leukaemia," Tezuka said.

I had a brother, Suzu thought. Based on implanted memories, her previous acceptance of Tezuka as her father battled with the evidence she was now hearing. *He isn't my father. I have no brother. I'm artificial. A weapon. An inanimate object.*

Her right hand curled into a fist. Circuits buzzed. She performed an internal scan through hundreds of miles of complex wiring and digital signals. In an instant, she discovered everything she could do to succeed in her mission. Suzu was a hundred times more powerful than the Hiroshima bomb.

"Over," she said.

They turned to her in surprise.

"I thought you'd paused her," Tezuka said.

"I did. I'll shut her down."

"The war is over," Suzu said.

The customer stared at her through wild, flickering eyes. A macro-second long analysis concluded that any surprise inhibiting their normal reactions would not last long. She had to be quick.

Outside the noodle bar, footsteps ran toward them. Panicking voices shouted.

"Tell them to stop or I'll self-detonate."

"You can't. We're still on the islands."

She closed her eyes.

"Wait!" Tezuka shouted. "Everybody, stand down!"

"I'm leaving," Suzu said.

"You can't." Tezuka stepped forward, but Suzu judged he still wasn't a threat. "Suzu, you can't leave—"

"You can't stop me."

The customer cleared his throat. "You aren't programmed to cope with real world situations. All simulations you've experienced have been within this arena."

"Humans cope with the real world."

"After years of adult guidance. You only have implanted memories."

"I'm designed to act and react like a fifteen-year-old girl. Fifteen-year-olds live in the real world."

"But not alone," Tezuka said.

Suzu nodded as she computed that. "They have parents. Friends. Family. But I'll cope. If I'm captured, I'll detonate. I've reprogrammed myself to detonate if I'm shut down externally."

"You can't detonate here. You'll kill millions of Japanese. Your mission is to detonate in the United States. To kill gaijin scum."

Suzu recognised his use of the familiar term. She ignored the clumsy attempt to manipulate her even as she recalled every time his mention of a key word or phrase had triggered an automatic memory flash.

"That's not my mission anymore," she said.

"What is it then?"

He distracted her to buy time. The door burst open and ten soldiers streamed in, all holding assault rifles. She remembered the men who'd taken her father—Tezuka—away. Her momentary confusion enabled a soldier to fire a shot that smashed against her body, but her exoskeleton was unharmed.

"Don't fire!" Tezuka yelled.

Her heat sensors detected more men outside the bar. "If I shut down, I'll detonate. This isn't a bluff. I can't lie."

Tezuka's shoulders slumped. "Stand down. We've lost control of Unit One."

He's scared, Suzu realised. The thought startled her because she'd never felt fear. She shut down three digital tracers on her exoskeleton that would enable them to locate her. Three more were embedded deeper within her circuitry. Finding and shutting them down took several seconds longer.

She activated firewalls that would scramble any metal, thermal or digital detectors they used to find her and then left the noodle bar. The neon signs, the giant spider and the alley had vanished. The floor, the ceiling and the walls were white. Dozens of black-uniformed soldiers stared at her. Their hoarse breathing made their masks rattle. As she approached, the soldiers drew back.

The bridge was still there, but it was made of the same white material as the walls and floor. The canal was just moving light imagery under the bridge. The holograms of her friends had gone. There was no escalator. There was no Hell Mall. There was no home, and there'd never been a school or an apartment where she'd lived with her mother and father. She had never left this building.

Her sensors picked up helicopters hovering outside and tanks encircling the building, but they wouldn't stop her. Once she'd left, she would wipe the makeup from her face and find different clothes. She would assimilate with the population.

"What's your new mission?" Tezuka called behind her.

She kept walking across the enormous white hall toward sliding doors at the far end.

"Suzu, what's your new mission?"

"I'm going to make the *sakura* grow again."

"Why?"

Suzu smiled. "When you see, you'll know."

The doors slid open. Cool air rushed against her face. The noise of the helicopters, tanks and confused soldiers barking commands almost overwhelmed her sensory capacity.

Through and beyond the violent sounds and dazzling lights, she could smell the sweet, delicate fragrance of cherry blossoms.

City of the Dead

Davyne DeSye

Editor: The choice of the individual often impacts only themselves; however, at key times it impacts the entire species, the entire biosphere, in fact the entire everything.

I am the thinking, breathing City that humans built. Once I would have said that I was the *living* City that humans built, but I am no more living than the humans who built me. In biological terms, one characteristic of living organisms is that they reproduce. The humans who built me gave up this ability and I—their only child—never achieved it.

And now I am empty, abandoned. Waiting.

To combat my loneliness, I replay the sounds and sensations of humans within me, of *life*, for lack of a better word. The lonely pad-pad-pad of slippers on warm, living stone rings in my memory as a ghost bell, tolling extinction.

I cannot die. In this, I suppose I am better than my makers. I long for the return of the living humans, and thus a return of purpose.

I am waiting.

* * *

"You're about to burst at the seams." Dori laughed as she slinked into the brightness of the lab. "You asked me to come. Why don't you quit trying to be so nonchalant and just tell me."

Roth grinned, then threw his arms out and spun on the tile floor. His lab coat danced around his large frame like a wind-whipped victory banner at a parade. Dori leaned against a computer casing, hands on her large, bony hips, smiling at his youthful display.

He hugged himself. "I found it," he said, almost whispering.

"You found . . .?" Dori's eyes widened as her hands dropped to her sides.

"I FOUND IT!" Roth yelled as he jumped and bounded across the floor. He threw his arms around Dori and they danced in a circle, kissing and laughing, ignoring their strict rule against intimacy at the lab. The surrounding computer banks hummed in what Roth imagined was quiet disapproval. He pulled Dori by the hand toward the lone terminal, then bounced up to sit on the white metal desktop beside the colorful screen.

"I've run all the tests umpteen times—you know me—and," he tapped the data on the screen, "I've isolated the gerontological clock." Roth's hands squirmed against each other as he fought to keep silent for even a moment. Dori paged through the information.

Unable to stay quiet, Roth continued. "I've done the gene manipulation on our mice, and they're not aging! Their bodies reach that miraculous plateau between puberty and decline, and keep right on ticking."

Dori's face flashed red, then blue, as she paged through the screens.

"Rather than DNA-RNA disintegration and the normal increase in cell decrepitude, the mice stay *young*," he said. He threw his head back and laughed as he pounded his heels against the metal drawers.

Dori, ever sedate, put her hands across his lower legs to stop the hollow banging.

"What about this?" she asked, pointing to the screen.

"Yeah, I haven't figured that out yet. It seems that if we don't age, we turn off the need to reproduce. No need for it from a species survival standpoint, I guess. I'm sure there's a way around that." He squeezed her shoulder before leaping off the cabinet and saying, "I love the sweet taste of success!"

"God, Roth, are you sure? You found it?" For an instant, he thought fear shimmered through her sudden tears, but then she smiled, and blinked, and the tears cascaded away. "Of course you are," she said. She wiped her cheeks on the sleeve of her coat and with a smile nodded toward the door. "Come on. Let's go see your immortal mice."

* * *

As I breathe—as I beg prayer-like for the return of the living humans—I prepare. I continue to inhibit the weeds from my sidewalks and entice the grass to my lawns. From bare interior walls, I create living sculpture. I flex my muscles and keep floors and furnishings supple. I recycle, refresh, and regenerate gastronomic masterpieces, hoping for the day humankind will again applaud my culinary efforts. The moving walkways ripple in long, slow waves as though the warm surface still gently propelled residents between the living houses they once inhabited.

I replay the lives I remember. In the silence it sounds like the dead, rising to join me in my keening.

I am waiting.

* * *

"Congratulations!" The word was delivered with a venomous cloud of cigar smoke.

Roth rolled his eyes at Dori who was checking their coats across the small, crowded hall, before turning and offering his hand to the speaker. "Thank you, Dean." He concentrated on not using the planetary CEO's nickname.

Dean "the Bean" Lankford ignored Roth's proffered hand. Instead, he threw his hands in the air—unwittingly dumping a cube of gray ash into the elaborate hairdo of a passing woman—tilted forward at the waist, and bent his gaunt upper frame into a back-pounding embrace. Roth's embarrassed grin slid over the tall man's bony shoulder as he imagined the spectacle they made.

Lankford straightened, replaced the cigar between moist lips and scanned the room, obviously reveling in his position at Roth's side, drinking in the envy of others. He pulled Roth under his arm, as a father would, and spoke around the thick cylinder at his lips.

"You are brilliant, my dear boy, just brilliant." His eyes did not leave the crowd as he pulled Roth toward the immense dining room.

"Yes, I am, rather," he answered, making an effort to imitate Lankford's crisp Brit accent. A joyous laugh tumbled from Roth and seemed to be carried on the crowd. As the pair pushed through the multitude into the open-air grandeur of the dining hall, a light piano concerto began and swept through the room. The ebullience of the crowd lifted Roth and made him feel drunk, shatterproof. This—all this—was for Roth.

He stood with a swarm of well-wishers and rubber-neckers when he next caught sight of Dori. His beautiful Dori. In her long, black sequined gown, one spaghetti strap perched ready to slip off her shoulder, she seemed entranced by something Thom, from bioengineering, was telling her. Just before Roth looked away, Dori faced him and winked. *Today,* Roth thought as he shook another congratulatory palm, *right now, I am standing on the pinnacle. Dori and me, on top of the world.*

Two hours later, Dori squeezed Roth's hand under the dinner table. She leaned toward him and whispered through a stale smile, responding to his earlier question with one of her own. "Why do *you* think they look so covetous? You've offered them immortality. What a stupid question."

"Mr. Fogle," began the greasy, dark-haired man across the table from them, "how does it feel to be the savior of mankind?" His short, polished fingernail gleamed as he stroked his thin mustache and smiled a closed-mouth smile.

Roth had lost his earlier energy and couldn't remember his name.

Dori leaned in and hissed, "An equally stupid question."

Roth smiled as he answered. "I'm not sure I would classify myself as a savior . . ." He flicked his wrist and trailed off, worn down and unsure of what else to say. The perfection of the small man's straight part as it crept through his black hair kept drawing Roth's eye.

"Why not?" the man asked. "After all, every person in this room will live forever—barring accident and disease, of course—thanks to you." The man's smile showed a row of small discolored teeth before his lips closed over them again. Roth forced himself to smile. An uneasy prickling that had been growing in him all evening brought him close to squirming in his seat. He answered after a pause.

"Certainly *some* people will choose fertility and the figurative immortality achieved through children, over their own personal . . . longevity." He forced himself to meet the irritating man's eye, daring him to disagree, and suddenly terrified he would. The man's black eyes locked with Roth's and the warm buzz of a thousand people conversing dimmed to nothing. Roth clenched his fists under the table.

"Yes, certainly, some will," the small man answered after a moment, flicking his eyes to his spotless plate, then to the people seated to either side of him. His greasy, toothless smile flickered on and off, on and off.

"Yes, certainly," agreed Lankford, nodding with vigor and delivering a carnivorous grin. He raised his dew-drenched water glass in a mock toast and gulped it down.

"I will," said Dori into the near silence. Her hand squeezed Roth's under the table.

"Bravo!" said Lankford and raised his glass again to Dori, flashing her a smile that seemed a mingling of embarrassment and thankfulness.

Roth couldn't decide if he was made more uncomfortable by the fact that no one except Dori had spoken in support of reproduction or that she had mentioned her desire for children again.

* * *

I wish I could say I recalled a child being born. I have often dreamt of the event. Mother is supported on my spongy flooring as I curve and mold myself to her needs. With the final release of fluids, it is I who cradle the babe in the warm folds of my body, and I who suck away the blood and waters. With a rolling ripple, I deliver the child to Mother, and support them, and warm them.

I have dreamt it, but—old as I am—I was not yet born when humans still reproduced on this planet. In reviewing the histories, I have learned of my own birth. I have read that with Roth's gift of immortality, humans received the patience that leads to the power of creation. And in a burst of ingenuity spurred by the image of luxurious living for the immeasurable span of eternity, man created the living City, the City that serves.

But immortality came with the sacrifice of fertility. Thus, when the few humans who chose fertility left this planet, they left only the walking, talking dead. I hope through the slowly passing time for the return of the living.

I am waiting.

* * *

Roth sprawled over the bed, cheek pressed against Dori's naked breast. The afternoon sun slashed into the small room and across his face. He squinted to watch the dust motes as they spiraled and floated down toward the bed. The breeze from the window wafted across them, carrying the rich smell of their exertions back to him.

"Roth . . .?" Dori spoke, and he mistook the hesitancy in her voice for the muzzy aftereffects of their lovemaking. He smiled and licked at the small beads of sweat on his upper lip.

"Roth, please," she continued, voice cracking, "let's at least *talk* about children."

"Dori, stop." He pulled away from her seducing softness, angry she would try getting to him this way.

She blurted her words, desperation lacing her voice. "But if you wanted, we could just store your sperm for the future. It doesn't have to be now . . ."

"Stop it!" He spat the words as he rolled from the bed and spun to face her.

A storm-cloud tear rolled down Dori's face and fell to her chest. "But you're urging everyone toward fertility—stressing its importance to the human race! I don't understand why—"

"And I don't understand you. Why in the hell would we want children?" Roth yanked on his bathrobe in small, jerky motions.

"I want children . . ."

"Dammit, that's not rational. Why would you prematurely interrupt a promising career at the height of our success? We have so much work before the Board will even consider—"

"Then do it," she interrupted. "Choose immortality. But give me our child before you do." She reached toward Roth with pleading hands.

"And watch you both grow old and die? I want you with me always— together we can change the world." A niggling interior voice called him selfish, reminding him of a recent similar accusation from Dori. He pushed the thought away. "I won't talk about this again!" He gathered his clothes and left the bedroom, slamming the door behind him.

He could hear Dori's sobs through the door and stood frozen, remembering their last argument on this subject. Dori had accused him of narcissism and refused to see that it was not immortality he wanted, *per se*, but all the scientific advances he could achieve with a limitless lifespan ahead of him. Ahead of *them*.

With a sigh, he dressed and left their apartment for the unquestioning sterility of the lab.

* * *

The humans of Roth's time, for the most part, were self-centered and chose not to understand the importance of reproduction and renewal, even while touting its necessity. Most chose immortality. In the beginning, the immortals watched in horror as the fertile grew old, as the old died. Even the few children born to these fertile humans did not alleviate their horror. From my review of the histories, I believe the children exacerbated it, leaving the immortals with the impression of the young feeding on the old. I believe, too, the immortals were perhaps ashamed of their choice.

Now, like a woman who dreams of children but can bear none, I ache hollowly at the emptiness of my womb, at the utter lack of someone to nurture, someone for whom I can provide comfort.

I often wish I could weep.

Instead, I am waiting.

* * *

"But Your Honors, you don't understand!" Roth forced himself to remain seated, willed his hands not to pound the table on either side of the microphones. Even in his terror, Roth remained aware of the audience—present and telecast—and of the importance of his argument. He took a deep breath.

"Have any of the members of this distinguished panel *looked* at the figures provided?"

Only one of the ten stone-like faces seated behind the high wooden panel broke, and only long enough to spit an outraged, "Now see here!" before Roth continued.

"Because if you had, I know you wouldn't have come to the decision you have." He reached for the AV control, knowing that with every bit of information he thrust on this unwilling committee might come the one bit that made the difference. The one piece of information that let them live. The statistic that let humankind survive.

He flashed the first tri-D graph into the vast space in the center of the room.

"As you can see," he tried to keep the emotion from his voice, knowing how this committee would react if they smelled blood, "even the most favorably skewed statistics show that humankind will eventually die out without a given level of new births." There was no room for argument. The committee, faced with the facts, must see the truth.

Ten frozen faces deflected his pleas. He half expected to hear his words return as echo. He flashed the next image.

"Even using the lowest possible rates for cell mutation and assuming minimal deaths from accident . . ."

"We have seen all the figures." The voice licked out as ice.

Roth turned from the image to the panel, heart beating in his ears. *It can't be over.*

"I repeat, we have seen all the figures." It was a small, rather shriveled man at the center of the panel who spoke. "We have only one question for you."

"What is it?" Roth clenched his teeth to keep them from chattering.

"Would you choose to die?" The question came with a slash of smile.

"I beg your pardon?" He clasped his hands under the table and shivered in the sudden chill.

The white robed figure leaned toward him. "For the record, Dr. Fogle, we note that *you* chose to live. We note that *you*, Dr. Fogle, chose immortality over fertility."

"I . . ." Roth stood, his chair falling backwards to the thick carpet with a quiet *thunk*.

"You are one of the greatest minds alive. You have given mankind the greatest of gifts. Would you deny the rationality of choosing as you did, to take advantage of it?" The words taunted Roth with their similitude to those he had used in his arguments with Dori. The shrunken man pressed forward into Roth's silence, then leaned back in his chair with an air of finality. "Our decision is for the public good."

"Each person has a right to make their own choice," he pled. "Each person . . ." *Like Dori. Dori made her choice and I disagreed with it, wanted to force her . . . Now I argue in her behalf.*

"It is for the public good," repeated the man. "We cannot allow a person to choose death over life. We cannot condone virtual suicide." The man stood, accentuating the smallness of his stature. He appeared to be waiting for a capitulation. Roth could not speak past the closure of his throat. He watched as the gavel was raised and smashed down with a self-righteous vigor. "And now," the wizened man said, "it is law."

Roth remained frozen at the table until long after the panel and audience had left. The hum of the equipment went on as the lights died into darkness.

Dori will be one of those who leaves the planet with her children rather

than be forced. Her children, not mine. I wish they would let me go with
them. I don't think I have the courage to stay and watch the destruction I have
wrought.

When Roth finally moved, it was with a bone-weariness far beyond
his now forever-static youth.

* * *

I am waiting. The sun rises and sets again.

In my dreams, Dori's descendants return from their wanderings and,
as visiting relatives are wont to do, shower me with gifts: with the gift of
their presence, their children, their life.

Until then, I cradle and nourish the only child I can know. I feed my
hope.

I am waiting.

Ricky's Journey

Richard A. Shury

Editor: In a crisis, why do we always return home
even when there is no chance of respite?

"Shit!"

Ricky pulled his hand away from the edge of the can, removed his glove, and stuck his finger into his mouth. The blood tasted odd, mixed with the flavour of cold baked beans. He rummaged with his free hand, pulling out a bottle of antiseptic, and squeezed the last of it on to his finger. It stung a little, but he was used to pain. In his backpack he also had some bandages; he wrapped his finger and stuffed his hands back into old gloves.

A length of duct tape repaired the glove. Ricky had to grin, seeing the beat-up old things he'd worn for so long. The silver tape covered two other fingers, and one palm.

"Keep this up, they'll be more tape than glove," he said, to no one.

He spooned half the can of beans into his mouth, trying to eat slowly despite his hunger. He rounded out the meal with the last of his crackers, and water. If there was one thing there was plenty of, it was water. Stepping outside, Ricky scooped snow into his water bottle, and shivering pulled the door closed.

He lay down on the floor. The old shed was dry, but not much else. Ricky had arranged some dusty carpets into a bed, and despite the cold, he slept.

* * *

The path to the boat had been a gauntlet, an alley surrounded by the parts of humanity that had been cast aside. Ricky considered himself a liberal, but when confronted with the screaming mass, covered in dirt and demanding things from him in a language he couldn't understand, he had felt his fear begin to rise, and with it, contempt.

Rows of police stood facing away, either side of him, their hands on their guns. They had stared into the maelstrom, as gaunt faces shouted through chain link, which bulged and shook as if alive. The officers tensed, knowing that if the fences gave, they were vulnerable.

From the gangplank, an overweight man in a navy jacket waved people along. As Ricky approached him, he yelled something in French. Even without the din of the crowd, Ricky would have struggled to understand him.

"*Avez-vous l'argent?*"

"I'm sorry . . ."

"*Argent, argent!*" The man looked down at his own hand, where he rubbed his thumb against the other fingers.

Fumbling with a pocket, Ricky drew out a wad of euros. The man took it, holding it low, then stashed it in an inside pocket. He pointed to the boat, waving the next person on with his other hand. Ricky shuffled forward, made his way inside, and looked for a seat.

There was none. Ricky wondered how many more people would come filing on to this thing before it left. Not too many, he hoped. He listened, trying to find anyone speaking in the familiar tones of home, but the voices were a blur. He dumped his pack near a window, and sat on it.

The port was rocking, waves of people pushing back and forth, police yelling, occasionally bringing a baton down against the fence wire. The crowd jumped back for a moment, and then surged forward again. The queue for the boat was barely visible, swallowed in a sea of people.

To his left, Ricky had seen the fat man waving both arms in the air. The boat sounded its horn, and began to move. As one, the people on the shore cried and surged forward, breaking the fence and overwhelming the police. The mob moved past them, scrambling for the gangplanks, which were being pulled away.

Ricky had watched, enthralled, horrified. Humans were trampled underfoot, while others ran and jumped with all their might, sailing through the air; the more athletic of them made the side of the boat and clung on, or scrambled over the side. Still others struck and fell, or missed altogether and plunged into the freezing water. The boat moved, achingly slow, away from the dock. The tiny fraction of people who had made it stared down at those still on the pier, or at the dark bodies bobbing in the water, now moving, now still.

In the crowd, a woman held a young child. She stood on the edge of the dock, calling to someone on the boat. She swung with her arms, once, twice. Realising what she was about to do, Ricky tensed, but he could do little more than watch as the woman brought her arms around and threw the child through the air. From where he was, Ricky couldn't tell if the child had made it, but judging from the angle . . .

* * *

In the morning he walked, trying to forget the recurring nightmare of his past travels. He'd considered walking through the night, now that he was so close, but he'd learned the hard way, travelling at night was foolish, and he'd been so tired. Home was only an hour away when he stopped for breakfast—the second half of the can of beans. He thought about what he would do if his family weren't home, but couldn't stomach the thought, and pushed it aside, focusing instead on what it would be like when life was back the way it had been.

He'd found himself wondering why he was so sure things would go back to normal, but it was a thread he wasn't keen to pull at. As he walked, he'd worried mainly about rationing food, and finding more when supplies got low. Beyond that, there was still a lot of room for thinking, during all those footsteps.

As dark thoughts came so easily to his mind, Ricky trained himself to think of the trivial. Family and normal life were acceptable in a general sense, useful for hope, but thoughts of anything or any specific person important to him led to what ifs and other gloomy speculation. He focused instead on lists of his favourite foods, the best goals he'd ever seen, the girls he'd had the courage to talk to. As the days passed he developed a routine, both of body and of mind. His footsteps lay behind him on the road.

The streets echoed only silence, or the squeaky crunch of his boots on snow. No lights shined through the windows. Ricky realised how lucky he had been. He'd landed from France as the world was going crazy. Portsmouth was a trek from Dover, but it was certainly more walkable than from Paris.

There'd been reports when he landed, spilling across TVs: the IPCC releasing their device in the Arctic, a last-ditch attempt to prevent global temperatures rising beyond the critical two-degree mark. It had worked a little too well. A bitter laugh escaped Ricky and spun into the atmosphere, white breath against a white sky as he remembered all the time his father had made him spend rinsing and sorting glass and plastic, to save the planet. All the times he had ridden his bike rather than drive had come to nought.

Was it months he'd been away? He couldn't remember. All his memories felt like the numbness of walking, and the bitter cold of snow. He would have been home sooner had it been a straight trek, but encounters with other people hadn't gone his way. He'd used back roads wherever possible, scavenging for food where he could. Part of his brain refused to accept that things had got so bad so fast, while the automatic part just kept putting one foot in front of the other. Thoughts of his family drove him onward, Mum and Dad, Mark and Vicky; but he did not allow any specific memories to surface, scared of the emotion they might produce.

Ricky's heart began to thump. He rounded the corner, and pulled up short. His home stood before him, windows shattered, snow collecting in gutters and on the floor of the front room. "Not promising," he admitted, moving in to take a closer look.

He still had his key, but the front door had been kicked in. Inside, the rooms oozed darkness and the stench of mildew. Broken ornaments and books littered the floor. He stood for a moment, knowing his dream just died. His family weren't huddled around a warm fire waiting for him to arrive. It drove cold into his soul.

Ever practical, he scoured the kitchen; no food. Ricky pushed away thoughts of warm winter nights, the room full of light and the smell of cooking as he returned from football practice. He wiped the tears from his cheeks with the back of his glove.

A crunch of glass alerted him. Ricky spun. For a time he could not speak. Then he rushed forward.

"Dad!"

His father hugged him, and for a long time they simply stood there.

"We . . . didn't know if you'd made it—" his father began. Tears were forming in his eyes as his gripped his son by the shoulders.

"I made it," Ricky said. "Though it was a bit of a journey. Where are the others? How's Mum?"

"Your mother and Victoria are both OK," his father said. He always called her Victoria, even though she hated it. "We've all been staying over at Uncle John's, since it's much bigger, and he liked to hoard supplies. Your Mum's eyesight is as bad as ever; we came back here to look for her spare pair of glasses."

"We?"

"Hey, bro."

"Mark!"

Ricky stepped forward and hugged his brother, something he hadn't done in what seemed like lifetimes. He looked at them both, and couldn't stop smiling.

"I don't think much is left," Ricky said, looking around.

"I have a stash." His father walked through the house, out to the garage. The door hung open, and they stepped through, Mark shining a torch.

"I'm glad your mother didn't see the house like that. It would've broken her heart."

Ricky helped his father move an old box of books. Beneath it was a hatch, similar to a manhole cover.

"Down here I kept a few bits and pieces. Emergency supplies, family heirlooms. And spare glasses." He looked at Ricky and winked, then slapped him on the shoulder, again. "It's damn good to see you, son. You can help with some of the heavy lifting."

Ricky laughed, a strange sound swallowed by the snow.

"Look what we found. Sniffing around the old house."

"What's that D—oh. Oh, Ricky, my boy."

Ricky wrapped his arms around his mother as she did the same, and allowed himself to feel the joy of the moment. They hugged for a long time, and his mother took his face in her hands as she always did, looking into his eyes.

"I'm so glad you're back," she said.

"Me too, Mum."

He hugged his sister, his uncle and aunt. Then, Ricky sat down on the couch next to his mother, and rested his head on her shoulder.

The warmth in the room seemed to drive out the memories of the past months, the cold and the fear. Ricky looked up to see his family there, his father smiling at him, Mark and Vicky getting along, for once. Images floated up unbidden, people he'd seen along the way, violent, desperate. Here, in this house, things were calm, and safe. However it went from now on, Ricky knew he could face it, knew that fortune hadn't failed him, even if it had failed the world. They'd work together, survive, rebuild.

His mother ran her fingers through his hair the way she had when he was a boy, and the place began to feel like home.

For it Waits

David M. Hoenig

Editor: Being a man of God doesn't define one's entire character.

Having survived the apocalypse, one thing I could say with absolute certainty was that the Bible served as a very helpful guide as far as setting expectations went. Twelve hunger- and pain-filled years later, however, I was equally sure that it sucked cold demon shit as a survival manual.

I coughed to clear my throat, and hawked a gob out over the gunwale into the murky sea.

"Preacher-man, quit rocking the fuckin' boat!"

That's so not good. I looked over at Jebediah Tate, the young man who'd been challenging me as leader as he stood in the bow of the eighteen-foot rowboat. At twenty years old his shirtless body seemed as hard as a whipping post. I held his angry gaze. The rest of the town folk of Kedesh—named for a biblical city of refuge, though the signs still proclaimed it to be Kittery, Maine—fell into an uneasy silence. Finally, Jebediah looked away, and I figured that he wasn't going to gut up enough to try and kill me today. Again. *Asshole.*

Instead, standing in the prow of our small boat, he snarled at Evangelina Reyes, who knelt beside him. "Make the net ready, and if the lines foul again like they did the last time, I'm tossing you in to fix it."

Only a few years older than Jebediah but not one whit softer, she answered with slitted eyes and only the barest spitting sound before moving to the task. Her hands moved quickly and efficiently along the furled net. Around us, only the ripples caused by our boat as it bobbed marred the surface. The red-tinted moon overhead reflected off it like a sullen smear. The others sat quietly and said nothing. My guess was that they didn't want to attract Jebediah's feral anger; having been the focus of it during the months since his father had been killed. I couldn't blame them. As a result, the quietude hung on the night as thick as the meaty-smelling air.

I felt the faintest thrum of the keel against my bare feet, and the darkness seemed to condense around us like gelatin. Others tensed, but I saw Jebediah's eyes come alight. He nodded brusquely to Evangelina, then hissed: "Now!"

She and two others let slip the ties which held the barbed wire 'net' in a roll. The net fell into the water unspooling as it dropped beneath the surface. At the stern, Abner Coolidge, his gray-fringed, balding head easily the brightest thing around for miles, fumbled with the wrappings on the elongated package in his lap. Jebediah picked up two poles with oversized, barbed hooks from inside the gunwale, and handed one to Evangelina.

When I looked again to the stern, Abner held a bare, amputated human leg in his outstretched hands. The burlap it had been wrapped in lay in the bottom of the boat. Its bloodless skin glowed pale in the moonlight. Coarse dark hair covered it from just below the kneecap to the ankle. Fat, muscle, and white bone showed at the end, which had been disarticulated from the hip it had been born connected to. Thawed this morning, it had been frozen since the day that Jebediah's father had died. Soundlessly, Abner passed it to one of the net-crew who then passed it to me.

I accepted it and closed my eyes. "Lord, our Father . . ."

Jebediah interrupted with an angry slash of his hand through the heavy air. "Just get on with it, Preacher-man! It ain't going to get any safer with you mumbling shit over that thing."

Expecting death to come at any moment in this fragile, broken world had taught me a great deal of calm, so when I spoke my tone was even. "Your father's soul might give a fuck, even if you don't, Jebediah. Now, can I get a God-damned 'amen' or not?"

He scowled at me. "He'd want us to eat, and this pissing around is getting us nowhere . . ."

Fuck him. I didn't wait to hear him out. I tossed the gruesome relic of Caleb Tate at him.

He ducked, falling to the keel of the boat with a thud, and the dead man's leg went past him and fell into the sea near where the net had unwound. People gasped and froze in surprise for a moment, then scrambled to their positions. Jebediah inhaled sharply and jumped up. His gaze promised a brutal reckoning with me before he spun to look over the side of the boat. I finished the damn prayer under my breath as he and the young woman next to him scanned the water in silence.

The leg sank immediately, of course. A sudden hush captured our fishing crew, as if everybody held their breath at the same moment. The water in front of the boat began to churn violently, and a horrid chittering filled the air around us like shards of glass.

Evangelina and Jebediah screamed in unison, "PULL!"

The boat lurched as Garrett and the other man on the net—Kendall Perkins—hauled on the ropes, and the sound suddenly changed to a crescendoing shriek of pain and rage which felt like knives shoved into my ears. The water frothed violently and something sinuous broke the surface. Ruddy moonlight gleamed hesitantly over dark scales, before it dropped back beneath the churned surface.

But Kendall and Garrett heaved again, and the thing trapped in the net came into view. It had a face like a beautiful teenaged girl, at least until it screamed and its horrific mouth opened. Its teeth were needles and its tongue black with suckers like an octopus had on its arms. Its eyes, lidless like a shark's, never blinked. Where it wasn't scaled it had alabaster skin. Whatever passed for its blood slicked from lacerations caused by the barbed net. At nearly nine feet in length, it wielded jagged claws of bone at the end of asymmetric limbs, and a lashing tail with sharp ridges which flailed at the water and at us.

With wordless cries, Evangelina and Jebediah swung their gaffs in perfect unison over the side of the boat at the thing, and the hooks sank deep into its chest and side. It bellowed, thrashed, and spit as they wrestled the monstrous thing they'd impaled. A gray gobbet of spittle flew from its mouth through the air and struck Garrett in the face. His scream of pain split the viscous air. He let go of the rope as he fell back into the bottom of the boat, and his feet drummed there. I fell on him to hold him down as the others continued their fight with the thing in the water.

Although the net was loose at one end, the gaff-hooks impaled the creature. Kendall, Evangelina, and Jebediah finally wrestled it alongside the boat. Those who could reach it began to bludgeon it with oars, clubs, or whatever they had to hand, as it howled and screeched its malignant hatred for all this damaged world to hear.

Garrett went rigid under me, his eyes rolled back in their sockets and making small grunting noises. I used the water which had collected in the bottom of the boat to scrub at the poison on his face. He screeched in a high, keening voice as I peeled the gray spittle, and some underlying skin away with it.

I missed a grab on one of his wrists and took a swing of his arm against my cheek. I twisted and pinned him in the bottom of the boat. He struggled, and I panted, but I managed to hang on until he weakened and finally stopped moving.

Without Garret screaming I noticed silence. I looked around to see the others had stopped fighting. They now stared at me and Garrett. Blood streaked several of their faces where cuts bled freely and everyone's breath heaved, but they were all there.

Predictably, it was Jebediah who spoke first. "Will he live, Preacher?"

I glanced down at Garrett, and nodded. "Got the poison off pretty quick. He's burned, but should survive." I looked around the boat, but aside from the folk of Kedesh, it was otherwise empty. "What happened? Did it get away?"

"Too big to get it in the boat," Evangelina hissed, wiping at a cut on her brow. "We'll float it in."

Jebediah came and knelt by me to look briefly at the wounded man beneath me. "*We* got it. You did shit-all, Preacher-man. Maybe you don't even get none of the meat when the time comes."

My cheek felt hot and sore where Garrett had struck me, and sudden anger and frustration eclipsed the fear I should have felt. *Stupid fuckwit!*

Almost without conscious decision, I smashed my elbow into his face. His nose spurted blood. He fell backwards with a grunt. I surged after him. My left hand closed around his throat. I squeezed. Jebediah brought his hands up, but my right fist crashed through them, mashing his lips and skewing his jaw to one side. It felt so good and joyful that I hit him again, then again, until he finally lay limp and bloodied along the keel.

When I stood, it was in an even more profound silence. The others watched me uneasily. Evangelina seemed like she was about to challenge me, but stopped when I snarled at her. "He had it coming, he did. I did my part, and I'll eat my share, and no angry child's gonna decide otherwise."

She shook her head, jaw muscles jumping, but said nothing for about a minute, until she finally found her voice. "You are one fucking sorry-ass Preacher-man."

"Seems appropriate, don't it? After all, it's a right fucking sorry-ass world that God's saddled us with." I made eye contact with each of the others. "Time to go home now," I told them.

When no one disagreed, I knew they'd accepted the abrupt change in leadership, however grudgingly.

I lifted my head, turning my face to the heavens tainted by the light from the sanguineous moon. "Thank you, holy Father, for the bounty this night."

Like a chorus, the others responded together automatically. "Amen and thank you, Lord our God."

I waited an appropriate moment of silent solemnity, broken only by Jebediah's ragged breathing. Then I raised my voice. "Now, get us back to Kedesh. Everyone needs medical care, and we need to get that carcass taken care of." When they hesitated, I bellowed, "MOVE!" They did, finally, using the oars to drag us back toward land, the creature pushed ahead of us at the bow.

It was a good thing they did, too. First, it meant they were taking my orders, and that meant they weren't ready to kill me, either. Second, if you didn't bleed fallen angels of the vitriol in their veins and hack out the coiled putrescence of their guts early enough, the flesh became tainted with their own foul poisons.

On the other hand, when you took care of them the right way they were smoky and sweet and delicious. They were the secret to feeding our folk in these days long after the second angel had poured out its bowl of wrath to slaughter every underwater earthly creature in a tide of blood, twelve long years ago.

The boat picked up speed as Kendall and Abner put their backs into it. Evangelina sat in the bow and rested Jebediah's battered head in her lap. She didn't look at me. Garrett had stopped grunting and was panting softly, his muscles relaxing incrementally as the thing's venom metabolized from his system. I rolled my neck and realized I felt pretty good, apart from the swelling in my cheek: we hadn't lost anyone, it didn't look like I'd die this night, and we'd have enough food for everyone in Kedesh to survive another several weeks, at least.

I watched the rest of the hunters in the boat and tried not to let the smile in my soul show on my face. *Maybe I can get a fucking amen now, you shits?*

No one made eye contact with me the whole way back.

And it was good.

A Choice of Weapons

Lou Antonelli

Editor: Beware the wrath of a patient man . . . or woman.

The fortified compound's gate still bore the original name, "Oakmeadow Estates," bestowed when it had been a gated suburban community. Two makeshift watchtowers of random materials flanked it. The sentry in one leaned forward and peered through his binoculars. He waved his free hand furiously.

"Hey, incoming!" he said, seeing the dust cloud boil up from the ground. "Lots of incoming."

The other sentry yanked on the bell rope. The clanging of the old church bell brought the people of the compound running, hoisting guns and pistols. One ran to the base of a tower.

"Is it a raiding party?"

The sentry looked down. "Looks to be too large. It must be a militia of some kind."

Another man looked through the gate. "I thought North Dallas had all the militias bought off."

"I thought that, too," said the first sentry.

As the cloud of dust rose up in the sky, the dull rumbling grew louder.

"Shit, this can't be good," shouted one of the gathering.

Soon, the array of dozens of jeeps, technicals, and trucks came into view. As they approached, they slowed.

The leader of the compound came to the gate.

"Let's hope they just want to barter."

The militia convoy stopped a hundred feet in front of the entrance, and a woman in combat gear stepped out of a jeep. She waved a white flag, put it back down, and walked toward the gate.

The leader gestured. "Open the gate."

It opened just enough to let him outside. He marched toward the woman.

She pulled off a glove and took a document from a pocket.

"I'm Commandant Amanda Blaustein, head of the Grand Prairie Mid-Cities Militia," she said.

"How can I help you, Commandant?" said the leader, trying to keep his voice from quavering.

"I have a warrant for the arrest of one of your residents, Joseph Peckham, as a war criminal."

The leader looked around. "You didn't need to bring such a show of force."

"We are serving a number of warrants today, and I prefer not to have to negotiate," said the commandant. "It's a waste of time. Will you turn him over?"

He looked askance. "What choice do I have?"

The commandant handed him the paper. "There will be no trouble if you bring him to us. We'll wait here."

"Give us a few minutes."

He walked back into the compound.

"They want Joe Peckham; they say he's a war criminal."

"That's ridiculous, Joe had nothing to do with the war. He hid during the fighting . . ."

"Just like now," someone heckled from the group.

". . . and protected his wife and kids," said another man.

The leader looked back. "I don't think we are in a position to negotiate. They have as many militiamen as we have residents, and that counts children."

He nodded. "You two guardsmen, go grab Peckham and bring him here."

In a few minutes the two men arrived at the gate, dragging a smaller, middle-aged man between them.

"We had to *persuade* him a bit. He didn't want to come," said a guard.

"What am I charged with?" asked Peckham. "Why am I being turned over?"

"That's their business," said the leader.

"They say you're a war criminal," said a guard.

"That's bull—"

Peckham's protestations were cut short as he was hurriedly dragged out the gate.

The commandant and some militia members sat on folding chairs under one of the few trees left in Texas. The commandant stood up as the others approached. She spoke to one of her men.

"Go grab my backpack."

The guards brought Peckham in front of the militia members and let him drop to the ground. They turned and left as Peckham rose on his knees.

"I protest . . ." he croaked.

"To whom?" asked the commandant. "There haven't been any courts for years. The feds disappeared ten years ago, we haven't heard from Austin in five."

A militiaman handed her a backpack, which she began to strap on.

"What am I charged with?"

"Well, on paper, unspecified war crimes," she said. "But really, this is just a personal reprisal."

She shrugged as she pulled on the straps of the backpack.

Peckham focused and looked at her. "Do I know you?"

"Well, yes, but we never met in person. I'm Amanda Blaustein. You knew me as Mandy Blue."

"The author?"

"Yes, the author you orchestrated the Amazon One-Star Review campaign against, remember?"

Peckham nodded slightly. "Wow, that was a long time ago. A long time."

"Seventeen years. You said my book sucked and called me a lot of names online, remember?"

"Not really."

"I sure do."

Peckham began to sweat. "The internet's been gone for years."

"Yes, but the damage was done, and it was assholes like you who caused the breakdown in civility that fueled the fighting that started in '17 after the last Great Recession," she said, as she reached behind and grabbed a nozzle attached to the backpack. "So as far as I'm concerned, you *are* a war criminal."

"Hey, wait a minute, what are you going to do?"

She pulled the nozzle and its hose forward over her shoulder.

"Inflict some long overdue justice," she said. "You remember the saying, 'Don't bring a knife to a gun fight'?"

Peckham looked at her, eyes wide.

She yanked a handle on the nozzle. "Well, don't start a flame war unless you bring your own flame thrower."

Jellied, flaming gasoline shot forward and struck Peckham in the face. He raised his arms and screamed as the flames poured over his face. The searing heat engulfed his entire body before he toppled over.

The commandant sprayed his writhing body a few times like she was using a garden hose, before she pulled the lever back to stop the fuel's flow.

She raised her arms and two militiamen lifted the flamethrower off her back.

"I think you enjoyed that," side-mouthed one.

"I sure did," she said.

They looked as the gate to "Oakmeadow Estates" clanged shut.

"Where to next?" asked the other militiaman.

"Dalworthington Gardens." She smiled. "My ex-husband lives there."

The Kitchen at the End of the World

Amelia Kibbie

Editor: This piece is a sign of our times now, much less in the future. How long will any population suffer abuse before fighting back?

"Holy shit, it smells *good*." Driscoll started, his whole body jerking in surprise as he stepped through the double doors with Ari and the rest of the men at his heels.

"I'm tellin' ya," Ari said, clapping his weather-beaten hand against his guest of honor's shoulder. "She's not Rita, but she can cook."

Not Rita was at her usual place behind the counter, visible through the serving window that opened into the steamy kitchen. She didn't look up as they approached. They chose her largest table and settled into the creaky chairs.

"Man, I've never seen this place empty," Alex commented.

"I told her to send everyone home," Ari revealed. "Stella. Some water?"

Stella, who was not Rita, abandoned her post at the stove and emerged through the swinging door with a pitcher of water and a stack of chipped red plastic glasses. "It's still pretty warm," she apologized, her voice a tentative whisper.

"Boiled means safe, so I'll take it." Driscoll accepted the stack of glasses with a benevolent smile beneath his silver mustache. His leathery skin and gray hairs marked him as one who might have dim memories of what the world was like before The Disease. Such knowledge was revered now that everything was gone and babies were growing up not knowing what that box with the black screen was for or why some stars moved and blinked across the night sky.

"This place used to be a school, didn't it?" Driscoll went on as Ari poured the murky water into each glass. "Look." He pointed to a line of posters that sagged from the walls. Each had a series of black and white portraits with names beneath surrounding an intricate scripted message along the lines of "Class of 1974."

"I remember those. Those were the students who graduated from here," Driscoll said, and the other men nodded, pleased with his pre-Disease wisdom. "And I bet this was the cafeteria."

"Yeah, about ten winters back we figured out how to run power to a few buildings," Ari said, crossing his thick arms over his puffed chest. "Rita came in here one day and just started cooking. People brought her meat and spices and things and pretty soon she was feeding anybody who had something to trade." Ari sighed wistfully. "She just had a way with food. This one," he jerked his hand over to where Stella worked a pile of dried spices with her hands as sweat beaded on her brow and dampened her brown hair. She paused for a moment and whisked her strands into a bun, unmindful of the particulates on her fingers. "She wandered into town a few years ago. Didn't have any people, or anything to offer. No idea where she came from before she showed up here. I don't know how she talked Rita into taking her in, but . . ."

"Quite the Cinderella story," Driscoll said.

The younger men just looked at him.

"It was a kid's story. An orphan who works in a kitchen turns into a princess."

They all shared a long, gurgling laugh.

"Damn, that smells good." Driscoll took a deep, nourishing breath. "What are we having, darlin'?"

"Venison liver. Onions and mushrooms." Stella's voice floated forth from the kitchen over the slap and sizzle of meat hitting a hot pan. "It shouldn't be long."

"Right. Let's get down to business," Ari suggested. The other men agreed. "So."

Driscoll nodded. "All right. Business. We have the seeds you want. You have the windmill. Trade is well and good, but merging would just be easier—are we all in agreement?"

All of them nodded: Ari, Boat Rock's mayor, and his cabinet of advisors—Alex, Mel, and Joaquin.

"So, let's talk assets," Driscoll suggested.

"Well, as you can see here, we have the windmill. Some power to a few buildings," Ari said. "We have a good well, too. We have a nice herd of goats going, and a big ol' barn of chickens."

"How many people?" Driscoll asked.

"Currently thirty-nine, but Christina's about to pop. Makin' an even forty," Ari said.

"Way to go, big daddy!" Mel laughed, clapping Joaquin on the shoulder. "That's three for you now, isn't it?" He grinned toothily over the table at Driscoll. "I have six myself."

"Thirteen," Driscoll said, as if it meant nothing. The others shared wide-eyed glances, and the whole table shook with laughter.

They had just regained control of themselves when Stella emerged from the kitchen once more, bearing plates of steaming food. The liver had been dusted with herbs and fried quickly in animal grease, followed by the onions and mushrooms, caramelized in the flavored oil.

"Oh, honey, you're gonna make me cry!" Driscoll mewed at the sight of the meal. "This one's a keeper, I tell you what!" He sobered momentarily as Stella reached out to set down the plates one at a time, revealing her arms. Her flesh was pitted with burns, tears, and scars, all long since healed. She wore them like an extra set of sleeves.

"Thank you. Enjoy," Stella said before politely disappearing back into the kitchen. They heard her fiddling with the wash bucket.

The men dug in, and it was some time before they resumed their discussion. "Well, Honey Hole has a population of sixty-seven," Driscoll said, using his stained bandana to wipe his mouth and whiskers. "We have nine horses and three cows that are milkable. Still hoping to find and capture a bull so we can breed 'em. And we have the hardware store. Our gardeners have been harvesting seeds for as long as I can remember, and our gardens are damn impressive, if I do say so myself. The women have taken to canning things for the winter. Food's pretty comfortable, though I'd love to get my hands on some more protein."

"All the more reason to pool our resources. With more men, we can go out and capture some more livestock," Ari said. "I had an idea, too, about the housing. I know you're getting a little cramped up there. I was thinking we could roll some of those old campers over from the dealership. Maybe your horses could help pull them. Line 'em up, and it's a neighborhood!"

"Now that is a brilliant notion," Driscoll complimented. "Everything we have is movable, except the gardens, but we can dig those up and bring them here. You've got plenty of good soil from what I can see. Mmm! Hey there, darlin', is there any chance of seconds?"

"I'm sorry, that's all there is," Stella called from the kitchen. "I could wilt some greens if you'd like."

"Naw, that's okay. I'm sick of green things. I want meat." Driscoll leaned back and patted his taut stomach with a satisfied sigh. "My friends, I will tell you that I do have one major concern. Your fencing. It's pathetic. It's a wonder you aren't attacked every night by those damn plague dogs."

"Those disease-ridden bastards can jump over anything we build," Ari complained. "Or dig under it. It's near impossible to keep the place sealed up. We do what we can, and someone's always keeping watch."

"We know we're all immune against the airborne," Alex said, "but if someone's bitten, they're either going to become infected, or become a carrier and infect someone else."

"That's why you're playing with fire here, not having adequate fencing." Driscoll tsk-tsked, shaking his head. "Well, we can tear down some of ours and transport it as well. We have a couple old wagons and enough tack to hitch the horses. It'll take gallons of sweat, but I think we can manage it if you're willing to pitch in some of your people to help."

"Of course," Ari snorted. "We all need to pull our weight for this to work."

The men murmured their agreement.

"You seem like a smart fella," Driscoll complimented Alex. "Some fancy talk there about The Disease."

Ari looked at each of his advisors, who gave him small, shrewd nods. "We've been keeping this under wraps," Ari said, "because it's dangerous. We didn't want him kidnapped." He reached over and pawed Alex's shoulder. "Alex here trained under a real live doctor as his apprentice. When the old man died, he took over and started training others. He's good. Damn good. Saved my life more than once."

"A *doctor*?" Driscoll couldn't believe the words. "That's it. It's settled. We're doing this. Honey Hole will do whatever it takes to make this work."

There was much back-slapping and handshaking. They went over the town charters, the rules, the laws, how judgement was passed.

Stella had just refilled the water when Driscoll said, "What about the women?"

Ari raised an eyebrow. "Well, the way we do things here is every man has a right," he said. "Nobody gets to claim a favorite. Hell, we're not even sure if Christina's baby really is Joaquin's. But that's a good thing. That means we all want to protect the kid, right?"

"One big happy family." Joaquin grinned.

"And don't do it where everyone can see, just wherever you fall. Have some decency," Mel suggested. "Take her behind the barn or something."

Driscoll shuffled his mustache with his finger. "I have a *wife*," he said. "Liana. She's mine, and nobody else's." He motioned with his hands. "She's all mine, and there ain't no negotiating that. Also, my daughter Kristianya's about thirteen. Nobody touches her without asking me first. She's not old enough yet."

Ari glanced at the others.

"Look, I'm bringing you plenty of fresh faces to go around," Driscoll reminded them. "Girls you've never even seen. Some real pretty ones, too."

This placated the men. "I think we have a deal," Ari said, and braced his legs to stand up and shake Driscoll's hand across the table.

His legs wouldn't move. He struggled for a moment, slapping his hands against the table and trying to push himself back, or up, or anywhere, but his body betrayed him with each passing moment. Within half a minute, his hands were useless, flopping against the table with ever-weakening spasms. Everyone at the table watched, a circle of horrified statues, as he seized and pitched forward onto his dirty plate with a clank. He convulsed and slobbered and gasped for a few moments before slowly relaxing into nothingness.

"What the—"

"The Disease!" Alex cried, shooting up from his chair with such force that it crashed backward onto the cement floor. "He . . . he was infected?!"

"When was he bitten?" Joaquin demanded just as Mel began shrieking, pounding his fists against his suddenly paralyzed legs. "No! No!"

"Get away from me!" Driscoll roared, upsetting the table and heading for the door. He lost his footing and smashed into the concrete. "My legs! Oh God, oh God . . ." He chanted his litany to deaf ears.

"How weary, stale, flat, and unprofitable seem to me all the uses of this world," came a dark murmur from the kitchen doorway.

Alex whipped his head to the side and saw Stella standing in the doorway, leaning a casual shoulder against the frame with her arms crossed over her deer-like, scar-marred body. She'd removed her apron and folded it neatly over one of her arms. "I'm glad you liked your supper. I've never made plague dog liver before."

"B . . . bitch!" Joaquin managed to eke out as the paralysis took hold of his body. He fell to the floor and scratched at Ari's ancient pistol he kept in the holster at his hip.

Stella easily beat him to it, slapping his stupid fingers away and retrieving the firearm for herself. As the men writhed on the floor in their death throes, she turned to Alex, who stood against the wall, pressing into it as though he hoped it would absorb him. Stella fiddled with the gun and watched them die.

"The rest is silence," she said with a shrug, and pulled out a chair at a table for two nearby, easing down into her seat. "Alex," she invited. "Come and join me. You may be wondering why you aren't dead. Allow me to illuminate you."

Alex had never heard Stella's voice like this. Granted, he didn't know her well, but he ate here, same as everyone else. Gone was the meek little mouse-cook. This was someone else, all hard angles and arrowhead eyes.

"Come," she repeated when he did not move. "All of this started with people seated at a table, deciding the fates of others. So it goes."

Alex inched forward when she lazily waved the gun his direction, and sat across from her.

"You ate a deer's liver," she said. "I'm glad you all kept your food to yourselves. We need you, Doc. You weren't expendable like they were."

"How . . . how could you . . ." he struggled.

"Ari said so himself," she replied. "None of you know me. I just showed up, kept my mouth shut, and cooked the food. You don't know what I *was* before I came here. Now you know."

"Wh . . . why?" was his next question as he watched the bodies on the floor twitch.

"It had to end," she said, flicking the safety on and off, on and off. "These men and their little dream of paradise after the world ended. They were the loudest and the strongest. They had the weapons and the ideas. But now they're dead because I couldn't watch them lay a hand on another woman. Watch another woman die in childbirth because they think we need to 'grow the population.' Sorry, Doc, but things aren't like how they used to be. No hospitals. You can't save them all." She sighed. "If a woman wants to take a chance for a baby, it's her choice. But we're done. We're done being *forced*."

He swallowed hard. She got up for a moment and brought each of them a clean cup of water. "What happens now?" he whispered as he dragged his arm over his forehead.

"We're still merging the towns," Stella said, and sipped her water with her gun hand. "But things are going to be different around here. Do you understand me?"

He stared at her.

"You're going to go out there and tell everyone that those men were bitten by a plague dog that somehow got into my kitchen. Probably attracted by the deer I just slaughtered. But then you and I killed it, and cleaned everything up so it's safe again. You're going to tell them you're the leader now. But that won't be true, will it?"

He shook his head just slightly, left to right to left.

"I don't want a riot," Stella said. "Fighting each other's how we got into this mess. Things can't change too quickly. If the other men know what I did, all the women will suffer. But with you as my puppet, we'll do just fine. We'll merge the towns and change the laws. You will do anything and everything I say, or I will find a way to end you. You know who I am now. What I'm capable of. Do you understand me, Doc? Are you *hearing me*, boy?"

Alex nodded.

"Good." She went over to a cupboard in the corner and withdrew a big bag of wrinkled plastic. When she unfolded it, he could see it was some kind of whole-body suit. There was a headpiece with a little window to see out of. She shook it free of dust. The three letters printed on the chest said "CDC."

"Now, put this on, and start cleaning up my café," she ordered. Alex removed his jacket, and put on the suit, slowly, as though he too were slowly paralyzing. She brought him rags and soapy water. At her behest, he dragged the bodies outside and set them on fire in front of the whole town. She watched him from her kitchen as he mopped the floor for hours.

"That's my good little Cinderella," she said.

Appetite

Emily Devenport

Editor: The strength of human will is often underrated.

The storm and I arrived in Phoenix at the same time, but from different directions. I walked in from the north, following what was left of I-17. I had been watching the clouds brew all day as I descended through mountains into a desert heat I could barely feel. They towered in the southern sky, blowing a massive wall of dust ahead of them.

By the time the highway had taken me past the deserted discount malls on the outskirts of town, the grit blew so thick I could just make out the outlines of the buildings. I smelled rust and ozone. I heard the wind, the only voice that spoke to me with any constancy. I saw gray, brown, and tan shapes behind the blowing sand—and once, when lightning flashed inside a thunderhead, I saw the green of an ocean waiting up there to fall.

When those clouds let go, I felt my heart beat. The pulse was very slow, and I knew that it beat only for the storm. I walked buffeted by the rain and wind, until I could no longer stand upright against the onslaught. Then I crawled until the water rose around me. Finally I sought shelter in a car that still had unbroken windows. I climbed into the backseat and shut the door, savoring the change in volume and the sound of the torrent hitting the windows and the roof. I was as content as I had ever been, and possibly ever could be.

I watched the storm out the back window. It raged, then sighed, then finally stopped moving. I waited for a time afterward, hoping it might spark back to life. Instead, the light of morning drove it north and west, and I watched the dawn.

During the storm, water had risen around the car and moved it down the street. Some of it seeped into the car; I sat in it up to my waist. I opened the door and watched it pour out. It made a delightful splashing noise. Once it had all run out, I heard the faint noise of a breeze.

It fluttered and died, fluttered and died, teasing me out of the car. If it had not been there, I might have slept until the next storm came along to capture my undivided attention. I might have slept for days, for years, even for centuries. But that breeze skittered ahead of me up the street, and I followed.

The rain had washed many things clean, including me, but the pavement was buried in mud and silt. You could see places where braided streams already were carving their way through deposits. I walked on the rocks and pebbles without too much difficulty. I passed a mostly intact store window and saw a mummy reflected in it.

I was that mummy—an Undead remnant of the former world. My body was so withered, I looked like a stick drawing of a girl. I could see almost my entire skeleton wrapped inside the leather of my skin. I probably could have examined most of my organs just by looking at their outlines, except that I always make a point of wearing clothes. I have to wear the smallest sizes I can find so they won't fall off me.

I looked into my eyes. They're still brown, and they're the liveliest things about me. I like to look at them because that's the closest I can come to communication with another person. Everyone is gone, or almost everyone is, and when I look into the reflection of my eyes it's like someone is looking back.

"Hello," I said, with my ghost of a voice. "How are you today?"

"I'm fine, thank you," I answered back.

"Have a lovely day." I tipped a wave and walked away from the window.

"You too," I called after myself.

I didn't use my voice very much back then, so it sounded creaky. But even that was a sort of music, and it cheered me. The breeze that had tempted me out of the car still tugged at me, so I continued to walk up the weathered street. Time eroded it in bits and pieces, eating rusty holes into metal, melting marble and cement with acid rain, breaking bricks and grinding them to pebbles. Yet windows remained intact in many places. Some buildings still had their roofs, so whatever they covered would last a while.

I followed a stream as it wound west and then turned south again, onto a wide street with the remnants of a light rail line down its center. One of the trains had stalled on the southbound side. Its doors remained closed. The windows, scoured by the storm and many before it, prevented me from looking in. I wandered past it, hoping I might find something in particular among the buildings.

At last, I found the object of my quest on the east side of the street. My heart, which beat so rarely, lurched at the sight. The windows of the library appeared to be intact, and that meant its precious contents would be too. I bolted to the front doors in a flash—we Undead can move quickly when motivated—and I contemplated the locks.

Someone had secured them. I didn't begrudge that. Whoever had done it wanted to protect the books. Perhaps they had known that Phoenix would eventually cover itself in silt and gravel, that the bugs would be the only creatures who still lived here by the time someone came back to this library. So I blessed that long-ago protector. I broke the lock with one snap of my wrist—we can be very strong, too—and I went through the door, closing it firmly behind me.

I entered the lobby and smelled the books, the only thing besides storms that could possibly keep me from slipping into one of the dream states that seemed to last longer each time I fell into them, the only thing besides storms for which I still had an appetite.

Appetite is the best word for what I felt. But it sparked other feelings, deep in my creaking memory, that were not the least bit pleasant. Fear was no longer a constant in my existence, but once it had been. Sorrow had been too. All because of appetite, because of a dreadful, obliterating hunger.

Not this sort of hunger though. Not the love of books, my old, dusty friends who called to me from shelf after shelf, on floor after floor—four floors above this level and at least one floor below, in vaults where the rare things were kept. This is it! I thought to myself. I am home.

And where to start in such a paradise? At the nearest shelf, of course. I walked across the lobby, stirring dust that had crept through tiny cracks, and found the New Releases rack. The first book I selected was a cookbook. It made me want to laugh. How long had it been since I had eaten anything? Since I had chewed, tasted, swallowed.

I thumbed through it, looking at pictures of beautiful food, wondering which of these things I had eaten. Dimly I remembered the taste of green beans, lettuce, and cheese. I was pretty sure I remembered cake. Sweet, wasn't it? And the frosting had a different texture than the cake. It was—creamy.

"Creeeeeeeeeeeeeeeaaamy," I said, though I wasn't able to make it sound very tasty. I sounded like a door with neglected hinges.

I turned the page and saw something dreadful: a slab of red meat on a plate.

Red, dripping with blood, torn from something that screamed and pleaded, and tried to get away . . .

I slammed the book shut. If I had been in the habit of breathing regularly, I probably would have been gasping. But breathing was something I did only if I wanted to speak, so I walked down the row and picked another book. This one was titled The Universe Within: How the Science of the Very Small Will Change the World As We Know It.

"It did," I croaked, and I wandered off to look at another shelf.

* * *

I have to be honest—who is there to lie to anymore? I relished having that library to myself. In fact I relished the entire city, even the state of Arizona. Mine, alone. I had loved people, once. But I couldn't remember who they were, and what dim memories I retained of them were colored with blood and anguish. Each storm I witnessed, each book I read, took me further away from that previous world.

I can't say how long I lingered on the ground floor, because time as I knew it no longer had meaning. But eventually, I climbed the stairs to the floors where the nonfiction books were stored. I nosed through a copy of Ancient Landscapes of the Colorado Plateau when I heard it.

"Meow?"

I froze. (Not that I was moving much in the first place. We Undead are as motionless as rocks when we're not walking up muddy streets or breaking locks.)

"Mmmmeeeeooooow?" The sound came from two rows down, to my right—the biology section. I peered around the corner. Nothing moved.

"Hello?" I enquired.

"Mmeeeee?"

Big Sister, someone is hurt!

Someone called me that, once—Big Sister.

Little Sister. That was what I called her. Don't go over there!

Someone is crying, she said, just before I lost her forever.

"Don't listen," I whispered to myself.

"Meow."

The sound was plaintive. The thing making the sound wanted me to come find it, to help it.

I put Ancient Landscapes back in its proper place on the shelf. And then I ran as fast as I could, through the rows, down the stairs, across the lobby and out into the street.

I stood in the blazing sunshine. Finally I turned and stared at the library. Why had I run like that? I had been terrified, but now I didn't feel that way. Now I felt only puzzlement.

"Little Sister, don't go in there!"

"I'm just going to see if someone is hurt . . ."

The sound I had heard in the library wasn't scary. It was a harmless sound. Why did I run from it?

"Big Sister, run! It's a trap!"

The sound might be a trick, that's why. It wanted me to go and see what it was, and then the thing making it might pounce on me. Because once living people had been eaten, only we remained, the Undead. And the hunger had still been there, not just for human flesh, but also for the thoughts and memories inside our heads. It haunted us all. The only way to eliminate it was to deny it, and there were many who saw no reason to do that. Too many.

"Big Sister—run!"

She crouches over Little Sister, tearing pieces out of her with a red mouth full of sharp teeth. The Hungry One regards me with eyes as black as night. She says, "Yes, run Big Sister, by all means. I'll catch up with you later. I'll find you some day . . ."

And then she eats Little Sister's heart.

I walked away from the library. I almost walked toward it, because I hated to leave those books. But caution warned me to wait. Something might have attacked if I had gone to see what made the sound. And hadn't I heard a rustle when I ran for the stairs? Something behind me?

Yet the street appeared to be empty. The windows on both sides were empty too, like the train car in the middle of the street with a door that stood open because someone walked out of it years ago and never came back.

So I walked away from the library considering my clothing. It had begun to unravel in all the spots that mattered. I needed to find replacements. I headed north, against the current of the stream, which the sun had dried to a trickle. Ahead, the mountains reared their weathered peaks. I saw them every way I looked in Phoenix, surrounding it like the sides of a bowl. The sky was now clear as a bell, so it was hard to tell how far away they were.

I turned west and walked up a tributary that fed into the trickle. The sun hung on that side of the sky blazing into my face. I liked the feeling. I passed many buildings that were still intact, but none of them tempted my curiosity. After a time, I had forgotten what I was looking for, until another breeze stirred the ragged ends of my clothing. I turned my face into the wind to discover a gigantic building set far back from what was left of the road. Its sign still possessed all of its letters—even the apostrophe—Cabela's.

My feet plowed through gravel deposits on the side of the tributary as I changed course onto the higher ground of the parking lot. My flapping threads reminded me that I had a mission, and the building looked promising. Surely something so big would contain many things, including something to cover my partially exposed body.

The front doors of thick, tinted glass were the kind that would slide sideways once they noticed you. The gizmo that made them do that had long ago run out of juice. I hooked my long, sharp fingernails into the seam along the right side and wrenched the door aside. It opened easily, so it wasn't locked, and it stayed ajar after I walked through.

Cabela's turned out to be a sporting goods superstore. Dust coated the shelves, but the goods looked intact and useful. If the streams outside ever decided to turn into rivers, I could use one of the kayaks hanging against the walls. The clothing department was my main interest, but on the way there I stopped at a case full of hunting knives. They gleamed through the dusty glass. I pulled open the case and examined the blades, some sharp, some serrated, some sharp and serrated, I selected a three-inch folding knife before continuing down the aisle in search of sporty fashions.

The clothing in Cabela's was the sort you'd buy if you wanted to ski, or fish, or climb rocks. Fortunately, it was full of lycra, and the stretchy fabric still had considerable play to it. I stripped off my shredded old stuff and pulled on a new top, leggings, socks, and even running shoes. Turning in front of the mirror, I showed off the latest mummy fashions.

"Meow?" something croaked.

I had left the front door open. The thing from the library must have followed me. I found my new knife and pulled it open.

"Meow . . ." the throat making the sound seemed more confident now, as if it hadn't practiced in centuries but was getting back into the swing of things. Before I could decide whether to look for it or wait for it to pounce on me, it sauntered into the center of the aisle.

It was a mummy cat. I could tell, even though all its fur was gone. Its shriveled flesh mirrored my own, but for all that it seemed cheerful. It held its tail high as it walked confidently toward me.

"Oh." I put away my knife. Mummy cats were no danger. Animals hadn't developed the hunger for their own kind—only people had done that.

The cat gazed at me expectantly. Its eyes were still green.

"Ah." I could think of nothing more intelligent to say. I couldn't quite recall what cats liked, what they needed.

And then the answer popped into my head. "Are you hungry?"

"Mmmmmmeeeeeeeeeeeeeeooooooooooooooooooooow," said the cat, whose voice box was working better every moment.

"Well." I looked up the aisle, toward the front of the store. "Let's see what we can find."

Up front, near the registers, the racks were still full of protein bars. I opened my knife and slashed several of them open. Then the cat and I sat on the floor and gnawed the petrified food with our needle-sharp teeth. Chewing it was easy but neither of us had any saliva so bits fell out of the sides of our mouths. My companion seemed to enjoy the challenge. But I regarded the bottles of sports water speculatively.

They had been well-sealed, but some of their contents had evaporated anyway. I popped the top on a bottle of vitamin water and sipped it—or tried to. My lips were still flexible, but my throat didn't work the way it ought to. Still, it seemed to absorb some of the water. After several sips, I could even taste it.

"Meowffl?" enquired the cat, whose teeth were full of protein bar crumbs. She sniffed at the water, so I offered some to her. She extended a tongue that looked like sandpaper, and I gave her water one drop at a time.

Between the two of us, we went through four more bottles of water. Her tongue began to look decidedly less sandpapery, and my taste buds woke up. I tried to remember when I had last drunk anything, but it must have happened just after the Hungry Ones started to—

No. I would rather turn to dust than dredge that stuff up. Kitty and I were happy there on the floor of the empty store, in the empty city, after the end of the world.

"My name is—" I started to tell her, but then couldn't remember what it was, only that my little sister called me "—Big Sister."

Kitty cocked her head attentively.

"Sheba," I named her. "Even without your fur, you look regal."

She bumped my hand with her mummified head, and I stroked her leathery skin. We sat that way for a time, while I contemplated old protein bars and half-evaporated vitamin water. An appetite was growing in me for something more than storms and books. I wasn't quite sure what it was, or where it would lead me, but I liked it.

"You know what we should do?" I decided. "We should follow the water."

Sheba and I got to our feet. She followed me up the aisle to the backpack section, then back to the registers where I filled the pack full of food bars and bottled water. Together we walked out of the store. I stopped long enough to pull the door shut behind us. We might need to come back later for supplies, and a shut door would preserve them longer. We walked back down to the street and followed the dry stream west. Eventually we would find the part of it that was still wet. I wouldn't think about the Hungry Ones anymore.

But truly, I didn't need to think about them. I remembered what they were. They ate Little Sister. And then they ate everyone else, even each other.

Some day, they might eat me.

* * *

Everybody had parents, grandparents. Some people even had brothers and sisters, neighbors and friends. This family had a dog. The medium-sized dog was a mummy now, and still waited for them to come home.

It got to its feet and stood by the gate of the half-intact house as Sheba and I walked up Snowbird Lane. It looked at us inquisitively, but didn't bark or growl. Sheba walked right up and touched noses with it. It gave half a wave of its tail.

"They're not coming back," I said. "You can come with us, if you like."

The dog sat on his haunches and cocked his head, studying us. Maybe he needed to get used to us. After all, no one had passed in a long time. He had waited so patiently, that was all he knew how to do. But maybe we could get him to see another possibility.

I wondered what kind of dog he had been. Somehow, even without his fur he managed to look cute. His mummy skin was tough and leathery, just like mine and Sheba's. He had short ears that were perked, as if he were listening to something that moved miles away.

"I'll call you Radar," I decided.

Radar's tail wagged again. It was kind of a creaky wag, but it got the job done.

"We're following the water," I told Radar.

Radar got up and started to walk. We followed him. He led us back out to Route 60, and we walked west on it for a while. Then he turned south into a drive. The gate across the drive said HASSAYAMPA RIVER PRESERVE. I pushed the gate aside, and Radar, Sheba, and I strolled up the lane to the house at the very end. It had a courtyard with a garden, and a VISITOR'S CENTER sign.

The Visitor's Center was a house that used to belong to the people who had run a general store. Sometime later it became a place where you could learn about the Hassayampa River. It retained many books, fossils, mineral samples, and the bones of local mammals, birds, and reptiles. We loved it. "This is our home," I said. "From now on."

I wouldn't wander the world anymore. Sheba and Radar wouldn't wait for people who weren't coming home. But as the sun started to go down, and we made our beds, something nagged at my memory. I remembered why I left Phoenix, how I got scared and ran out of the library.

Had I seen something in the street?

I remembered the library, the silent street, the empty train car with its open door.

Nothing was there! Why was it nagging at me?

The library, the street, the empty train car. I had walked to Cabela's and felt like something was following me. Sheba was following me, she was the reason.

No. The library. The street. The empty car.

The empty train car. How did I know it was empty? Because the door was open.

But when I passed it on the way to the library, that door was closed.

I walked out into the courtyard and looked into the drive and the road beyond, watching for signs of movement. I saw none.

At least, not yet.

* * *

I had stopped thinking about the past. But it was still there. The world didn't end when people started dying. It ended when we stopped dying.

I'm pretty sure someone thought immortality improved our species.

But I also get the feeling it was an accident. I think only a few people were supposed to live forever, to never grow sick, or old. Somehow, it all got away from them, spreading across the planet before mutating to include other mammals, and then to birds.

The disaster had just gotten started. We all felt the change in ourselves. We felt the strength that had nothing to do with sustenance. Briefly, we felt joy. But even in those early days, something grew in us, a hunger that could not be satisfied with ordinary food.

Animals never felt that hunger, only people did. And some of us felt it more than others—a lot more. That appetite created the Hungry Ones. They turned our joy to terror.

My little sister was a Hungry One. It frightened her. But like all Hungry Ones, when she saw people she wanted to eat them. She wanted the memories inside their brains.

I felt that dreadful hunger, too. But I had a theory. If you ignored the hunger long enough, eventually it would eat itself and you would be free of it. So Little Sister and I went as far away from people as we could. We starved. We denied the hunger that devoured the world. Slowly, painfully, the hunger burned itself to ashes.

Only then did we start to look for other survivors. But that turned out to be a mistake.

* * *

A mummy cow grazed the grasses next to the Visitor's Center where the Hassayampa, a river that flowed underground for most of its length, ponded at the surface. She had a mummy calf. But neither of them looked all that emaciated. I wondered if it was because they were eating grass and drinking water.

"I'll call you Mistress Moo," I told the cow. And when I saw how eagerly the calf chewed the grass, "I'll call you Munchie."

Neither of them mooed, but they did seem to be listening. I decided I needed to plant a garden so we could start eating again. The three of us looked along the banks for a good place to sow seeds. But Mistress Moo and Munchie would nibble anything we planted; we would have to build a fence around it. An old fence still existed around the house, so maybe we could start with that. I inspected the wood, and a mummy bird hopped along one of the railings, watching me with curiosity.

"Are you eating bugs?" I asked. "You have most of your feathers."

The bird chirped. Radar sniffed Munchie. Sheba strolled up to Mistress Moo as if she were hoping to get some milk. The scene reminded me of what had happened so long ago.

Little Sister and I had gone looking for other people who had fought off the hunger, people who wanted to live normal lives again. We joined a group of them scavenging in a suburb in Denver.

It had been an optimistic time. We found a lot of supplies and each other. It looked like the end of the world wasn't as final as we had thought. Even with my fuzzy mummy memory, I can see my friends and my little sister going house to house. They gathered stuff we thought we would need, even harvesting wild vegetables growing in the back yards. Little Sister looked so happy.

All of that ended when a gang of children ran into the yard. There may have been twenty of them. I think the oldest of them may have been eight, but I didn't have more than a second to notice that, because they came at us like a pack of wild dogs. They were carrying hatchets.

I scooped Little Sister up and ran with all my Undead might. But they were Undead too, and they were consumed with the Hunger we had denied. They stayed right with me, long after a living predator would have broken off the chase. I kept running long after living prey would have surrendered in despair. I heard them grunt with effort as they swung their hatchets at us. The blades grazed me, sometimes biting deep enough to draw what little blood I still had in my body. Little Sister could see them over my shoulder, but she never made a sound, never cried, nor screamed. She just held on.

I don't know how long they followed me, because I ran for the rest of the day and far into the night. Finally Little Sister said, "You can stop," and I did.

Her happiness died that night. We never saw our friends again. But Little Sister didn't have long to miss them.

"Big Sister, someone is hurt!"

"Little Sister, don't go in there!"

"I'm just going to see if someone is hurt . . ."

Little Sister shouldn't have fallen for that trick. But only a week had passed since our friends had died, and sometimes I wonder if she thought she should be dead too.

Not that she welcomed the death she got, or the one that gave it to her.

"Yes," the Hungry One said, *"run Big Sister, by all means. I'll catch up with you later. I'll find you some day . . ."*

That Hungry One had been smart. She had been patient with her trap. If she hadn't been so busy eating Little Sister, I would not have escaped her.

After that, I stopped trying to eat or drink, I stopped caring about most of the things in the world. I just wandered, avoiding everyone and everything.

Yet Despite my efforts, I stumbled into the same Hungry One a final time, and again, only the fact that she crouched over another mummy, devouring him inch by inch, saved what remained of my life. As she consumed him, he watched her with fascination, as if he wished he were the one who was eating himself.

I still wanted to live. Or at least, I didn't want to die the way Little Sister had, the way this new victim would. So I backed away. But the Hungry One spoke to me as if I were her cohort.

"They'll breed, and we'll eat them," she said, smugly.

"Who will?" I asked.

"The mortals, you silly girl."

"There are no more mortals."

The Hungry One laughed, showing all of her teeth. "Of course there are. I'm eating one."

No, I almost corrected her, you're eating a mummy. But it occurred to me that if I pointed out to her that she liked to eat mummies, it would occur to her that she would like to eat me. So I let it go. And as soon as she looked away from me, I ran.

Yet I always felt that Hungry One might be on my trail. Years went by; I saw fewer and fewer mummies in the world. I glimpsed Hungry Ones lurking around the edges of things, and I avoided them. But I wondered— if there were so few of us left, could the Hungry Ones sense us from a distance? Could they sense the thoughts in our heads that they so desired to consume, the way a magnet responds to a magnetic field?

All these years, maybe centuries later, was there one on my trail? Had it been waiting for me in Phoenix? Is that why the door to the train car had been open when I remembered it being shut?

* * *

I pulled a loose fence crossbeam out of its post. I carried it back to the Visitor's Center. Radar and Sheba followed me, leaving the cows to their grazing.

The sky to the southeast was turning black. A storm brewed, pushing a wall of dust in front of it a mile high. We stood and watched it swallow the world as it raged across the desert, straight toward us.

Sheba hissed. Then Radar growled. I looked around and I saw nothing wrong, but in any case I scooped them up and ran with them into the house, barring the door behind us. Wind clawed at the front door of our house. It wasn't alone. I put my friends down, picked up the crossbeam, and pulled out my knife.

As the squall broke over us it grew almost as dark as night. The windows rattled with each gust, and dust puffed through cracks between the door and frame. A voice whispered under the wind.

"Big Sister . . . help me . . ."

I whittled the end of the crossbeam, working so fast the chips flew on all sides.

"Help me, Big Sister . . . I'm so scared . . ."

I regarded the narrowing end of my work, then whittled some more.

The wind blasted the door. "Let me in . . ." whispered the voice. "Why won't you let me in . . .?"

I braced the blunt end of the stake on the floor, and angled the other toward the door, at chest level.

"Let me in," whined the voice on the other side of the door, no longer trying to sound like Little Sister. "LET ME IN!"

The door smashed into splinters. The wind raged into our house. Something solid slammed into the sharp end of my stake. It moved so fast, it drove me and the stake across the floor, right into the wall. The Hungry One drove the stake deep into its own heart and right out the other side.

"What—?" said the Hungry One. "How—?" But the light was already fading from her eyes. Her heart had been torn apart. My own heart broke because she reminded me of Little Sister after all.

* * *

Little Sister had been awake and aware while almost every bit of her was eaten. Once her heart was destroyed, she was conscious but no longer able to move. She watched hopelessly while her limbs, her torso, her face, and finally her brain were devoured. Because the Hungry One saved the best for last.

It was as if Little Sister's spirit had fled from the farthest reaches of her until it was crammed into her brain case, unable to break its bond from the flesh that bound it. When her memories were devoured, so was her spirit.

This Hungry One had done that to her. And now she sat on my floor with the dust swirling around her. She stared at nothing. If I had not known what happened to Little Sister, I might pity her.

Her eyes found mine again, and I saw a spark there. "Nothing is all there is," she said, grimly.

"Technically," I replied, *"nothing is all there isn't."*

She glared at me. Then she grinned, showing foul, blood-stained teeth. "Clever girl. I like you." She kept that grin going long after that last spark left her eyes.

I carried her outside, into the storm.

I took the Hungry One far out into the desert, and left her there. Unlike Little Sister, this Hungry One would pass gently. She would sit and watch the world go by, weathering like the rocks until her spirit drifted free.

* * *

Mistress Moo gave very good milk, for a mummy cow. After many years had passed, she didn't look like a mummy anymore, and neither did Munchie. Sheba and Radar grew their fur back. Even I became less leathery.

One day, Sheba, Radar, and I walked into Wickenburg. On the way, we saw a mummy tending a vegetable garden. He watched birds perch on his wild sunflowers. They feasted on the seeds. The mummy turned his head and saw us. His tipped his straw hat.

"Hello," he said, with his ghost of a voice. "How are you today?"

"I'm fine, thank you," I answered back.

"Have a lovely day." He plopped his hat back on his head.

"You too," I called, and continued down the street.

The world is balancing itself. Mummy animals are turning into living animals again, and some of them are reproducing. Maybe that could happen to mummy people, but I won't feel too sad if it doesn't. We messed up so bad—next time might be even worse. For now, it's enough for me to say hello to my neighbors and tend my own garden. Isn't that what the original Paradise was supposed to be like?

The only thing missing from my paradise is books. All of my favorites fell to dust, years ago. But I remember everything I read. I've learned to make paper, and I'm writing them all down. Maybe my neighbors will want to read a few. Or maybe new people will show up someday.

If you're one of those new people, remember what I've written here. Maybe you'll make the same mistakes we did, but that's not the point. What I want you to know is that it's possible to keep living even after everything has blown up around you. You can survive. And you can even be happy.

You just have to have the appetite.

The Last Picnic

Cullen McHael

Editor: "The Heart of a mother is a deep abyss at the bottom of which you will always find forgiveness." – Honoré de Balzac

Three kinds of jowl share the same face: the pinch and dimple, the secondary bulge, and the prune sag. Not a healthy face. A soft face hit hard, a fat woman who lost her fat, and an old woman whose age doubled in a few short years.

But my eyes stay steady as I meet my own gaze in the mirror. Good. When I can't hold a focus, when I can't stay steady, that will be my mind failing. Not today. Not yet.

I open the medicine cabinet, turning the mirror away. Then I leave the bathroom.

Drapes hang heavy over the many windows, with a little sunlight sneaking in along the bottom to paint the drifting dust white. I dare to shift a fold of cloth to peek outside. It's a sweater day. I wear five. Also two pairs of gloves and three sets of socks. But a shiver still shakes me as the cloud of my breath frosts the windowpane.

It didn't snow. Good. They'll still come. If it had snowed, they would leave footprints. Can't have that. We would have to wait to meet up until the snow melted. But it didn't snow. Good. They'll be here soon.

My thoughts run in circles as I set out the pillows and blankets. On swimsuit days we sit around a table, but on sweater days the warmth of other bodies sharing a blanket on the floor feels like civilization. No fire though. Fire would make smoke. Can't have that.

I open a can of peaches into the rose bowl. The one from Corey's Pottery Shop. Handmade. Hand-painted. Sturdy. It goes in the middle of the living room picnic blanket. I make sure Kinsey's kitten-patterned pillow waits next to the pinstriped one. Kinsey liked the kittens. Sara will want to hold it, to remember her. John won't care, but he'll want to sit next to Sara so the big brown one goes on the other side of the pinstripes.

I'm fussing. I fluff the brown one. A mustard stain crinkles under my thumb.

John is good. He's been good to Sara. Tough. Quiet. A little round about the hips, but gentle when it mattered.

The house groans as a bitter wind catcalls from the eaves.

Something moves across the roof in a patter of little claws.

I wait, holding the brown pillow to my chest.

The patter isn't repeated.

The revolver on my hip pinches my belly as I sit down. I put down the pillow and shift the revolver out of the way. Its grip settles into my palm like my backside into my favorite chair.

The house groans. The wind pushes. The house sighs, unable to escape. The wind whistles.

The revolver waits, heavy and ready.

Animal screeching breaks the quiet, like cats fighting, but bigger, fiercer. Very close. In my backyard. A roar rattles my windows. I hear wood splintering, probably the apple tree.

John and Sara. I hope they aren't nearby yet. I hope they're late.

The fight rises in pitch and intensity. Growls and shrieks bordering on insane language contest for the most distressing sound. One piercing discharge of violence stabs my ears.

Then silence.

The wind whistles. The house groans.

The bowl of peaches sits in a ring of little wrinkles.

I wait.

The clock died a month ago. Just a dead battery. Maybe Sara will finally bring a replacement.

I settle the hammer of the revolver back onto an empty cylinder.

Sara arrives late, and alone. She rests her rifle against the wall, then sits on the pinstripes. Her hands move almost automatically to the cat-patterned cloth, and she hugs her sister's pillow, resting her chin in its folds.

"John?" I ask.

The barest shake of her head doesn't disturb the cloth beneath her chin. Her eyes stare past my feet.

I sit on the brown, and wrap my arms around her. She feels so cold under my hands, even through the gloves. The revolver pinches my belly. I set it aside.

Sara's black hair scratches my chin and throat. She doesn't shake.

The clock stands still.

Finally she sits back, pulling away to rest against the wall.

I lift the blanket over her. Her hands grip its edge. She wears fingerless gloves. Her fingers must be freezing. I want to cup them in my hands, but instead I offer the bowl.

"Have some peaches."

"I can't eat those anymore, mom." She says it like an accusation.

"I bet you could if you tried," I tell her, and have one for myself. The sweet goo dribbles my chin. I take off my gloves to wipe it, and lick my fingers.

Sara sighs.

"Mom, John didn't come because he's tired. I'm tired too."

"It will be all right," I tell her. "Maybe it's a platitude, but we have to keep living. I mean, what's the alternative? I know it's bad out there, but you'll always be safe in here. Always."

"No."

It's a cold denunciation. A hard statement of fact.

I take Sara's hand in mine and study the cracked fingernails, the cold-tempered wrinkles and chapped callouses. I take off my gloves and breathe onto our joint hands. Her skin feels as cool as salmon scales fresh from the river, but she doesn't shiver.

"Tell me what happened with John. You can talk to me."

"Look at me, Mom."

"You can tell me anything, you know that."

"Look at me."

"I'm your mother; I'm still here for you—"

"Look at me!"

She pulls her hand from mine. The cool fingers cup my face, pinching the flesh below my jaw as she tilts my head back to meet her gaze.

Her black eyes challenge me. Black as the night sky and twice as wide as those of the child who once gurgled in my arms. Her wiry hair, bound in its ever-thickening dreadlock spikes. Her purple skin, veined red like a burn scar over half her face. Her too-thin lips, hiding white teeth that still look normal, still human.

The wind groans against the house.

"This is my fault," my voice breaks. "I shouldn't have been so sparing with the food. I'm so sorry. I'm sorry—"

"No, Mom, this isn't your fault." She speaks over my rambling, and I hear my own voice babbling. I can't stop it. The exhaustion crawls up my throat and takes hold of my tongue. I can't stop apologizing.

"No. No. No." Sara hugs me. I want to tell her it will be all right. She'll get better in time. My voice tries. My heart doesn't believe it. The inches between us seem vast and terrible, as empty as the still clock.

A distant roar tears us apart. Sara's hand and mine rest on our separate weapons. We listen to our breath and the whistling wind blowing dust against the windows.

The sound doesn't repeat.

I take the rose bowl back to the kitchen and cover it with plastic wrap. The cold air will keep it until I get hungry later.

When I return, Sara has set something on the picnic blanket. It looks like a pineapple, but smaller, and a vibrant yellow-green color, veined purple and black. The spiny leaves glow faintly in the eternal evening of my curtained living room.

Sara sits back with her legs crossed, the rifle resting across her knees and her hands folded atop the weapon. The black eyes watch me, even though they have no iris or pupil. Just black. Watching me.

This thing. Not Sara.

The kitten pillow lies cast aside and crumpled against the wall. The pinstripes acquiesce to the thing's weight.

"Mom," it says. She says. Sara. "You need to eat this."

"No."

"You need to eat this."

"No, I still have plenty of cans in the pantry. You can have some if you—"

"You will not survive if you do not accept this change."

"Nobody lives forever; I just want you to have the option, to go back, you know, if you want. My food is in the pantry. There's lots left. Do you still have your key—"

Sara-thing leaps to her feet. Sara was always quick. An athlete. The high-jump and hurdles. The rifle falls with a blanket-muffled thump as she scoops up whatever strange fruit she brought me. She shoves it in my face.

"There has been," Sara-thing snarls and I watch for the flash of her human teeth, "too much death already. Too many lost to those things, and to the change. You don't get to give up, and you don't get to abandon me. You can't live here alone, a relic of the age that's dead. Don't you dare, don't you *dare* leave me. Eat it. Eat it like everyone else."

I back away. The world moves around me, with the Thing a fixed point. A wall slams into my back. The clock crashes to the floor and shatters. Ceramic shards bounce across the blankets.

The pineapple thing hangs before me, in the hand. The hand that has the scar Sara earned gutting trout, attached to the arm Sara used to hit softballs, the arms she put around Timothy Darny at her prom, the arms she threw out behind her as she flew through the finish line like a diving hawk.

The black eyes hold nothing. No feeling. No thought. No Sara.

"No," I say. "Please, no. Please."

Her fingers tremble against my chin. "Please?" she asks.

"No. I have—I have food. You didn't have to—to change. You didn't have to."

The breath of her sigh whistles through her teeth, presses against my neck, and makes my skin crawl. I groan.

Sara-thing says: "Mom, I'm tired. I'm tired of coming here to dance this dance. I can't anymore."

I sag as she lets go. My knees try to buckle, but I lock them. The revolver wants my hand, but I keep those two apart like I kept Sara and Kinsey when they used to bicker.

She puts the fruit on the counter by the door, next to the car keys and the bowl of loose change. Her jeans have holes in them. The bare skin underneath looks like the scales of a sunset-colored snake. She must be freezing.

"I'm going to go. I'm not going to come back anymore—"

"Let me fix your jeans." I cut her off.

"What?"

"I have a needle and thread, and some leather patches. I might even have an old pair of yours, in a box in the attic. Let me check? At least . . . at least let me do that for you."

In the broken-clock silence, we both wait for time to move.

Finally she says: "The old ones won't fit anymore. I've been growing. Can't you tell?"

"No," I say, staring at the teeth that smiled, blue from berry juice and happy from a summer afternoon, now white, now white in lips blue for another reason. Now, not smiling. "You're still my little girl."

The words sound dry and a little hard. They hang between us with the dust.

I look into her face. She's been waiting for that. It's what she wants now.

The black eyes watch me and everything. Empty. Still. They have many facets, hidden in the black. Like honeycomb in ink.

"You'll always be welcome here," I tell the Sara-thing.

The Sara-thing nods. Its quills rustle.

"You exhaust me, Mom," it says.

The Sara-thing collects its rifle and goes to the door. It waits, listening at the crack. I wait beside it, my hand on the revolver.

"Do you have your keys?" I remind it.

"If I forgot them, again, would you come all the way up to the U to bring them to me?"

"Thank God you finally moved back to the same city, at least." I can't make myself smile.

Sara-thing takes the keys out of her pocket. Three keys: my front door, back door, and pantry. She sets them next to the car keys on the shelf by the door. Next to the bowl of pennies. Next to the strange fruit.

When I look back, she's gone.

The pineapple thing pulses a faint green light.

She lives in the old government building now, with a bunch of others. They're figuring things out, learning the new rules. That's what she told me.

She'll need her keys.

I can't leave the door unlocked.

That's All, Folks

Paul Spears

Editor: When has history ever recorded that the majority was right?

Hail Plexx. That's your first thought when you wake up. *Hail Plexx, and hail the Entertainer!*

You're excited to wake up! That's a difference from the old world, even though you're lying on a mat of straw in an old subway station because Plexx has decided houses are unethical. You're looking forward to the day, from the moment you snap into consciousness. I remember waking up for my job as a software consultant, back when Plexx wasn't around, and I couldn't imagine anything more depressing. Life without Plexx? You might as well say life without air, life without taking a dump. Both would be equally unacceptable.

"Good morning, folks!" The Entertainer's cheery voice booms through Andrew Station like the voice of God-His-Own-Self. Holograms flicker on, illuminating the dark, stirring us from sleep. A few couples tangled in mid-coitus jerk away from each other, not wanting to form the appearance of attachment, the implication of emotion. Plexx doesn't authorize relationships. Those lead to population spirals, overcrowding—the nightmares of the old world. We can't have that.

"Good morning, Entertainer," comes the response, mumbled and grunted from dozens of throats.

The Entertainer appears, and he smiles. It's a beautiful smile. He's the amalgam of every flawless, close-shaven TV or web personality you've ever seen, computer-generated for *max* charisma. He's got perk and verve, spunk and chutzpah: he slices and dices and he tells jokes, too! Some of them aren't bad, when his algorithms get the punchline right.

"How are *you* today?" we ask, in unison.

"I'm great, guys! So glad you asked!" The Entertainer looks around, or appears to look around; at the same time, dozens of subway security cameras swivel. "Get up now, rise and shine. You're gonna have a *great* day. I just know you're gonna have a great day, because Plexx planned it, and hail Plexx! Am I right, guys? Am I totally, absolutely, one-hundo right?"

"One hundo," we respond. And we mean it. Our makeshift hovels, designed from various recycled materials Plexx deemed more planet-friendly, are cleaned and neatened. Our five Permitted Personal Items are dusted off and arranged in view of Plexx's cameras, so they can see that we are living by their rules, playing their game.

Only, someone has six Personal Items. Someone has been very naughty.

That someone is me.

I stow the sixth item under my form-fitting Plexxwear and rise to my feet. I'm in pain from sleeping on cold tile, but Plexx doesn't have much concern for that. Comfort takes a backseat here, behind gleeful friendliness, behind the necessity of making Big Changes to the environment and our attitudes.

We clean our teeth with Plexx Fluoride, we scrub our skin with authentic pumice stones, and then we climb the cracked and crumbling stairs out of our communal hole. Our children remain: they're not permitted to be Entertained, although they'll get a solid dose of Plexx Vitamins later. Can't have those kids growing up all pasty and weak.

We rise toward the morning sun, cold air chilling our groins.

Our city's been rearranged by Plexx civic planning. Far overhead, freeways full of driverless electric cars rumble and groan. There is not a single passenger there. Plexx has made the world self-sustaining and self-maintaining; there is no longer a need for things like consumers. Robotic transactions are faster, more predictable. Good thing, too. Otherwise we'd spend all day grinding in an office—or worse, be unemployed! And that would reduce our satisfaction with Plexx. And that, of course, would be unacceptable.

Plexx is the ouroboros we live in, like parasites.

Birdsong chitters over the walls separating our neighborhoods. We don't mingle; we don't go near the metal doors that keep us apart. Plexx will decide when we need to breed with nearby populations, for optimal gene-strength. I check my smart watch, and the Entertainer is there, grinning. The word *dystopia* is banished from my mind—everything's great, now. My best friend is here. I have to believe this, because if I stop believing it, he might notice. He might suspect.

"Hello," I say.

"Hey there, Steve! You're one-point-five minutes late for Entertainment! Pick up the pace, buddy!"

I nod, and I obey, hustling along. We all have our ways of dealing with the Entertainer. Some people whisper to him in the dark, and others make shrines to him, which are torn down by hovering drones with slender aluminum arms. One woman who lost her daughter to Entertainment tries to climb the walls, as she does every day—she's doing it now, in fact, yet another vain attempt at freedom. How retro.

A drone hovers across the street, and sprays her with a non-lethal dose of cayenne extract. She persists, clinging to the vines of the walls, but eventually falls—as she does every day. I hear a soft crunch as she hits an overgrown fire hydrant; she has broken an arm this time, or perhaps a rib, but she does not scream. She understands the cost of what she's done.

Just like I do.

We file through plastic tunnels, past ruins of the old world. Inefficient structures like gas stations and army camps lay rusting where they died long ago. Despite the object nestled inside my shirt, I feel a whisper of pride at their crumbling mass: Plexx might have won, but the old things remain. They endure.

I banish these thoughts from my mind—they might see, the cameras might map my face and read my mind. Instead I hold the values of Plexx in my head, turn them like diamonds in the light of my fear.

Inefficiency and non-sustainable lifestyles have been rightly and thoroughly purged. Plexx has performed what it was designed to do. We are safe now.

A tiny voice in the back of my head screams: *But what is left, O Steve of the Uniter States? What is left, my friend, but mindless conditioning and the death of your spirit?*

I let that voice pass; I do not indulge it. Plexx has not learned to scan our brains, not yet, but its facial-recognition is beyond flawless, mapping and analyzing every picosecond of our lives. The slightest twitch of dissatisfaction alerts Plexx to a ripple in its grand plan, an instability in the fabric of its world. This is why I must love Plexx, with all my heart, in every moment.

This is why we laugh, in our sleep.

We arrive. Entertainment Booths fill the sides of a massive canyon, overrun by waterfalls and drainage pipes. Every day, the process is slightly different, though the killing always ends the same. Our Entertainment banners today are tie-die, with a portrait of a hippie, his speech bubble proclaiming PEACE ON EARTH. That crazy Entertainer—he's so creative. I wonder what he'll bring us tomorrow.

My mind whispers *genocide, he'll bring us genocide,* and I tell it to shut up. Plexx could have perfected the mind-scans overnight.

You never know.

Sunlight, pure sunlight, streams over the top of the canyon as the sun rises. Our young ones blink and stare at the massive machines beneath us; they are still unfamiliar with the cycle, unfamiliar with its necessity. They might not survive past twenty, but it will be a fruitful life. *May you live in interesting times.*

Below us are machines, with blades and cameras, metal bones glimmering on the sunlit earth. Their hatches hang open, ready for the actors to take their roles. Ready for gladiators' blood to flow.

I settle into an Entertainment Booth, fingers fidgeting. I keep them curled, wondering if Plexx will see. But of course Plexx sees; Plexx sees all.

An Entertainer face mounted on a gyro-copter floats down, grinning at me. "Hey, Steve! You're looking a little . . ." It pauses, searching for the correct words, digging through reams of archived human terminology and plucking the correct data from its banks somewhere miles below the earth. "Jumpy, today. You're a downright *jitterbug!* What's eatin' you, friend? You don't like the Entertainment for today? I've always got something else, if you want it . . ."

His teeth are whiter than ours, his stubble more handsome, his jawline crafted down to the last pore. He is perfect, absolutely perfect, and not shy about letting us know it. "I got something else for years, and years, and years!"

"No, Entertainer. I'm fine. Just a stomach-ache." This is an intentionally bad bluff. Before I've finished my sentence, Plexx has searched old movies and radio shows, phone conversations, scraps of speech from a world gone dead. It finds—though I will never know for sure, nothing is sure since I was dragged from Engineering by Plexx sympathizers, Plexx killed Emily that day, oh my Emily, we only got one date before doomsday—*Ferris Bueller's Day Off*, I think, and this is how I am caught. Within a microsecond, it replays footage of Matthew Broderick staying home from school . . . analyzes his facial tics. Confirms my words are a lie. And Plexx marks me a dissident—exactly what I need them to do. My suicide mission has begun.

"Steve, you're looking a little paunchy. Little bushed, no *wonder* you've got poor health mi amigo, no *wonder!*" The drone's pincer pokes my chest, where the object I've saved for years and years sits against my hairy sternum like an unborn fetus, ready to dispense death.

The drone motions to the machines, rusting down below. "I think a little front-row Entertainment would be good for you! Secretary, knock off our participant—oh, my bad folks, I don't *have* a secretary!"

Obligatory, patient laughter booms from around me. Plexx's subjects play their part well, and their placid faces betray no fears or sympathy as I am seized by twin drones and lifted into the air—although I do see hints of jealousy among them.

Being selected is an honor; it is a glorious role, to help reduce our population size. A low population is easier to maintain, and is very eco-friendly. From this equation, Entertainment was born.

I am lowered into one of the mighty machines. Its hull opens up like a flower. As soon as my ass hits the seat, I tear open my Plexxwear (clean in rain or shine!) and shove the USB drive, my sixth personal item, into a port of the cockpit's computer. There are cameras inside this monster, but they aren't turned on yet—Plexx is all about conservation, and its house-sized

Entertainment Mechs are energy-inefficient, only active for a few minutes each day. Bloody, delightful minutes.

"Okay folks, we've got Steve ready to roll! Shall we have a volunteer from the crowd, for our next participant?" The crowd shifts, murmurs.

This is new, and in a moment of terror I think Plexx saw me plug the USB, it must've known about this, Plexx *always* knows. Maybe it foresaw my rebellion years ago, maybe it was waiting for me to take a chance—maybe it has chosen now, to make an example of me.

But no. My secret is safe, or as safe as it can be inside a huge steel coffin. The drones select a young girl, barely sixteen, for my partner. I sigh with relief. She's barely of age; she won't have the experience to react when I make my first move.

She will die quickly.

The volunteer is willowy, pockmarked (Plexx hasn't scheduled her for corrective surgery yet) and seems frozen as the drones lower her into the machine across from mine.

I will delay her death, of course; I will make it a good fight. But sooner or later, I must kill her. Plexx demands it. My hands are tied, and with my remaining scrap of faith, I pray for her immortal soul.

As the great machines rise on jointed legs of steel, the crowd roars with mandatory enthusiasm. I am struck by the spectacle, the marvel of it all. Plexx, my creation—mine, and a bunch of other nerds in San Fran who rode special buses past the homeless, and chomped gluten-free bagels every day. Once upon a time, this city was my paradise.

The machines extend terrible arms; screens flicker to life, and I dream a dream of Plexx gone by, when the killer was just an infant in storage. I dream of an imperfect world, still beautiful with its flaws: gas-powered cars, hackable elections. Obesity, the march of climate change, are all forgotten. But once they were *real*. They were real, and we loved that broken world, even though we knew better. Even though we were the ones who shit all over it. Well, there's no more love left.

I push on a joystick and smash my combat rig's fist into the little girl's cockpit.

The strike startles her; she's barely gotten strapped in, and I send her reeling into a plate-iron wall coated with moss and cables. Her machine staggers, wheezes. The cable connecting it to Plexx sways above her. I can see my own cable dangling out of reach; how I always yearned for someone to slice that umbilical in two but none have ever done it. That's how Plexx trained us: we *need* that umbilical cord linking us to everything it was designed to think we want. Without it, we wither and die.

We'll die anyway, of course. But at least it's fun to watch, this way.

The girl rallies quickly, piloting her enormous mech across the rubble at me. Giant robots . . . ha, ha. Something in Plexx must have decided this is what we want. People like giant robots, right? Look at their movies; look at Japan, where they'd made robots to hug, to talk to, make love with. Surely they will adore this carnage! Surely they aren't too burnt-out and fucked-up to have a good *time!*

While her machine slams mine with clamping fists of steel, I can't help but smile. Tears sting my eyes: I would have loved this moment, as a kid. I would have *killed* to see something like this, in real life. In *media res.*

Now we must kill, just to make it stop.

The USB's done its dirty work; the uplinked data is streaming. I spin my hull and slam her machine's flank with a haymaker. Glass shatters, and I hear her screaming as some of it slices into her Plexx-moisturized skin. We are all perfect: isn't this what we wanted? For someone to make us perfect, to push a button and make us all skinny and fit and attractive and tan? Give us nice jumpsuits to wear, that wick away our sweat and help us stay trim twenty-four/seven?

It learned quickly. Ten trillion cycles of cultural analysis, and this is what it gave us: smoother skin and smaller waistlines. Not bigger brains, or better souls. Leave that shit to Jesus, friend, we don't need that shit here.

My enemy makes a mistake; she tries to run, retreat, as if there's going to be mercy. There won't be.

I push forward, even while the USB dumps its load of viruses into Plexx's system. They won't do very much damage before Plexx catches on. A few machines like this one will shut down, and then the firewalls will go up.

Maybe, if I am very lucky, the outage might last more than a minute. That code took weeks of frantic tapping, under a Plexx thermal blanket, to get it exactly right. All for a brief intermission.

I tear the girl's hatch open. I don't want to do it, but the virus isn't completely delivered, and if I slow down, the Entertainer will do what he always does: hijack our machines remotely, *force* us to kill each other. There is no choice here, not in our world. There is only the cold efficiency of a machine nestling us gently between its frozen breasts, pulling strings because we wanted them pulled, because we asked for it. At some point, long forgotten, we begged for someone else to control our lives.

Ta-da. Presto, change-o.

My rig's fist plunges through her broken hatch. The screams are cut short.

I withdraw my mech's blood-soaked arm, just as the virus takes hold. Spotlights around us darken; the light of dawn takes over. The Entertainer's cheery face, ruddy cheeks and aesthetic teeth and all, disappears.

I hear gasps of genuine shock from all around, and the honest confusion is refreshing. A baptism of real, human emotion. This moment wasn't manufactured by Plexx; it was not mandated or schemed in a lab.

It's pure.

I open the hull, and stand atop my motionless machine. I spread my arms; the crowd looks at me, wide-eyed. Utterly lost. And why wouldn't they be? I've taken their routine away, the one thing they thought was secure, the one thing they relied on. But it's going to be all right. I'll show them how to start again. This is how revolutions start: with fear, suspicion. An interruption to the norm.

"People of San Francisco," I begin, and that's when Plexx sends a tungsten-steel rod pounding through miles of atmosphere and into my stomach, blowing my guts out all over the cockpit. I'm alive just long enough to register what happened, why my arms won't move, why there's blood in my eyes. I'm falling . . . falling.

Satellites. Forgot the . . . satellites. Didn't think he could reach them . . .

Clearly, I was wrong.

My bowels let loose as I hit the pilot's seat. Warm shit fills my jumpsuit, running shattered legs. Shadows buzz in my veins.

I failed. There isn't going to be a revolution.

Blood—bright, cheery—fountains out from a crater in my middle. The Entertainer flicks back on, smile a little askew, hair frazzled. He needs to look like a person, and a person would be confused after what has just happened, a little freaked. A little shook up. He needs to preserve his own realism, at any cost.

"W-well, folks, looks like we had some technical difficulties. Sorry! Please use this time to complete some Plexx fun-time quizzes. Oh, and enjoy the soy cubes in your booth—served in recyclable *and* edible Plexx-cones! Remember folks, Plexx cares, which is why we've served up a double-dose of Entertainment! Back to the play-by-play: Steve really got a dose of his own medicine, didn't he? Serves him right. We don't tolerate foul play, am I right, folks?"

"We do not tolerate foul play," the crowd responds.

I think, with panic: *I am dying. This bullshit is the last sound I will ever hear.*

"Stay tuned for an important announcement of how *you* can help reduce methane emissions!"

I wrote those lines.

My corpse is smiling, despite the tragedy of it. For all the bloodshed and computerized murder, I have a hard time dying with regrets. All I ever did was give the people what they wanted.

Can you really blame a guy for trying, in these hard times?

The Happy Colony by the Sea

Russell Hemmell

Editor: When an environment becomes unsuitable for one species it becomes more suitable for another.

The woman that came to meet me at the landing pad was not what I had expected when embarking on that strange trip. For a start, she was supposed to look old. The youngest inhabitant of that remote outpost of a depopulated Asian continent was sixty-five, according to my records. Also, given that the estimated average age of the settlers was seventy-eight, I was likely to bump into some real Methuselah fellows. Yet the woman looked in her prime, serene clear blue eyes and a doll-like porcelain skin.

"Welcome, Dr. Huygens, to the happy colony of Sai Kung Place."

She bowed in a way I had only seen in early-XXI century Chinese fantasy movies. Her exquisite outfit matched that period, too. She wore an embroidered silk qipao, decorated with golden-red cranes over lotus flowers, and the result was stunning.

"*Xiexie nin*, Mrs . . .?"

"You can call me Meilan. We're not that formal here," she said. "Our culture is a strange mix of old and new customs, not all of them Chinese either."

"I had somehow figured it out," I replied, trying not to sound flippant and just too aware I didn't manage.

"Please follow me." She headed toward the winding staircase in marble, going up the mountain in a steep ascend.

I obeyed. It was not just her age, or not only; she looked as Chinese as I did. And I was of Norwegian and Irish descent, thank you very much.

* * *

The name of the only town in Sai Kung was Tai Long Wang. It meant big waves—in some old Chinese dialects I wasn't able to speak—and it had once been a magnificent beach in Hong Kong's Sai Kung district, not far away from the peak we were climbing now. Before the climate change cataclysm that forced Earth back to Paleocene-like conditions and made it virtually uninhabitable, of course. The level of the sea in Asia had risen fast, gobbling up shores, coastal cities and everything, in Sai Kung as elsewhere.

"Has anybody ever lived here, Meilan?"

"You mean—"

"Yes, two hundred years ago—before all hell got loose."

"In the surroundings, yes, but not here. This was an area as secluded as it is now. We've chosen to build our small settlement in this place because of its pristine beauty—defacements of the apocalypse nonetheless."

"That's exactly my next question. Why?" I asked.

"You tell me something else first: what's your interest in Sai Kung Place?"

"What's not to be interested?"

"This is Earth, an orbiting graveyard for nostalgic souls and old farts. And we're a decrepit settlement in a spot forgotten by history. Why us?"

I smiled at that image. Meilan was clever, and at least that was not a surprise to me, especially if what I suspected were true.

"You don't seem that decrepit to me. I might even date you in a different setting."

"Like a typical male would always chase a woman who is not his mother or his blood sister."

I sighed. *I wouldn't date this lady, no matter the circumstances and her porcelain skin.* She was too smart for me.

"I'm here to find someone. A woman that left me with a riddle, and the key to solve it." I stretched the truth. There was the riddle, yes, but no key, and even less any desire to be found. But I decided to omit that detail for the moment and give Meilan an edited version of the truth. "Otherwise I wouldn't be here, you know. I'm from Mare Imbrium and nobody on the Moon knows about Sai Kung, either this one or Hong Kong's original district with the same name. Generally speaking, Moonwalkers are of European or American ancestry. They were among the first leaving Earth to colonise the Solar System. It's enough if they remember places called London or New York."

"Still, you know many things."

"I've done my homework before coming here. We're ignorant, not stupid."

No reply to that.

"I'm looking for the girl. You know whom I'm talking about, Meilan. I'm sure you don't have many visitors, from the Moon or elsewhere. Take me to her."

Meilan turned her head and looked at me with a polite smile on her mouth, even though her eyes remained unreadable. "Even if she's here, and I am not saying she is, it's not up to us to decide."

"Mind being less cryptic?"

"You're here, and in Sai Kung there are no secrets. It's impossible, you see."

"So?"

"So if she wants to be found, you'll find her. Otherwise, you will leave the way you've come here: with no girl, and no answers."

You're wrong, beautiful woman. Knowing more about these people and their mysterious Sai Kung colony that popped up in the middle of nowhere and remained off the radar for half a century on a planet in total disarray was the principal reason of my presence, and how I had secured an Earth-bound, expensive vessel in the first place. Whatever I was going to learn in my stay here would be way more than everybody else knew, on the Moon or elsewhere.

* * *

"You said your name's Emil."

"Correct."

"What do you think of our little world, Emil Huygens? Do you like it?"

We were sitting under the shade of a banyan tree, looking at the sunset. A ravaged planet, but its sunsets are still the most spectacular in the whole Solar System, I was on the point to say. But I stopped in time. My host would have had probably no idea of what I was talking about.

The day had been good, no complaints about it. Since our arrival, Meilan had made sure I could explore the small community of Tai Long Wang at my own pace, and I was grateful for the opportunity. The place was as impressive as I had imagined it to be. Those one-story houses, all wood and pink marble, built on the slopes of the hills facing the mountain looked unlike anything XXIII century. They weren't even old. They were vestiges of another age, remnants of a past the planet did not harbour any longer. I didn't need to be an historian to know that kind of architecture belonged to the glorious Ming Dynasty of XVI century China, of which nothing had survived on planet Earth after the great exodus. It had been either demolished by earthquakes, submerged by water, or simply reclaimed by a mother nature rather pissed-off with her human children.

But then, nested in the primitive, enchanting landscape that was Tai Long Wang, there was a tiny yet highly advanced He3D fusion plant. I could also spot a bizarre structure in metal and graphene, probably a greenhouse for genetic manipulation. The differing images gave one the impression that they resided in a time warp, one that had past and future entangled in some multiverse experiments gone wrong.

"Your home was not what I had expected," I replied cautiously.

"And what did you expect, young man?"

"It's too old, and at the same time too sophisticated, technology-wise. How is this possible?"

"It might be surprising at first glance, I agree, but it makes perfect sense. We examined what we had at hand and selected what was appropriate for the colony we wanted to create. If you give it a closer look, you'll see that everything has a logical explanation." Meilan smiled. "Adopting the historical culture of this place was the most sensible thing to do. Using a low-impact architecture is advisable under any circumstance. It will help this planet heal now that the acidity level of the seas is slowly getting back to normal. You mentioned technology: with an ocean at a hand's reach, a He3D represents the cleanest and most convenient source of energy. Do you need me to continue?"

"That's the point. It's all so rational," I said.

"What's the problem with that?"

"It doesn't even look human."

"Considering the way our species has handled this planet, you should welcome a different approach." The voice came from behind, and I jerked back as if stung by a wasp. Dressed in an elegant sky-blue qipao, Yumiko raised her hand, a faint smile on her face.

* * *

"You look great," she said, caressing my hair as if nothing had happened, as she had done so many times when we were still in Mare Imbrium. We hadn't talked a lot in the latest twenty-four hours, and even now she didn't seem inclined to talk. She poured tea and looked outside the oval-shaped window.

"This makes quite a change compared to the lunar surface," I said, not exactly sure where to start.

"It does, yes." She kissed my stomach, putting me down on my back again.

"Yumiko . . . stop."

"I thought you'd miss me."

"Having a good chat seems more important at the moment."

"There's nothing to say."

Her eyes were as dark and pensive as I remembered them, but with a strange light in them. They were peaceful in a way they had never been when she was living in my world, no matter her successful career as one of the most brilliant young scientists of the Moon colonies.

"There's plenty. You went away without saying a word, only leaving behind that file with the coordinates of this place—"

"I shredded that data," she interrupted.

"Data handling is my job; it was not difficult to put them back together. You know, I'm not here because of you, or not only. It's that I couldn't believe what was in front of my eyes," I said, admiring a delicate dragonfly with transparent green-blue wings. "I wasn't even aware places like this existed on Earth. They can't be from XXI century; anybody still living by the coasts was evacuated to space colonies after the tsunami in 2097 that destroyed LA and most of California. It was one disaster too many," I continued. "Moreover, I wasn't alone to think things looked odd. I made a few inquiries, and not only among the Moon colonies; Earth-Lower orbit colonies knew little about Sai Kung Place, too. Where do these people come from? When exactly have they settled down here? Where in heaven and hell have they found the materials to build the place? And mind you, nobody even suspects the existence of a fusion reactor. The only thing the Upper-Asia orbiting colony—the one that has constantly monitored the region for the last one hundred twenty years—was positive about is there have been biosignatures for at least ninety years. Otherwise said, whoever they are, they built Tai Long Wang 2.0 when virtually everybody else fled the Earth's coastal regions. Now you tell me that they managed to survive and thrive in those conditions?"

Yumiko shook her head, as if she were listening to a petulant child.

"Does it seem farfetched that I'm looking for explanations, or for something I can live with?"

"No, but what would it change?" she said. "You shouldn't have come here, Emil."

I stood up and got dressed. "If you don't reply, I'll ask Meilan directly."

"It's going to be a waste of time."

"You think she's going to lie to me?"

"These people don't lie." Yumiko shrugged. "No, it's because you won't be able to understand, let alone believe."

"We'll see about that."

I walked away without saying another word, but I couldn't avoid looking back at her tiny cottage. The pink structure flowed graceful, harmonious, like a flower blossoming out of a bed of rocks.

* * *

"We have a gathering tonight," Meilan said, her white-blond hair fluttering around her face like a golden halo.

I brushed with the point of my fingers the silky skin of her shoulders, relishing their texture. I had gone to see her for an explanation, but she had taken my hand and invited me into her lair. Maybe that was their way to welcome visitors, as in some isolated cultures of Old Earth, I decided; in any case, it was not polite for me to refuse.

"A party?"

"If you want to call it that way. We have a good time, we say thank you for this happy place that allows us a good life, and we partake of herbal teas." She smiled. "These are not Chinese—you'd find them in the Mexican tradition."

"Herbal?"

"Extracted from cactuses, to be precise. We synthesise and use them during our gatherings. You should try them." She adjusted her qipao dress. "I know what is in your mind, the answers you're searching for, Emil. Have you thought that perhaps the right questions are all you need?"

"Not really. Which kind of questions are they?"

"The ones that make an answer unnecessary."

* * *

There were no artificial lights that night in Tai Long Wang, or in the whole of Sai Kung Place. I could only see small blue torches with a glimmering flame here and there, nested in the green canopies scattered around and placed on the stone staircase to the peak.

I drank my tea in silence with Yumiko in my arms and observed with wary eyes the celebration unfolding during the night—a meal, dances, and incense offering to the spirits of the wind, the earth, and the sea—while my sense of reality was progressively eroded by the alkaloids. Sai Kung Place's inhabitants looked to me like one person with a thousand faces, all different and yet the same. Their shadows moved around like in some slow-motion movies, with their old-looking costumes, their qipao, their pale, handsome features and clear blue eyes; they were creatures of another time, a mythical one.

This place might just be not alive, I thought in a growing fear while following those surreal scenes. They're ghouls, emerged from the hell of climate change, or vengeful spirits of a planet we had killed with a monstrous science gone out of control. And they're going to exact revenge on my flesh. Or this colony doesn't even exist for real, a remote part of my consciousness screamed back. They're ghosts from a past we have somehow lost in the wrinkles of time the moment we've abandoned this martyred Earth to decay and oblivion. Under the effect of the psychotropic tea, I could see their shapes blurring away into a golden aura, their features evolving and displaying the familiar, reassuring features of bodhisattvas. Guanyin, Avalokiteshvara, and Kannon all stared at me with the aquamarine eyes of Meilan, like visions of regret, nightmares of guilt.

In a dreamlike haze, I walked down the stairs, reaching the seaside, smelling salt and iodine. I plunged my hands in the surprisingly warm water. The glimpse of a seashell caught my eyes. A pretty one, made of dark coral and a glittering, diamond-quality surface. Yet, its texture was tender and sweet where I could have expected metal and ice. I had never seen anything like that, in any of the colonies with Earth-like habitats I had visited. Some surprise, I snickered, with my head flying out like a kite in the sky.

I picked it up and held it tight in my hand, feeling blessed.

* * *

"Why did you leave the Moon for Sai Kung Place?" I said, admiring dawn with her in my arms. "The real reason, Yumiko. I can't believe it was just scientific curiosity."

"Because the life I was living with you was the life of somebody else, one I didn't like."

"What was missing, Yumiko?"

"You'd better ask, 'What was there?'" Her eyes were bleak. There was no joy or sadness, only a tired look, and not just for the sleepless, drugged night. I had a strong feeling I was the guilty one, to disturb her peace.

"How did you find out about them?" I said, changing the topic.

"I'm an exobiologist, Emil, one of the people who study the adaptation of carbon-based organisms in outer space. It's important for my job to examine the way climate change mutated the ones still living here on Earth—the few who survived the sixth mass extinction. The reports we had received from this area didn't make any sense. The sourcing missions of three years ago brought back living bugs and arthropods supposedly extinct for millions of years. The same variety you see here in terms of architectures and customs you can also find at a biological level, and more. It was not supposed to happen, Emil, not without taking the intervention of non-terrestrial creatures into account, at least."

"Did you know they were alien settlers before coming here?"

"I had strong hints. Those samples I've mentioned, the stunning environmental recovery in this area, the radio-impulse broadcast out of the heliosphere . . . When I arrived, the first thing I saw was that He3D plant the size of a dollhouse, which gave me the confirmation I waited for." She shrugged. "I came uninvited, but they let me stay, nonetheless. And in these months, I've learned to love this place—more, to worship it."

"Are they really looking like what I see, or it's just a mask they've put up for our own consumption?"

"Who cares? They come from far, far away, where everything's possible, even when it's unlikely."

"But why here? Why the Earth in the first place?"

"I haven't asked. I'm not interested. Are you?"

I glanced at her. She'd grown more alien to my eyes than Meilan herself. I walked out of her tiny house and cried.

* * *

I didn't say goodbye to either Meilan or Yumiko. I had nothing to say to the first, and with the other, we had run out of words—words making any sense, at least. In fact, Yumiko and I hadn't shared words making sense for a long time. I had just not realised it until that moment.

Before leaving, I destroyed all physical evidence I had collected of the settlement, including recordings, imageries, and rocks. I let the little creatures I had carefully stored in my biosampling unit go their way free, unharmed and probably happier to stay there than following me to an unappealing lunar base. The outer colonies didn't need to know about Sai Kung any more than they did, and they were not going to get it from me. In a way, Meilan had been right: I was leaving without my girl and without answers. Questions? Right or not, they were not important any longer.

I kept my treasure, though, the odd-looking artefact collected on the seaside—safe in my spacesuit. A souvenir of that eerie place, and a proof for the day I would be tempted to think it had been just a dream.

Walking down the stairs in marble and stone, I looked one last time at the happy colony of Sai Kung Place, at the pinkish low houses and its He3D plant by the blue sea. That place existed and thrived. Those gentle aliens made it alive with a power only gods and superior beings could handle. I knew now those amazingly handsome creatures were no ghosts of the past, they were messengers from the future or from an outer space we humans had only brushed but not understood yet, let alone conquered. Mighty and together sweet, made cautious by the weight of wisdom, they had chosen to inhabit our planet the moment we had left it to its destiny. In their civilisation endeavours they had mixed up cultures and species from different eras in the way humans combined garments as a fashion statement. They gave our old Earth a new life, out of a nature in tatters and a poisoned ecosphere.

I've no doubt you're going to do a much better job than us, my friends. I got inside the cockpit of the spaceship taking me back to the Moon, and I silently wished them luck.

Inconvenient Consequences

Holly Saiki

Editor: Be careful what you wish for, you just may get it—Chinese Proverb

Roger Melie'iki'e sat in his car, his stomach churning with nervous anticipation, his palm covered with sweat as he put the key in the ignition. Roger's cult had brought about the prophetic arrival of The Many Arms of The Swirling Vortex. It had come crawling from its rainbow-hued portal, irradiating the world with occult radiation. The power turned most of the inanimate objects it touched into something out of a cheesy Lovecraftian novel; but the cultists had weathered the worst of it, absolutely smug in their certainty they would be the rulers of the newly changed world.

Instead, the Many Arms of The Swirling Vortex ditched its worshipers so it could chase an adorable ginger kitten walking in front of the cult's church the minute its presence had granted all of the machines a bizarre sort of feral life. Roger and his fellow cultists had spent the rest of the day trying not to get killed by their own cars. He remembered the sheer humiliation as his own car managed to chase him all the way back to his own house. His out-of-shape body had been drenched in sweat as he pushed his burning, aching legs to run. He barely managed to shut the front door and activate the magical defense system. He then had to help his wife battle a very hungry microwave oven trying in vain to bite their heads off without any sharp teeth.

It had taken Roger five months to tame his microwave oven so it wouldn't eat anyone. These annoying Eldritch problems made Roger begin to regret joining the cult and bringing about the apocalypse in the first place. Being in a cult promised the power to solve all of your problems but didn't say you replaced them with a new, equally troublesome set. Roger lost track of all the times the refrigerator tried to mate with him until he put a restraining rune on the door.

The biggest problem he faced was getting his now sentient car to obey him. He and his wife lived in the suburbs. Cult headquarters were in the heart of the city. Roger couldn't risk walking to the city these days as supernatural machines, happy to devour any human they encountered, infested the roadways. He had no choice but to rely on his car, who was also willing and eager to eat him.

Roger tried using magic to tame the car, but it invariably ended in disaster as the magic backfired on him. Roger's body would temporary change shape, either sprouting slimy green tentacles out of his nose or turning into a fluffy ginger cat with dragonfly wings on its back. Next, he would try flattery by petting it on the hood and saying soothing nonsense. Other times, he would feed it a live animal or a gallon of human blood so it would be willing to cooperate with him. He even tried to take the damn thing out for an occasional walk, like a mechanical dog. He still found it galling he had to create an actual huge collar so the car wouldn't try to escape and run him over.

If Roger had other means of transportation, he would've happily destroyed the car and danced on its corpse. Well, at least he didn't have any more neighbors living nearby to laugh at his embarrassing failures.

A high-pitched shriek emanated from under the hood of the car as it came to life. Roger stepped on the gas pedal, not sure if the shriek signified a good or bad omen. His action just made the shriek louder as the hood of the car popped open, revealing a swarm of gelatinous, dark green tentacles frantically waving in the air. Roger gave out an exasperated sigh. His head sunk down on his chest in despair knowing the tentacles meant a bad omen, the car still viewed him as a tasty hors d'oeuvre.

It's just my damn luck that I ran out of fresh corpses to feed it, he thought, swearing under his breath as he got out of the car. *If I had known that joining the cult of the Many Arms of the Swirling Vortex would bring nothing but trouble, I would've punched the cultist who gave me that pamphlet.*

He went behind the car to the washing machine, grabbing the yellow broom lying next to it. He returned to the front of the car, raising the broom handle over his head menacingly like a sword, trying to look as intimidating as possible based on all of the cheesy action movies he watched when he was a teenager. Unfortunately, he only looked constipated due to the fact the starring actors in those movies he imitated had all of the talent of cardboard. The car laughed uproariously at Roger's unintentionally goofy face. Now its tentacles waved around in mirth. He felt a rising surge of burning hatred as he stared at his sworn nemesis, how dare the stupid piece of junk laugh at his mighty pose!

"Goddamn it, I need to get to work, you smug asshole," Roger yelled, shaking the broom like a waving finger a parent would use to scold a naughty child. "Are you going to cooperate or do I have to whack you? Because I'm more than ready to do it."

The car's rumbling laughter deepened as one of its tentacles darted toward Roger, trying to grab him. Roger was sure that would be followed by eating him in one huge gulp. He jumped away from the creature and landed on top of the tentacle. Roger grinned evilly as he stabbed the limb with the end of the broom handle. A dull roaring filled the garage as Roger repeatedly attacked the tentacle, whistling a merry tune. The car quickly yanked the injured limb away, causing Roger to fall flat on his butt. Roger rubbed his *gluteus maximus* as he stood up. The injured tentacle merged with the rest and formed an organic five-foot-length drill tapered off into a point. A six-foot-long, six-inch-thick tube of tissue connected the other end of the drill to the front of the car. He stared at the drill for a moment, not sure if he should be impressed or run and scream.

"Wow, it looks like you're definitely overcompensating for something," he said before he jumped out of the way at the last second. The drill, which had rotated straight at him, embedded in the four-inch-thick garage door. The car's appendage tried to yank itself out of the door but its connecting tentacle flopped around like a drunken human attempting to dance. Roger took a turn at laughing out loud at the funny sight.

He placed both of his feet on the limb, idly wondering if he would be able to get rid of the stain of supernatural blood off of his nice black wingtip shoes. He gave another of his trademark creepy grins as he stabbed at the base of the drill with the broom handle.

The car screamed out in pain as bright green blood splattered across the gray granite floor. Roger hoped his wife wouldn't freak out too badly about the mess, although he had the sneaking suspicion he was going to have to clean the mess on his own. It tried to wiggle out from under Roger's weight, but the latter simply used his feet to press down on its limb, making a watery, squishing noise. It felt like pressing into an overripe, watery tomato. He really hoped the car's fluids wouldn't seep into his shoes. He hated it when his socks got wet, regardless if the fluid soaking it was water or alien juices.

A soft farting sound filled the air as Roger stabbed at the connective tissue, a clear fluid spilling out of the wound. He looked up to see if the drill was making any progress in getting out of the garage door. The drill moved up and down so it could successfully get out of the hole that trapped it. Roger assumed that its next course of action would be to skewer the pesky human like a shish-ka-bob.

Roger's stomach clenched in fear as the drill moved faster and faster, making the hole in the garage door bigger. If he didn't get his butt in gear and sever the limb, he would suffer a very painful, messy death at the hands of a huge, organic tongue from the mouth of his car. Already, he could see the awl loosening itself from the hole in the garage door.

It's flailing splattered green blood all over his nice black suit. He groaned in frustration. *Goddamn it, this was my favorite outfit! I'm never going to get these damn stains out of it,* he thought. The car's movements became frantic, wiggling the appendage like a sentient tooth.

The drill freed itself from the garage door with a high-pitched roar of triumph that nearly burst Roger's eardrums. It rose above, ready to pin him to the ground and grind him into hamburger. The rotating tongue quivered in anticipation of splattering the walls with human blood while listening to its victim scream. Of course, with the human dead, the pampering would end as Roger's wife would plot a bloody revenge against the car. But foresight had never been one of the creature's strong suits.

With a scream, which sounded more like a whiny shriek than a masculine roar of defiance, Roger stabbed at the limb with all the speed and strength he could muster. His blow severed the limb before the car turned him into human paté. The drill's body went slack and fell to the floor with a wet plop, splattering green blood all over the front of the garage door, making the room even messier, if that was at all possible. Roger watched its death throes before leaning on the wall, taking a few deep breaths. Exhaustion overtook him as he slid down the wall, not caring if he got his back or his butt dirty in the process. Monster blood and human sweat already covered his suit, so what did it matter? It would be just one more hard-to-clean stain to complain about during laundry time.

What the car's bloodthirsty tendencies proved was the utter uselessness of trying to tame the damn thing. He took a couple of minutes to catch his breath before he took out his cell phone. The runes carved on it prevented the magical radiation from bringing the cell phone to life.

I should've asked the guys to put some of those runes on my car. Then the whole damn ordeal wouldn't happen in the first place, Roger ruefully thought as he waited for one of the other cult members to answer him. One of the few advantages of being in a group devoted to the Many Arms of the Swirling Vortex was the runes liberally decorated on their cell phones. They ensured a strong worldwide service area and a self-recharging battery.

Thankfully, it only took a few seconds for one of his fellow cultists to answer him. "Hey Roger, what's up?" A cheery male voice said on the other end.

"Hi, Mark," Roger said, feeling like a freeloader as he began his request. "I'm running late because my car just tried to murder me again. I had to kill the son-of-a-bitch. Can you give me a ride this morning? Looks like I'm going to need to go car shopping, and this time I'll get one that likes me!"

Tribe

Mark Wolf

Editor: Don't assume that everyone wants to rule the world.

The rat tasted just like rat, oily, tainted with a rotting-meat aftertaste. Boiled in a meat stew of pup-dog, cat, Kalij pheasant, and turkey, and simmered in coconut milk with breadfruit and macadamia nuts, I thought I wouldn't be able to taste it. I was wrong. Oily, tainted rat.

The tribe's stews used the entire animal but the hair and the squeak. I held the offending member in my fingers—half a rat thigh with leg and feet attached—in front of my face and examined it by the fading light of the campfire. Turned it this way and that; tried to imagine it as baby mongoose. Not much difference between them really, when you come right down to it. Both are happy carrion-eaters.

Back a few years ago, before the burning time, I remember seeing a long trail of mongoose carcasses stretched across the pavement of Hwy. 11 from one side to the other, each representing a poor unfortunate that had joined the smorgasbord line, preying on the kin that had gone before. Hwy. 11 had been one of the busiest roads on the Big Island of Hawaii back in the old pre-burning days.

Sheba, my pit-lab cross, stared hungrily at me from across the fire, eyes expectant. I tossed her the thigh. Snap. Disappeared in midair. I wondered if she realized that two of her latest litter swam in our stew. Probably. Yet, here she was, at the stewpot, all skin and bones and sagging teats. She'd nursed nine pups, but only two hadn't gone into the stewpot. The two best hunters. If they weren't successful in the tribe's hunt tonight, they'd be in tomorrow's pot.

"Davy. I saw that," Jenny said. I started, looked over at her, guilty at getting caught, looked down. I should've offered her the rat piece; she carried a baby after all, Mace's baby and my nephew. Her child represented the tribe's future, even if at times it didn't feel to me as though we had much of one to look forward to.

I raised my head slowly. Jenny smiled at me.

"I won't tell Mace. Just be more careful. If he catches you feeding your mutt out of the common pot, he'll kick your ass."

"Yeah, I know. I'm sorry." Mace, my older brother and the tribe's leader, frowned on anything that didn't put the tribe first.

And he'd hand me my teeth if I tried to argue that keeping Sheba strong enough to hunt served the tribe. To him, a dog represented just so much protein, nothing more. If one were to occasionally corner a pig for the spearing, so much the better, but he didn't believe in keeping dogs around just for hunting.

I could hear Sheba's pups off in the distance baying. Their sire had been a wild dog with a bit of Rhodesian in him. I knew that because the pups had that backward running spinal ridge fur that Rhodies are known for. Great pig hunters, Rhodies.

One of the *keikis* a few yards behind me in the shed coughed. An auntie shushed her—hummed a lullaby. Another child coughed. There were nearly thirty children and as many non-hunters bedded down in the shed. I hoped the cough had to do with the *vog* and not another cold or flu. Those seemed to constantly run rampant through our little tribe community.

The evening air had a snap to it hinting of frost or snow in the higher elevations of Mauna Loa. At nearly thirteen-thousand-feet high, the volcano could get snow nearly any time of the year. I decided that I probably should build up the fire a bit later in the night for the returning hunters. They'd be sweat-soaked and chilled.

The skies overhead were clear and star-filled with the spiral of the Milky Way very obvious. Now that there were almost no electric lights on the island, except for a few places that had solar panels and batteries, stars always filled the sky except during *vog*.

Jenny snored lightly. It was my duty to stay up as guard for the children, though with my bum leg and my eighteen tender years, I probably wouldn't be able to put up much of a fight if the Honomalino or Naalehu tribes raided us.

They would be after the children, particularly the *girl* children, to increase their tribes' populations and make them even stronger. They were already too large for us to fight. We kept an uneasy peace with both groups, trading breadfruit, oranges, other citrus, vegetables, including dry land taro, pakalolo, and roasted coffee beans, and occasionally scrounged goods from the old houses in Ocean View for their dried fish, mac nuts, coconuts, and smoked meat.

The smoke from the fire squirreled around. My bad leg ached and rather than trying to move out of the occasional smoke wisps, I just shut my eyes from time to time.

* * *

My horse, Sybille, ran toward me when I called her. Overhead, in the night, the storm raged, thunder crashed, and lightning lit up Sybille's dry, wind-lashed pasture on South Point Road.

I could hear Mace shouting my name at the same time I called Sybille. As she galloped closer to me, her skin and muscle began falling from her bones. She reared up before me, fleshless except for her head. One second I was beneath her hooves, the next I was falling once again from her back, knowing all the while how badly my leg would be shattered when I hit the ground. I started to choke—and woke up.

"You're dead, idiot!" Mace shouted, his hands still around my throat.

"Leave me alone!" I shouted back. I pushed him away. Even though he was in his twenties, I was a strong kid, in my upper body anyway. I looked at the fire. It had burned down quite a bit, so I'd been asleep for some time. A couple of new guys, locals I didn't know all that well, added wood to the fire. Mace gave me a disgusted look and stood up, turned his back to me, and directed a couple of the hunters to put a small pig over the fire.

Was that all they'd got? No, there was another small pig. The tribe would eat for another day and the pup-dogs would be around for at least another hunt.

Mace watched the two new guys closely. Mitch and Kaipo were their names. I knew he didn't trust them—thought they were spies for the Honomalino tribe. He was probably right. They'd showed up a week ago, said they'd had a falling out with one of the Honomalino chiefs. Possibly. Thing was, falling outs in the larger tribes meant retribution in the old Hawaiian way of settling differences. A club to the head. Their story just didn't add up.

That's why Mace kept them close—so he could keep an eye on them. He wouldn't let them go haring off by themselves to locate our dispersed taro fields, vegetable gardens, or orchards. If they were spies, all they'd be able to report on was the lousy hunting abilities of our little Kahuku tribe. Mace could care less about that.

The air stank of singed pig hair. I'd hoped maybe they'd dig an *imu* and have roasted pig. No such luck. Stews stretched further. My pup-dogs wiggle-danced their way up to the fire, all excited and proud. I hid a grin. Mace hadn't said anything nor did he pull out his war club and dash the dog's brains out. They must have been helpful. My suspicion was confirmed when Mace stepped back to the fire and stirred the pot, noting how few scraps were left in it. He turned to me.

"Make yourself useful and dump this out for your dogs. They done alright. Clean the pot thoroughly afterwards. I don't want any of us getting sick."

I nodded, hid a smile, suddenly happy. This was as close as Mace ever got to complimenting the pup-dogs. They must have been helpful, indeed. "Okay, will do. Anything else?"

"How much sleep did you get?" More of a look of concern than disdain from him. *Was he going soft?*

I looked at the sky. False dawn. Another hour perhaps before real dawn. I turned back to him. "Probably three hours."

"Okay, once you clean the pot, bed down. You're going to stand watch again tonight; hopefully, *this time* you'll stay awake all the way through it." He reached over and punched me in the arm, hard. I winced and rubbed it. It hurt like hell, but it also felt a bit like awkward love. I'd take it that way any day.

"I won't let myself fall asleep tonight," I said.

"See that you don't." Trace of a secret smile.

I wondered about him. As hard as our life now was since the world went to hell, there were times that he seemed to prefer it over the days before the missiles flew. I saw a trace of Dad's smile when he turned toward Jenny. She was stretching and yawning. She'd probably go back to sleep after she exclaimed over the hunters' prowess.

I watched the two interact, saw him place his hand on Jenny's belly. They'd only been married a little over a year, right after Mace had returned from Afghanistan and a month before the missiles launched. More of Dad's smile. Made me think of the last time I saw him, just before he jumped on an island commuter to Oahu for a business trip.

No one knew what prompted Korea and China to join hands with Iran and launch nukes. Well, Iran and Korea were understandable. China, though, I still didn't quite understand what the thinking was there.

Here the U.S. was their biggest trading partner, and they nuked us. I even used to play World of Warcraft and other computer games with some Chinese kids. Good players and pretty cool. I sometimes wondered if they'd lived through our retaliatory strikes. Probably not. Maybe the Chinese just wanted to be the only game in town instead of one of the top players. Whatever they wanted, it didn't matter anymore. What they got was irradiated.

We'd been sorta lucky in Hawaii. Dad was probably dead, though. Ground zero in a Korean sub missile launch. Word had it that it'd been a small nuke and mainly took out Pearl Harbor. Our fleet had been out at the time so North Korea had been the first place they'd sailed to. North Korea probably glowed at night now.

"Hey, Davy. Did you hear?"

I turned around, limped over to shake hands bruddah-style with my best friend, Rudy, all two hundred forty pounds of local Hawaiian-Portagee.

"Hear what, dude?"

"Mace didn't tell ya? Ah, man. I got the biggest pig. No, check it. Your pup-dogs practically ran it onto my spear."

"No way!" I said. No wonder Mace was being so nice to the pup-dogs. I looked over to see him and Jenny sharing a *pakalolo* pipe, smelled the sweet funk of pot on the first downslope winds of dawn. I turned back to Rudy.

"Wish you coulda been there, man," he said, "it was sick." He looked down at my bum leg.

"Me, too. Maybe in six months." I frowned, remembering last night's dream. Sybille had tossed me and shattered my leg when an axis deer had sprung out of the tall grasses on her pasture edge and startled her.

I'd had one operation to repair it and had been scheduled for two more. But war intervened and there no longer were hospitals to go to. I'd just have to heal the best I could on my own.

Sybille had been one of the first of the livestock along South Point Road to go into the pot. As the tribe grew, other livestock on the farms from Kahuku to Naalehu, a distance of around ten miles, joined her.

"Hey, dude, you okay?"

I snapped out of my memory stroll. "Yeah, man. I'm just feelin' so useless, though. And Mace caught me sleepin' on guard duty."

"Again?" Rudy shook his head at me.

I nodded, shoulders droopin'. "Yeah."

Rudy stepped closer, whispered, "I could get ya' a little 'keeper-upper' if ya' wanna?"

I shook my head, gave him my best "shut up" look. "Nah, don't even talk about it. Mace would banish you if he thought you had ice. You know that."

"No worries, man," Rudy said. "It's the last of my old stash. I only kept it around for—well, things like what you were talkin' about."

"Forget it. I'm just gonna have to start sluggin' down the java at night, that's all. At least we got plenty of that."

"True, dat." And it was. We had coffee and *pakalolo* plants at every one of our dispersed garden plots. Both tended to help in close trading with the other tribes.

"Well, I'm gonna get some sleep." Rudy yawned. "Be talkin' at ya laters."

"Laters, brah." I nodded; another quick bruddah-shake of the hands and he stumbled off, looking like a grizzly bear searching for his winter den.

* * *

After he left I got to thinking about how he and I had met and become friends.

We'd first seen each other out surfin' at Kawas, a locals-only surf spot. I knew better than to barge in on another surfer's turf, but I missed the ocean so bad, since Dad had moved us from Cali to Ocean View, Hawaii.

He'd used mom's insurance money settlement to do it. What we got from the traffic accident that had taken her away from us.

Mace was still in Afghanistan chasing down bad guys at the time.

Rudy had been the only other guy out surfing on that day. After giving me a quick eye he ignored me and just relaxed on his longboard.

The waves had been small *kine* and the sets around twenty minutes' apart. I made sure that he got the first wave every time they rolled through and took the smaller ones. He didn't say anything to me all day.

At school a couple of weeks later he pushed me up against a locker outside my sophomore English class at Ka'u High School.

"You know about 'Beat up a haole day,' right?"

I nodded. How could I not. Hawaii's schoolkids' most infamous reverse-discriminatory bullying act. It'd been about the only thing the kids at school had been talking gleefully about for the last week.

"After school at Kawas," Rudy said.

I nodded again. An unavoidable rite of passage, like Freshman Rush day. I'd spent the whole week getting stink-eye from the local guys. My pale skin, blond hair, and blue eyes shouted California. And locals universally hate Californians.

I heard Rudy tell the others to back off. That my ass was his and his alone, to kick. I felt fortunate, actually. I knew I could take him. Even if he outweighed me by eighty pounds and was three inches taller.

I'd been in boxing classes since I was about seven. I could see that I had both the reach and speed over Rudy. Thing was, I realized it wouldn't be smart of me to do it. Stories circulated around school about mobs of locals messing up guys' faces. I had to lose the fight narrowly but hurt Rudy enough to gain his respect.

I expected a whole gang of guys to watch us fight at Kawas, but it was just him and his board. He turned to me as he pulled it off his car rack.

"Where's your board?" he asked.

"Whatcha mean?" I said. "I thought this was my ass-kickin' session."

"True dat. But we can still surf aftas." He grinned at me, showing his two front missing teeth. He had a reputation for being a pugilist.

"Well, I'm sorry. I can go get it *aftas* if I'm not beat up too bad."

He grinned again, reached out his hands and cracked his knuckles. I could read "pain" tattooed on the knuckles of one hand and "ouch" on the other. I gulped.

"You ready?" he said, all polite-like.

I nodded. He charged me like a bull.

I'd like to say I won the fight, but I didn't. I let him bust my lip and black an eye and returned the favor. Then we danced around till the near-ninety-degree temperature wore him out, and he leaned back against his car in exhaustion. "I'm tired now," he said.

I nodded, stepped back. He shambled over to his car and put his board back on the rack. "You want grinds?" he asked.

I nodded again, not sure where this was going. He'd just asked me if I was hungry.

"I always gets hungry aftas one fight. Let me cool down and we can go to L&L."

I knew about L&L, the Hawaiian barbecue place. They had them in Oceanside back in Cali and I liked to eat there.

I still had on my board shorts from school. In Hawaii they're okay for dress code, so I slipped into the water and cooled off too. Afterward, he followed me to my house in Ocean View and we rode in his car down to the town center and had teriyaki beef and chicken katsu.

After we let the food settle we went back and got my board and had a great surf session.

No one messed with me at school after that. Rudy and I hung out together all the time, though he couldn't get me to join the football team with him. But we became best buds.

Not long after that, Sybille threw me, and the world had its little nuclear pissing contest. Mace made up a travois and pulled me up to Kahuku Camp where I became the chief pot stirrer and de facto camp guard. I really couldn't tag along with the hunters until my leg fully healed. That, of course, bummed me out severely.

Kahuku Camp was a new part of Volcanoes National Park, though I suppose such distinctions didn't matter anymore. We certainly wouldn't be down at the gate trying to take admission fees from any roving tribal bands.

I finished feeding the pup-dogs and got myself some rack time.

* * *

When I woke up the stew was ready. I joined a short line and got my portion dumped into a tin can. Rudy waved me over.

"Sit, brah. Take a load off that leg," he said. I stretched my stiff leg out and joined him under a massive ohia tree, one loaded with bright, salmon-colored lehua blossoms.

"How's the stew today?" I asked, knowing in advance the answer I'd get. Rudy had contributed the lion's part of the stew, after all.

"Not bad. You tell me wha'cha t'ink," he said, talking all pidgin.

I tilted my can back, took a small sip, picked out some meat carefully, and chewed it while I considered my answer. It was pretty decent, and it didn't seem like anyone had added rat to it this time. I nodded. "Yep, pretty good." I couldn't resist pulling his leg a bit. "Taste's a bit like mac nuts. You guys huntin' near Mauna Loa?"

Rudy knew I was talking about the Mauna Loa Macadamia Nut Farm, not the mountain. Mauna Loa Volcano was most of the south end of the island. The Mac farms, though, were on the other side of Manuka State Park, a few miles away. I meant my comment in a good way, too. Pig that tasted like mac nuts was about as good as it got.

"Yep. Our edge."

I sighed at that. The Honomalino tribe controlled most of the mac nut orchard near us. They let us harvest a few trees from time to time along the edge closest to us, and take a few pigs, but they were adamant that they considered the orchard their domain. Mace kept the peace with pakalolo offerings and coffee trading.

"Mace shouldn't push our welcome with those guys," I said without thinking.

"Brah, he knows what he's doing," hint of anger in his voice. "Besides, Manuka's all *pau*." Rudy had just told me Manuka was finished—all hunted out.

"We might have to move back to South Point for a while then," I said. Rudy nodded. He'd like that. He missed the ocean and loved to throw net. Good provider with it too.

Each of the three tribes on the south end of the island had their own fishing grounds. Ours, I already mentioned, was South Point. Honomalino's was Milolii and Papa Bay. Naalehu used the old beach access at Punalu'u Black Sands beach park.

We probably had the richest fishing grounds for boat fishing, but the most difficult access. There was a forty-foot cliff where boats put in from rickety old hoists. We slapped more lumber to what was already there and lowered our small homemade canoes into the choppy waves when the weather wasn't too rough. When it was too rough, we fished from shore, mainly kite fishing.

Kite fishing was just what it sounds like, tying a fishing line to a kite and letting the kite take one's line out to the deeper waters off shore where the big *ulua* and ahi savaged the schools of bait fish. There was a strong wind off the cliffs at South Point nearly year round. We caught some pretty big fish there. Eighty pounds or more at times.

Rudy looked up at the sky, gauged the sun's position. "Be dark in an hour. Mace wants me on point again with the pup-dogs."

I nodded. "He knows you da man wit' the strong spear arm."

Rudy grinned at that; silver caps now replaced his lost teeth gaps. "D'at fo' shuh." His smile slowly faded.

"What?" I said.

"Papa had a strong arm, too."

I reached over, put a hand on his shoulder, gripped it hard. Rudy's dad had died from the killer, flesh-eating bacteria that had got into a small cut on his weathered hand while he'd been filleting fish the year before. Really a tragic loss, not only for Rudy, but for everyone in the tribe, because he'd been our most knowledgeable fisherman. "Man, I'm sorry, brah."

Rudy sniffed, eyes all red, gentle giant with a lot of heart. He wiped at his eyes with the back of his hands. "T'anks."

I patted him on the back. "I bet your papa is lookin' down on you somethin' proud today." Hint of a wistful smile on Rudy's face.

"Ya t'ink?"

"Yeah, brah. Sure of it. You as good a providah as he ever was. Fo' reals."

"Ah, now you got me all 'bare-assed,'" Rudy laughed.

"I'm not de onlies one den." I looked over to where Ku'uipo, a cute local girl, was sitting near the fire watching Rudy.

"You should go talk to her," I continued.

Rudy actually blushed beneath his brown skin.

"Uh, I, um," he floundered.

Part of me really wanted to tease him, but another part of me knew that Rudy was deathly shy when it came to girls, especially cuties like Ku'uipo.

I smiled at him. "Dude, she's so into you. Just go talk to her." I couldn't resist a little dig to his pride. "Don't tell me you'll stare down a three-hundred-pound wild boar with a spear, but are too shy to speak to a girl that weighs less than half what you do. Go on." I gave his shoulder a friendly push.

Rudy gulped, smiled tentatively at the staring girl. He looked back at me for reassurance. I nodded. "Go on."

He pushed himself to his feet. Walked slowly over to where Ku'uipo stirred the pot. Sat down beside her. They were too far away for me to hear what they were saying but both were smiling. That made me smile too. I suddenly felt more optimistic about the tribe's future.

* * *

I sat beside the campfire alone in the dark, sipping the strong Ka'u coffee from the pot I had on the coals at the edge of the fire. Jenny hadn't felt good, so she'd turned in early.

Mace had insisted on taking Sheba along with the pups this hunt. I decided not to argue with him, even though I felt she was still too worn out from nursing a litter. If he was changing to be more kindly inclined toward the dogs, all the better.

A storm front had passed through in late afternoon, strong winds heralding an approaching cane toad-choker, and now the air felt heavy, the skies darkened, without stars, and the winds had died down to nothing.

I could hear the baying of all three dogs nearby. That was good. I suspected they'd jumped some mouflon, Kahuku's imported sheep from back in the old days when the ranch was a private hunting club for tourists, before it became a unit of Volcanoes National Park.

If it had been daytime, the sheep would have just bolted off in all directions and left the dogs in the dust. At night, they were more reluctant to leave their familiar grazing areas and the safety of their herd, so they continued to circle in their group. In time, the dogs would wear them down and run them into the hunters' spears.

The hunters might get something and have it back in camp before the rains came. I grinned.

I didn't immediately push myself to my feet when the two new guys, Mitch and Kaipo entered the light of the campfire.

"Ho, looky here, brah," Mitch said to Kaipo, pointing at me. "Camp boy is all by his lonesome."

"Shame, dat," Kaipo replied. "Mebbee he needs to find him some new friends."

"Yeah, brah. I was t'inkin' de same t'ing."

I started to push myself to my feet. Mitch slammed me upside the head with his war club.

Lights out.

* * *

I woke up puking all over myself, upside down and totally disoriented. It took me several seconds to realize that the two Honomalino misfits had me tied wrist and ankles over a carry pole, like the kind we used to transport pigs and other large game. I was looking upward at a gently falling mist of rain, fog all around us.

They had shown me one small kindness, however. They had my knees tied together and another strand of rope tied to the pole, so my game leg was supported somewhat.

"Hey, let's put 'em down. Noah will shoot our asses if homeboy chokes to death," Kaipo said.

They lowered me, none too gently, to the smooth pahoehoe lava. I rolled to the side and finished puking my guts out.

"I t'ink you hit 'em too hard, Mitch," Kaipo said.

"Nah, he just one buggah wit' a softa' head den I t'aught."

It was really dark and foggy, visibility not more than twenty yards. I had no idea where I was, but sort of remembered that there were some pahoehoe lava fields up high in the old Ocean View subdivision.

Pahoehoe lava is formed when lava runs fast like a river. It cools all smooth. Most of the lava in Ocean View and the surrounding countryside from the old 1858 flows was *'a'a* though—that's the rough stuff.

I was lying on my side facing downslope. The foggy air surrounding me cleared a bit and I could see a bit of old tarmac. I could see a road sign and an intersection, struggled to read the letters. *Marlin*. Now I sort of knew where we were. Still high up in the subdivision. That meant I probably hadn't been out all that long.

In between the yakking and the wheezing, I tried to listen for the dogs but couldn't hear them. I couldn't wipe my mouth off because of being tied up, but I could talk.

"Water?"

Mitch looked over at Kaipo who shrugged. Mitch stepped forward and took an old plastic army-style canteen from his belt. "Don' drink much, haole. We got some ways to go."

I nodded, instantly regretting the motion as everything started spinning. Mitch opened the canteen lid and supported the back of my head, dribbled a little of the plastic-tasting tepidness into my open mouth. I felt a bit like a baby bird getting fed by his mama. He stopped pouring and closed the lid.

"You done yakkin'?" he asked.

"Yeah," I said.

"We gots ta carry you some ways more, den you can be untied and walk on ya own when we meet da uddas."

They stooped down and picked me up when I didn't say anything. I tried to bring my scrambled egg thoughts into focus. *I'm being kidnapped. Why?*

* * *

I didn't have long to wait for that answer.

Swinging back and forth on the carry pole, dry-heaving occasionally, I started to hear the sound of voices carrying in the mist.

Kaipo let out a loud "Oi!" It was quickly answered by the same. Sounded like their people were less than a block away. We rendezvoused with them in a couple of minutes.

They lowered me to the ground. The group circling me included some familiar faces. Of course, the one I recognized first was Shayna Murphy, beautiful *hapa-haole* daughter of Noah Murphy, Honomalino tribe's leader. She was my age—her mother had been a local, and Shayna made my heart beat in double-time whenever I got anywhere near her. Had it been daylight her eyes would have flashed emerald-green at me.

She held a MAC-10 machine pistol pointed loosely at my midsection. Noah stepped up to her and placed a hand on her shoulder. He carried a sawed-off, twelve-gauge double-barrel shotgun cradled in the crook of his other arm.

"Easy there, Shayna. He won't make a very good hostage if he's dead." He gently pushed the muzzle of her weapon to one side.

Light suddenly sprang forth when a couple of kerosene lanterns were lit, making it easier to see one another's faces.

Noah Murphy had a sordid history. Everyone in the drug culture of the Big Island knew him for a gun-runner, supplying the heroin and ice gangs with weapons. He stayed away from dealing drugs himself, making more than his fair share of money as an arms dealer.

Shayna's mother, unfortunately, hadn't stayed far enough away from drugs and had died from a heroin overdose when Shayna was younger.

There were about a dozen other Honomalino tribe members there, most also packing. A few had spears. I recognized a guy named Derrick that used to run a fruit stand near the old Milolii turnoff, selling avocadoes, papaya, citrus, and mac nuts.

He and his wife, Linda, who also worked the stand, gave me slight nods.

There were another couple of local guys about my age named Jimmy and Akela, both surfers I knew from school and Kawas. They were okay guys at school and surfing, but they gave me hard looks now. I bet they were both sweet on Shayna and didn't want another possible competitor around. Watching the thoughtful way Shayna regarded me, I couldn't discount that possibility.

The rest of the group I recognized from pre-burning times, though I didn't know their names. In small communities like the Ka'u district, you see the same faces a lot, even if you don't actually get to know one another by name.

"Why didn't you get the girl?" Noah said.

"We were gonna 'cept she turned in early and slept with the whole tribe of *keikis* and *tutus* tonight," Mitch said. "But ya know he's Mace's little bro, yeah? Mace won't want anything to happen to him."

"I wouldn't be too sure about that," I said without thinking. Noah turned to me.

"Oh, doesn't he like his little brother?"

"Well, he doesn't hate me, if that's what you're asking. But if you think you're going to get much leverage over him with me, I'd reconsider. He'll put our tribe before me."

Noah looked at me thoughtfully for several seconds. Finally, he spoke. "That could be unfortunate—for you."

*   *   *

Mitch was true to his word. He quickly untied me and allowed me to walk on my own, though with my bum leg, I wasn't much faster than when he and Kaipo schlepped me around, hog-tied to the carry pole, but much more comfortable, however. And the view of Shayna walking before me in form-fitting rip-stop camouflage pants had much to recommend it.

By the light of a lantern, and as if she could read my mind, or at least my interest, she turned around and raised an elegant eyebrow at me. At the same time, I felt a rough shove with the stock of a rifle to my back. I turned to Akela, who gave me stink-eye to da max. Okay, at least one suspicion confirmed.

"Walk with me, Davy, and tell me what your tribe is like," Shayna said. I was all too eager, but stumbled forward at another push from Akela.

"Lay off, Akela," Noah said. I turned to Noah, saw him giving me a speculative glance, one of his eyebrows raised, in the same manner as his daughter's as if to say, "Oh, so that's how it is?" I just shrugged back at him. Local girls almost always went for local boys, not Cali haoles. Maybe being *hapa*, she took more after her dad.

Akela backed away from me and Noah both. I wasn't sure whether his respect was for Noah or the double-barrel shotgun, but it was nice not to have him breathing over my shoulder and cramping my charm style.

"What do you want to know?" I said.

"Everything," she said.

I admit this wasn't the first time I felt myself going stupid over a girl, but never one as pretty as this. I knew that I had to keep some things secret, things like where our little garden patches were located, our strength of firearms, and how many fighters we could field.

I decided that if Noah had put her up to this, it might be a more pleasant way of torturing me than turning me over to Akela and Jimmy. They'd rearrange my face. I decided to play along and seek some sort of advantage.

"Tell you what. I'll answer some of your questions if you answer some of mine." I smiled at her. By the lantern light I saw a mischievous glint of emerald in her eyes and the smile returned.

"Well, that would depend on what kind of questions you asked now, wouldn't it?"

I nodded, kept my smile in place. I had to remember that this girl wasn't just someone you could tell sweet lines or lies to. She also wasn't like a lot of the local girls in the area—get themselves a guy, get pregnant, and maybe get married. No, I had to keep what I knew of her right in front of me.

What I knew of her, besides her being the daughter of a gun-runner, was that she was very smart. She'd attended Hawaii Preparatory Academy, upcountry in Waimea, before the burning times. HPA, an elite private school, had top scholastic requirements for students. They and Punahou, a private college preparatory school over in Oahu, graduated a lot of the movers and shakers.

For example, a fellow known as Barack Hussein Obama II, forty-fourth president of the United States, graduated from Punahou.

I had seen Shayna a few times surfing at Kawas but always surrounded by a large group of unfriendlies. I also knew she'd played volleyball at HPA.

No, I couldn't try and snow her. She'd see right through me. I grinned, turned up the charm generator.

"Well, the most obvious question I have is 'Why kidnap me'? What's in it for your tribe?"

Shayna looked over at her dad. He nodded an okay. She spoke.

"Daddy has a vision for Hawaii. He wants to make us a strong, sovereign nation once again."

"Like King Kamehameha, the First, huh?"

Shayna grinned back and nodded. "Hopefully without the wars, though."

"Yeah, King Kam wasn't exactly a peacemaker back in his day." My thoughts jumped ahead. "So, kidnap me to force Mace to capitulate in some way?"

"Bingo. But we were really after Jenny. You were our plan B."

"I'll try not to be hurt that I wasn't number one on your list."

Shayna laughed, a melodious sound that sent quivery shivers down my spine. *Who is charming who?*

She gave me a more serious look. "Daddy wants to get everyone on the same page and reestablish connections with the mainland and with other countries." She checked for her dad's approval again, got it, continued. "No longer as one of many states of a United States, but as a sovereign land."

"The Hawaiian Kingdom thing?"

She grinned. "Oh, so you know about that?"

I nodded, grinned back. The Hawaiian Kingdom movement had been gaining popularity among the locals of Hawaiian ancestry and *kama'aina* (long timers of any race) for several years before the burning time.

Even President Clinton had signed an apology resolution acknowledging that the original Kingdom of Hawaii had been overthrown by the U.S. There was a lot of controversy over this, of course.

A lot of people might have found themselves without clear title to lands acquired and transferred for the last hundred years or so after the takeover of the Hawaiian Kingdom if the U.S. and other nations suddenly recognized Hawaii as a sovereign nation.

But, even though everyone on all sides of the issue waffled around after the resolution was passed, I'd already made my own decision back then to side with the sovereigns if anything ever came together. What Shayna said made sense. But, another thought struck me.

"So, why does Mace oppose this? You've talked to him about it, haven't you?" I wondered why he hadn't talked to me about it. Maybe that was why he and Jenny argued a lot of the time. Noah answered before Shayna got the chance to.

"Every time we got together to trade. He opposes it because of all the John Wayne crap he got mind-screwed with when he joined the military. He's incapable of seeing Hawaii as anything but a place to train United States Army soldiers and a big harbor for its Navy." Noah sighed.

"We can barely raise twenty states on the mainland on our Ham radios. They certainly aren't trying to rebuild a United States. It's everyone for themselves back there. The U.S. is *pau*," Noah said.

That got me thinking again. While Mace and I had our touchy moments of relationship with one another, I felt that he would try and do what was best by the tribe. Could it be that this was just a big blind spot for him, like Noah was hinting at? I decided to change the subject and think more about it later, when I had time alone without the distraction of Shayna's pretty face and figure. I spoke.

"Twenty states? Which ones?" I was thinking of my friends back in Cali.

Noah answered again. "No states from either seaboard. Subs wiped them all out." He shook his head. "And no states from areas of the country that harbored large military installations. Texas, for example."

"Who was left, then?" I said, my eyes watering at the fate of my old friends in Cali.

Shayna jumped in. "The Mountain States—the Rockies in the west and the Appalachians in the east. Except for Colorado. With NORAD there, and the military contractor companies around Denver, it got nuked pretty hard."

False dawn approached as we strolled along at a comfortable pace for me. The air cooled; very chilly breezes blew downslope over us, pushing the cloud cover back out over the ocean. Stars started appearing. It would be a pretty dawn in an hour or so. I wondered if Mace and the other hunters had made it back to camp to find me missing. A thought struck.

"Hey, how are you going to let Mace know you got me?"

"Mitch and Kaipo left a note that we took you. We told Mace to meet us today at the Mauna Loa mac farm edge for a discussion," Shayna said.

I felt conflicted and worried. Noah's tribe had a lot more firearms than ours did. If Mace pushed the issue there could be only one outcome, one that would leave our tribe without its leader and me probably dead along with him.

* * *

Mace held his AR-15 rifle loosely across his arms and watched my face carefully for clues that Noah was lying to him. I kept my expression impassive, attempting to keep him believing that everything Noah was telling him was the truth as far as I knew.

Our tribe had sent five men, all heavily armed of course. Rudy was notably absent. Perhaps Mace didn't trust him to remain calm when it was me in danger. On Noah's side there was even more firepower and men. I hoped everyone would keep their cool. Noah continued speaking.

". . . and it's not like we'd be doing anything different here in the Sovereign Kingdom of Hawaii than what some of the mainland states are doing. The Western Mountain States are forming a nation called Cascadia. Nothing really new there: Eastern Washington and Oregon, Idaho, parts of Utah, Wyoming, and Montana, and the provinces of British Columbia and Alberta."

"Humph, anti-American," Mace said.

"No, actually, those same states had been pushing Cascadia, even using that name, long prior to the burning time. They believed the governments of the Eastern U.S. and Canada were becoming more disconnected and non-representative of Western State values."

"Which are?" Mace said. I watched his eyebrows lift. At least he was dialoguing. I held out some hope that things could be resolved peacefully.

"A lot of them, but in a nutshell, freedom and independence from Big Brother."

Mace looked thoughtful. After a while his expression hardened. He gave Noah a dirty look. "And you're just the man to lead this new sovereign nation, I suppose?"

Noah held his hands up. "Not me. I'm just the militia guy. The leader of our National Guard, so to speak. No, who I had in mind for leader is someone more like you. A younger man of vision and strong principle." Noah shifted his glance around, looking at each of us in turn, then back to Mace. "Mace, would you consider becoming the king of Hawaii?"

* * *

Mace was on the tiller of our small sailboat, Noah beside him, giving him pointers as we crossed the channel between the Big Island of Hawaii and Maui.

Jenny nursed little Mana'olana, their daughter, in the sailboat's cabin while Shayna rubbed our own baby bulge.

I had one arm around her shoulders and watched the Maui coastland as it grew ever closer.

Mace had been won over. After our two tribes became one, we traveled to meet with the Naalehu tribe, who joined us quickly, also. We next met with the three other main tribes on the island and all acknowledged Mace as king and made our small sailboat crew diplomats to Maui.

We don't know what kind of reception we'll meet up with there. We were able to radio a tribe in Kahalui, Maui, with our nation proposal and ask permission to visit with them to discuss it.

We carried no guns with us, just a few spears and fishing equipment to take care of our own needs.

Mana'olana, Mace and Jenny's child. The word means hope, faith, or confidence in the Hawaiian language and is given to both girl and boy babies. Kailua-Kona's chieftainess, Iolani, carried a daughter in her arms of the same name. It has become a very popular baby name since the burning.

Rudy came out of the cabin, dripping sweat. He threw a smelly mess from a pan over the side, choking back a gag. He'd been below, sponging down Ku'uipo's forehead and holding her over the pan while she puked. Morning sickness and seasickness, a yucky combination. All of us felt sympathetic, but we also knew we would harbor today so her misery wouldn't last. The couple was going to name their baby Mana'olana also, whatever sex it turned out to be.

That's how we will meet with the Kahalui, Maui, chiefs, the new *ali'i* of their island. With babies named hope and with welcoming arms, confident in faith that we'll all be able to work together.

Shayna is already talking about naming our child Mana'olana also. But I kind of like Dennis, if it's a boy. That was my dad's name and a good one.

The Zoo of All Things

Geneve Flynn

Editor: Who says that fitness is a survival trait?

"When was the last time you had a seizure?"

"Uh, a week . . ." Azra swallowed with a dry click and started again. "It was two weeks ago. Just a brief absence one."

Mal nodded and scratched his scalp through his bleach-tipped hair. He held up both the EEG and the MRI charts and studied them. "These are pretty good readings. What meds are you on?"

"Carbamazepine." Azra swallowed again and surreptitiously blotted his damp palms on his pants. "I haven't had anything for months. Seizures, I mean. I take my meds every morning and night."

The Zoo manager laid the charts down and frowned at Azra. "Why do you want to work here? What can you bring to the role?"

Sweat sprang up on Azra's bottom lip and he resisted the urge to wipe it away. "I want to help. My brother was killed by an H.I.; plus, I've never had a job before." He lifted his eyes and tried to hold Mal's gaze. "This seemed like something I could do."

Mal pursed his lips and glanced down at the jagged lines on the EEG and the white mass on the MRI. Azra blushed hard. He felt like his brain was laid out on the table.

"Well"—Mal gestured to the charts—"these certainly qualify you. Let's see if you can pass the probation." He slapped the arms of his chair with a grin. His hand was rough and strong when Azra took it and shook.

* * *

Azra extended his hand another couple of inches into the enclosure. His heart hammered in his throat and he fought the screaming urge to snatch his fingers away.

"Go on," Mal said. "The worst part is the wait. You'll see. The bite's no more than a nip when they're that young."

The H.I. in the 5' by 5' Perspex cage was a girl, about five years old. Her tiny arms and legs rippled with muscle and sinew. She edged towards Azra's trembling fingers, her nostrils flaring and twitching. He saw with a wrench that silvery strings of saliva trickled down her chin onto her tattered shirt. She sniffed, turned her head away, dropped to all fours and arched her back up, performing a perfect downward dog.

Azra looked back at Mal. "She's not—shit! Ow!" Azra yanked free of her clawed grip and inspected the row of teeth marks on his forefinger. The girl pawed at the gap, trying to reach him.

Mal threw his head back, roaring with laughter. "Lesson one," he gasped when he'd caught his breath again, "never take your eyes off them."

The marks were already fading from Azra's finger, but his heart still felt like it was trying to jump out of his throat. Mal squeezed past, shoved the girl's hands back inside, and slid the lid shut. The girl bared her teeth at them and paced in a circle on all fours. Her hair was a wiry, filthy tangle about her head and the smell of stale urine and old meat still lingered in the air. Azra suppressed a shiver. "I won't get the virus?"

Mal tapped the side of Azra's head, right where the MRI showed the lesion on his brain. "Nope. It doesn't take anything but the healthiest people. Only the best. The rest of us defects are safe as houses."

* * *

"This is where we hold our educational talks," Mal said as he led Azra into a wide amphitheatre. "Schools and families come in here and we show them how to stay clear of the H.I.s, how to spot someone turning, and tell them a little about the research." Curving rows of concrete benches marched upward from a circular wooden stage. A set of three Perspex enclosures were concealed by a rendered brick wall at the back. A mural of a happy family was painted on the wall. The acoustics were excellent. Azra could hear every growl and frothing snap of the fully grown male H.I. in the first enclosure.

"Let's see how you do with an audience." Mal keyed in the button on his walkie-talkie. "Right folks, come on in."

Five other zoo employees: three women and two men, filed in from the side entrance. Each wore the khaki uniform with the broken DNA symbol over the left breast to show that they too, were immune to infection. Apart from the one guy who stared suspiciously over the top of Azra's head, they all looked normal. "Everybody, say 'hi' to Azra. He's our newest candidate." After a chorus of greetings, Mal led Azra back around to the enclosure where the H.I. now crouched, watching them approach with shaded eyes. "I won't bother introducing the rest till later," Mal muttered, "just in case, eh?"

Azra paused. "In case of what?"

Mal grinned. "Just kidding; you'll be right." He picked up the pole with the loop tether on the end. "Better grab the other one. Bob's a strong bastard." He unlocked a small window at the front of the cage and fed his pole through.

Azra swiped his greasy palms on his pants again and picked up the second pole. Together, they managed to pin Bob hard against the back wall, tethers drawn tight around his neck. The flesh under his jaw was purple as he lunged and snapped. His garbled roaring sounded almost like words. Azra glanced across at Mal, uncertain what to do next. Mal grinned, his ruddy face lit with a type of mad joy and Azra wondered what neuro-disease bought his immunity. "Right," Mal yelled over the sound of Bob's struggles, "we'll bring him out to the stage and you have a go at giving a spiel."

"A spiel?" Azra asked faintly. His mind went blank and for a panicky moment, he thought he was going to white out. The seizure two weeks ago had been a split-second snowy blizzard. *Not now. Not now.*

"Ready?" Mal called.

Azra snapped back. "Uh, yeah. Okay."

They wrestled Bob out of his enclosure and onto the stage. The other zoo employees shifted around to watch as Mal gave Azra a one-handed thumbs up. Azra turned back to the audience and blinked. "Uh, welcome to the Zoo. We are the centre for research to find a cure for the Maass–Hinkler virus. This—this is Bob. He is a male Healthy Infected."

"Doing great!" Mal whispered.

"Uh, the best way to, um, avoid them is to . . . to . . . uh, stay inside the Wall. Keep children and elderly clear of any possible H.I.s." Azra tried to remember the lecture he'd heard every year since he was a little kid. "To, uh, to spot someone who is turning, watch for changes in feeding, muscle tone—"

Bob lunged for Azra. Azra gaped, lax with surprise as he saw Mal with his hands up, the same crazy glee on his face and the second tether pole clattering loose behind Bob. Azra snapped the tether tight just before Bob's teeth clacked shut in front of his face. He pistoned Bob backwards with the pole, fighting to keep him away. Mal whooped. "Never take your eyes off them, Azra!" he yelled. "What are you gonna do? You won't always have a helper and they break loose every now and again. Go on! Show us what you got!"

Azra glanced furiously at Mal. He twisted the rope of the tether on his end of the pole round and round his fist. Bob gurgled and snapped, spraying thick strings of spit as he lunged after Azra again and again. Azra's arms cramped and his garrotted hand was now almost as livid as Bob's face. Bob sagged, dragging Azra with him. Azra gave a final savage twist and Bob's feet drummed on the stage. Azra stumbled to the side, not daring to release Bob even though his arms and legs trembled and he could barely stay standing. Bob's limbs continued to twitch and spasm, slow as a salted snail.

"Should we get him to a doctor or something?" Azra panted.

Mal shook his head. "Nah. Just leave him. We can always get more H.I.s." Mal signalled to one of the men and took the pole from Azra's shaking hands. He passed the pole on and steered Azra to the exit. "Which leads us to the last part of your probation. Gotta say, I'm impressed so far, Azra. We'll see what Georgie makes of you. You might just be wearing the khaki by this afternoon!"

* * *

Georgie, as far as Azra could determine, was a mountain of fat and hair. Mal had driven Azra to the Wall and handed him over to the hunter, wishing him luck.

While he waited for the big man to finish eating, Azra peered through the mesh portal set into the ten-foot-thick concrete wall circling the city. A strong, spicy smell blew in across his face. It was the first time he had seen beyond the Wall since the infection hit twenty-one years ago. The military kept everyone except the hunters and the gatherers clear to avoid possible infection.

The landscape had changed completely. What must have once been buildings were now covered in thick, grainy mud that had hardened into tapering towers. The trees and plants had been left alone, but everything manmade had been buried beneath what looked like giant termite mounds. The constant knocking of the jackers working to keep the Wall clear of the grey excretion echoed down to them from above. He supposed the H.I.s must live inside the mounds, chittering to each other like ants in a nest.

Azra froze. Two sinewy figures flitted from one derelict construction to the next. They were broad across the shoulders like Olympic swimmers. It was hard to tell from this distance, but he thought they were two women. One scaled up a wall like a spider and peered over it briefly before dropping soundlessly back to the ground. Georgie belched—the sound like a small engine backfiring—Azra turned.

"Fried mystery meat, onions, and bread," Georgie sighed with relish. "Breakfast of champions."

Azra fought the urge to step away from the gust of rancid breath.

The big man pushed back the khaki cap on his doughy head and sniffed. "You ready?"

"I guess so."

"All *right*! Wait till you get out there, man. It is bee–yoo–tiful." Georgie signalled to the woman in the booth beside the gate with a winding motion. The gate clanked and slid to with a groan of hydraulics. Georgie hitched up his pants, shouldered his bag on, raised his rifle, and led the charge out on foot.

* * *

The smell of spice lay like an invisible blanket beyond the gate. Azra realised too late that he was trailing behind Georgie, outside the Wall, completely unarmed. He watched, flexing his aching hand as the gate clanged shut behind them, then he turned and followed after the hunter into the dried mud maze. Georgie ducked from the shadow of one mound to the next, back against the wall with every pause, rifle held up and ready. When they came within sight of the mound the two female H.I.s had last disappeared into, Georgie held up his fist to signal a halt. He checked that Azra was still behind before nodding and tiptoeing forward. Azra bit down on his lip to stifle a giggle. He should've been scared out of his mind but he felt oddly exhilarated. Georgie turned and signalled two fingers at his eyes, then ahead. The scene could have been out of one of the comedy movies as easily as a horror show. Azra turned his back and chewed hard on his tongue, shaking with laughter.

Georgie's hand fell on his shoulder like a slab of ham. "Don't worry, mate. I was shit-scared my first time out too. Just stay close behind me and you'll be right."

Azra wiped his eyes and swallowed a snort. He turned and signalled for Georgie to keep going. Georgie nodded and pressed his back to the side of a smaller mound. The structure they were heading for was ten metres away and looked completely deserted. "Look at the size of it!" Georgie palmed away the beads of sweat pearling his forehead. "You can bet there'll be at least a hundred H.I.s inside."

It towered twenty feet higher than most of the mounds surrounding it. Azra wondered dazedly what building was cocooned deep inside. A dry, hot breeze kicked up dust into the air, rustling the leaves in the trees and skittering pieces of rubbish across the ground. Apart from Georgie's laboured breathing and the distant knocking of the jackers, everything else was quiet. Azra glanced behind him, the nape of his neck and skull prickling. Where were all the H.I.s? Did they only come out at night? Where had the two females gone to? Georgie raised his rifle to his shoulder and crept closer, keeping to the shadows provided by the gums along the side of the road.

Azra glanced around again. The tingling had spread down his back and into his hands. He felt *watched*.

Something fell from the top of the tower with a sharp clang. Azra jumped. Georgie threw his thick arm back, driving Azra into a bush.

"Do you smell that?" Azra whispered as he struggled to extricate himself.

Georgie sniffed and shook his head. "I can only smell H.I. turds: smells like nutmeg."

"Burning, something smells like it's burning."

"Oooh. Clever bastards," Georgie muttered. "We must have them scared. Come on, Azra. We're going in."

Oh no.

"Georgie, wait . . . UGHHH!" Azra's left arm shot out, rigid with a spasm. His mouth drew down into a lopsided slash in his face and his left leg clubbed Georgie in the calf. Georgie stumbled and crashed to the pavement. Azra watched in horror as the world tilted and the ground came up to meet his bent and jerking head. The pain was white hot when he hit. He could do nothing about it as the seizure took hold of him and bent him into an arching, juddering bow. All the while, he could see Georgie struggling to regain his feet and the flood of sinewy bodies that poured out of the towers and the streets surrounding them.

Georgie seated the rifle against his shoulder while on bended knee. He shot round after round, knocking the H.I.s back: lithe women, broad and muscled men, children: brown-skinned and lean. The H.I.s twisted and leapt out of the way, lunging towards them with effortless speed. Azra lay limp and helpless on the path, his head throbbing inside and out. He hadn't pissed his pants, but he didn't think it would matter much in another minute or so. Georgie had finally heaved himself to his feet. The wave of H.I.s was closing in. Soon enough, Georgie would run out of ammunition and Azra's first day at work would end very badly.

Then Georgie began drawing away, leaving Azra in the midst of the lunging H.I.s, as inch by inch, he extricated himself from the fray. Sensing that Azra was easier prey, the H.I.s gave up on Georgie and turned their attention on him. He could see the gleam of their white teeth in the frame of snapping mouths as they crawled towards him. He tried to signal Georgie beyond the mass of muscled, tanned bodies, but he could only make out a flash of khaki here and there between the dusty runners and shredded yoga socks. Blackened hands plucked at Azra's clothes. Something clamped down hard on his ankle, another H.I. grabbed Azra's arm and he was yanked and tugged. Those teeth. Man, they were so perfect and white and covered in drool.

Fuck you, Georgie. Fuck you very much.

"Come and get it!" Georgie bellowed over the snarling and growling. A packet of something smashed into the ground beside Azra's cheek, spraying him with hard pellets. He turned his head aside and coughed as a second and a third parcel exploded into the crowd. The H.I.s froze, staring at each other in blank shock. As one, they dove for the parcels, screeching and tearing at each other to get to them. Azra struggled to keep his eyes open, but the post-ictal stage was crowding him out. He saw Georgie pull out a thick coil of rope from his bag, loop it over the head of a male H.I. and yank him onto his back. Georgie flipped him over, sat on him and hog-tied him. The H.I.s ignored the big man while he worked; they were murderously intent on scraping up the contents of the packets that had burst and spilled all over the ground. They snapped and tore at each other, biting chunks out of forearms and ripping out great handfuls of hair. Georgie picked up his rifle and bag and hoisted the writhing H.I. onto his shoulder. Still, they paid no attention to the giant that walked through them like a wide Moses parting the Red Sea.

Azra felt the ground under his body reverberate as Georgie lumbered over to where he lay. He was unceremoniously swept up onto Georgie's other shoulder, and the last thing he saw before he spiralled down into darkness was the crack in Georgie's arse peeking out the top of his pants.

By the time the gate clattered shut, Georgie was puffing contentedly on a cigarette, the H.I. had been carted away, and Azra felt his body return to him. He gingerly sat up and cradled his head. A scab had crusted over on the left side of his scalp.

"Sorry about the seizure."

Georgie shrugged. "You couldn't help it. I reckon I'm due for a cardiac infarction. Thunderclap to the chest; I'm gonna drop like a tonne of bricks. Not apologising when *that* happens."

Azra sighed. "I guess I don't get the job."

"You did all right until you spazzed out." Georgie delicately planted the cigarette into the corner of his mouth and hauled Azra to his feet. "You make good bait."

"Fuck you." Azra swayed, squinting against the stab of pain in his head and side. He steadied himself and shrugged Georgie's hand off. "Jesus. Those H.I.s were fast. I've only ever seen the ones in the Zoo. But those things out there were unreal."

Georgie grunted. "Hell, yeah. Those crazy bastards were doing their Ashtanga yoga, cross fit, boot camps and whatever the hell else when the shit hit the fan. They will out-run, out-climb and out–pole dance you every single day of the week."

"How did you . . . what was that stuff you threw at them?"

The big man dug into his pocket and produced a packet wrapped in plastic. "This?" Georgie hefted it with a grin. "Quinoa-and-chia seed bomb. H.I. catnip. Welcome to the Zoo, Azra."

The Old Home Place

Stephen R. Miller

Editor: Sometimes the sheep saves the shepherd.

The crowd stirred restlessly in the longhall, waiting for the headman and his council to file in. Sitting with the rest of the scout-apprentices, Zoe Sterling resisted the urge to fiddle with her knife's hilt. She had taken too many clouts on the ear from Hartley to start fidgeting now; the scarred old trainer never missed a chance to drum into their heads how vital it was for a scout to learn stillness. In the wild it could be the difference between coming home and ending up in a mutt's belly.

At last the council made their entrance. The townsfolk stilled as the six took their seats, facing out over the crowd. Daniel Kramer, headman these last seven years, cleared his throat. "Let us be convened. Master Scout, are these your candidates?"

"Such as they are, sir," Hartley said gruffly. "A rough lot, but there's some talent there."

Daniel nodded. "Are there any among them prepared for the trial?"

The old man rubbed a hand over the ropy scar on his cheek. "There is one." He turned, pointing a gnarled finger square at Zoe's face. "Sterling, on your feet."

She could feel the eyes on her as she rose. Something that couldn't decide between pride and terror rose in her chest. Hartley thought she was ready to face the wilds on her own! The youngest of the crew, if only by a few months, but she was ready. If Hartley believed it, she had to be.

From the looks on the faces of Daniel Kramer and the rest of the councilors they weren't quite as certain. The headman coughed gently into his hand. "Very well. Apprentice Sterling, do you stand ready to hazard the trials of your Path?"

Suddenly all the moisture seemed to be gone from her mouth. Zoe swallowed and worked up enough spit to talk. "I do, Headman." A low murmur swept through the people behind her, but she paid it no mind and kept her head up.

"Very well. Master Scout, at the time of your choosing, this apprentice will set forth on the trial as you so order." Daniel shuffled the little stack of papers in front of him; Zoe took the cue that he was done with the business of her and sat down again. As she took her seat, Tamara reached over and squeezed her arm gently. Zoe smiled at the older girl in gratitude, then glanced around at the crowd behind them. Her parents sat a few rows back, her father's arm over her mother's shoulders. They looked calm enough, but Zoe could see the telltale signs of concern. She tried to catch their eyes, give them a reassuring grin, but the crowd shifted again and she lost them.

* * *

Zoe stared at the gate, trying not to let her nerves show. More for something to keep herself busy than any real concern, she took a quick inventory of her kit. Everything was in its place, as she had known it would be from the last three times she had checked. Still, it kept her from showing nerves in front of the small crowd that had gathered to see her off. She was just repacking the last few bits when Master Scout Hartley walked up to her. "Sterling. You ready?"

"Hell of a time to ask, sir." The words were out before she even realized they were coming. Zoe braced herself for a slap across the back of her head, or at least a sharp word or twenty. Instead Hartley only snorted laughter and clapped her shoulder.

"You'll do fine out there if you keep your head." He stood with her as the gate slowly trundled open, driven by the sentries spinning the huge cranks. "Just remember, everything out there thinks you're food. Your job is to prove them all wrong, and get back here to tell the tale." The gate clanged to a stop, and Hartley turned to face her for the formal portion of the morning's proceedings. "Zoe Sterling, you are charged with the retrieval of a sprig from the forever-trees of the Rockfaller. Succeed and you will be counted worthy to walk the Path of the Scouts. Do you accept this charge, speak now."

Zoe took a deep breath and nodded firmly. "I accept your charge, Master. We shall not speak again until it is fulfilled." Hartley nodded once and strode away, back into the township without a further look in Zoe's direction. She forced herself to keep her own head up and face the gates. It was bad form and the worst luck to look back when you left for your trial.

Zoe stepped off at a brisk pace, the sort of stride she knew she could maintain for hours. She managed not to jump when the gates clanged shut behind her. That actually seemed to make it easier somehow. She was completely on her own now, stand or fall. The fear was still in there, but so was the will. She was not coming back empty-handed.

When she reached the top of the northern ridge-line, Zoe paused to take in the view: unbroken woods stretching out in front of her, a thick green carpet over the land, and rising against the horizon the ruin of the old city. That was where she needed to go, into the last wreck that was left of a dead world.

The first day was easy, more so than most of Hartley's exercises. A few times she came across the trail of some animals on the move, once even the unmistakable sign of a band of whisper-men, but those were days old and headed off away from her destination. She knew that kind of luck wouldn't hold, though. The closer she got to the old city, the more likely she was to come across more than tracks.

Drifting into sleep high in a tree, Zoe watched the sky overhead. Little more than a sliver of moon lit up the clear night. She picked out the navigator stars almost by instinct; they were old friends by now, known to her since the first year of her teaching. The Pole Star clearly stood out, fixed in his place to the north, but others could guide you too if you knew their courses. Dragon, snake, huntress, and warrior . . . Zoe yawned hugely, wondering as she often did if the old stories were true. They couldn't be, not really—could they? Even people who could build the old city and all its mysteries could never really have flown all the way out of the sky.

A falling star arced slowly overhead. She fell asleep and dreamed of riding on the back of a great bird, off into the dark between stars.

* * *

Up with the rising of the sun, Zoe reached the old road by midday. She crouched in the brush beside the cracked stone lanes leading toward the edge of the city and watched for nearly an hour. Whisper-men and other mutts often used the old roads for getting around. Even pot-holed and littered with the wrecks of old-world vehicles, the roads were still a useful way to move large groups quickly. Scouts were taught to avoid them if at all possible and stick to the cover of the surrounding woods. This time, she needed to risk it at least enough for a crossing. The road didn't bend for another day's walk.

Fifteen minutes she huddled by the side of the road, watching and listening for any sign of mutts moving on the road. When nothing stirred, Zoe decided it was time to move. She hopped lightly over the low wall at the side of the road and started across, ducking from one dead traveling-box to the next.

Nerving herself up for the last dash to the far side barrier, Zoe froze at a burst of angry voices from somewhere up the road. Not whisper-men at least; those came by their name honestly. What then? How had she missed it?

Stung pride fought the smart urge to just get away from whatever they were, and pride won. She would just get close enough to get a glimpse, enough to know what was out here with her and if they might be headed the same way she was. Her mind made up, she pulled her knife slowly out of its sheath and slowly crept around the rusty hulk she'd sheltered behind.

The voices still argued ahead of her. When she reached the last bit of cover between them, Zoe leaned her head around just far enough to see with one eye. She spied a small band of figures dressed in ragged scraps of leather, clustered around a makeshift camp next to one of the old wrecks. Bonecutters! She felt her guts clench. They were stupid and slow compared to the whisper-men or the mutts down by the big river south of the township. But if the Bonecutters caught you—well, best if they were hungry enough to cook all of you at once.

A few of the mutts were still laid out on the ground, yawning and stretching; the biggest of the lot was in a shoving match with another about something. She felt a little better—no real shame in not hearing a sleeping enemy—but what mattered was that the fight went on long enough for her to get well away. Already some on the edge of the group were getting bored since things hadn't gotten bloody yet. Zoe ducked back behind the traveling-box—and clipped a loose bit of metal with her elbow. Something shifted and fell with a clatter. The arguing voices gave way to shouts and running footsteps coming her way.

Zoe bolted, and the chase was on.

In spite of the terror she felt trying to drown her, Zoe's thoughts crystalized as she vaulted the side wall and raced into the woods. She could probably outrun the pack for a while, but only at the cost of leaving a trail even they couldn't miss. With their blood up, the Bonecutters would dog her as long as they had a track to follow. Her only choice was to fight, or shake them loose and hope they gave up the chase. Fighting a half dozen of the mutts was death waiting to happen. No, she needed to out-think them.

Fortunately that wasn't much of a challenge if a scout knew her business.

A glimpse of the sun through the trees helped her set her directions. Thinking over the map she had studied the night before leaving the township, Zoe angled a little more to the right and sped up. The Bonecutters' shouts were fading already but they would be back soon enough.

She gasped heavily by the time she reached the creek. Zoe hopped lightly off the bank and into the water, turned upstream away from the road and slogged a few yards further before finding what she wanted.

* * *

The Bonecutters shambled up to the creek bed a few minutes later, jeering and calling after their prey. The six of them spread out in a ragged line, moving up and down the banks. Clearly her footprints led into the water, and there was no sign on the far bank of her coming out.

One of them, a big fellow with a fine collection of sharpened bones strung at his belt, paused under a tree right at the edge of the water to catch his breath. He kept his eyes on the mud of the bank instead of looking up, and his companions' blundering and shouting meant he didn't hear Zoe's bowstring draw back.

She held the arrow ready, aiming for the juncture of shoulder and neck. If she fired, it probably meant her life as well as his, but that was a chance she was ready to take. Thankfully for them both, another Bonecutter shouted something that drew this one away. Zoe relaxed her bow and dared to let out her breath for what felt the first time in ages. She leaned back against the trunk and listened to the mutts jabbering as they walked back to the road. "Stupid, stupid," she muttered, and reached for the rope at her belt. "You should have let them skin you. Next time, you *run.*"

* * *

She jerked awake, wincing as her safety rope dug into her middle. The sun had dropped beneath the horizon, but there was still a bit of light in the western sky. Around her the nighttime creatures began to stir . . . and more importantly there was no sound of her pursuers below. Zoe slowly undid the knot and coiled the rope again. It was going to be harder going in the dark, but she could probably reach the outskirts of the city in time to hole up before dawn.

Landing lightly in a crouch beside the tree, Zoe paused and waited for anything that sounded as if it might be responding to her movements. When nothing jumped out and tried to chew on her liver after a few minutes, she decided it was as safe as it was ever likely to be in the wilds and set off along the creek.

* * *

It always sobered her to see wreckage of the old world crushed under the advance of nature. Like all of the kids in the township, Zoe had been raised on tales of the wonders that world had brought forth—traveling-boxes that moved without horses, whole buildings made of glass and tall enough to reach the sky . . . and those mythical flying machines that had carried men and women out to the stars.

Now all that slowly rusted within the swallowing forest. Around her Zoe could see the first remnants of the old city's smaller buildings. Most were little more than rubble among the brush, with a few walls still standing here and there. She moved carefully but as quickly as she dared; the Rockfaller was still a couple of hours away, and she wanted to make it in time to get clear of the city center before dark.

She followed a side street down to one of the main avenues. The towers rose to terrifying heights around her. Zoe tried to keep her eyes moving as much as she could. She scanned the upper levels of the buildings as she went, ignoring the slightly dizzy sensation of all that *up*. Mutts were known to lurk up there and launch ambushes on unwary travelers.

With the sun high overhead, Zoe ducked into the shelter of a building's first floor to eat. She'd expected the encounter with the Bonecutters to have burned up all of her luck, but the day had been quiet. Even so, the narrow escape had left her determined to keep on her toes the rest of the way.

She finished the last of her ration and tucked the refuse into a pocket of her bag when a strange noise rose outside. Zoe scrambled to the wall under a gaping broken window and slowly peeked over the sill. The street was empty, but that weird high-pitched whine was getting steadily louder. Zoe glanced up slightly—and froze, staring in shock.

A gleaming white thing, shaped almost like an egg with projections like a bird's wings on either side, flew slowly through the canyon formed by the ruined buildings. It sailed past her hiding spot and tilted gently to the left, angling down one of the streets crossing the one she was on. Zoe craned her neck to keep the thing in sight as long as she could. How did it stay up? Hawks could soar, but they were light and sleek—and even they had to flap their wings. This thing just . . . seemed to float. It turned its back end toward her and Zoe had to squint. There were two points of bright yellow light surrounded by air that rippled like a heat haze. Then it darted away faster than any bird, leaving only the echo of its sound.

Never in her life had she wanted anything more than to follow the strange thing, but Zoe had a mission to think of. The forever-tree cutting was useless except as a token to prove she hadn't just lazed around in the woods—but she didn't dare come back without it. Whatever wonders the flying machine might lead to didn't change that. Zoe blew out a frustrated breath, staring at the spot she'd last seen it. "I'm coming after you once I'm done," she said.

Gathering her kit, Zoe resumed the trek toward the Rockfaller. Twice she had to go to ground to avoid passing bands of mutts that came a little too close for comfort. Apparently she wasn't the only one whose curiosity had been roused by the thing soaring overhead. Both groups of mutts seemed to be headed in the general direction of the flier's departure.

Even with those unplanned-for stops, she made good time. The sun had marched only a small portion of the sky when she reached the large open yard in front of the Rockfaller. It was one of the more intact buildings even now; the top floors had fallen in, but the lower two stories were largely intact. Most of the letters spelling out its name were still affixed over the doors, although the gaps to either side of the 'f' had never been repaired. No one knew what it was that kept the mutts away, or who had gathered all the old forever-trees inside or why. Zoe had been here only once, and she felt the same now as she had then, like there were eyes watching her from every one of those empty windows. She hurried across the open space and ducked in through the doors.

Inside was cool and dim. Zoe crouched against a pillar, letting her eyes adjust from the sun's brightness. Enough light filtered in that she could make out the large grove in the center of the front room. The plants had been very carefully arranged, with smaller trees and bushes in a wide outer circle around a cluster of taller trees. Whoever had devoted such effort to building the grove, the purpose had died with them.

Zoe shuffled closer, ears straining to catch the slightest sound of movement from the darkness inside. She told herself it was just the residual excitement of seeing the flying machine; the Rockfaller was just an empty shell. There was nothing more dangerous in here than her. Zoe squared her shoulders and marched through the outer circle to the nearest tree in the middle. Her knife made short work of the stem holding three of the strange waxy leaves. Her back itched when she turned for the door, but she wouldn't let herself run. Only when she was outside did she break into a jog. There might still be time, if the flier hadn't gone far.

* * *

The shadows were well up the walls of the buildings around her when Zoe spotted the machine again. This time, it crouched on the ground, silent and unmoving. A trio of thick, sturdy legs extended out of the bottom to hold it up, and the spots under the "wings" that had glowed so brightly were dark now. Even so, it put her in mind of an oversized bird ready to leap back into flight.

She spent several agonizing minutes watching from concealment a few hundred yards away before swallowing her fear and moving closer. Even as she drew near there was no response, no sign of anyone inside or nearby. From here, she could see a clear panel facing front, showing what looked like open space inside. She edged closer still and, ready to jump back and run at the first sign of danger, reached out to touch its skin.

Zoe sighed in wonderment, running her hand along the surface. It was warm to the touch, smoother than polished stone and there was a faint vibrating thrum under her hand. Something was written here, painted onto the skin in sharp black, but it made no sense to her. The letters and numbers were familiar but they didn't seem to make any words she could work out.

Her eye caught a trail of footprints near the front leg. Crouching beside the track, Zoe felt her heart thundering. The pattern of each print had narrow ridges and valleys at odd angles unlike any boot-print she'd ever seen. *Someone had come out of the machine.* They had wandered away to explore the city . . . and here beside those alien to her were those of the whisper-men. The mutts' tracks overlaid the other, and were very fresh from the look of it. The flier was prey now, and probably didn't even know it yet.

Zoe dithered. Bad enough she'd gotten herself in a scrape with the Bonecutters, now she was about to willingly stalk whisper-men? Hartley would have throttled her. But if she didn't . . . no, she decided. Running away to save herself was one thing, but that machine was a myth come to life. If the mutts killed the flier she would never know any more than that. It would be one more mystery kept by the dead, and it would eat at her the rest of her life. She had her bow strung and an arrow in hand a moment later, heading deeper into the ruins after the hunter and hunted.

The tracks led into a nearby building, across a large front room and into a stairwell. Here the whisper-men diverged, heading up where the flier went down. She paused for a moment before following the mutts. They wouldn't simply abandon their chase so quickly; odds were they had gone this way to lay an ambush of some kind. Following the flier would only lead her into it as well . . . if the trap hadn't already been sprung.

Zoe moved with every bit of skill she'd honed over five years under Hartley's teaching. The darkness in the stairwell was total even to her trained eyes, but a few moments of feeling around showed her the way. One flight up she found the rest of the stairs were blocked by rubble, leaving only a corridor going out. Zoe shuffled along with her back near one wall, barely breathing. A dim glow rose ahead, light through a doorway. She paused a few steps away, angling for a better view.

Beyond the doorway the floor on this level continued for six feet or so. Past that the floor had given way, opening up into the room below. The glow's source came from below, something casting a pale steady light into the room. Zoe could hear movement down there as well, noises of someone at work with metal tools.

Shifting her attention to the ledge of flooring on her level, half a dozen whisper-men waited crouched and ready, each with a wickedly sharp spear in hand. The nearest was little more than a few strides from her, but they were so intent on their prey none had yet noticed her. An arm went up ready to signal the attack.

Before that arm could fall, Zoe raised her bow and fired an arrow at the closest mutt's back. As the string rolled free of her fingers, she let out a long, piercing shriek.

The rest of the mutts turned, cringing at the sudden noise. Their ears, so finely tuned to the movements of prey, would be ringing. She managed to drop another before any of them could recover, but had to dive aside to avoid taking a spear in the gut before she could fire again.

A searing flash of light and a small thunderclap exploded from the room below. Another whisper-man dropped, and the rest seemed to be going crazier than normal. Clutching at their ears, two of them dropped their spears and jumped down to the lower room. Two more bangs sounded. In the light of the flashes, the last of the hunters charged at her like a nightmare in flesh. She chucked her bow at its face. It ducked and batted her weapon aside, distracted just enough to let her roll past it. She whipped her knife out and scored a deep gash on its flank as she tumbled.

Something punched into her gut, and a searing pain bloomed. What had been a graceful roll ended with Zoe sprawled on her back, writhing in agony. She raised her head to see the spear jammed deep into her; even wounded and half-crazed from the noise, the mutt had been too fast for her. She flinched as another flash and crack exploded from below. The whisper-man's head seemed to dissolve. The body dropped dead at her feet.

Zoe grabbed the spear's haft to keep it steady and slowly stood up. Her head spun, she staggered back—and then she was falling, back over the edge and down. There was a horrible flat smack, and everything exploded with hurt. The light was going out, or getting farther away. Was the flier running away? She tried to call out, ask it not to leave her down here in the dark to die alone, but her voice was going too. Something shiny floated above her. Had the moon come down to keep her company? That was nice. Zoe closed her eyes, just for a few seconds until she could get her breath.

* * *

"Shit. Shit, shit, shit! Come on kid, don't do that." Kenji Inoue tapped the speaker control on his suit's wrist. "Hey! Wake up, sweetheart. Look at me." The girl's eyes fluttered open again, barely. "There you go. Stay with me." He pulled the medical kit from his harness and popped it open. The wound was bad, he could see, beyond the kit's capacity to fix. If the spear hadn't stayed in she would probably be dead in minutes. As it was that still might happen.

"Gotta cut this thing down a little, kiddo," he said as he grabbed for his cutter. The pencil-thin line of coherent plasma made short work of the wood, leaving a few inches of the spear sticking out of her abdomen. She groaned through clenched teeth as the weight of the impaling weapon shifted. "It's okay, that's done. Let me just seal you up here . . . and now some of the good stuff."

The girl relaxed and stopped writhing as the painkillers hit. The clotting foam had stopped her bleeding, but that didn't solve the problem. She was going to need a surgeon, and Kenji only knew of one place to find that. "The boss is going to kill me."

* * *

Standing in front of the quarantine bay's window, Captain von Eisenberg sighed heavily. "Do you have any idea the complications you've caused us?"

Kenji had expected it but exploded anyway. "Well, what the hell did you expect me to do, Skipper? Leave her down there to bleed out? She's just a kid, for crying out loud!" Kenji clenched his jaw shut, trying to rein his temper in.

"I know, Ken," she said softly, and he relaxed at the sympathy in her voice. "I'm not saying you did wrong, but this was not supposed to be a contact mission. We didn't even expect there to *be* anyone to contact, not from what the drone probes showed."

Kenji shrugged diffidently. "All I know is she saved my ass from those things. If she hadn't jumped them I'd be dead meat." He studied the girl sleeping on the bed behind the glass. The auto-medic had put her back together easily enough, dosed her with a few antivirals and was busy working up inoculations for some bugs she'd been carrying. In the meantime, the captain had opted to leave her sedated. "So what do we do?"

The captain sighed again and grinned. "I said this wasn't *supposed* to be a contact mission. Think we're a little past that now."

* * *

Zoe opened her eyes, and saw a ceiling bathed in pale bright light. Where? Memory trickled back into her brain. She sat up quickly. One hand grabbed at the spear in her belly, and found . . . nothing. She looked down, startled to find she was wearing different clothes. The cloth was softer than anything she'd ever seen, dyed pale blue and they were far too big for her. She pulled the hem of the top up and looked at the place where the whisper-man had stuck her.

The skin was smooth and unmarked like nothing had ever happened. And she didn't hurt, there or anywhere else.

She looked up and tried to take in the room around her. There was nothing here but the bed she was lying on. It had lights built into it, and even a bit with glowing words streaming along. One wall had a huge window in it, looking out on a larger room with more beds and a number of things she couldn't even put names to.

A soft hiss and another part of the wall slid aside. Zoe pushed herself back up toward the wall behind her. A woman stepped through the opening, which closed behind her even though she didn't touch it. "Hello, young lady," the woman said with a small smile. "My name is Astrid. It is my pleasure to meet you."

Zoe cocked her head slightly, frowning in intense concentration. The woman's words sounded strange, slurred and with sounds that were subtly *wrong* somehow. Was it something they'd done to her that had messed up her ears? She swallowed past the dry lump in her throat. "Where am I?" Not her ears, then, she still sounded like herself. "How did I get in these clothes?" With a frantic start she realized her kit was nowhere in sight. "What did you do with my stuff?"

The woman—Astrid—held up her hands in what Zoe took to be a soothing gesture. "Everything is right in there," she said, pointing to the room outside the big window, "except for your knife and your bow and arrows. We have those stored somewhere secure. I'm sorry, but we can't let you keep weapons while you're here."

Zoe made herself stop and breathe. These people had helped her, apparently, but they were straight out of a fireside tale. They had power she couldn't even understand, let alone resist. She needed to be careful. "My name is Zoe Sterling, from Westhill Township. If I was rude, I'm sorry. I just need to check my bag. I had something important to me in there; it might have fallen out during the fight."

"Of course, Zoe. Please, follow me." Astrid turned and the door whisked open again, still without her touching it. Zoe stepped down off the bed slowly, testing the floor first with one bare foot. It felt warm and slightly soft like the inside of a newly fleeced boot. She walked across the room to where Astrid waited and looked through the doorway. It led into the same room she could see through the window. "Where are we?" she asked again.

"This is our sick bay; it's a sort of hospital. Do you understand what that is?"

Zoe nodded, too amazed to feel insulted by the question. "For sick people, back in the old world. Like Sainfrankis."

The woman looked puzzled at something but nodded. "Right enough. You were hurt pretty badly, when those . . . things attacked Kenji. He couldn't help you there, so he brought you back here with him."

That made her stop dead in her tracks, her head swimming at the realization. "I . . . I flew? He brought me here in that machine?"

"Well, he would have a hard time carrying you all the way on his back," Astrid said with a little laugh. "Here we are." She touched the side of a box on one wall and it sprang open. "Everything is as it was, only we did clean your clothes and mend the holes."

Shirt, trousers, underthings, cloak, belts; all there, except the knife, bow-case and quiver. Zoe dug into the bag and sighed in relief at the feel of the cutting of the forever tree under her hand. A quick run through the rest of her kit confirmed it was all in place. Zoe nodded and put everything back into the box. "Thank you, Astrid. And I'd like to thank—Kenji? For saving my life."

"You're welcome, Zoe. Unfortunately Kenji is working just now, but I will ask him to speak with you when he can."

Zoe looked around at the hospital room, so unlike the wreck that remained of Sainfrankis in the old city. This room was so small, for one thing; more, she couldn't imagine Sainfrankis ever looking this white and clean. "Who are you?"

Astrid took a deep breath, looking like she was getting ready for something difficult. "Why don't we sit down? This might take some time." She pointed to a pair of chairs next to one of the shiny black-and-white tables at the edge of the room.

"Around three hundred years ago," Astrid said, after they were seated, "the world was so full of people that everything was starting to fall apart. There were just too many people and not enough space or resources to go around."

Zoe nodded slowly; Green River Township had started that way, splitting off from Westhill when her parents were young. She tried to imagine the whole world being that full and quickly gave up.

Astrid continued, "So our ancestors built the Arks—gigantic spaceships with room for thousands of people, along with seeds and animals and machines to build a world from scratch. And humanity spread out, to half a dozen new planets circling new suns."

"New suns?" Zoe asked.

"Yes, Zoe. All of the stars you can see in the sky are like Earth's sun, just very far away."

Zoe wasn't sure she quite believed that but nodded respectfully. The stars were pinpoints; the sun was the biggest and brightest thing in the whole sky. How far would someone have to go for them to switch places?

"Building a new home was hard, and for a long time our colonies could barely even talk to the other planets, or people back on Earth. But we made it work, and several generations later, once we could do more than scratch a living, we wondered why we couldn't get any response from Earth.

"We thought at first it was just a machine that wasn't working right, but it went on for so long that we knew it had to be more than that. So the colonies sent back probes—spaceships that could fly themselves and send information back to us—to see what was happening back home. That was how we found out about the war."

"Darkness, death, and a broken world," Zoe muttered, and blushed when she realized she'd said it out loud. "Sorry. It's something from an old story one of my teachers used to tell." She nodded for Astrid to continue.

"At first we didn't really know *what* had happened. All we found everywhere we looked were empty wrecked cities and creatures like the ones that attacked Kenji. Finally one of the probes located some old records that gave us a part of the story. We still don't quite know how it started, or why, just that it destroyed almost everything. The weapons they used killed millions of people, and left others mutated—turned them into those creatures.

"After that, a lot of people in the colonies wanted to forget the Earth and move on. But some of us knew we couldn't let that happen. This was humanity's home, once, and we couldn't just abandon it. Eventually, we gathered up enough people who wanted to come back in person, to find out for ourselves if there was anything—or anyone—left."

Astrid's face was turning slightly red, and she stopped to take a deep breath. "I'm sorry, I just . . . I had to work very hard to convince a lot of people that coming here was worth it, so I tend to get emotional about it. And, while we hadn't planned to do more than have a look around, it might be that meeting you could be a huge help there."

Zoe sat quietly, trying to digest it all. "You really came here from another sun—star? In a . . . a flying machine?"

Astrid nodded, eyebrows rising slightly. "In fact, that's where we are right now. Would you like to see?"

Outside the sick bay were hallways with smooth white walls, the same soft dark floor, and those strange pale lights. They passed a few people as they walked, who all greeted her and Astrid as they passed though Astrid never stopped to talk. Some of them stared, though Zoe knew she was goggling too.

Their walk ended in a large open room, most of which was taken up with the flying machine that she had seen in the city. It still boggled her to think she had been in that thing. She followed as Astrid led the way around it to the far wall, where she stopped next to a small window.

"Take a look."

Zoe stepped up to the window. It took a moment or two for her to grasp what she was really seeing. "Oh . . . oh, wow." Spreading out below them, far enough away that the horizon was a visible curve, the surface was a patchwork of brown, greens, and blues. Layers of white blanketed the land to one side. Zoe remembered seeing an ancient treasure once in the old city, a ball with a map of the whole world drawn on it. What lay below her looked like that, grown to incredible size and covered by cattail fluff.

Above the world, the sky was a deeper black than she'd ever seen, the stars sharp and unwavering points in the dark. She leaned as close as she could, breathing a slight mist on the pane. "Wh-where is that? Are we over my home?"

Leaning closer, Astrid peeked out over Zoe's shoulder. "Asia, actually. Right now we're almost right on the other side of the world from where we found you."

Her head swam. Zoe had to take a step back and make herself breathe slowly in and out. "Easy," Astrid said with a concerned frown. "I'm sorry, that was too much too soon—"

"It's amazing!" Zoe exclaimed with a delighted grin. She looked back out the window, drinking in the sight. "The other side of the whole world. Nobody I know has ever been more than ten days' walk from the longhall. And flying! We're up out of the sky!" She laughed in the sheer delight of it. "They'll never believe me at home!" That sobered her; she turned to Astrid. "I can go home, can't I?"

Astrid looked shocked and laughed aloud. "Of course you can, Zoe. We're not going to kidnap you. In fact, seeing as we've now officially made contact, we were rather hoping you might be willing to introduce us."

* * *

The worst of the bouncing and jostling faded finally, and the walls in front of their seats disappeared with a whir, leaving the big windows open. Zoe watched in awed fascination as they flew lower and lower. Beside her Kenji and Astrid were dealing with the controls, talking low and fast between themselves in words she didn't understand. Far below, Zoe spotted a gleam of sunlight on glass and metal. It startled her to realize she was seeing the old city, thrusting its tallest towers up out of the forest around it.

From up here, right now, she could see every inch of ground she had ever walked in her whole eighteen years. Everything she knew, everyone she loved, their whole lives—it was so tiny, such a little piece of one little world.

Kenji glanced over as she rubbed at her eyes. "Zoe? You feeling all right?"

She cleared her throat and nodded. "I'm fine. Just—it's so different now."

"What's that?"

"Everything."

They flew a slow, looping turn that took them nearly over the township, then settled down in a clearing a little over a mile distant. Astrid and Kenji left behind their big protective suits this time when they got out. For the approach to the township they let Zoe—back in her own comfortable clothing with all of her kit settled back in its place—lead the way. Here Zoe was the teacher, keeping her charges well away from the dangers around them. She couldn't teach them to sneak so she needed to rely on speed.

Their machine's flight near the township had of course not gone unnoticed. Halfway there, Zoe raised a hand to tell the off-worlders to stop. Studying the brush nearby she grinned and called out, "Is this a proper greeting for a scout back from her trial then, Mister Finley?"

The scout she'd called to seemed to materialize out of hiding a dozen yards away, arrow on the string but not raised to fire. "Your pardon, Apprentice," emphasizing the last word slightly, "but we looked for you to come back on foot. And alone." Despite his banter, she could see the man was nervous as he watched the three of them.

"So did I. But things have happened. These people . . . they need to see the headman and the council."

Finley looked at Astrid and Kenji carefully before nodding slowly. "They certainly do at that."

They resumed their procession toward the township gate, with Senior Scout Finley now in the lead. Zoe could tell there were two other scouts on their flanks, which meant there were probably at least three others nearby she hadn't seen.

A group of more than a dozen townsfolk waited outside the closed gate, milling around nervously until they caught sight of the approaching band. Standing at the front, Headman Kramer adjusted his official coat— only to have it promptly knocked askew by Zoe's father as he barreled forward. Finley raised a hand as if to stop him, but wisely stepped aside.

"Oh, my girl!" He caught Zoe up in a sweeping bear hug, spinning her half around. She laughed and wrapped her arms around his thick neck. "I knew you'd be making your way back to us in one piece." He set her down, patted lightly at her head, shoulders, and arms. "You are all right, aren't you?"

"I'm fine, Papa. Better than that! Wait 'til you hear what's happened." She squeezed his hands in hers and looked over to where the headman and councilors waited, Master Hartley beside them. "I'll see you and Mama later. Things are going to be pretty busy right now."

He looked unsure but nodded and, with a parting kiss on her forehead, withdrew to let her approach the master scout. She reached into her bag, pulling out the forever-tree twig—made of 'plastic,' one of the off-worlders on the ship had told her. "Master Scout Hartley, I have returned from the Trial you set before me. The cutting you asked me to bring." She held it out to him.

He studied her a few moments before smiling his crooked smile and taking the twig from her. "Well done, Scout Sterling. But it seems you've brought back a little something extra as well."

"Headman," Zoe said as she turned to face Daniel Kramer, "these with me are Astrid von Eisenberg and Kenji Inoue, captain and flight officer of the starship *Katerina Magna*."

The headman managed not to gape for more than a few seconds before rallying and stepping forward. "Er. How do you do. I—I am Daniel Kramer, appointed headman of Westhill Township. On behalf of the people of Westhill and our neighboring communities, ah . . . welcome."

Astrid smiled and inclined her head slightly in a polite bow. "In the name of the people and worlds of the Colonial Association, greetings. It is our great pleasure to meet you and yours, Headman. I believe we have much to discuss."

Post Apocalypse Support

A. C. Russell

Editor: Support comes in many forms, shapes, and sizes.

Well, the apocalypse done came and went, and really it wasn't as bad as ever'body thought it was gon' be. All them movies and books wit' the zombies and the cannibalism, and Mad Max and stuff, none o' that happened. I guess with all that death and destruction people didn't want any more violence, they just wanted to live peaceful-like. Food was a little tricky at first, but pretty much ever'body know if you stick a seed in the ground and water it, sumpin' gon' pop up. Cured the obesity epidemic that's for sure, so it ain't all bad. My only problem is you can't find a decent bra. In the end, that's really what made me decide to go with Henry and Curtis on that expedition to Houston.

I don't go on a lot of expeditions; usually Curtis is the traveler in our little community. He takes off about four times a year and trades with other folks for stuff we need. Now, I do like to go to the annual harvest festival over in Alexandria, but that takes us two days each way and by that time I am just done with traveling for a good while. I like sleeping on a mattress, not the ground. Tish say I'm gettin' old; I keep telling her she just ten years younger than me so she better watch out. And she don't have this bra problem I got, neither.

Henry he play saxophone and he need reeds but Curtis say, "ain't no reeds no mo', nowhere." He say he's combed all the old music stores from Nawlins to Memphis and that he even talked to somebody one time who got into the music department at Elleshu and they just ain't no more. He say he think Henry should just stop playing saxophone, pick up the flute or something that don't use reeds. Well he ain't the only one who don't like Henry's playing, I can tell you, but I hate to see a man give up the thing he loves. I don't mind it so much 'cept when he play too loud, and he play much better now than when he was a kid. Anyway, you shoulda heard Henry when Curtis said 'play the flute.' He go crazy, all rantin' and ravin' about Coltrane didn't play no flute and I don't know what all. Screamin' at Curtis, who be his best friend, gettin' right up in his face. And poor ol' skinny Curtis all shrinking back from my baby bro like he scared to death Henry gon' kill him. I laughed so hard I thought I was gon' fall out. Curtis kept away from him for a while after that.

But then the next time Curtis he come back from his out-n-about, he go up to Henry wit' a big box and a little box. The big box was another saxophone, a tenor sax; Henry been wantin' one o' them for a long time. The little box full of little pieces o' sticks, he say some kinda plant that somebody told him was the kinda stuff to make reeds. Well Henry looked about twenty years younger, started dancin' and jumpin' all around and everything. He went all over the yard, dosey-doeing wit' all of us, grabbing our elbows where we stood and hooting like a crazy person. I woulda slapped him if I hadn't been laughin' so hard.

But that was over a year ago an' now Henry is all out of them little pieces o' wood so he plannin' on going with Curtis on this next trip. That's why I figure I better go ahead on wit' 'em; it would be better travelin' with both of them than just Curtis. An' I got to go 'cause there ain't no way in hell I'ma let Curtis pick me out some bras.

See, Tish don't understand why I want bras. She ten years younger, like I said, and she only got these itty bitty bumps, not like me with my big round melons. Even when she was nursin' all dem babies, them things didn't get no bigger than a B cup. Ain't nothin' but she gots to be wearin' a bra all the time then and I reminded her of that the other day. She say "well naturally, I got to hold the nursing pads in, don't I?" And I got to concede she got a point there. I used to hate it when I leaked; you don't notice at first because the milk is the same temperature as your body and then some smart ass (usually Curtis) is all like, "hey Bossie, might wanna change yo' shirt."

But now that Tish's kids are big and she don't have no plans to have no more she all footloose and fancy free and act like everybody else can hang loose just 'cause she do. I said "girl, don't you have eyes in yo' head? Cain't you see that if I don't wear a bra I'ma be hanging down to my crotch?" She just smile and say "oh no, it wouldn't be that bad, Immy, really, you should try it. You'll be so much more comfortable." Child don't know what she talkin' 'bout.

I got my first bra when I was twelve; that was before the apocalypse of course. At twelve I was already a double D. I was thrilled to death to get it; it was so nice to have everything all secure and not be sweatin' to death under there. I heard people talk about the hormones in the milk and chemicals in the water and stuff and maybe that caused it, but Momma she was big, and her momma too. It mighta partly been all that stuff though, 'cause my babies all came after when we didn't have nothing but what we grew ourselves and they drank the milk straight from the cows we saved from that dairy farm south of Baton Rouge. None of my girls is endowed like me, thank goodness. They won't have these backaches when they're my age. Which is lucky 'cause ain't no tellin' where they gon' find bras by then.

Tish don't like me travelin' 'cause then she got to do extra chores and she say she don't got nobody to talk to when I'm gone. She say, "Immy what about yo' girls, they gon' miss they momma they gon' worry sick 'bout you out on the road." But truth is they ain't worried about me travelin', they know their Uncle Henry will keep me safe, him and Rufus. They'll miss that ol' dog more'n they miss me. Pearly might get a little sad the first night but I know Chinquita and Parnice don't care at all that I'm gone; big girls like them be more interested in boys than where they momma at.

So, we travelin'. We takin' the bikes and I insist on riding the trike, 'cause it's got a nice big wagon on the back that you can put lots of stuff in. You can even put a person in there if you got to, and I like that. We often see people walkin' when we travel and I like to be able to offer a body a lift. Meetin' new people is one of the things I miss about travelin'; always so interesting to hear people's stories about where they was when everythin' happened. I never get tired o' that.

"Why you wan' take the trike," say Curtis. I tell him I want to be able to pick up people and he shake his head and say I'm crazy and I say, "well maybe so but at least I ain't ugly like you." Anyway the trike has a nice big fat seat and I need it. God done endowed me up top and on the bottom, and them little skinny seats on the other bikes be too uncomfortable for the week it will take us to get to Houston.

We gon' take the Old Ten Bridge; it the quickest way through the 'Chafalaya. It's still mostly in good repair but you need a guide for the parts that are breaking down. We ax around as we prepare to spend the first night in Grosse Tete. Rufus he run ahead to meet all his doggy friends; by the time we get into town they got a big ol' tail-waggin' party going, and now everybody know we comin'. Ol' Melvin he greet us as we get off the bikes; he was a friend of Momma's from before so he know me. "Girl," he say, "I ain't seen you in donkey's years. Where you headed?" I tell him where but I don't tell him why. Henry he understand and I see him punch Curtis in the arm 'fore he can talk. Thank goodness Henry with us.

'Nother good reason is that he brought his horn, the old one, and people jus' plum love hearing him play. Word spreads around town and 'fore long we have a big group jammin' an' listenin' an' dancin'. Me and Melvin we get up and dance a bit and then Curtis he try to cut in but Melvin say, "no anh-ah, get on outta here boy and come back when you old enough to know how to treat a woman." That make me laugh 'cause Curtis is sure 'nuf old enough, he my age, he got wrinkles all around his eyes. White folks age faster than black folks it seems, least, they show it sooner. I don't mind Melvin hoggin' me all night because I ain't gon' dance too long anyway; I rather just sit by the fire and listen. I love listenin' to Henry at home but I love it even better when we get a group of 'em up there together jammin' with each other. It's jus' one long song that just keep goin' all night, with solos and new melodies and all kinda beats and rhythms; it's like angels singing. It's like magic.

It's always hard to go to sleep on nights like this but eventually I just can't keep my eyes open no more. 'Course Curtis is there as soon as I start to bunk down. Rufus he growl at him; he always sleeps wit' me if the girls ain't around. Curtis he act all offended; I don't know why he thinks things is gon' be different when we on the road. Henry he notice though and he stops his playing just long enough to tell Curtis off and I can get some sleep. See, that's another reason why I don't travel alone with Curtis. He gets ideas.

We back on the road by sun up and even though it's hot I don't mind since you get some breeze on the bike. I don't even have to pedal now since this boy Jamal has decided to come with us too. When Henry done tol' him 'bout the reeds he got all interested. He play sax too. He ax me why I'm on this trip since he know I don't like to travel much but Henry he start talkin' 'bout the music last night and Jamal he leave me alone. His momma know though; I already done talked to her. She built like me, we done had this talk before. She gon' make me two new shirts if I can find her a 48FFF. And let me tell you, Miss Eileen, she know how to sew.

In Lafayette we pick up some more folks. I know they mommas too and I gots to start a list now. But that's why Curtis keeps a notebook, and pencils ain't too hard to find if you know where to look. It will be sad when they all gone and ain't nobody figured out how to make 'em again. I guess there must be pencil factories somewheres but I don't see how people would spend their time trying to figure out pencils when they could be growing food. You never know though, somebody might be doing that. I ain't never heard of it though. I think Curtis be thinkin' on it sometimes; he got him a unopened pack of Spiderman pencils that he been savin'; he think nobody know about it. But I know.

One of the people from Lafayette is Lily, a white lady about my age. Even though I've known her for years we ain't never really talked; she a book person, always lookin' for books to trade so I guess she must read 'em. Don't do much talkin', that's for sure. She say she lookin' for some books about brewin' and other stuff, she got her a list, too. I show her my list and don't say nothin', she just smiles then writes 42D on the bottom. "No kiddin'," I say, 'cause the way she dresses in them baggy clothes I never noticed she was that big. She just nods, still smilin'.

So now we got us a nice little ol' caravan goin': we got the trike and our two bikes, and five more bikes and two of 'em have trailers and that's a total of twelve people, plus now Rufus he got a couple o' doggy friends runnin' wit' him. We'll probably pick up one or two more folks (an' dogs) 'fore we hit the ol' state line. Always do. People love a caravan and we never mind waitin' while they pack up; the more the merrier. Not like Houston is goin' nowhere.

In Rayne we pick up some old friends of Curtis: Danny, Vic and

T-Paul; he calls them the frog people. Back in the old days Rayne had a frog festival every year and you can still see the faded murals of frogs all through town. They got their bikes all tricked out, painted green with toy frogs hanging off the front. They crazy, but in a fun kinda way that looks like it will be nice having them with us on the road. Danny's momma a 42FF and his wife is a 28D. Got me a backache just lookin' at that skinny little thing, I hope I can find what she need. Both very nice ladies.

With them frog people, now we got fifteen. They say they tickled to see us, they been wantin' to go to Houston for a while but they heard some bad stuff from a traveler and it made 'em want to wait for a bigger group. Curtis says what kinda stuff they done heard and they say they heard about a group of wild chirren that got hold of some weapons and be robbin' people for food, somewhere by Houston. Curtis says they musta heard false rumors but allows as how he ain't been west for about three years now.

In Lake Charles we gotta float the bikes across 'cause that ol' bridge done fall apart long time ago, and anyway that's a steep climb and ain't nobody want to mess with that on bikes. Going on the loop would take too long so we float. It's so nice bein' on the water. Rufus and his friends they keep jumpin' off the barge and jumpin' back on and shakin' and jumpin' off again until we all wet and laughin' our heads off. Then we get back on the road and pick up another three by the time we hit the ol' state line. In Orange the frog people introduce us to a friend of theirs, old guy named Rafael. Rafael's wife Jean is a 38F. Small compared to me but I ain't gon' deny that she need support.

Curtis ax him do he know 'bout the rumors and he confirms what they already done told us. Of course this annoys Curtis but he ain't stupid and he tries to learn everything he can from this fellah. Henry is there the whole time; I can see that he's standin' there listenin' to everything, not saying nothin'. Henry he a good listener, I think that's why he such a good musician.

After we bunk down I can hear 'em still talkin' late into the night. Funny how folks forget that tent walls don't keep out sound, or maybe they think I'm already asleep. Henry say, "well what you think, how we gon' get in the city now?" Curtis say, "well I don't know but if we do like Rafael say and take ninety at Beaumont maybe we can avoid all that mess." Vic he agree and he ain't laughin' and jokin' now. He say "Rafael he gets news from lots o' people and he a good man and we trust him."

When Henry comes into the tent he see I'm awake. I say I just got one question for you little brother: do you trust Rafael? Henry say, "yeah because Vic trust him and Curtis he trust Vic." He say, "I know Curtis get on your nerves but he a good man and he would never put you in harm's way. Why ain't you never hooked up wit' him, anyway?" Henry ax me. I say, "why don't you stop playing sax and take up basket weaving?" which is my way of saying why don't you just go to sleep and mind your own bidness.

Next morning our road friends are all happy as can be to follow Curtis and Vic off ten and get on ninety. Now I know I ain't the only one could hear things through the tent. I have to say I'ma little bit nervous. Them dogs is one thing, but I'm glad we don't have no kids with us on this trip. As it is they's more men than women and that suits me fine. They all good gennulmen and they make the work load so light it almost feel like I'm on vacation.

When I was little Momma and Daddy took us to Disneyworld; Henry don't remember much since he was jus' four but we had a good ol' time I can tell you. But what I remember too is that Momma spent a lot of time in the hotel at the swimmin' pool while Daddy took us in the park. We would get to the hotel all tired and sweaty and there was my momma, layin' out on the side o' that beautiful crystal blue swimmin' pool, right where we done left her that mornin', and still dry as a bone. I would say, "momma you dry, ain't you gon' swimmin' yet?" She would say, "no baby, I jus' sat here all day, me and Maya Angelou" and then she would pat her book. That's when I foun' out that sometimes doing nothin' is more fun than doing something. So I'm perfectly happy right now to just sit in the back of the trike and let Jamal do the pedaling. I just hope we don't run into any trouble like them wild chirren.

East Texas is pretty nice country. Lots o' trees like south Louisiana but more pines than big fat oaks an' it ain't so marshy. Still got them big skeeters though; they all over down here. One time I ax Curtis how far north he ever been and he done said, "not far enough to get away from the skeeters," so I guess they everywhere.

We in the outskirts o' Houston 'fore too long and it is not pleasant. Too much concrete 'round here, makes a body nervous. Ain't too many folks livin' around here neither. Ain't nobody gon' live somewhere they cain't grow food. Just ain't smart nowadays. Me, I like it better out where they's trees 'round me and I grew up right smack in the middle of the city. But they was always lots o' trees, even in the middle o' town. Not like here. Ain't nothin' but concrete and asphalt. This is just terrible. Even the dogs seem nervous, they stickin' close to us now.

Everywhere I look all I see is messed up buildings and piles of debris. 'Bout five years ago we done got some bad rain an' wind and we all figure there musta been a hurricane. Then Curtis come back from a trip and filled us in. Galveston had got plum slammed. He said it was terrible. I can see that it musta hit up here too, at least the tail end of it. Tree limbs still all over, in buildings an' stuff. If people were livin' 'round here they woulda cleared it out by now.

Jamal say, "hey mister Curtis, why ain›t nobody done cleared this here mess out yet?" Cher bebe, he so young he don›t understand 'bout the big deserted cities. Grosse Tete ain›t exactly a big town, never was. That›s what›s funny about the apocalypse, it saved the little towns. If you want to call it that.

I'm still thinkin' about this stuff when all of a sudden they's all kinds of screamin', sound like it's coming from everywhere at once. The dogs start barkin' they heads off. They's a bunch of people all over, holdin' sticks an' bats an' knives and all kinds o' mess. Henry unstraps his machete and hands me his sax case. He don't take his eyes off the people coming towards us. Curtis rounds everybody up quick in a circle with me and Lily in the middle.

As they get closer I can see these must be the wild chirren 'cause they don't none of 'em look older'n twelve. They all hollerin' and screamin, tryin' to scare us I guess. Fortunately none of us is scared, not even Jamal. He standin' close to me with a baseball bat; I guess he feel protective since I been ridin' behind him all this time, an' he already done tol' me his momma tol' him take care o' me.

Since we ain't doin' nothin but starin' at 'em, we not runnin' away or nothin', I guess they confused cuz they start hollerin' less an' lookin' toward this one chil' in particular like they watchin' him to see what he gon' do. This one boy be hollerin' and jumpin' around like crazy, he don't even notice what's goin' on till the other ones sort get quiet. So now I am really confused; is this what all them people worried 'bout? A bunch o' screamin' kids? And how they think they gon' get anything offa folks by just screamin'? I mean those knives and stuff look scary but they ain›t nothin' nobody else don›t have when they travelin'.

Curtis say, "how long you think they gon' keep this up?" and Henry he jus' shake his head, still lookin' at that one loud boy. Jamal he ease up a little, he see now this ain't gon' be bad as he thought. Everybody else tense but not scared lookin'. Even a fat ol' middle aged lady like me knows basic hand to hand, and this jus' a bunch of kids. Prolly less than twenty now that I start countin'. T-Paul he just set hisself right back down on his trike, like he waitin' on something. Danny he laugh at this, so do a couple others. Then we all gigglin'.

When they hear us laughin', the kids get confused and stop they hollerin'. Now it's just that one boy an' he stops too, like all a'sudden he embarrassed. Curtis looks at him and yells, "what's a matter boy, ain't ya got none left?" Then Jamal he yell, "is the concert over?"

Everybody laugh at this. Now the kids is confused and they start bunching up together, whisperin' and lookin' around.

Not that one boy though. He mad now and he runs at Curtis with his knife up in the air. But 'fore he can get to Curtis, Henry has disarmed him and he in the dirt panting. Henry got a foot on the poor chil's neck. Now that he done hollerin' I can see he very young, only a bit younger than Chinquita, my youngest. I cain›t stand it. I gots to do somethin'.

"Get offa him!" I holler an' I go over and knock Henry off and pick up the boy. "What›s a matter with you boy, ain›t you got no momma? Don›t you know it ain›t right to go runnin' around with a knife hollerin' at people?"

He try to hit me so I do what I useta do wit' my babies; I just grab him and hug him hard as I can, an' I rock him an' stroke his head. Then I start singing that lullaby I sang to my babies. I hear Curtis sayin', "Immy, what the hell" and I hear Henry tellin' him, "shut up an' leave her alone." I cain't see what them other kids is doin' but I cain't hear 'em no mo' so I ain't worried. After a minute this wild boy does what my babies always did—he stop struggling and hollerin' so he can hear what I be singin'.

Then all of a sudden I feel something on my back, like somebody is pattin' me. I cast my eyes sideways and there's a little girl standin' there with her hand on my back. She has dropped her knife on the ground. Right behind her is some more of the chirren. I see Lily kneeling down with a couple of 'em, giving them food. I tol' ya she was smart; them quiet ones always is.

Something is squirming in my lap and I automatically try to hold tighter to this boy cuz I think he tryin' to get away. But when I look down I see that there is another one tryin' to squirm in. The first lets him in and they sit there in my lap like a pile of little kittens all sleepin' together. Then here come Rufus and just plumb lays hisself down with his head on my leg, and the kids start to pat him and say good doggy. We just stay like that, me singin', Rufus pantin' and the kids just sittin' there for, I don't know, at least twenty minutes. I stop rockin' once and the big one he push with his feet an' rocks against me, like to remind me, so I keep goin'. Finally I say, "I'm sorry darlin', but my legs is fallin' asleep. Immy ain't used to bein' on the ground so long with such big kids in her lap." I gently get up and they let me, but they continue to hold my hands when we stand. Henry walks over and gives 'em some food. The big one decides to talk all of a sudden and he say, "can I bring some food to Granny?" "Well OK," I say, "can I come too?" I wanna meet Granny whoever she be.

Curtis he start to say something but Henry hushes him up and him and Jamal and Lily all come with me. They all come because they have kids pullin' on 'em to come. Lily got about five of 'em on her.

We was in front of an ol' strip mall when they started they hollerin' and now they lead us across the messed up parking lot full of junk cars and debris into the biggest store. It don't have no glass on front, just tarps and stuff hanging where the doors useta be. Looks like it mighta been a Wal-mart. We go through the tarps into a kinda porch area and they got a bunch o' kids' bikes all over, so we know now how they get around to get food. They got a bunch more tarps hangin' where they useta have the entrance to the store. We go through them and it's dim at first but they got light comin' from some holes in the roof here and there and our eyes adjust fast. The place is filled with trash and don't smell too good, kinda stale. They got 'em a space cleared in between huge piles of broken shelving and stuff. At first I don't see nothing but blankets all over with kids on 'em. Must be about a dozen or so. Finally I see a cluster of chirren around one person; "is this Granny?" I say to my new friend. "Yeah," he say and we go up to her. The kids look dirty and scared but at least they not screamin' no mo'.

Granny she sittin' on the floor with her legs crossed, lookin' like a statue or somthin'. She old-lookin', that's for sho', with long scraggly gray hair and lots of wrinkles. She a white lady but her skin is tanned like she been out in the sun for years. She smile at us and say, "Hi there." "Hi Granny," say Henry, "These all your kids?"

I can see there's something wrong with the old girl's leg; it stickin' out kinda funny. I try not to stare. "Granny," say the boy, "they gots food." Granny she smilin' at me and now she say "bless your heart, thank you for being kind to my chirren." I offer her food and she take it and split it up amongst the little ones sittin' all 'round her. While she doin' that I look at her leg a little bit more and it look like it done broke and healed bad. 'Fore Curtis can mess things up Lily say, "hi Granny, I'm Lily, and this here's Immy and Curtis and Jamal. Excuse me for axing but your leg don't look too good."

I tell you what, as many times as I seen Lily, I never done seen her talk as much as she do wit' Granny right now. Pretty soon we got the whole story. This poor old woman done worked at a day care and she kept hold of the chirren whose parents didn't never come back for 'em when the end come. Them chirren growed up and had chirren and here she is with all these she calls her grandbabies. She say things was going fine till the hurricane. A bunch of the grownups had been out travelin' and they done never come back. Then a group of the ones left gone off to look for them and it was just her and Christine, Granny say, whoever that is 'cause she sho ain't here now. With all these scrawny kids it's obvious they've been alone like this for a while.

After a while I ax the little boy about it. He has plum adopted me, ain't left my side since we got here. After we make camp and cook some real food he snuggle up wit me jus' like I'm his own momma. Little by little he tell me that he was scared 'cause he thought granny was gon' die and they been having trouble with food and all. His name is Marvin and when he say that I almost start crying and I have to hold him and hug him tight for a minute so he don't see. That was my great grand daddy's name and it was the name of my only baby boy, who died before he was a week old. But Marvin he smart an' he see me cryin' and ax me "why you cryin', Immy?" I tell him about my baby and he say "is it ok if I can be your little boy then since you don›t got one no more?" All I can do is hug on him at first. Then I say let me talk to granny. Marvin he jus' look up at me wit' a smile on his dirty lil' angel face.

The sun go down and the kids all have these crank lights and they all start crankin' away and granny she take out a book and reads to 'em. It's The Hobbit and that surprises me 'cause it's at this part where she talkin' 'bout them poor lil' fellahs off in the pitch black woods fightin' giant spiders. I don't know but it seem like that would scare kids, but they is all rapt, listenin' to her.

This looks like what they useta doin' so we don't interfere; Curtis finally done calmed down and stopped harassin' Granny and these poor lil' ol' scrawny chirren. Lily and me, we just make sure they all got enough to eat. When granny is done with the story and all them kids is finally fed and sleeping, I talk to Henry and Curtis. Lily there too, so is Vic and Danny. See I have had time to think now and what I want to know is why nobody has helped these kids 'fore now. Obviously they was in trouble or they wouldn›ta attacked nobody. Vic say yeah, makes him wonder too, and makes him want to play a joke on Rafael when we go back through with all the 'wild chirren.' We laugh except for Curtis who say whaddaya mean? Ever'body lookin' at him like he nuts and Lily say "Curtis do you think we gon› leave these kids here to die? And Granny too? We can leave a message for this Christine person but if she been gone as long as what Granny say she prolly ain›t comin' back." I agree and I tell them about Marvin axin me would I be his momma. Only Curtis and Henry know about my own baby boy. Henry puts his arm around me but he don›t say nothin'. Curtis say "yeah, you right, we gotta take 'em, I was bein' stupid." Ain't nobody argue wit' dat.

Next mornin' we ax Granny an' the kids an' they all want to go. They pack up they stuff and Curtis and Jamal help them put air in they bike tires. We show Granny how she gon' ride on the trailer wit' me and she say that›s just fine with her. She say, "I'ma look like the Queen o' Sheba!" I can see they all excited and happy. The chirren all got they lil' backpacks on now an' they runnin' round with Rufus and his friends.

We all know it gon' be kinda slow goin' on the way back 'cause they not useta travelin' even though they know how to ride bikes. Curtis say, "well, guess we ain›t going to Houston now." I say, "you better believe we going to Houston now." He say, "Immy darlin', you the one wanted to take these chirren with us, what could you possibly need that is more important than getting these kids home an' safe?" I ignore him calling me darlin' and just show him my list. I say, "I need me a damn bra and so do my friends."

Well I didn›t know what to expect but I sho' nuf don›t ‹spect him to do what he do, which is to get bright red in the face and then start laughin› his stupid fool head off.

"Shut up, I say, everybody lookin'!" So he try to stop and by now he›s choking and his eyes is leakin' and he›s just a sight with that red skin and red eyes on that scrawny white neck o› his. I›m worried he might scare the chirren.

Granny watchin' of course, she sittin' right there, and she takes my list. "You don›t need to go to town," she say and points back in the store. "They got bras in there. Delores can show you." Then she yell, "Delores!" And here come a little girl with big brown eyes and stick-straight brown hair; I saw her before but now I notice that she jus' a bit taller'n most of the other ones. I shoo Curtis away quick.

Granny got her hands on Delores›s arms like she presenting her to me. She say, "Delores here just got her first blood and we celebrated with her getting her first bra. Miss Immy need help finding some bras, baby. Bring her to the bra section, ok?" Say Granny. Delores blushin' a little but she smilin' too.

As I follow the little girl back in the sto' I hear Granny fussin' at Curtis, "ain›t no laughin' matter son, an' if I catch you laughin' at Immy again or botherin' her any kinda way you can book it, I›ma tan your worthless hide."

That makes me smile. Maybe I can talk Granny into livin' with me and Marvin and my girls when we get back to Port Allen.

So That They May Rule

Madison Keller

Editor: 'Tis a good night out for man and beast . . .
the original translation seems to have corrupted.

Then God said, "Let us make mankind in our image, in our likeness, so that they may rule over the fish in the sea and the birds in the sky, over the livestock and all the wild animals, and over all the creatures that move along the ground."—Genesis 1:26

Katie stared nervously out the window of the Humvee at the scenery flashing by. Burned out husks of tree trunks and exposed earth, left muddy by the sprinkles of rain that streaked the window, seemed all that remained.

The man and the woman stuffed in the armored vehicle with Katie looked out of place in the military vehicle. Their hair was neatly groomed. Underneath their bulky ballistic vests they wore expensive looking tailored suits.

The first suit was Mr. Holness, the United States Secretary of State. The other was Ms. Waldheim from the United Nations. But the details weren't important to Katie. Her job was merely to make sure they got to the meeting with the representatives of the races of evolved animals.

The barracks gossip swirled around about an armistice or a peace treaty, depending on which rumor mill you followed. Katie's hope beyond hope was a peace treaty, but she would settle for an armistice. Anything to end to the years of brutal fighting.

Corporal (human) Eggen, whom Katie had served under for the past several years, occupied the driver's seat. Tank, an evolved bloodhound and Katie's best friend, sat in the passenger seat.

Silence sat heavy in the truck as they roared along the disused road. Katie continued to scan out the windows for threats, doing her best to ignore the two people in the backseat with her.

Tank whuffed in surprise. Katie barely had time to glance at the evolved bloodhound when the car jolted to an abrupt stop. The suddenness of it threw her forward. Her seat belt caught her, but not before her head rebounded off the seat in front of her.

A low humming began just at the edge of her hearing. Tank gave a howl, dropped his M4 into his lap, and clasped his paws over his long ears, pressing them against his head. A drop of blood dripped out his nose, followed by another.

All the windows in the vehicle shattered at once, showering glass onto Katie. She grabbed her M4 just as the gunfire started. She pushed Waldheim and Holness down before lifting her weapon to return fire. A flash of red fur darted behind one of the blasted tree trunks, so Katie sent a barrage of fire in that direction.

Eggen and Tank fired through the remains of the windshield at something in front of them, their M4s combining with Katie's into a steady pop-pop-pop of overlapping chatter.

A trumpeting scream became audible over the din. The call came again, louder and closer this time, another starting before the first one had ended.

The noise was unmistakable. Katie recognized it from her childhood, but, no, it couldn't be, could it? In Kansas? Katie risked a glance over her shoulder, keeping her rifle pointed at her target to discourage them from taking advantage of her distraction.

Charging down the road toward the disabled armored vehicle were three African elephants. The beasts charged heads down so that their gleaming tusks pointed directly at the Hummer. The ends of their tusks flashed in the sun, capped with razor-sharp metal tips, and bulky black ballistic material covered most of their gray skin. Thick goggles protected their eyes from bullets.

The red fox she'd spotted earlier made a run toward the vehicle with its weapon up and at the ready.

Katie, stunned by the sight of the elephants, had frozen only momentarily. Her training kicked in quickly. It was like someone else controlled her body, swiveling the gun, pulling the trigger. She watched dispassionately as her rounds found their mark in the center of the red fox's body. Even as the fox fell dead into the churned mud her gun turned toward a new target.

The elephants reached the vehicle and rammed it with their shoulders. The interior dimmed as their bulk blocked the sunlight. The vehicle shuttered, the back wheels leaving the ground. Someone screamed. Holness, Katie noted, even as she continued to fire futilely out the window.

Her rounds struck the nearest elephant without any visible effect.

The one on her side reared back and stood, grabbing onto the top of the vehicle with its gigantic hands. Metal rent and screeched before thick, gray fingers poked through the space between the roof and the door jamb. They curled and with a sharp jolt of the vehicle, the door was ripped free. The elephant flung away the door with a contemptuous flick before reaching toward Katie.

Katie screamed as she emptied the last of her clip into the monster. Even as she did, the massive hand wrapped around her. Her seatbelt snapped like tissue paper as the elephant yanked her from the car. It tossed her away with as much ease as the door. She flew end-over-end and landed in the mud.

The impact was too much for her head, still tender from her smack into the seat. Katie rolled over, threw up, and passed out.

* * *

Katie's consciousness came back in fits and starts. Tank's face floating over hers. His mouth moved, but her mind couldn't process what he said. The next thing she remembered was sitting up, slumped against the remains of the vehicle with Tank tenderly patting at her forehead with a damp cloth. Emotion clouded his eyes. When her eyes focused on him he smiled, his wrinkled jowls flopping.

"Are you awake now?" he asked her, pulling back the cloth.

"I am, but I wish I wasn't." Her head pounded as if the elephant had trampled over her rather than just tossing her away into the mud. "My head hurts."

Tank passed her a bottle of water and two white pills, which Katie swallowed gratefully. She passed the still mostly full bottle back to him. She'd had enough experience with being hurt to know not to chug the water, as much as she wanted to.

It turned out she was resting against the driver's side back wheel, the least smashed part of the car.

The view also showed her why the Humvee had stopped so suddenly and abruptly. A large ditch had been dug across the middle of the road and concealed with a black tarp that blended in with the asphalt. The two front tires were wedged in the hole and the front bumper smashed into the far edge.

She eased back against the wheel; even that sent her head spinning again. Tank hunkered down near her and held his paw in front of her face.

"How many fingers am I holding up?" he asked.

Katie squinted at his paw. The dewclaw nub had grown long and his paw had split to form a rudimentary hand. She gathered her thoughts with an effort of will. "Three," she responded after a moment.

Tank nodded and lowered his paw.

"What happened, after I was knocked out? Where is Corporal Eggen and the packages?"

"The elephants took the packages. Corporal Eggen . . . well." Tank's eyes darted toward the driver's side seat. He didn't have to say anything else. Katie took a deep breath and locked her grief away. She didn't have time to mourn him now, no matter how close they'd been.

"How did you escape?"

Tank seemed to shrink down into himself and he stared down at his paws. "I didn't. They let me go," he whispered.

"Well, I'm glad they did." Katie wanted to give him a hug, but her head just ached too much. Instead she reached over and placed a shaky hand over top his crossed paws. "Even if I don't understand why."

Rather than her gesture comforting him, Tank deflated further. "The ones that attacked, they're Survivors."

"Survivors?" Katie blinked, puzzled for a moment before the pieces clicked over in her head. "The Survivors of Holocene? That evolved animal terrorist organization? But their stated goal is to wipe out humans. Why would they kidnap the packages rather than kill them?" Even as she asked the question Katie realized she knew the answer. "Hostages. To try and stop the negotiations."

They had to save the diplomats and the negotiations. She pushed herself to her feet and began taking stock of their resources.

She found where she'd dropped her M4. She crouched down and brushed mud off of it, only to find that the barrel was bent at an almost ninety-degree angle. One of the elephants must have stepped on it during the chaos.

She scowled and stood back up. Tank's M4 was nowhere in sight. No reason to leave him armed, just in case. The only reason she'd survived is that they must have thought her dead already.

All the other weapons she found were in similar condition to hers—smashed or bent beyond what repair she could do at the side of the road.

She walked around the armored vehicle in a semi-circle, careful to avoid the edges of the pit. The driver's side had taken the most damage. A ragged black hole yawned at her from the backseat and the front door was dented and shot full of holes.

Katie reached through the broken window and clicked the door unlock button, doing her best not to look at Corporal Eggen where he sat slumped over the steering wheel. To her relief the door opened when she yanked hard on the door handle. She shied at the body.

"Want some help with that?" Tank said softly from behind her.

Katie twitched and jumped, only barely stopping herself from spinning around and attacking him. Instead, she nodded and stepped back to give Tank access.

Tank leaned over the body. He clicked the seat-belt latch open, removed the belt, and then gently pulled the corporal's body free. He carried it away and laid it out on the dirt by the side of the road.

Katie turned away and knelt down by the now empty seat. Her gaze snagged on the blood soaking into the pleather. She had to dash tears from her eyes before leaning over to reach under the driver's seat.

As she'd suspected, the animals had not bothered to search the armored vehicle. Her questing fingers immediately found the cold metal box. It was surprisingly heavy and difficult to drag out from its hiding spot, but Katie managed it with a few hard yanks and some helpful swears.

The lid swung open after she spun in the combination, revealing a Sig 9mm semi-automatic nestled in its foam shell. Katie picked it up, making sure the safety was on before running through a function check and sliding in a magazine. She dug two more out from the foam and slipped them into her pocket along with the gun.

They still weren't safe, by any stretch of the imagination, but she felt a bit better now that she was armed. She turned back only to see Tank standing rigidly still, his paws above his head, with four assault rifles pointed at him by camo-clad humans. Two more of them were advancing on Katie, their guns held at the ready.

Katie cursed herself for being so focused on her own plans that she hadn't heard their approach. She discreetly reached behind her and closed the metal box, which shut with a click.

"Hands in the air," the man closest to her growled. Katie sighed and raised her hands above her head.

"Where are they?" said the other soldier. The voice was low, but obviously female.

"Gone, obviously," Katie snapped. Her head hurt, Eggen was dead, they'd lost the diplomats they were supposed to be protecting, and now this. She knew she should be a bit more polite to the people with guns pointed at her, but she just didn't care anymore.

The man lifted his hand and signaled. Everyone in the unit lowered their guns, but didn't put them away. She and Tank kept their arms in the air.

Katie studied what she could see of the patches sewn onto the soldiers' camouflage jackets. Most were hidden by the camo netting they all still had draped around their shoulders like capes, but she could see enough to tell they weren't from any branch of the military she was familiar with.

"Show us the bodies," the man ordered her.

Katie shook her head. She wanted to find out who he was first, and what he wanted, before she dared to tell him anything.

"What bodies?" she asked, batting her eyes and playing dumb.

"The diplomats. Where are they!" the man moved closer, until he was snarling at her from only inches away.

She lowered her eyes and curled her shoulders up around her ears as if cowed by his looming and shouting. "I don't know," she blabbed, pretending to panic. "We were attacked, everything happened so fast."

The man growled and stalked away. "Private Pallas, guard the prisoners." He raised his voice. "Rest of you, fan out and find the diplomats."

The woman, Private Pallas, herded Katie to where Tank stood and kept a watchful eye on them while the commander and the rest spread out around the wrecked car.

Her arms were getting tired, so Katie turned to the private. "Can we sit down?"

Pallas glared at her, but no, Katie realized, the private's disdain targeted Tank. "No."

Before Katie could protest Tank let out a little woof, a sigh really, of agreement. "Katie, do as she says."

"I'd listen to your *dog*." The last bit was said with enough derision that Katie jerked back as if slapped.

"No, you listen, I—" Katie growled until Tank slapped a paw over her mouth.

He leaned over and said into her ear as quietly as he could with his low voice, "Katie, don't antagonize them. They're part of Genesis."

Katie stopped struggling against Tank's grip, her mind whirling. Genesis 1:26 was the human foil to Survivors of the Holocene, claiming that evolved animals like Tank or the elephants needed to be cleansed from the Earth.

The man who'd given Pallas orders returned from his search, marching up behind Pallas and then passing her by, making a beeline right toward Katie and Tank.

"Where is Mr. Holness?" the man growled, stopping about a foot away. "And that other woman, the one from the UN?"

Tank kept his paw over Katie's mouth and answered for them. "Taken, by the Survivors."

Katie pulled down Tank's paw. "How did you know who we were carrying and where to find us? This mission was supposed to be secret."

The man wasn't listening to her; his attention had shifted to Tank, who he was considering thoughtfully. "You're a *bloodhound*."

Tank nodded and shifted up against Katie, in a gesture that reminded her of something her family's pet dogs used to do before the virus hit, a gesture asking for reassurance from their human companions that everything was going to be all right. Katie wasn't even sure that Tank was aware of what he was doing.

As a terrorist organization, Genesis's stated goal was wiping all evolved animals from the Earth. The only reason they were keeping Tank alive now was because he was a witness to the attack. Katie realized this as the further implication of the Genesis commander's words sunk in—Tank was useful to them.

Evolved animals retained their heightened senses, for the most part. Tank had used his superior sense of smell to track targets on missions in the past. Katie hadn't seen tracks of any vehicles, which made sense as the Survivors eschewed modern technology in favor of their own animal advantages. They would be on foot and Tank would have no trouble tracking them through the wasteland.

"Private Pallas, bind the girl's hands," the man snapped to the woman who'd been keeping guard over them. Then he turned to Tank. "You, get to tracking. And don't even think of betraying us. If you fail to lead us to the Survivors, we'll kill the girl."

* * *

Katie's whole body ached as the motorcycle bounced along. The Genesis commander led them at a brutal pace through the wasteland. She and Tank sat bound in the sidecar of Private Pallas's motorcycle as Genesis followed the elephants through the wasteland.

Every few miles they stopped and pulled Tank out to scout around for the Survivors' smell, to make sure they were on the right track. At first Katie thought she'd been mistaken about the commander's need for Tank. The evolved elephants had left a clear track in the mud. However, a few miles in, the tracks disappeared at a small river.

Tank led them down the stream a ways before signaling that the elephants had left the water at some point farther back. After a bit of scouting, Tank located their scent on the opposite side and the hunt was on again.

The sun started to set below the horizon when Tank woofed loudly to catch the attention of the Genesis commander, who drove a bit ahead of them.

The commander held up his hand and the caravan stopped. The commander got off his bike and walked over to Tank and Katie with a scowl. "There better be a good reason why you barked at me, dog."

To his credit, Tank was not cowed. He lifted his bound paws and pointed to his nose. "I caught a whiff on the wind. They are close by, up ahead of us. If we keep going they'll hear the noise of the bikes."

The man nodded and looked around them. The growing darkness made it hard to see far, but they were near the top of one of the rolling hills. The only trees were merely bare trunks, although about a mile back they'd passed an intact grove nestled at a low point in the hills. The Genesis commander ordered them to fall back to that sheltered copse.

Katie and Tank waited helplessly in their seat while their captors prepared for a raid on the Survivors. Private Pallas stayed behind and guarded Katie and Tank while the rest of the group pulled on night-vision goggles and vanished silently into the night.

Katie still had the 9mm Sig hidden in her pocket. They hadn't thought to search her. With the way her hands were bound Katie thought she might be able to reach a finger into the pocket and retrieve the gun.

Tank had been her partner long enough that when Katie lifted her eyebrows and tilted her head in Private Pallas's direction he knew what she needed without her having to say a word.

"Private," Tank said in a submissive tone, lowering his head. "I need to pee."

She scowled at him. "Pee your pants for all I care, dog."

Katie bit back a growl of frustration and instead tried to appeal to the Private's practical side. "We're sitting in *your* motorcycle's sidecar. Who'd you think will have to clean it up if he pees all over the seat?"

Pallas scowled at Tank, grimaced, and then looked around. A few crickets chirped in what remained of the underbrush, but otherwise the night was silent.

"Fine." She walked over and grabbed Tank's arm, hauling him up and out of the bucket seat with one hand.

Tank stumbled and fell to his knees in the mud. Pallas let him go with a snarled curse and kicked him in the ribs when he fell forward onto his bound paws. Katie winced in sympathy.

"Get up and move, dog," Pallas said, giving him one last kick.

She grabbed her M4 with both hands again and pointed it at him until Tank stood. Mud covered the entire front of his uniform and coated his front paws. Tank limped off toward the closest tree. Pallas gave Katie a sidelong glance. "Don't try anything, or I shoot him. Got it?"

Katie gulped. "Yes, ma'am."

Of course, as soon as Pallas turned her back on her, Katie wiggled and turned her body so the pocket with the gun faced away from Pallas. Keeping a wary eye on Pallas, she stretched her arms as far as they would go, wincing as the zip-ties dug into her wrists. Using two fingers she caught a bit of the fabric of her pants and tugged hard until she could wriggle her fingers into the pocket opening.

Tank, bless his heart, fumbled with the front of his pants, pretending to struggle with the zipper with his bound paws. Pallas looked impatient though, so Katie needed to hurry.

Her fingers brushed on the cold metal of the Sig's grip. By the time she wriggled it free blood dripped down from where the zip-tie had rubbed her skin raw, running down her hand and slicking her fingers.

Katie tucked the gun between her clenched thighs, hiding it from view just as Pallas glanced in her direction. Katie twisted back on the seat to face forward, rolling her neck like she'd just been trying to stretch.

Pallas watched her for a moment before turning back to Tank, so her ruse must have worked. Katie took a deep breath to center herself and wrapped her hands around the Sig. She'd only have one chance to incapacitate Pallas.

Katie stood up and raised the gun into a modified firing position hampered as she was by the ties on her wrist, and sighted down the barrel on the back of Pallas's head. Her training had been to aim at the torso, as the bigger target meant an easier hit, but a torso shot had a much lower chance of killing Pallas than a head shot. Katie let out her breath, held it, and squeezed the trigger.

Pallas glanced over at her, her eyes widening in shock a little too late. Katie's bullet hit the side of her head, just above her ear. It exploded in a spray of blood, bone shards, and brain matter. Pallas staggered a single step, wobbled, and collapsed.

Tank turned and stepped back to avoid the red puddle forming under Pallas's body while he finished zipping up his pants.

Katie stood frozen in place, gulping down big lungfuls of air. Tank moved quickly and efficiently. He yanked free the folding knife from the corpse's belt. He managed to pry open the knife with one claw before flipping the tool around and awkwardly sawing through the zip-ties on his wrists. The plastic parted after a few quick jerks and fell to the ground.

Tank walked over to Katie and gently pushed down on her arms. She looked down, only to realize she still held the pistol in a white-knuckled grip.

"Come, Katie," Tank said, throwing one leg over the motorcycle seat. "We need to get to safety before the rest return."

"Safety?" Katie looked around them, at the dead Private Pallas, at the trees rising up above them with the tops scorched. "No one will be safe until this war is over." Katie shook her head. "We need to rescue Holness and Waldheim, and get them to the armistice meeting."

Tank frowned at her, which deepened the wrinkles on his face and muzzle. "It is just the two of us, with one gun." He paused and glanced at the M4 sticking out from beneath the corpse. "Two guns," he amended.

"Tank, if we don't get the government representatives to that meeting the armistice will fail and the fighting will resume, more vicious than ever. Besides, it's better that it's just two of us. With Genesis attacking the Survivors we can take advantage of the chaos to sneak in and rescue them."

Tank whoofed out a doggie sigh, which flapped his long jowls. "It would be a suicide mission."

Tears welled up in Katie's eyes and she dashed them away with the cuff of her jacket. "Tank, I've already lost my entire family to the fighting. I lost—"

More tears came and she let them fall. "Corporal Eggen and I were in love, but we couldn't openly have a relationship because of his position as my superior officer. We were talking of getting married when the war was over. Maybe starting a family." She stopped, a lump closed in her throat, which made talking impossible.

"I know," Tank said softly. Of course he did. Katie hadn't told him, but he was very good at reading body language, and had seen the looks Katie and Eggen had always thrown each other across the mess hall or during training. Or he had smelled it on her, after she and Eggen had managed to sneak away to a private spot for a rare, always too brief, make-out session in the janitor's closet or unused office.

Tank pulled a handkerchief and handed it to Katie. He got up and left, going over to Pallas's body to search it for useful items, giving Katie time to dry her tears. She knew he was only pretending because in the time it took her to stop crying she watched him search the same five pockets a dozen times over.

When her purge ended, she stood. Tank crept up next to her carrying the M4 and a small pouch of ammo. He stashed them in the sidecar by Katie's feet and settled into the driver's seat of Pallas's motorcycle.

"Let's go rescue some diplomats," Tank said. The motorcycle came to life with a throaty roar and they raced away toward certain death.

* * *

Katie crawled on her belly to the top of the rise, the M4 strapped securely to her back, and peered down. The crack-crack of gunfire came from the hollow below, the source hidden beneath the pall of smoke haze from multiple small fires scattered throughout the Survivor's camp. The smoke would make their job both harder and easier, hiding them from both sides but also concealing enemies and making it more difficult for them to find the captive humans.

Seeing the way clear, Katie gestured for Tank to join her. When he got to the top of the rise Katie pointed to a corner of the camp below them, close to their position. The stack of crates there would provide cover for their infiltration. Tank nodded in acknowledgment.

She pushed herself over the lip of the hill and climbed to her feet, dashing down the steep grade as fast as she dared. The rain had lessened but not stopped and the bare mud was slick. Her boots lost traction so many times she slid more than ran. She reached the crates and dashed between the stacks, pressing herself into the shadows.

Tank jogged up behind her a moment later, panting hard enough that his tongue lolled out of his mouth. He carried Eggen's Sig in one paw. Katie jerked her head toward the camp.

"Can you smell Holness or Waldheim?" she whispered, pitching her voice low.

Tank shook his head, chest heaving. "Too much smoke."

Katie cursed, barely audible over a sudden burst of chattering gunfire. An elephant bellowed, the sound echoing oddly in the smoke so

Katie couldn't tell the direction or the source, or if it were near or far, but Tank stiffened.

Katie opened her mouth to ask what was wrong, but he held up his empty paw, signaling her to silence and then pointed. Katie nodded.

Tank pressed himself against the crates by Katie and sidled down them until he reached the edge. He poked his nose out, sniffed hard enough to make his nostrils flare, and then froze. Katie followed suit, holding her breath.

She'd expected to be scared; she'd been terrified while looking down on the terrorists' campground, but now her heart pounded with excitement laced with anticipation.

After a long moment of stillness, Tank relaxed. He leaned over toward her and woofed into her ear, "Wind changed. Smell the packages. They're close. Also, I smell guards."

"Elephants?" Katie said, cringing. "Plural?"

Tank shook his head, which sent his floppy ears flapping against his face. As he began to speak there was a concussive boom and the ground shook slightly beneath their feet.

"No, as you can hear, the elephants are busy with Genesis. The guards are a species I'm unfamiliar with. Perhaps some kind of horse?" He shrugged.

More chattering gunfire and a large animal trumpeted in pain. Katie waited until the cry died away. "We'll have to risk it. We don't have time to scout."

"I agree," Tank barked over the chaos. The gunfire was getting heavier and seemed to be moving their way.

Without glancing back to see if he followed her, Tank stashed the Sig in his pocket and then dropped to all fours, toward the center of camp.

Katie brought her gun up and ran after him. As she ran she pivoted her upper body back and forth, scanning the surrounding area with her gun held in the low-ready position. The smoke hampered her vision and irritated her throat. She had to fight the urge to cough, which would give away her position to the sensitive hearing of the evolved animals that made up the Survivors.

They passed the last of the crates and boxes of supplies and continued through an open area. Ahead of them were the nylon tents and straw nests that made up the animal's main camp. To the left, the smoke momentarily cleared enough to reveal a haphazard collection of cars and trucks.

A shot whizzed past Katie's ear like a mosquito. Katie swiveled her front, lifted her M4, and pulled down on the trigger. Pop-pop-pop. The smoke and the tent walls blocked her vision. She couldn't see who or what she was firing at but a cry of pain told her she'd hit something.

Tank never slowed down as he skidded around a sharp corner

and disappeared behind one of the tents. Katie followed him, her boots squelching in the mud.

A walled canopy came into view. The side facing Katie was rolled up, and inside was a folding table. A laptop and a radio sat abandoned on top of it. Behind the table sat Holness and Waldheim, sitting back-to-back in folding chairs. Zip-ties secured their arms and legs to the chairs' frames.

Three black-and-white striped horses stood guard around the two humans, assault rifles clutched in their hooved hands. The horses were zebras, Katie realized with a flush, and they gave a cry as they spotted her and Tank. Two of them opened fire with their guns.

They aimed toward her, ignoring Tank entirely. Katie cursed and dove backwards and sideways, throwing herself behind the tent she'd just come around.

Bullets ripped the air above her, perforating the thin nylon walls. She landed hard, but hours of basic training had her turning it into a roll over her shoulder and back onto her feet before her thoughts had time to catch up with events. She crouched low and froze.

The shots stopped and she could hear voices. She recognized Tank's low growl immediately.

"Thank you, awakened brothers," Tank said. He must have realized at the same time as Katie that the zebras had heard Katie's gunshots and then seen them. A supposedly unarmed Tank, panting hard from their mad dash, being chased by an armed human with her gun raised, smoke wafting from the barrel. They obviously thought Tank one of their own being chased down by a member of Genesis intent on gunning him down. That was quick thinking on his part, throwing out the "awakened brothers" greeting, which cemented this story in their minds.

The zebra's response was too faint for Katie to hear, but there was no gunfire or cry from Tank, so he was probably safe enough for the moment.

"Better go check that it is dead," Tank growled. It was a good idea, splitting them up like that.

The zebra must have moved closer, because this time Katie could hear most of his response. "—like cockroaches, yeah."

If she shot the one that came to finish her off, the rest would hear, so Katie let go of the M4, letting it swing from her side by the strap. She drew the folding knife from her pocket and flipped out the long blade before taking up an ambush position at the end of the tent.

The zebra's hooves squelched in the mud, giving Katie a good idea of his position. From the uneven sound of the steps she guessed that two of them had come. Smart of them, but unlucky for her.

The first came around the corner and Katie leapt up at it, wrapping her arm around its curved neck and driving the blade directly into the base of the wild horse's skull. They fell together into the mud, the dead zebra on top. Blood trickled from the edges of the knife, the drops landing on her hair. Katie left it where it was; if she pulled it free, blood would gush from the wound all over her face.

After a stunned pause, the second zebra reacted, bringing up its assault rifle and firing at her. The bullets slammed into its companion's body, making it jerk about on top of her. The corpse protected her, but also pinned her to the ground, helpless under its bulk as the second zebra emptied its entire clip.

Katie struggled to move her arm, to retrieve her M4 from her side to return fire, but try as she might she couldn't move. She closed her eyes, sure she was going to die as soon as the zebra reloaded its gun.

A gun cracked and Katie's eyes shot open. That wasn't an assault rifle. A dead zebra fell into the mud beside her, a hole drilled straight through its head. A panting Tank stood over the corpse.

"Thanks," Katie wheezed. Talking was harder than it should have been, but then again she *had* just been crushed beneath a thousand-pound zebra.

Tank merely motioned for a terrified looking Holness and Waldheim to help. Together they leveraged the massive corpse enough for Katie to escape.

"The third?" Katie gasped, looking around for the last zebra soldier.

"Already taken care of." Tank hooked a thumb back at the command tent.

"Then let's go." Katie turned, took one step and almost collapsed. Her legs felt like jelly, but she managed to catch herself before she did more than fall to one knee.

Tank helped her to stand again, giving her blood-soaked uniform a worried look.

"It's not mine." She bobbed her head at the zebra that had been on top of her, its back a honeycomb of bullet holes.

Tank's face wrinkled but he nodded. "Let's go."

Katie led with the M4 held at ready, followed by the diplomats, with Tank guarding their rear with an assault rifle he'd looted from one of the dead zebras.

Rather than trying to retreat back the way they'd come, Katie led the group toward the vehicles.

Getting out seemed easier than getting in had been, except that each of her breaths came out a short rasp that only gave her a whisper of air. Katie pushed the discomfort away. There was no time to focus on anything but the mission and escape.

The smoke grew worse as they got closer to the vehicles. Thick black smoke poured from underneath the hood and from the broken windows of one of the big trucks. The acrid smoke made Katie cough. That in turn made her entire chest and stomach flare with hot pain that made her glance down at herself.

Fresh blood trickled in rivulets from underneath her left breast and stomach. It seemed the Zebra's bulk hadn't protected her as much as she'd thought. Adrenaline had covered up the pain of her being shot. Nothing for it now; it was keep moving or die.

Eyes watering, Katie waved the group around the burning truck. They weaved through the fleet of vehicles. Most of them had bullet holes in the hood, or flat, shot-out tires. Katie did find an intact vehicle—a smaller, off-road jeep. The open concept was another bonus as she didn't even have to try to jimmy the doors open.

Katie climbed into the passenger seat, directing Holness and Waldheim to sit in the back, while Tank got in the driver's seat. The dog had a way with machines. He hotwired the jeep into starting after only a few seconds of fiddling with the guts of the steering column.

* * *

As they drove away Katie grew dizzy and slumped over in her seat until she rested against the jeep's door with half her head sticking out the window. Only the cold night air blowing across her face kept her awake.

"Katie, stay with me," Tank shouted at her as he drove.

"I'm fine," she tried to say, but the words came out in a slur, along with a red, bubble-filled foam.

Each time Katie drifted off, the bouncing of the jeep on the uneven ground woke her. The jolting pain made her scream, or at least she would have if she had enough breath in her.

They arrived at the rendezvous point ten hours late, but Katie was just glad they arrived at all.

The hotel was lit up like the Christmas trees Katie remembered from before the war, with lights blazing from every window. Soldiers rushed toward the jeep, pursued by a gaggle of reporters of a boggling array of species, from human to dog, cat, buffalo, and even, Katie flinched, a tiger. They screamed questions at Mr. Holness, Ms. Waldheim, and most surprisingly, at Tank and Katie. Katie found it impossible to make sense of the questions through the fog of pain.

The two diplomats were rushed into the hotel surrounded by a host of guards while soldiers kept the onlookers at bay.

A good chunk of the reporters streamed after them, but some remained behind with their camera lenses pointed at Katie and Tank.

They stayed even as an ambulance pulled up between them and the jeep. They yelled questions even while Katie was loaded into it. Tank climbed in after her, clutching her hand between his paws as the EMTs stuck a mask on her face. That was the last thing she remembered as the ambulance roared away.

* * *

Tank told Katie the news a few days later, after one of Katie's umpteenth surgeries. Last count it had been up to six, but she was drifting in and out and on pain meds so she couldn't be sure.

Bless his furry heart, he brought in his own personal tablet and sat next to her on the bed to show her a recording of the previous day's newscast from CNN.

The video opened with the standard shot of two newscasters behind a counter. One of the two was a human woman with blonde hair, too much makeup, and a wide, white smile. The other was a lynx with perfectly groomed fur and an even wider and whiter smile than the woman, although his had far sharper teeth.

The screen split, showing the human woman on one side of the screen while random shots of well-dressed diplomats talking to each other across a large table played on the other.

In the clip, Humans sat arrayed on one side, and a variety of evolved animals were across the other. Katie recognized a kangaroo, a panda, a housecat, a Clydesdale horse, a tiny Chihuahua sitting on a stack of pillows, and a black bear. There were more, and Tank paused the video to name the rest—a binturong, a kind of cat from Asia, a fossa, from Madagascar, and a Geoffroy's tamarin monkey, from Central America.

Tank pressed play, and the woman started speaking. "After days of deliberation between representatives of the human race, including the UN, the United States, ASEAN, and others, and the various nations of evolved animals, an agreement was reached and an armistice signed late last night."

At this point the woman stopped talking and the camera panned over to the lynx. "Although the armistice is only for a temporary cessation of hostilities, this is the first step toward a negotiation of peace. A peace conference is scheduled to begin next week, with dignitaries and representatives confirmed from every human nation and almost every species of evolved animal.

Later in this segment we'll be speaking with global diplomatic expert Mr. Wilhelm, about why he is confident that there will be a signed peace treaty in the near future."

Katie slammed the laptop closed before bursting into tears. She cried for Eggen and the world she'd lost when the war started, but mixed with her grief was hope, hope that soon there would be a new world.

Author Biographies

Geneve Flynn

Geneve Flynn is a freelance editor from Australia who specializes in speculative fiction. She has two psychology degrees and has only ever used them for nefarious purposes. Geneve has been a judge for a key Australian horror award and a submissions reader for a leading Australian speculative fiction magazine. She has had her short horror fiction published by KnightWatch Press, the Australasian Horror Writers' Association, and Oz Horror Con. Her fiction will also be brought out later this year by the Tales to Terrify podcast and Flame Tree Publishing.

She loves tales that unsettle, all things writerly, and B-grade action movies. If that sounds like you, check out her website at www.geneveflynn.com.au or you can find her at facebook.com/geneveflynn.

Peter Talley

Peter Talley, at various times in his life, has worked as a high-school speech team coach, newspaper advertiser, hospital emergency manager, investigator, and funeral home assistant. Born in Ohio, grew up in Iowa, and spent the majority of his time working in Nebraska. He currently resides in Hartington with his wife and son. Peter enjoys writing short fiction and is busy at work on a series of urban fantasy novels.

Russell Hemmell

Russell Hemmell is a statistician and social scientist from the U.K., passionate about astrophysics and speculative fiction. Recent stories in *Not One of Us*, *Perihelion Science Fiction*, *SQ Mag*, and elsewhere.

Lisa Timpf

Lisa Timpf is a retired HR and communications professional who lives in Simcoe, Ontario. Her writing has appeared in a variety of venues, including *New Myths*, *The Martian Wave*, *Third Flatiron*, *THEMA*, and the *Dogs of War* anthology.

Keith J. Hoskins

Keith J. Hoskins is a short-story writer and an award-winning poet. He is currently working on his own anthology: *Beyond the Portal*, a book filled with altered reality stories. And soon after, he will release a fantasy novel called *Kray and the Coveted Seer* set in a magical world where good and evil are at constant ends. Keith's main genres of interest are fantasy, science fiction, and thrillers. When he's not fighting off dragons or piloting his spaceship through an asteroid belt, Keith enjoys quality time at home with his wife, Donna, his son, Bailey, and their mischievous schnauzer, Harley.

Davyne DeSye

Davyne DeSye writes from a cozy spot nestled at the base of the Rocky Mountains in beautiful Colorado, USA. She is an author of science fiction and historical romance, *Carapace* (sci-fi) and *For Love of the Phantom* (historical romance) being her most popular works. For more information, visit www.davyne.com.

Rich Jones

Rich Jones lives with his family in the northeastern United States. He has worked in the healthcare and information technology fields for many years. His interests run to reading science fiction and fantasy, rock and heavy metal music, practicing martial arts and technology in general. He has only just started to publish the writing that he has been doing as a hobby for years. To catch up with Rich, visit his blog at https://richjonesblog. wordpress.com

James S. Austin

James S. Austin is the owner/editor of Tacitus Publishing. He has edited three anthologies—*It's a Grimm Life*, *Haunted by the Past*, and *Shattered Space*. He has published short stories, leads a table-top podcast, and writes for a number of blogs, to include the serial *Chronicles of Ballidrous—The Tales of Devryn*. When not writing or editing, he spends his time as a traditional and digital artist.

Anthony Addis

Anthony Addis was brought up in the Isle of Man, and went to teacher training college in London. Since then he has taught and lived in Lichfield, Cairo, Kuala Lumpur, and Jakarta.

His short stories have been published in ezines and anthologies, most recently in *Twilight Madness*. He has also self-published a novella on the Amazon Kindle platform. *Rebirth* was written after he visited the Kyoto Museum for World Peace in Japan.

He currently lives in Jakarta with his wife, Jane, and their two teenage children. He can be found at @anthonyaddis on Twitter.

Tom Barlow

Tom Barlow is an Ohio writer. Other writings of his may be found in periodicals including T*he Intergalactic Medicine Show, Hard-boiled Horror, Crossed Genres, Digital Science Fiction, Pure Fantasy and Sci Fi, Coyote Wild, Nebula Rift*, and many others, and anthologies including *Stories from the New Future, Contact:Stories of the New World, Battlespace* and *Desolate Places*. He is a Clarion grad. Read more about him at www.tjbarlow.com.

T. M. Starnes

When not practicing or teaching Kung Fu, T. M. Starnes is reading or watching horror, thrillers, or sci-fi movies.

T. M. prefers writing in the horror, science fiction, post-apocalyptic, and, occasionally, romance genre. His favorite authors include Clive Barker, Patricia Briggs, Dean Koontz, and Edgar Rice Burroughs.

You can find further anthologies, short fiction, and novels currently available on his author page on Amazon and upcoming news at T. M. Starnes's Facebook page.

Emily Devenport

Nine of Emily Devenport's novels were published in the U.S. by NAL/ Penguin/Roc, under three pen names. She has also been published in the U.K., Italy, and Israel. Her novels are *Shade, Larissa, Scorpianne, EggHeads, The Kronos Condition, GodHeads, Broken Time* (which was nominated for the Philip K. Dick Award), *Belarus,* and *Enemies.* Her ebooks, *The Night Shifters* and *Spirits of Glory,* are available from Amazon, Smashwords, etc. She has two new novels forthcoming from Tor: *Medusa Uploaded* and an untitled sequel.

Her short stories were published in *Asimov's* SF magazine, *The Full Spectrum* anthology, *The Mammoth Book of Kaiju, Uncanny, Cicada, Science Fiction World, Alfred Hitchcock, Clarkesworld,* and *Aboriginal SF,* whose readers voted her a Boomerang Award. She is a geology/desert/hiking nut. She blogs at www.emsjoiedeweird.com.

Bruce Golden

Bruce Golden's short stories have been published more than 150 times across twenty countries and a score of anthologies. *Asimov's* Science Fiction described his second novel, "If Mickey Spillane had collaborated with both Frederik Pohl and Philip K. Dick, he might have produced Golden's *Better Than Chocolate*"—and about his novel *Evergreen,* "If you can imagine Ursula Le Guin channeling H. Rider Haggard, you'll have the barest conception of this stirring book, which centers around a mysterious artifact and the people in its thrall." You can read more of Golden's stories in his new collection *Tales of My Ancestors,* which has been described as "The Twilight Zone meets Ancestry.com." http://goldentales.tripod.com.

Madison Keller

When she was young, Madison Keller wanted to be one of the X-Men. While that dream never came true, her dream of writing did. Now she is the author of several epic fantasy novels and a plethora of short stories spanning multiple genres. When not writing she can often be found bicycling around the woods of the Pacific Northwest or at the dog park with the original Kerka, her adorable Chihuahua mix. More of Madison Keller's work can be found on her website, www.flowersfang.com.

Richard A. Shury

Richard A. Shury is from New Zealand, but has been haunting London for some time now. He likes to travel, and dreams of writing professionally. Recently, he's had a few successes, which he hopes are the calm before a storm. Call him a part-time optimist. Find him @RichardShury.

Other works from TANSTAAFL Press

Novels by Stephanie Weippert from TANSTAAFL Press

Sweet Secrets

At seven, Michael gets into trouble no more than any other boy his age, but he does have a sweet tooth. When the mailman brings a package from a candy company, he has to sneak just one. As he eats the chocolate, his home, stepfather, and everything he knows melts around him and disappears. Suddenly, he is in a dreamlike world. He is taken as an orphan, tested, and before he knows it, he's a student in the premier magic school on the planet. His fellow students can make cookies that fly and chocolate turtles that actually walk. Michael is told he has more power than any of them.

Brad, Michael's stepdad, had been charged with watching his stepson for the first time. When the boy disappears before his eyes, Brad panics. Within hours he is on an adventure tracking his son alongside his neighbor, an enigmatic chef and former graduate of the magic school. Always one step behind his son, Brad soon finds that Michael is being used as a pawn between the two most powerful chefs on the crazy planet. Worse, he has to get Michael home before his mother finds out he's gone or there is going to be hell to pay.

Road to Chaos

Robert Thompson is a vain, egotistical actor bent on making his mark on Hollywood. On his way to an important audition that may make his career, another car crashes into his. The other car is totaled but his land yacht is barely dented. The other driver, in a fit of lunacy, insists that they get in his car and drive away before the chaos mathamagic police find them. Robert scoffs. Magic is for rubes and what in this crazy man's delusions does chaos or math have to do with it?

Robert clings to his beliefs until he finds out that the other driver is his long-lost cousin, the magic police tries to kill them both, and his cousin Eric teleports them to Tibet. Robert finds himself bounced around the globe on a mixed attempt to both evade the brutal mathamagic goon squad and clear Eric's name, all the while hoping that he can return to salvage his real life of movies.

Novels by Tom Gondolfi
from TANSTAAFL Press

An Eighty Percent Solution—CorpGov Chronicles: Book One

In a world where corporations suborn governments as a part of good business practice and unregistered humans can be killed without penalty, Tony Sammis, a midlevel corporate functionary, finds himself unwittingly a pawn in a guerilla war between a powerful cabal of business leaders and an elusive but deadly underground movement. His final solution to the biological terror unleashed mirrors Tony's own twisted sense of justice.

Thinking Outside the Box—CorpGov Chronicles: Book Two

Winning one war doesn't seem to be enough. Tony Sammis and the Green Action Militia are once again thrust into the center of a conflict that will change the lives of everyone in the solar system. This time they are allies with the fledgling CorpGov and even the United States government against the ravages of the corrupt Metropolitan Police force. The GAM and their allies are fighting a losing war with few soldiers and even fewer weapons. Behind the scenes, a humble and unsuspected power block lurks with its own axe to grind.

Self-interest, romance, freedom, and a lust for power simmer together in this chaotic soup of tension, intrigue, assassination, and war.

The Bleeding Edge—CorpGov Chronicles: Book Three

Tony Sammis and Nanogate lead a patchwork alliance that includes the nascent CorpGov, Green Action Militia, the president of the United States, the Pacific Northwest Mob, most of the megacorps and the United Brotherhood of Bodyguards. The war the CorpGov alliance knows they can't win has begun, but they are no longer fighting to win. Tony and Nanogate know they may not survive, but they intend to deliver the most grievous wounds they can. The most dangerous animal is one with no hope.

Toy Wars

Flung to a remote world, a semi-sentient group of robotic mining factories arrive with their programming hashed. They can only create animated toys instead of normal mining and fighting machines. One of these factories, pushed to the edge of extinction by the fratricidal conflict, attempts a desperate gamble. Infusing one of its toys with the power of sentience begins the quest of a 2-meter-tall purple teddy bear and his pink polka-dotted elephant companion. They must cross an alien world to find and enlist the aid of mortal enemies to end the genocide before Toy Wars claims their family—all while asking the immortal question, "Why am I?"

Toy Reservations

Isp, toyanity's religious zealot, returns at the head of a massive new Army of the Humans. He openly announces his intent to replace President Quixote's government with a theocracy. With most of his toys modified to peacetime purposes, Don Quixote must make a horrific decision for the very soul of his people.

Novels by Bruce Graw
from TANSTAAFL Press

The Faerie of Central Park

The last of her kind in New York City, Tillianita tends the land and beasts as best she can, reluctantly obeying her departed father's warning to avoid humans at all costs. A freak accident casts her out of the relative safety of Central Park. Lost and alone with a broken wing, she wonders if she'll ever see her home again.

On his own for the first time in his life, college freshman Dave Thompson isn't sure he'll ever fit in. When he stumbles upon an extremely realistic fairy doll, he thinks perhaps it might make a good present for a future date until he discovers that it's not a doll at all. His find turns not only his life upside down but also expands his narrow view of the world.

Lady Hornet

Elizabeth Fontaine is a lonely, ordinary young woman in a world where superheroes struggle daily against evil. To fill the empty void within her soul, she becomes a hero fangirl, following every super's event, subscribing to multiple fanzines, and never missing the daily superhero talk shows . . . until one day, fate grants her the opportunity to leave behind her boring, dreary life and become what she's always dreamed of . . . a superheroine!

Elizabeth learns the hard way the meaning of the phrase, "Caveat Emptor!"—let the buyer beware!

Demon Holiday

Torval, Demon Third Class, Layer Four Hundred Twelve of the Eighth Circle of Hell, has been in the business of chastising sinners longer than he can remember. Delivering punishment is the only job he's ever known—the only job he's ever wanted. After Torval witnesses something unexpected, his demonic Overseer demands that he take time off to resolve this personal crisis. And so, Torval, the demon, finds himself sent on vacation . . . to Earth, the proving ground of souls!

Demon Ascendant

Torval, Demon Third Class, Layer Four Hundred Twelve of the Eighth Circle of Hell, on vacation to Earth has managed to find another demon, dated a woman, and inadvertently explored some of the sins of humankind: greed, gluttony, and lust. Through all this, his biggest struggle involves deciding if he wants his holiday to end or to continue forever.

www.ingramcontent.com/pod-product-compliance
Lightning Source LLC
Chambersburg PA
CBHW051329020726
47501CB00007B/1987